Jinx came out fast. She jabbed her heel hard into the guy's instep, then shot her knee up with all her might into his crotch. He howled, and the other women on the bus applauded. When we got to our stop, Jinx slipped away and left Sally standing there, dazed to discover the bus was nearly empty.

The driver smiled as she got off. 'You sure gave it to him. I bet he never does that again.'

Sally just stared at him.

Sometimes I feel really sorry for her. It's going to blow her mind when she finally really understands and accepts what Roger is learning about the rest of us. We're like a can of worms. I knew Roger was going to get us untangled eventually. He was smart. But then, what could he do about it? I mean, here we were. Of course, if he could kill us off, since there would be no bodies to get rid of, I guess that would be the perfect crime.

Daniel Keyes was born in Brooklyn in 1927, and worked as a merchant seaman, editor and university English lecturer. He won the Hugo Award in 1960 for the short story that *Flowers for Algernon* was based on and the Nebula in 1966 for the full-length novel. In 1968 *Flowers for Algernon* became the Oscar-winning film *Charly* and has now sold over five million copies worldwide. He died in June 2014.

By Daniel Keyes

NOVELS

Flowers for Algernon
The Touch
The Fifth Sally

COLLECTIONS

Daniel Keyes Collected Stories

NON-FICTION

The Minds of Billy Milligan
The Milligan Wars
Unveiling Claudia
Algernon, Charlie and I: A Writer's Journey

THE FIFTH SALLY

Daniel Keyes

WEIDENFELD & NICOLSON

First published in Great Britain in 1981
This paperback edition published in 2020 by Weidenfeld & Nicolson
an imprint of The Orion Publishing Group Ltd
Carmelite House, 50 Victoria Embankment
London EC4Y 0DZ

An Hachette UK Company

1 3 5 7 9 10 8 6 4 2

A CIP catalogue record for this book is
available from the British Library.

ISBN (Mass Market Paperback) 978 1 4732 2379 0
ISBN (eBook) 978 1 4732 1540 5

Typeset by Born Group
Printed and bound in Great Britain by Clays Ltd, Elcograf S.p.A.

MIX
Paper from
responsible sources
FSC® C104740

www.orionbooks.co.uk
www.weidenfeldandnicolson.co.uk

For my daughters, Hillary and Leslie,
and for my wife, Aurea, who is always
there to encourage and help.

Part One

One

OKAY, I'M DERRY, and I got elected to the job of writing all this down because I'm the only one who knows what's been happening to us, and somebody's got to keep a record so people will understand.

Now first of all, it wasn't my idea to leave the apartment on a rainy April night. That started with Nola thinking about those Greek tragedies she's always reading and being in a real depressed mood. Then she remembered childhood summers at the beach, and she decided she wanted to see the ocean again. She took the subway from Manhattan to Coney Island and started to walk. All the rides and games were boarded up, and the streets between Neptune and Mermaid Avenues were deserted except for a few poor drunks wrapped in newspapers, huddled in doorways. It made her feel worse, as if time had frozen, waiting for summer crowds. She thought Coney Island on a drizzly April evening was the most desolate place in the world.

Except for Nathan's. She remembered Nathan's used to be open all year around, an oasis of light and warmth, and she drifted toward it now. There were a few people out in front on the sidewalk, sipping coffee out of Styrofoam cups, eating French fries, and 'the most famous hot dogs in the world.' If I hadn't been on a diet, I'd have bought a juicy one smothered in mustard and sauerkraut. There is nothing like the smell of hot dogs and french fries on a drizzly night. But Nola wanted to see the ocean. She paused and looked at the clock to check her watch and fix the time in her mind. 10:45.

I saw three young guys in patched jeans and studded denim jackets passing a pint in a brown bag, tilting it upward and eyeing Nola as she walked through the dark alley between Nathan's and the Frozen Custard stand. She headed toward the seashore, remembering summertime twenty years ago. She'd play on the crowded beach building drip-castles, and then she'd slide into the water to wash off the sand.

As she moved under the dark boardwalk, she smelled wet sand and kicked off her shoes and felt it gritty between her toes. The idea of dying at sea had always haunted her. She was thinking, Homer's wine-dark sea, as she walked toward the blackness of it and took off her plastic rainhat and tossed it in the sand, but the sands were filthy with garbage and dung and condoms washed ashore after having floated on the sea like messages from another time. And why, she wondered, was she thinking about condoms when she was a virgin about to abort her own destiny? Perhaps she should have left a message, too, saying she couldn't live this fragmented life anymore and drowning was better than slitting her wrists.

Thinking about it gave her a headache. It felt good to take off her blouse and skirt and feel rain on her skin as she walked along the deserted beach toward the purring surf, dropping her clothes. She walked through the wet sand to where it became hard, and then mud, and then the water bubbled up between her toes, and when it receded the waves pulled the mud out from between them and made little channels. She looked at her illuminated watch to fix the time.

11:23.

4

She felt the water, warmer than the air, and her feet became alive while the rest of her became chilled, then numb. And that, she thought, must be the opposite of the way Socrates had felt after drinking the hemlock – his feet and legs slowly turning to stone.

Stupid time to have a headache. She fought the neck pain and the head-splitting thoughts that kept saying *no . . . no . . . no . . .* Someone was fighting her.

The water was warm to her knees and then to her thighs, and it lapped around her as she paused and let it caress her there. Soon she would be in the lap of the gods. She, like Athena, born full-blown from the head of Zeus. But as the water lapped, she shuddered and moved deeper, and found that when you contemplated death your own navel became the center of the universe.

How would it feel to breathe salt water? What if she were really a mermaid, and instead of drowning were to sink into the kingdom of the sea, and with a flip of her tail enter the regions of Neptune along with Captain Nemo and . . .? Oh, God, she had never finished *Moby Dick.* Maybe not finishing a book was a sin that would send her floating through limbo, doomed never to know the ending. Maybe her punishment would be to swim eternally against the current of endlessly turning pages, to be beaten back constantly into the Sargasso of unfinished stories.

The water felt good kissing her breasts now, like a demon-lover, but then she moved past the waves, and her shoulders went under, and she grew warmer and became sleepy as she moved in slow motion.

From behind her came shouts, 'Hey! There she is, in the water! Get her!'

Glancing back, she saw three dark figures coming across the beach toward her.

'Leave me alone!' she screamed.

They splashed in behind her. She tried to throw herself under, tried to breathe water, but it wouldn't stay down. She grew dizzy, sputtered, the brine bubbling through her nose. Someone caught her hair and then grabbed her arms, and when they pulled her out she was gasping and wheezing and crying.

Oh, God, please let me die . . .

She thought they were going to give her artificial respiration, so she went limp. Instead, they dragged her under the boardwalk, and one of them dropped his trousers. The one holding her right arm said, 'Hey, let me!'

'Shit,' the one without trousers said, 'I saw her first. You get seconds. He gets thirds.'

'Thirds? Hey shit, man!'

Then she knew they hadn't dragged her out to save her. 'Don't!' she gasped. 'Please let me go!'

The one who was going to get thirds grinned. 'You were gonna feed it to the fishes anyway. We'll have a little fun, and then we'll throw you back. Okay? You'll never miss it.'

'Yeah,' said Seconds. 'We're just borrowing it.'

The headache was still there, nagging, insistent, but she fought it off. She could handle this herself. She had gotten out of dozens of tight spots. She could talk her way out of it. They could be outwitted, outmaneuvered.

Seconds and Thirds had her arms and legs spread-eagled, and Firsts climbed on top of her.

'Fellas, you don't want to do it here on the sand,' she said. 'Why don't you come over to my apartment? We could have some wine. And I've got some aged cheddar, and we could have some music and—'

He kissed her with whiskey breath and cut her off. She twisted and turned, moving her body to keep him out.

6

'It's like wrestling an alligator,' Thirds said.

'We shoulda waited till she drowned,' Seconds said.

'Help!' she screamed, 'Rape! . . . Somebody! Help me!'

Then Nola split.

It didn't take Jinx long to figure out what was happening when she found herself out there wet and naked in the sand, pinned down by two pairs of hands and one guy with his pants off, trying to get in.

'Who the hell got me into this?' she screamed.

'Hold still a minute,' the one on top said, laughing, 'and you'll enjoy it.'

'You sonofabitch! Get the hell off me!'

She twisted and turned, rocking first to one side and then the other. She managed to twist her head sharply and reached Thirds' hand. She bit hard and hung on, clamping her jaws like a lock-wrench. He screamed and let go, and she swung her right hand down and caught Firsts by the balls and squeezed, digging her nails with all her might. Now he became the bronco, arching his back and then collapsing beside her.

Seconds was so surprised he let go, trying to back-crawl like a crab, but Jinx flung sand into his eyes before he could get away and went after him.

She clawed and kicked, and then got her teeth into his shoulder and tasted blood. He tore loose and ran. So did Thirds. Only Firsts was left, still unconscious. She punched him in the face, smashed his nose, and then looked around for a piece of driftwood or an old board to castrate him with. She wanted him dead and rotting for the gulls to pick at.

Then she heard the car overhead. Looking up, Jinx saw the flashing red and blue lights through the cracks in the boardwalk. The last thing in the world she wanted was to face the cops. She had no intention of being taken down to the station house and asked: Did you lead them on? Did you let them pick you up? What were you doing naked on the beach alone? Did you ask them for money? Have you ever had sexual relations with strange men before?

As much as she would have liked to stay out awhile, steal a car and go joyriding or go see the auto races, she figured she'd better get out of the way. That was always the way it was. Somebody started something she couldn't finish and got cornered in a lousy situation, and then left it for Jinx to deal with. She heard the footsteps clattering down the boardwalk and saw flashlights glaring, and she figured, okay, let somebody else tow this wreck in.

When Sally woke up in Coney Island General Hospital, she didn't know anything about the night before. She saw a fat, motherly nurse standing over her bed, smiling at her. Sally had learned, over the years, that it was better to keep quiet after a blackout so she could figure out how much time had passed and what was going on. She didn't want people thinking she was peculiar. She glanced quickly at the wall clock. 9:53.

The nurse looked at her as if waiting for her to say, Where am I? or What happened? But Sally knew better than that. She saw the white-on-black plastic name tag: A. Vanelli, R.N.

'Do you know where you are?' Vanelli wore a fat, pasted-on smile, but her voice was thin and sharp and slipped under Sally's skin like a needle.

Sally frowned. 'Is there any reason I shouldn't?'

'Well considering you were nearly raped and almost tore the guys apart, I thought you might be upset.'

'Yes,' Sally said calmly. 'Of course I'm upset.'

'Do you remember what happened?'

'Why shouldn't I remember?' Sally clenched her fists under the sheet. She was terrified, but she'd learned to hide it pretty well.

'When the police got to you, you were unconscious.'

Sally looked away, relieved. 'Oh, well, in that case I couldn't be expected to remember could I? You're not expected to remember what happens when you're unconscious.'

'I need to get some information from you,' Vanelli said, pulling her pen out of her side pocket and rearranging pages on her clipboard. 'Name and address?'

'Sally Porter, 628 West Sixty-sixth Street.'

Her eyebrows went up as if to ask what Sally was doing so far from home under the boardwalk in Coney Island, but still smiling, she said, 'Next of kin? Husband? Family?'

'I'm divorced. It's been a year. My husband has custody of my ten-year-old twins. There's no one else.'

'Are you employed?'

'Not right now. But I was planning to look for a job, when this happened.'

'Do you have medical insurance?'

Sally shook her head. 'Just send me the bill. I can pay. I get alimony.'

'The doctor says you're all right. You can leave whenever you're ready.' She lowered the clipboard and carefully put the pen back in her side pocket.

'I want to talk to someone,' Sally said. 'A psychiatrist or a psychologist. Which is which? I get them mixed up.'

'A psychiatrist is a doctor,' Vanelli said, and the eyebrows went up again. 'Why do you want to see one?'

Sally sighed and lay back. 'Because I tried to kill myself three times this month. Because something inside is forcing me to do things. Oh, God, help me before I lose my mind.'

9

Vanelli flipped the clipboard up again, methodically took out the pen, clicked it, and made an entry. 'In that case,' she said, her voice scratching against metal, 'I'll arrange for you to talk to our psychiatric social worker.'

A half-hour later she brought a wheelchair and took Sally up the elevator to the fifth floor, down the long gleaming corridor to the social worker's office. The name on the door said Ms. Burchwell.

'I'll leave Sally with you,' Vanelli said, placing the chart on her desk. 'She's been discharged from Emergency.'

Ms. Burchwell was about sixty, a small, birdlike woman with harlequin-shaped glasses and blue-tinted hair who gave Sally the impression that if she was startled by what she heard, she'd fly away.

'Let me get some background,' Ms. Burchwell said. 'How old are you?'

'I'm twenty-nine. Divorced. High-school graduate. Two children – twins – a boy and a girl. My ex-husband has custody.' She'd given the litany so often it came out like a telephone recording. She knew Ms. Burchwell must be wondering why the husband was given custody of the twins.

'I need help,' Sally said. 'I need to talk to someone about these feelings I have.'

Ms. Burchwell looked at the top sheet on the chart and frowned. 'Before we proceed, Sally, you must understand that suicide is no solution to any problem. We have a form here I want you to sign. It states that you agree not to attempt suicide while you are working as an outpatient with me, or anyone recommended by me.'

'I don't think I could sign that,' Sally said.

'Why not?'

'I might not be able to keep the promise, because I have the feeling I don't control everything I do.'

Ms. Burchwell put her pencil down and looked into Sally's eyes. 'Would you please elaborate?'

Sally clasped her hands. 'I know this is going to sound crazy, but at times I feel other forces inside me. Something or someone is doing things I get blamed for.'

Ms. Burchwell sat back, tapped her desk with her pen, and then leaned forward to write something on a pad. She tore off the page and handed it to Sally.

'This is the name and address of a psychiatrist I know on the staff of the Midtown Hospital Mental Health Center in Manhattan. He also has a private practice. He doesn't usually take on patients who have tried to commit suicide, but because of your feelings that it's beyond your control, he might make an exception.'

Sally looked at the name. Roger Ash, M.D. 'You think I'm crazy?'

'I didn't say that. I'm not trained or equipped to handle your problem. You should see someone who can be of more help to you.'

Sally sat quietly and nodded.

'I'm going to call Dr. Ash and tell him about your case. But first I want you to sign the no-suicide contract.'

Sally picked up the pen and slowly wrote out *Sally Porter*. I slipped out and signed it, too – *Derry Hall*. Ms. Burchwell pretended not to notice, but her eyes widened, and when she stood up to end the interview, Sally realized Ms. Burchwell had flown away.

Sally left the hospital and as she walked the two blocks to the elevated station of the Brighton Beach Line, she tried to remember how she had gotten here and what had happened, but it was all a blank. She was alert and on edge in the subway all the way to Manhattan.

An hour later she got out at Seventy-second Street, took

the crosstown bus to Tenth Avenue, and walked the six blocks south to the apartment. It was almost dark and she clutched her purse tightly, looking around nervously as she headed toward the brownstone building. She was glad to see there were customers in Mr. Greenberg's tailor shop next door. She always tried to get back before Mr. Greenberg closed the shop. Even though the little tailor was over seventy-five, she felt safe going up the street knowing someone was there.

She ran up all three flights, examined the door to make sure it hadn't been forced, and let herself in. She checked every one of the four rooms, in the closets, under the beds, double-checked the bar locks on the windows, and when she was sure the apartment hadn't been broken into, she relocked the three locks on the door, pushed the guard bar into place, and threw herself down on the bed.

Tomorrow she was going to get help, she thought. The psychiatrist would know what to do. She would tell him everything.

I had planned to come out and do some shopping tomorrow, but I figured I'd stay out of the way and observe. Why not? Listening to Sally try to explain us to a shrink ought to be interesting.

Two

SALLY WENT to Dr. Roger Ash's private office on Fifty-seventh off Lexington Avenue wearing her favorite flowered print dress. She wore her long black hair braided into a crown, like those faded photographs of her grandmother from Poland. If it had been me, I'd have worn the blonde wig.

She sat in the reception room with her hands folded in her lap as if waiting for services to begin. When the nurse finally sent her in and she saw the psychiatrist was good-looking, that scared her. I thought he was great – my favorite leading-man type. He was in his early forties, real rangy, and I'd bet he played basketball in college. A lock of his black hair kept falling over into his eyes. But it was his eyebrows that really got to me – you know? – black and bushy, and they went across and almost connected and made a straight line. I find dignified, mature men very attractive. He was going to get all my cooperation.

I really tried to get out to talk to him, but she kept rubbing her neck where I gave her a headache, and she hung in there. She didn't dare let go in front of him, and that made me sore because I really wanted to have him meet me. I could tell by the way he was looking at her that she wasn't making any impression. His deep-set dark eyes were just calm and professional. That's the way most men look at Sally. She's so washed-out nobody can get interested in her. I told myself: Derry, your turn will come. She can't keep you locked in forever.

'Ms. Burchwell called and spoke to me about you,' he said. 'I've been looking forward to meeting you, Sally. May I call you Sally?' His voice was deep and rich like the announcers on the evening news.

She nodded but looked down at the floor, and that annoyed me because I wanted to watch his eyes.

'Now I'm here to help you, Sally. Why don't you start by telling me what's bothering you?'

She shrugged.

'Something must be bothering you, Sally. You told Nurse Vanelli at Coney Island General Hospital that you tried to commit suicide three times this month. But she also said you spoke of something inside you forcing you to do things.'

'I don't want you to think I'm crazy,' she said.

'I don't think you're crazy. Why should I? But if I'm to help you, I have to know more about what's bothering you.'

'Losing time bothers me.'

He studied her. 'What do you mean?'

Her whole body shuddered. She had never thought she would reveal her secret to anyone. But something in her mind kept saying over and over, *Trust him. Now is the time to tell. Now is the time to seek help.*

'I know it sounds peculiar,' she said, 'but when a man gets – you know – forward with me, or when I feel in danger or I have to act under pressure, I'll get a headache, and when I look up time has passed, and I'm somewhere else.'

'How did you explain that to yourself?'

'In the beginning I used to think everyone was that way. I'd see them walk out of the room angry and come back smiling, or the other way around. Or I'd watch two people being friendly, and suddenly one would get violent.

14

I thought they'd just blacked out and lost time the way I did. But now I realize it's not so. And the suicide attempts scare me. Something's very wrong with me, Dr. Ash. I don't know what it is, but it's hell.'

'Try to relax now, Sally, and tell me about your past. I need to know as much about you as possible.'

At first she felt panicky, as she always did when she had to talk about herself, but she breathed deeply and started talking fast.

'I'm twenty-nine. No brothers or sisters. I'm divorced. I married Larry a year after I graduated from high school – just to get away from my stepfather. My real father – Oscar – he used to be a postman – disappeared one day. Just didn't come back. And Fred married my mother six months later. I never had any friends. I kept to myself even when I was very little.'

She stopped to catch her breath, and Dr. Ash smiled at her. 'You don't have to rush through it, Sally. Slow down. Tell me about your mother.'

Sally stared at the floor. 'She never permitted me to get angry. She beat me if I did. She slashed her wrists when I was about nineteen, right after I left home. I didn't believe it for a long time, because she was Catholic. Fred's Baptist.'

'Are you a religious person, Sally?'

'I don't go to church much anymore,' she said. 'I guess I'm all confused about religion. I'm confused about a lot of things.'

'Tell me about your ex-husband.'

'Larry is a salesman in the garment industry. He's successful because he's such a great liar. Oh, God, the terrible lies he told the judge about me. He said I disappeared for weeks at a time. Do you know he said I had a violent temper, and that I stormed out of the apartment one day and ran off to Atlantic City and gambled away five thousand dollars of our savings? God, he lied, and lied, and lied, and the judge gave him the twins. Then last month Larry went back to the court and told the judge I bothered him with late phone calls and threatened his life and the lives of my children. Can you imagine that? And he said I worked as a go-go dancer in a nightclub. And that was a lie, too, because my job at that place was just cleaning off tables. Fully dressed, I assure you. And it wasn't only for the money. I mean, the alimony is more than enough. But I've got to work. I've got to do something. But the judge believed Larry's lies and canceled my visitation rights.'

She suddenly realized she had raised her voice and put her hand to her mouth. 'Oh, Dr. Ash . . . I'm sorry . . .'

'That's all right, Sally. Nothing wrong with expressing your emotions.'

'I never shout.'

'You weren't shouting.'

She blinked several times. 'Wasn't I? It sounded like shouting in my head.'

'Well then,' he said. 'I think we've covered enough history for one day. I can see how painful it is for you to go over the past. We'll take it a little at a time.'

If only Sally had let me out, I'd have set him straight and saved us all a lot of time and energy. I tried again, but she was still fighting me, the muscles in the back of her neck and on her scalp tightening and twitching so I was afraid she'd have a convulsion. Jesus, all I wanted to do was help. I figured, well, okay, I'd bide my time. Sooner or later Dr. Roger Ash was going to have to come to me.

'What's wrong with me, Dr. Ash?' she said.

'That's something we'll have to find out, Sally. Today, I'll give you some tests and a complete physical examination, and then tomorrow I'd like you to see me at the Midtown Hospital Mental Health Center for a sodium amytal interview.'

'What's that?'

'It's a drug, commonly known as the truth serum—'

'You don't need that. I wouldn't lie.'

'Of course not, Sally. That's not the point. The drug will relax you and let us go deeply into your thoughts and feelings without the barriers that block us from finding out what's troubling you.'

'I want to be well again, Dr. Ash. I want to be able to live without always watching the clock, terrified I'll discover I've lost another five minutes, or an hour, or a day, and not know where it went. You have no idea how horrible that is – not knowing where you've been or what you've done. You've got to help me, Dr. Ash.'

'I'll try, Sally. But in return you must promise you'll abide by this agreement you signed with Ms. Burchwell.' He picked up the folder and shook his head. 'I'm sure she told you I don't usually take on patients who have tried to commit suicide. Because of your unusual time-loss problem and the feelings you describe of inner pressure, I've become interested in your case. You're different from the kind of patients I usually see, and I want to help you. But you must promise not to hurt yourself.'

She nodded tearfully. 'I'll try.'

'That's not good enough,' he said, jabbing his finger at the folder on the desk. 'Not just *try*. I insist on a definite commitment.'

'All right,' she said. 'I promise not to hurt myself.'

I wished she'd asked him why he didn't take on patients who tried to commit suicide. Not that her promise would do any good, because she wasn't the one who wanted to die – that was Nola. But I figured, okay, I'd help keep an eye on Nola until we'd seen what Roger Ash could do.

When she left Roger's office, I could tell she was scared. She took a taxi right home. After she paid the driver, she started toward the house, but Mr. Greenberg waved to her through the window of his tailor shop. He was a thin, wizened old man with white hair and a stoop that looked as if he were bowing.

She wasn't sure he meant her at first, but he came to the door and called to her. 'Miss Porter, you have here some clothes that have been here a long time. You want to take them out? – I say take them out?'

'Clothes? Mine? I don't remember.'

She followed him inside, and turned, startled, as she noticed a male window dummy dressed as a policeman: cap, badge, nightstick, and all.

She laughed. 'For a minute I thought he was a real policeman.'

Greenberg had to turn his head at an angle to look up at her from his stooped position. 'That's Murphy,' he said. 'I just bought him secondhand. Ain't he handsome? I'm going to put him behind the glass door at night to frighten crooks away. I been robbed four times already – I say four times already. They stole customers' suits. It's terrible.'

'But what good would a window dummy do?' Sally asked.

Greenberg was looking through clothes on the rack, pulling several down and laying them on the counter. 'It's not the dummy who does anything. A policeman's uniform in the doorway will have a psychological effect. Maybe the crook will decide to rob some other store – I say some other store.'

'Why do you call him Murphy?'

Greenberg shrugged. 'He'll get along better with the other policemen than if his name is Cohen – I say Cohen.'

He pushed the garments toward her. 'Comes to $18.98.'

She looked at the bright red dress, the tailored black suit, and a blue sheath.

'Those aren't mine,' she said.

Greenberg peered up at her. 'What do you mean? It says here right on all three tickets, "Porter, 628 W. Sixty-sixth Street."'

She examined the pink tickets, trying to hide her confusion. Often before she had discovered clothes in the closet that she had no memory of buying. There were always credit card sales slips, or cash receipts. This was the first time she had ever forgotten bringing clothes to the tailor. But she couldn't let him know.

'Besides,' he said, 'I remember when you made me take up the hem on the red dress. Teasing an old man like that. I told you I was old enough to be your grandfather – I say your grandfather. I remember because you wasn't like that when you had me let out the blue dress or weave the cut in the black suit.' He opened a little plastic bag he had pinned to it. 'You left this silver flying-fish pin in the pocket of the suit.'

Then he gave her a grin, clicking his false teeth. 'But anytime you want I should take up a hem, I assure you it's my pleasure – I say it's my pleasure.'

She remembered none of it. Flustered, she paid the bill. She rushed out, nearly knocking over the dummy in the police uniform, and took the clothes upstairs to the apartment. She was so confused she started toward the door on the second floor instead of the third. Then, not seeing her name on the door, she backed away and ran up to the third floor.

As usual, she checked the door lock and its metal plate for signs of forced entry. She unlocked the heavy gray metal door and let herself in. She looked around her, not knowing for a moment what to do with the clothes. She studied them closely, trying to stir up some memory of buying them. Nothing. She hung them in the bedroom closet, far back out of sight. Some day she would have to figure out how her name had gotten on the receipt and who Mr. Greenberg had mistaken her for. He was old and nearsighted. That was it. He had mistaken her for someone else.

She took off her shoes, put them carefully in the shoe bag, hung her dress neatly on a hanger, and washed her pantyhose. Then she cooked herself a TV chicken dinner and ate a package of Twinkies for dessert. Although the place was immaculate, she dusted, vacuumed the living room, and rearranged the stuffed animals neatly on the bed.

She didn't understand why she was so tired at eight o'clock, why she got up so sleepy in the morning and felt washed out through most of the day. Tomorrow she would have to find a job. The alimony payments alone, she decided, wouldn't pay for the psychiatrist. She wondered what kind of job to get, but caught herself yawning. She'd think about it in the morning. She showered, washed her hair, drank a glass of warm milk, and picked up a detective story to read in bed. But she was fast asleep by the time her head hit the pillow.

What she didn't know was that I liked to stay up late and watch the late, late shows. ABC was running a Bogart festival this week. When she was asleep, I came out, made some popcorn, and curled up to watch Bogie and Hepburn in *The African Queen*. I'm just crazy about those old movies.

In the morning Sally woke up in the armchair in front of the TV set and panicked. She called the operator to find out the date, relieved to discover she hadn't lost a day.

After coffee and a corn muffin, she decided to get a job. She wasn't sure where to begin and kept thinking of things like the last job, operating a machine that squeezed the plastic handles onto the screwdrivers.

Now, I've given up talking to Sally because hearing voices freaks her out. But I've discovered if I think very hard, I can influence her. I remembered seeing a Waitress Wanted sign at a restaurant called The Yellow Brick Road on the East Side a couple of days ago when I was out jogging. So I concentrated on the name of the place. It didn't work at first, because what she did was pick up the Yellow Pages. (At least she got the color right!) And she started calling restaurants, starting with the A's, asking if they needed an experienced waitress. I figured she would never get down to the Y's. So I tried extra hard, and I knew she was getting more and more confused. Finally, I just yelled it out: 'They need a waitress at The Yellow Brick Road!'

She got so scared she dropped the receiver and let it lie on the table while she stared at it. Then she picked it up and said, 'Hello?' a few times, figuring the operator or someone must have spoken to her over the phone, but all she got was a dial tone. Then it clicked into place, and she let her fingers do the walking down the list of restaurants until she got to The Yellow Brick Road, Seventy-second and Third Avenue. And thank God they had a big ad: CAFÉ AND RESTAURANT. ENTERTAINMENT AND DANCING NIGHTLY. She dialed, and got someone called Todd Kramer, who said he was one of the partners and if she was interested in the job she should come down for an interview.

She looked through the clothes closet, trying to figure out the best thing to wear for a job interview. I was trying to get her to pick out Nola's brown pants suit or my blue dress. But she put on the matronly houndstooth check, and I gave up. What's the use of trying?

The Yellow Brick Road had a long yellow canopy from the street to the double glass doors. Sally walked under it and then followed the yellow-brick carpet down the stairs, through the corridor, past the doors marked 'munchkins' and 'munchkinettes,' and ended up on the yellow spiral pattern in front of the Emerald City Bar, where a fat bartender was wiping glasses. The place was darkened except for a light over a table across the dance floor where some men were playing cards.

It was so plush and glamorous that she became frightened and turned to leave.

'Help ya, lady?' asked the bartender.

'I had an appointment to see Mr. Todd Kramer. About the waitress job?'

The bartender pointed with his bar rag to the card table. 'Blond fella.'

'Maybe I shouldn't disturb him while he's playing cards.'

The bartender studied the spots on a glass. 'In that case, you'll never get to talk to him.'

She was torn between interrupting the card game or leaving without the interview. Finally, clutching her purse, she headed toward the table, embarrassed at the loud clicking of her heels on the empty dance floor.

The men looked up as she approached. The handsome blond one with the high forehead and the bluest eyes she ever saw, had a toothpick in his mouth tilted up at a jaunty angle. He reminded her of a movie riverboat gambler, except that he wore jeans and a wrinkled denim shirt.

'Mr. Kramer?'

He glanced up from the cards, looked her up and down without interest, and then looked back at his hand. 'Raise five,' he said, and threw in some toothpicks. His voice was surprisingly soft and low.

'I'm sorry to disturb you,' she said. 'I'm Sally Porter. I called about the waitress job, but I could come back—'

'Hold on a minute,' he said. Then he leaned forward and grinned as he slowly looked around the table. 'Three tens,' he said.

'Sorry, Todd,' said a small man with a face like a seal, 'I caught a little straight.' He gloated as he raked in the pile of toothpicks.

Slamming his cards down in a fury, Kramer pushed his chair back as he jumped up, and it fell over. 'Sonofabitchin' cards,' he shouted. 'Deal me out a couple of hands.'

He got up and walked ahead of Sally, crooking his index finger without looking back at her. 'Goddamned lousy inside straight,' he muttered. 'I really think that sonofabitch was cheating.'

He led her to one of the stools at the bar and sat beside her. She was flustered and confused, and she knew she was going to queer the interview. So I started pushing out. Sally usually fights the headache, but this time she was in a panic – as she always was about job interviews – and she felt the chill and saw herself slipping away. The last thing she did was look up at the clock over the bar, that old trick she learned when we were kids to know how much time had passed during her blackouts.

3:45.

Well, thank God. It was about time I got out.

Todd Kramer frowned and looked at me with his head cocked, just like he'd studied his hole cards. 'What's wrong?'

'Hey, what should be wrong?' I said. 'You need a waitress, and I'm the fastest, most experienced waitress you're going to get this side of thirty. Just what this place needs – the wicked witch of the West Side.' I caught his eye, crossed my legs, flashed him some thigh, and smiled.

His Adam's apple jiggled. 'You turned that on like a light-switch.'

'I always do a light switch. I used to be a fashion model,' I lied. 'We don't waste it until the camera is ready and the lights go on. Now, I notice you've got entertainment here too. Well, I'm no Judy Garland, but if the mood is with me, I can sing and dance, and I look damned good in a short skirt.'

'I'll bet you do.'

'Do I get a tryout?'

He studied me from behind those blue eyes. I'd gotten him interested. 'Come back at five-thirty and meet my partner. Eliot has to okay anyone we hire. You'd be working with him more than me. I'm really the silent partner here. I've got other interests.'

'Like what?' I asked.

His eyebrows went up. 'Things.'

'I'm really interested,' I said. 'I love to know all about what people do.'

'Well, during the harness-racing season I moonlight at the New York Raceway. But I'll be here most of the time.'

'Oh, the trotters. I love them. What do you do there? You're too big for a jockey.'

He laughed. 'A friend of mine is the special-events manager. If someone has a political organization or a convention or group fund-raising project, I help him work out the publicity gimmicks.'

'That sounds like fun.'

'It's work.'

'Could I ask something else?' I said. 'I don't mean to pry. Just curious.'

He nodded.

'How much were those toothpicks worth?'

He took one out of his pocket and put it into his mouth. 'A whole box costs just forty-nine cents,' he said. 'But we buy them by the case.'

'I meant in the game. You were using them instead of chips, right? What were the stakes?'

'Nothing.'

'Nothing?'

He looked at me like some people do when they're peering over their reading glasses, except that he wasn't wearing glasses. 'I don't play cards for money anymore,' he said, nibbling at the toothpick. 'This was just friendly poker to pass the time.'

'I hope you don't mind my asking,' I said.

He shook his head, still looking puzzled, as if he was trying to figure me out. 'See you at five-thirty.'

When I left, I decided not to let Sally out again before the interview with Todd's partner. She'd just blow it. And since I'd be doing most of the work, I figured I had a right to an advance on my share to do some shopping and get the kind of dresses I like. I could never understand Sally's crummy taste in clothes, always two years behind the right length. I was always embarrassed whenever I came out and found myself the object of pathetic stares. Once I clipped some photographs from the *Sunday Times Fashion Section* and left Sally a note trying to set her straight. But she went bananas when she saw the pictures and the note, so I never tried that again.

I went to Bloomingdale's and picked out a blue spring outfit for the job interview with Eliot. I squeezed into a size ten and decided I'd have cottage cheese for dinner. The others don't give a damn about their figures, and it's always up to me to take off the pounds.

*

I got back to The Yellow Brick Road at five-thirty, and they were setting up for the evening. The crystal chandelier was rotating now, throwing emerald specks all over the floor, the ceiling, the walls. Waitresses in emerald-sequinned halter tops and short skirts were setting the tables.

The poker game was just breaking up, and Todd was putting his toothpicks into a plastic baggie. 'Eliot'll be here in a few minutes,' he said. 'Why don't you just wait in his office?'

'Hope he likes me.'

'You're a woman, aren't you? No offense intended.'

I laughed. 'None taken.'

He led me into a back office that had photographs all over the walls, most of them autographed pictures of beautiful starlets hugging a fat, gray-haired businessman in a pin-striped suit, signed: 'To my good friend, Eliot.'

Five minutes later the door opened, but the man who came in bore only a faint resemblance to the pictures. He was real thin now and wore tan slacks and a blue silk sport shirt open at the collar, with a heavy gold medallion around his neck. Big diamond rings glinted on the fingers of both hands, and his hair was dyed black.

'Eliot Nelson,' he said, and seeing my open mouth, he nodded at the photographs. 'Some difference, huh? Went on a crash diet last year and lost over a hundred pounds. Like a new man, huh? Not bad for forty-five.'

He smiled. His eyes crinkled and his jaw jutted out. Everything about him looked thin and leathery, but with his puffy cheeks and double chin and the bags under his eyes, he looked like a smiling, friendly bulldog.

'You look twenty years younger,' I lied. I figured he had gone through some kind of middle-age crisis, and I could sympathize with the diet.

'So you want to be a waitress. Any experience?'

'I've waited on tables everywhere from greasy-spoon diners to fancy restaurants. My last job was at the Deuces Wild in Newark.'

He nodded and gave me a hungry look. 'Okay, we'll try you out. You can start the dinner hour tonight. You must have made quite an impression on Todd. Usually, he doesn't give the women a second glance.'

'You won't be sorry,' I said. 'I'm really good, and fast.'

He slipped his arm around my waist. 'Fast I like, but not too good, I hope.'

I patted him on the cheek and said, 'Fast on my feet and good with my hands. I've got a black belt in karate.'

He laughed and threw up his hands. 'Just kidding. But maybe we can Kung Fu sometime. C'mon, I'll introduce you to Evvie, the head waitress. She'll set you up.'

Evvie got me an emerald-and-yellow-sequinned uniform and showed me where to change. She introduced me to the other waitresses, the cooks, the kitchen help, and the busboys, showed me where the menus were, and went over the system for placing orders.

'The only thing you got to look out for is Eliot,' she said.

'What do you mean?'

'Ever since he lost the weight, he's become a regular stud. The old Don Juan has Roman hands and Russian fingers. A regular United Nations.'

'I'll watch for him,' I said, laughing.

'It's not funny when he corners you behind the counter or in the kitchen. I'm black and blue all over my thighs and my butt from his pinching. He's been through three wives and seven waitresses that I know of firsthand.'

'How about the other one?'

'Todd? Always used to be too much of a gambling man to have time for the ladies. But now that he's joined

Gamblers Anonymous, you never can tell. He might redirect his energies.'

'I appreciate the warnings,' I said.

As the newest waitress, I got the station farthest from ringside, so I had a chance to watch the maître d' greet and guide the customers to their seats. I watched Evvie write out the orders, go back to the bar to call in the drinks, and then turn the slips in to the kitchen. Easy enough.

Finally, a party of six was seated at my station. Just my luck it was three middle-aged, grouchy couples, and I could tell right away my first party was going to be a stiff.

'Anything from the bar?' I asked.

'A very dry vodka martini,' said one of the men, winking at me. He was big, with the thick neck of a football player. I figured him for a used-car dealer.

'Cancel that,' his wife said. 'Leonard, if you have even one drink, I'm getting up and walking out of here.'

He canceled the martini, sulking. And none of the others wanted anything from the bar, either. I took their dinner orders, and on the way to the kitchen I told the bartender to make a very dry vodka martini without the olive and to put it into a water glass. I managed to avoid being pinched by Eliot as I picked up the drink.

When I went back to the table, I pretended I saw something wrong with Leonard's water glass. 'There's dirt in this one, sir. I'll get you another glass.' I substituted the martini and winked at him so he'd get the idea. 'No charge for the water.'

When I came back with the seafood and prime ribs, Leonard winked back at me and handed me the empty glass. 'I'd like some more water, please.'

He slipped me extra to pay for the martinis and added a five-dollar tip. As he was leaving I asked him what his line was, and he said he owned a fish market.

I handled the other tables quickly and efficiently, kidding with the women customers and joking with the men who flirted. It was fun. Of all the jobs Sally ever held, I'd always liked waiting on tables best, because no matter what kind of place it is, I like meeting all kinds of people and trying to guess what they do or where they're from. And, let's face it, it's always exciting to find money on the tables after they've gone, or to see how they've appreciated your service when they add a big tip to their credit card slips.

The part I don't care for is closing down the station and setting up for the next meal, filling the salt and pepper shakers and the condiments, and wiping the ketchup bottles, and setting out the tablecloths and silver. So I figured I'd let Sally handle that. After I changed my tips into bills and tucked them into my bra, for safekeeping, I stepped aside.

Sally came out, dazed. As she remembered it, she was sitting on a bar stool asking Todd Kramer for the job. She glanced up at the clock. Six hours and fifteen minutes had disappeared. It was ten at night, and she was in a sequinned, low-cut halter top and a very short skirt. The place was still nearly empty, but now the tables were cluttered with dirty dishes, the aisles had papers and napkins on the floors, the other waitresses were sitting at the bar counting their tips.

'Hey, baby, how 'bout another scotch 'n soda?'

She heard the voice, saw the short, fat customer out of the corner of her eye, but she wasn't sure his call was for her. She stood there, unable to move because her mind wouldn't control her body.

'Anything wrong?' said a soft, low voice.

She looked up into Todd's concerned face. He was chewing on a toothpick, studying her. 'No. Just a bit of a headache. I . . . I . . .' Then she saw the order pad in her hand. 'I can't remember where I put my pencil.'

'You have it in your hair.' He reached up, slid it out, and handed it to her. Then he put his hand reassuringly on her arm. 'You've done a great job tonight. You're a fine waitress. I think that customer is trying to get your attention.'

She got herself into motion and went to the fat guy waving his glass at her. She took his order for a scotch and soda, but when she turned away she felt his hand sliding down her behind and squeezing it.

She let out a screech and dropped the glass. It shattered, and she ran out of the dining area into the ladies' room and tried to compose herself.

Now, that's what I mean. She shouldn't have gotten flustered and taken him so seriously. She should have kidded with him, played him along. Guys like that. And then everything goes smoothly and you get a nice big tip. So what if he grabs for you? A little feel doesn't cost you anything. But not Sally. She goes up in smoke if a guy puts his pinkie against her breast. She sat in the john telling herself she had to hang on. Things like this had happened often before, but now Dr. Ash was going to help her understand why. He had to help her take control of her own mind.

She felt a lump in her bra, reached down, and found a roll of bills. Forty-three dollars. Well, she thought, whatever she did tonight, she hadn't done a bad job. Todd Kramer had said she was a good waitress, and the tips proved it.

When she came out of the ladies' room she felt in control, but edgy. She jumped when Eliot asked if she was okay. She didn't know who he was, but he looked like one of those middle-aged dance hall Romeos.

'Just a little tired,' she said, guardedly.

Eliot smiled. 'Go ahead and take off,' he said. 'I'll have one of the other girls finish up your station. First night can be a strain. But Todd and I want you to know you don't have to worry. The job is yours.'

So he was the partner who'd hired her. She'd never have guessed it.

She thanked him, and when she saw two of the other waitresses head back to the room marked 'Employees Only,' she followed them, confused at first because she didn't see the dress she had worn that morning. She stalled around, waiting for the others to get dressed, and when they took their clothes and hung up their uniforms, there were three others left – a green pants suit, a blue dress, and a yellow and red skirt and sweater. She went back to the bathroom and sat there until the other two waitresses were finished. Only the blue dress was left, and she tried it on. A little tight, but she hoped it was hers because otherwise she was going to have some explaining to do.

When she came out, Eliot winked. 'See you tomorrow night.'

She nodded, but she was thinking that she had no intention of ever coming back here. They were very nice, but it was far too hectic and fast for her.

Three

NEXT DAY Sally went to the Midtown Hospital on Lexington and Fifty-second street. From the outside, the Mental Health Center wing looked like any other glass and chrome office building. Maggie Holston, Dr. Ash's thin nurse with the chipmunk cheeks, took her to an examination room and stayed to take notes.

'Now I like to explain as much as I can to my patients,' Roger said. 'Sodium amytal will help us get past the blocks in your mind, help you remember things you've forgotten. Once you're under, I'll use a process called age-regression, taking you back to your childhood to help uncover some of the people and events that might shed light on your problems.'

Sally was real scared. I could feel her trembling. He gave her the shot, then had her count backward from one hundred. By the time she got to eighty-eight, she started skipping numbers, getting them all confused, mumbling. Her mouth felt full of cotton balls.

'Now, Sally,' he said. 'Don't go to sleep. Stay awake and concentrate. Let's go back to your childhood. When I count to five, you'll be back at the time before any of the blackouts or forgetting. You'll open your eyes and see it all in front of you, as if it were on a TV screen happening to someone else. And you'll describe everything you see and hear and smell. Do you understand me?'

She nodded.

'All right then. One-two-three . . . four . . . five!'

She opens her eyes, looks at the TV screen in her mind, and tells him what she sees.

She is very little. Her father, Oscar, a thin stoop-shouldered man with a pencil-line mustache and sleepy eyes, takes her with him on his mail delivery route, letting her carry the letters to the mailboxes or hand them to the ladies who wait at the front door and who pat her on the head for being such a good girl. One woman gives her a piece of pie, and she dribbles the hot apple filling on her green dress. But Oscar doesn't notice. He walks off smiling to himself like he's chuckling in his sleep. When his leather mailbag is empty, he gives Sally a piggyback ride in it. She's so happy. She knows he loves her very much, and she loves it when he tells her fairy tales from his bottomless magic mail-pouch at bedtime every night. But once, when she's four years old, he stops at The Shamrock for a couple of quick ones and hoists her up in the bag to sit on the bar, and she's frightened because twice before he has gotten very drunk and wandered off leaving her behind. He had also lost her once at the circus in Madison Square Garden after drinking from a hip flask, and once on the subway he got on the train without her. She kept pushing through the crowd, crying and screaming, and when the policeman picked her up, she shouted, 'My daddy is lost! I got to find my daddy!'

One day, after he lost a sackful of mail, he disappeared for good. Her mother said he probably got drunk and fell into the Hudson River and drowned, but Sally never believed that. And to this day, whenever she sees a postman's uniform, she rushes to see if it's a tired-looking man

33

with sad, sleepy eyes and a pencil-line mustache, laughing to himself. She's sure he thinks he's lost her somewhere and he's looking for her.

'Very good, Sally. Relax now. It's all coming back to you. Can you see your stepfather and your mother?'

The channel switches, and now Sally sees their one-room house, and she describes it. It's night. The place is a mess. The big double bed is rumpled, and next to it is her cot. The wood-burning stove is crackling. Her mother is sewing. She has become fat and wears a shapeless housedress. Her dark brown hair is tied back in a bun. The lines under her eyes makes her look like someone who cries too often.

Sally, sitting on the floor playing with her dolls, sees her new stepfather, Fred Wyant, turn off the TV set. He gets up from his wicker easy chair and says, 'Vivian, put the kid away.'

Her mother says, 'I'm tired, Fred. I've got a headache—'

Fred glares at her and tilts back the cap he always wears, even in the house, and now it shows the dent in his bald skull where his head was busted in a drunken brawl.

'I said put the kid away and let's go to bed.'

Her mother's shoulders drop and she sighs. Her face, once very soft and beautiful, has become puffy and pasty in the cheeks and under her eyes, so that she looks like a face of dough that has sagged.

She drops her sewing back into the basket and puts Sally and her four dolls into the closet, and Sally begins to cry softly because being in the dark frightens her.

The TV screen in her mind goes black, Sally says, and she hears the sound of something – she guesses it's a chair – wedged up against the closet door. Sally pushes, but the door won't budge. After a few minutes the bedsprings start creaking, and she imagines them jumping up and down on the bed. That's how it sounded when she would bounce on the bed and her mother would scream at her to stop. She imagines the two of them jumping up and down on the bed to make it creak that way, but she doesn't understand why she can't watch. She figures it must be very bad to jump up and down on the bed because her mother always shouts for her to stop when she does it, and when they do it, she's locked in the closet.

When her mother opens the door and lets her out, Fred is sleeping in the bed, snoring as usual with his mouth open so she can see his missing front teeth, and Sally crawls into her cot.

Tears run down her cheeks and she trembles as she recalls the time her mother forgets the chair, or doesn't get it under the knob. Sally is able to push the closet door partway open and sees both of them naked by the yellow glow of the night lamp. They aren't jumping up and down. Her mother is on her knees with her behind up, and Fred is on her, pumping the way dogs do. His face is flushed and his head looks too big and round for his thin body, and he's grunting.

When Fred gets off and Sally sees that thing he's been sticking into her mother, oh, God, does she get scared. She faints.

Remembering it, Sally cried out and rocked back and forth, perspiration streaming down her face. She felt the stabbing pain in her neck and eyes, and right there in the examination room she blacked out.

Bella opened her eyes and looked around, wondering what the hell was going on, but when she saw Roger she perked up, wet her lips, and used her throaty Mae West voice. 'Hi, handsome . . .'

His eyes went wide and he started to say something, but he didn't. He glanced quickly at Maggie and caught her attention with a slight warning head shake. Her mouth was open.

When Bella saw she was on an examination table she sat up, swung her legs down over the side and ran her hands down her hips. Still doing the Mae West, she spoke in a husky voice.

'Well, whatever I got, Doc, I hope it's not gonna stop you from comin' up and seein' me sometime.'

When they still didn't speak, Bella dropped the impersonation and laughed. 'You both look like the patient died and came back to life. I hope it's not an antisocial disease.'

Roger found his voice, but it came out hoarse. 'Would you give me your name for the record.'

'You making a record? I don't hear any music.'

'I mean for the record of our conversation.'

'Oh, that kind of record. My name is Bella. That means "beautiful" in Italian. I don't speak Italian, but a talent scout who was *very* interested in me, once told me that.'

Roger nodded, and I could tell he was struggling to keep his cool.

'Could you tell me your age?'

'Over eighteen,' she said and giggled.

'Do you know where you are?'

She looked around. 'Well, I'm on an examination table and you've got a white coat on. Maybe this is a movie set for *General Hospital*, and I'm trying out for a part.' She stretched out and put her hands behind her head, settling her body in a very suggestive position. 'I'll do anything to get started in acting. I'm very talented.'

'I'm a doctor, Bella. And I'm here to help you.'

Bella laughed. 'Boy, have I heard that one before.'

36

'This is Maggie Holston, my nurse. I'm Doctor Roger Ash, your psychiatrist.'

She sat up suddenly. 'A shrink? Hold it, Buster. I'm not crazy.'

'Of course not,' he said. 'But I'm here to help you deal with your problem.'

'I don't have any problems.'

'Does the name Sally Porter mean anything to you?'

She leaned back and stared at the ceiling in disgust. 'Oh, shit! So that's what this is all about.'

'Then you do know her.'

'Not personally, but I've heard about her from someone who does.'

'Who's that?'

'Derry.'

'Derry who?'

'Just Derry, is all I know. But I've also seen Sally's clothes and read some of her letters, and I can tell you she's the dumbest, straightest, most boring person I ever heard about.'

'Why?'

'Derry says all Sally ever wants to do is stay home and take care of the house. All she ever thinks about is getting her twins back from her lousy ex-husband. She never wants to go out dancing or to a show. She never gets high. God, what a crappy existence she lives.'

'What's her relationship to you?'

Bella thought about it for a moment. 'I don't really know.'

'How does it work then? Are the two of you ever in contact at the same time? Are you ever out when Sally is?'

'Well,' she said, 'it's like when you've got to pee, and you find all the doors to the booths in the ladies' room are locked and you can't get in because the slots say 'occupied.' You wait around, you hear the sounds of crapping and the

37

flushing, but only one person can use a booth at a time. But, like I said, Derry tells me about her.'

'Then you don't know what goes on in Sally's mind?'

'I didn't know she had a mind.'

'Are you ever aware of the things that happen when you're not out?'

'Only what I can figure out. Like once last year I came out, before the divorce, I found she was at a wedding reception. Very unusual, because I'm usually the one who goes to parties. But Sally and Larry – that's her ex-husband – were invited, and suddenly I was on the dance floor and this guy was holding me close, and I could feel his hard-on against me. And then I knew why I was there. Sally just doesn't know how to handle men.

'So me and this guy danced all evening, and it turned out he was a friend of the bride. I didn't even know the wedding couple. But this guy was a live one. We went to his hotel room, and he undressed me in bed and kissed my breasts, and that was the last thing I remembered until the rain on the window woke me up early in the morning and the guy was gone. I heard later from Derry that Sally got into a hell of an argument with Larry over it, and I figured out that was the final thing that led to the divorce.'

'Do you know anything about Sally's attempted suicide?'

Bella looked surprised. 'Did she try to bump herself off?'

'You haven't heard about it?'

'Well, I haven't been in touch with Derry for a while, so I'm behind on the latest gossip. But she'll tell me eventually. She's fascinated with people and the things they do, and she loves to talk about things. You ought to meet her. I think you'd like her.'

'I plan to. Not today, because it's late, but possibly at our next session. And I want to thank you, Bella, for being so helpful.'

'Any time, Doc. I think you're kinda cute.'

He looked uncomfortably at Maggie, and then he gave Bella an awkward smile. 'Thank you, Bella. Now it's time for you to close your eyes and go back to sleep. I'm going to count, and when I reach the number five, Sally will be awake, feeling good, and she will remember as much of this interview as she wants to. Sally, you will be able to remember all of it, or some, or none.'

When he finished counting, she woke up and looked around, dazed and scared, and she didn't remember anything. That upset her because it felt just like the blackouts.

'I can't stand it,' she sobbed. 'I want a normal life. I want to be able to go to bed at night and get up in the morning without this awful worry. Am I crazy, Dr. Ash?'

Roger said, 'You mustn't think that. This isn't insanity.'

'Then what is it?'

He paused for a minute, glancing quickly at Maggie, and then back to Sally, as if he was feeling unsure about what he was going to say.

'I know this may be difficult to accept . . .'

'Please,' she said, 'I feel as if my whole world is falling apart.'

'I can't be certain, of course, but I believe you're dealing with a mental state that we're seeing more and more of these days. Up to the mid-1940s there were only about a hundred and fifty recorded cases, classified psychiatrically as hysterical neurosis, dissociative type. Since then, thousands more have appeared, and it now has its own new classification, called "dissociative disorders." '

Her brow wrinkled and she shook her head. 'I don't understand. What does that mean?'

He paused and then leaned forward. 'Did you ever see a movie called *The Three Faces of Eve*?' She shook her head. 'I never go to the movies.'

39

'Have you ever read a book called *Sybil*?'

She shook her head, but her body started to tremble. 'I didn't read it, but I heard about it. What do those things have to do with me?'

'What did you hear about *Sybil*?'

'A woman with a multiple personality . . .' Her eyes widened and she stared at him. 'Are you saying . . .?'

'I'm not certain, Sally. But I have reason to believe that this multiple personality syndrome is part of your problem.'

She was dazed. She knew he was absolutely wrong. It was the most ridiculous thing she had ever heard. But she didn't want to contradict him. It was wrong to contradict a doctor. If she told him she didn't believe it, he would probably send her away and not help her anymore. And she knew she needed help. Only if she got better would the judge let her have the children back. So she had to be careful not to insult Dr. Ash.

'Have you had a lot of these cases?' she asked.

'You're my first,' he said.

'Is it because of my mult – because of what you said – is that why you agreed to treat me, even though you don't usually accept suicidal patients?'

'To be completely honest with you, yes.'

She didn't know if it was a good thing or not, to have something he had never treated before. She was certain she didn't have this multiple personality. But she wasn't going to argue with him. As long as he felt she had something he was interested in, he would continue to treat her. And that was all that mattered.

'Do you get any warnings, Sally, before you black out and lose control?'

'Usually, before the headache there's a funny feeling, like a chill and electricity in the air.'

He made a note of that. 'It sounds almost like an epileptic's aura, the warning before the seizure.' Then he sat back and tapped the pencil on his desk thoughtfully. 'You should be able to work, live, and cope with the world while we're struggling to solve your problem. It may take time to find the key, but we'll do our best to help you. I'll see you twice a week to start with – Mondays and Fridays at ten – then we'll adjust the sessions as needed. I'll see you on Friday.'

'I trust you, Dr. Ash. Whatever I've got, I know you'll find a way to cure me.'

'We will, Sally,' he said. 'At least we'll try.'

When she left the hospital, she tried to feel what it would be like to have multiple personalities, with different people inside her. But it felt silly even to think of it.

He was wrong, of course, she thought. But if he continued to treat her, he would find the real problem, and then he would be able to save her.

The crosstown bus was crowded. As Sally held on to one of the handgrips, a big young man with pimples, his hands in his pockets, pressed up behind her, rubbing against her. She tried to change position, but he shifted every time she did, and she was embarrassed and confused – too ashamed to say or do anything. And he kept going at it strong. She could feel his hard-on right up against her, rubbing . . . rubbing . . . She felt the chill – what Roger called the aura – and then the headache, and I knew what was going to happen. I just kept to one side.

Jinx came out fast. She jabbed her heel hard into the guy's instep, cursing him with words I don't repeat, and then she shot her knee up with all her might into his crotch. He howled, and the other women on the bus applauded. When we got to our stop, Jinx slipped away and left Sally standing there, dazed to discover the bus was nearly empty.

The driver smiled as she got off. 'You sure gave it to him. I bet he never does that again.'

Sally just stared at him.

Sometimes I really feel sorry for her. It's going to blow her mind when she finally really understands and accepts what Roger is learning about the rest of us. We're like a can of worms. I knew Roger was going to get us untangled eventually. He was smart. But then what could he do about it? I mean, here we were. Of course, if he could kill us off, since there would be no bodies to get rid of, I guess that would be the perfect crime.

The week went fast. I enjoyed working at the restaurant, and the tips rolled in. Eliot was really impressed. He asked me for a date, but I managed to put him off. I just couldn't wait for Friday to come. I wanted to see Roger.

Sally showed up at his private office right on the dot of ten.

'We're going to do something different today, Sally,' Roger said. 'Instead of the drug, I'm going to use hypnosis, and we'll be able to retrieve a lot of childhood things you've forgotten. Is that all right with you?'

She nodded.

'Now I want you to look at the reflection of this gold pen in the light. I want you to keep your eyes on it and listen carefully to my voice. Watch it closely and concentrate on my words, and soon you'll begin to feel very sleepy.'

It was fascinating. I never saw anyone hypnotized before except in the movies. Frankly, I didn't think it was going to work, because I heard somewhere that you have to be intelligent to be hypnotized, and Sally isn't very bright. But she was trying very hard to please him, staring at the glint of gold, and Roger's voice was smooth and low and she was growing numb. Then her mind went blank the way it does just before she falls off to sleep. Those are the times I usually come out, but I stayed put to see what he was going to do next.

'When I count to three, you'll open your eyes, but you'll still be hypnotized. I'll ask questions, and you'll be able to answer them and speak with me naturally and easily. What number did I say I would count to?'

'Three . . .'

'Good. One . . . two . . . three . . .'

'Now tell me, Sally. Do you know someone named Bella?'

'I had a doll once, when I was little. I called her Bella.'

'Tell me about her.'

'I pretended she was real, and I talked to her.'

'Did she ever answer you?'

Sally was silent for a moment. Then she whispered, 'They gave a play in school, about Snow White and the seven dwarves. Queen Bella was such a funny witch-queen I pretended my doll was her, and then later my Bella-doll talked to me.'

'Did you name any other dolls?'

She nodded.

He paused, but she just sat there, thinking, *Wait until he asks.*

'When was that?'

'At different times.'

'What were their names?'

'Nola.'

'And who else?'

'Derry.'

'Any others?'

She sighed, relieved he had gotten it out of her. 'Jinx.'

'Did anyone else know your dolls' names?'

43

She shook her head. 'I never told. They were my private friends. I named Derry from the middle part of Cin-*der*-ella.'

'I see. Why did you want to name her for Cinderella?'

'Because that was my kitten's name.'

He waited, but so did she.

'What happened to your kitten?'

'She died in her first life, even though she was supposed to have nine lives. My stepfather, Fred, lied to me.'

'Was Derry the first doll you named?'

'No.'

'Tell me the order in which they came.'

'Jinx was first. Then Derry, then Bella. Nola was last.'

'Now Sally, listen carefully. I'd like to speak to the first one, to Jinx. Do you think she'll speak with me?'

Sally shrugged.

'All right then. When I say the words "*Come into the light*," you'll drop back into a sleep and the other person will come out and speak with me. When I say "*Go back into the dark*," that person will return to wherever she came from. What words will I say?'

'*Come into the light*, or *Go back into the dark*.'

'Good. Now, Sally, I want to speak to Jinx. I want Jinx to *come into the light*.'

Now the minute he said he wanted to speak to Jinx I was surprised. I figured after what Bella told him about me, he'd want to talk to me. I didn't think he'd want to go in order. But it wasn't the right time to bring Jinx out. If he did there'd be trouble. He didn't know anything about Jinx, and he just wasn't prepared to meet her. Maybe it wasn't right, but when he said 'Come into the light,' I took it on myself to come out instead. Jinx would have gone on a rampage.

44

'Hi,' I said. 'I know you sent for Jinx but I figured you and I ought to meet first and have a talk about her, because she's a very dangerous person.'

'And who are you?'

'Derry.'

'How are you, Derry?'

'Not so hot.'

'What's wrong?'

'Well, it used to be a lot easier for me to get out than it is now. In the beginning I'd slip into Sally's mind like a hand into a glove. Now my time out is cut down.'

'What do you want, Derry?'

'To be a real person. To be out all the time, so I can ski and sail and fly. I'd like to try skydiving.'

'Have you ever done any of those things?'

'Once I tried skiing during a "getaway weekend" in Vermont. Sally never did figure out that twisted left ankle. Now I'm into jogging.'

'How do you feel about Sally?'

'She's about the dullest person I ever knew. You have no idea what a drag it is to have to spend your days watching the soaps and game shows and cleaning up the house. You vacuum one day, and do laundry the next, and wash windows the next, and so on and so on. God, it only gets dirty again, and pretty soon you're starting all over. It's not my idea of living. The only time I have any fun is when I'm waiting on customers.'

'Could you tell me why you came out instead of Jinx?'

'Well, I heard you ask to speak to her. And I figured I ought to come out first and sort of warn you. Jinx has more hate packed inside her than you can imagine. And she's clever and sly. She'll wrap you around her finger, then stick it into the fire.'

45

'Would she do me any harm?'

'All I can say is if you ever talk to her, make sure she doesn't have a weapon handy.'

'Has Jinx ever killed anyone?'

'Not yet. But I tell you she's capable. And she's getting stronger. She thinks life is one big demolition derby. Get into your car and smash up everybody else before they get you.'

'You seem to know a great deal about Sally and Jinx. Yet Sally spoke of you only as the memory of a doll. Could you explain how that works?'

'Well, I'm the only one who knows what's going on in all the minds, Sally's and those of the others, what they're doing or thinking when they're out. I'm the only one who can see things happening even when I'm not out. But I don't control any of them. Whoever is out is free to do what she wants because they're all different people. The others know me, and know what I've told them about each other. Except Sally. She still doesn't know we exist, but she knows something is wrong.'

'But how does it work when you're not out? How do you know what's going on?'

'When I'm out, I know things through my own senses. When one of the others is out, it's like I'm perched in a little corner of each mind. So I know what's happening, but I know it only the way that person would see it. For example, Jinx doesn't feel pain much. So it doesn't frighten me to get slapped or punched when she's in control. Nola's nearsighted, so if she doesn't have her glasses on, everything is blurry. When it's Bella and she's dancing, I feel the beat of the music. So I see the world in a lot of different ways. I haven't had much schooling, but I've picked up a lot of stuff through the others.'

Roger looked at me, nodding and pulling on his ear. 'Derry, would you tell me where all of you came from?'

'We're just here,' I told him. 'We always have been, ever since Sally named the dolls. I don't know how it happened, but after that we became the real people of the names – only she doesn't know it. Now can I ask you a question?'

He seemed surprised, but he nodded.

'Okay,' I said, 'this therapy you're doing for Sally. Does it mean the rest of us are going to die?'

Roger seemed surprised. He fumbled around for words as if he hadn't thought about it before. 'No, of course not. I mean, it's not death. It's . . . well . . . let me put it this way. The technique will be to let Sally become aware of each of you, to accept you intellectually at first, and then emotionally. Later, we'll bring Sally and the other personalities together to communicate with each other so you can cooperate and live a tolerable existence. Finally, by hypnotherapy, I'll try to merge you all back into one mind. You'll become one person instead of five.'

'That sounds awful!'

'Why?'

'I'm me!' I said. 'How would you like it if someone decided you should give up your freedom, and tossed you into the pot with four other people, and told you not to worry because you'd come out with a nice new personality, like a mulligan stew?'

'It won't be that way, Derry.'

'How do you know? You told Sally you never had a case like us before.'

'That's right. I haven't.'

'The other doctors don't seem to be having much success,' I told him. 'Nola read all about *Sybil*, and *The Three Faces of Eve*, and what their doctors did was get rid of the other

47

personalities. At least they thought they did. But then she read an article about how killing off the others didn't work, because different ones were created.'

'That's exactly why I don't intend to cut you off or do away with any of you. You were one personality before you split. Now I want to put you back together, merge you into one.'

'All the king's horses and all the king's men couldn't do it.'

His brow furrowed, so I knew I'd upset him. I said I was sorry and I'd do whatever I could to help.

'It's in your interest to cooperate with Sally,' he said, tapping the desk with his forefinger. 'Help her keep the job. You're the one who got it in the first place, aren't you?'

I nodded.

'Then help her keep it – to earn a living, keep things stable, keep occupied.'

'So you can make me disappear?'

'It won't be like that.'

'She should be the one made to disappear.'

'What do you mean?'

'Well,' I said, 'she doesn't know anything about any of us, or what's going on, and I do. I know what each one is thinking and feeling. So I should be the real person, shouldn't I?'

'It doesn't work exactly that way, Derry. You see, according to many of the therapists who work in this field, most multiple personalities develop one persona who knows all the others – just as you do. What we refer to as co-consciousness. They call this personality "the trace." In fact, it is suggested that the therapist try very quickly to get in touch with the trace to find out about the others, and to get the trace to cooperate. But the trace is not the real person.'

That really sank me. I was hoping the fact that I knew what was in all the minds meant I was really the real person and Sally only thought she was. 'The trace, huh? Derry the trace. Well, that sounds pretty important to me. Okay, I'll cooperate, but not for nothing. I'll make you a deal.'

He looked surprised. 'What kind of a deal?'

'You get her to change her life-style, tell her to dump that old-fashioned hairdo and buy some decent clothes and help me with the diet by cutting out rich desserts, and I'll cooperate. At least I should be able to enjoy life while I'm tracing around.'

'I'll talk to Sally about it.' The way he swiveled around in his chair and looked at me I knew he was going to tell me to go back into the dark. I did.

When he brought Sally back, he gave her suggestions about the things I'd said. Then he told her that in the future all he would have to do to hypnotize her would be to say, *He knows what's in the darkness*, and she would go under. Those other two lines he gave her before – *Come into the light* and *Go back into the dark* – would be used for moving from one personality to another.

'But you will respond to these words only when I say them. No one else, using those words, will have any effect on you. Do you understand me, Sally?'

She nodded. He told her that when he counted to five she'd awaken and feel refreshed, and she'd be able to remember all of the session, part of the session, or none of it.

She didn't remember a damn thing.

That weekend was pretty much of a drag. I kept waiting for some sign she was going to change, the way Roger had promised she would, in return for my cooperation. But she walked around so scared and jumpy that I was about to give up hope. Then, about a week later, Eliot stopped her on the way out and asked her for a date. That's right. Not

49

Bella or me. He asked Sally for a date. Of course, it was his mistake, and she was about to say no, but then something in her head clicked with what Roger had told her, and she blushed and said okay.

'You're off Wednesday night,' he said. 'I'll meet you for a drink at The Lion and Crown, and then we can go out and have a good time.'

Wednesday she wandered around the apartment, feeling lightheaded and off balance. She forgot about the date for a time, and she started to wash the windows. She looked up at the bright sunshine reflecting on the apartment building roofs, trying to remember what she had to do. Someplace to go . . . someone to meet.

I pushed her finger on the window, writing in the dust. E-L-I-O-T. She thought she'd done it herself, and then she remembered she was supposed to meet him for a drink at The Lion and Crown.

She glanced down at the black and white checked dress she was wearing. So dowdy-looking, she realized for the first time. She had liked it when she bought it, but suddenly it seemed wrong . . . especially wrong for meeting Eliot at a bar. She didn't know why it was suddenly so important for her to wear the blue dress. Ordinarily she would have fought the desire to do something as impulsive as this, but Dr. Ash had said she shouldn't fight the urge to dress differently. As much as she despised the vulgar blue dress, she had to keep that promise. She just hoped Eliot wouldn't think she'd worn it for him.

The Lion and Crown was crowded when Sally arrived exactly at six. It was an imitation English pub on Madison Avenue with dark paneled walls and dark wooden tables and chairs. Eliot waved from a back booth. He was wearing a lavender silk shirt, open at the neck, matching slacks, a white jacket, and a shark's-tooth necklace.

'Yez wanna orda?' the waiter asked in a Brooklyn-Italian accent.

'I'll have a Diet Pepsi,' she said.

Eliot ordered a pint of bitters.

The waiter brought their drinks. Eliot pointed at her Diet Pepsi. 'I used to live on that stuff. You saw the pictures of me in my office, when I was real fat.'

She nodded, sipping her drink. 'You look like a different person.'

He glowed. 'You know what they say. Inside every fat person there's a thin one screaming to get out. You're looking at what was really inside. Now I'm out. Let the fat one scream his head off. I'm staying out.'

She felt a shudder without knowing why. Her hand trembled, clinking the ice, and she put the drink down.

'I'll bet you feel better too,' she said.

'Feel like a youngster again. That's why I went over to Switzerland. They've got a clinic there I heard about from one of our customers. A regular fountain of youth. Those Swiss doctors know all the secrets about keeping people young. Diets and gland extracts. Cost me nearly ten grand, but I figure it's worth it to turn back the clock. My doctor here nearly fainted. He said now I got the body of a thirty-year-old.'

He looked deep into her eyes as he said it, and it sounded like a proposition.

'As long as you're healthy,' she said.

'I been thinking about you the past few days, Sally. I think you're a terrific looker. Interesting, changeable, mysterious. You've got me all worked up wondering how you're going to act next. One minute you're distant and withdrawn, like you'd fall apart if I touched you, and the next minute you're cool and in control. You work that floor during the rush like no one I've ever seen. And you handle those fresh dudes like a woman who knows what's going on and where she is. Then other times you're like a lost little girl. It sort of got me to wondering how a woman could be almost like two different people. You know what I mean?'

Sally sipped her diet drink, set the glass down slowly, and leaned back against the cool leather of the booth. 'I – I have no explanation for it, Mr. Nelson. But you know women are changeable . . . moody . . .'

He shook his head as he stared at her. 'I got the feeling there's more than that. Please call me Eliot.'

'Look, I don't know what you want of me, Mr. Nelson. I agreed to meet you. I didn't think we were going to get involved in this heavy talk about my moods. You ought to know women have times when they're edgy and moody, and that's all there is to it.'

'I'm sorry. I didn't mean to upset you.'

'I'm getting a headache. A very bad headache. Excuse me, Mr. Nelson, I've got to go to the powder room.'

She slid out of the booth and stumbled toward the washroom. The pain was between her eyes and at the back of her head. A chill made her shudder, as if her body were charged. Inside the washroom, she went to the sink and splashed cold water on her face. She knew if she just relaxed and slid into the darkness of her mind the pain would go away, but she didn't want a blackout. She had to hang on and fight the urge to run and hide behind someone else in every sex-charged situation. She had to stay out front and face the world. She had to . . . she had to . . . oh, dear God . . . please . . . no . . .

Bella smiled at herself in the mirror.

She ran her tongue over her lips and looked at her teeth. Then she rummaged in the purse for lipstick, lip gloss, anything, but there was none. And no eye liner, not a goddamned thing. She looked so pale and flat. No depth in her face. Thank God for the dress at least. Not one of her own, but it would do. She pulled at the neckline to show more cleavage. She wanted to see some shows and go dancing . . . She planned to have a hell of a good time.

She started to walk out of The Lion and Crown, right past Eliot Nelson.

'Sally, where you going?' he called.

She turned and walked back. She knew she'd never met this guy before. Middle-aged, she thought, but with those lavender threads he looked like the swinging type. She went back and sat down at the table.

'Hi,' she said. 'Hey, you're cute.'

He looked surprised.

'What's the matter, Sally? You're acting strange.'

'Why don't you just call me by my nickname – Bella.'

'Bella?'

'And what should I call you?'

He looked around as if to see if anyone else was observing. 'Most of my friends call me Eliot.'

'I don't see any wedding ring, Eliot.'

He laughed. 'Damned right. My third wife walked out on me two years ago, and I've been having fun ever since.'

She ran her fingers up and down his silk shirt and pouted. 'Fun is the magic word. I bet you're a good dancer, Eliot. I've got the sudden urge for some rock and disco. I haven't been dancing for a long time. Would you like to hold me in your arms?'

'You're different again.'

She smiled and ran her tongue over her lips. 'The better to fascinate you, my dear.'

'Do you remember what we were talking about before you went to the john?'

She thought about it. 'Not really. I guess I wasn't paying much attention. What the hell, we're out for a good time, aren't we? I mean I don't go too much for heavy talk. Do you like to dance, Eliot?'

'Yeah, sure, but I was thinking about dinner, and maybe a movie.'

'Oh, crap on the movies. I love the live theater, though. I want to do things. I want to see a show, go dancing, get drunk and have a good time . . . not necessarily in that order.'

'Okay, Bella. You want to eat first?'

'Hell, I can always eat. I want music and lights and rhythm. I haven't been dancing in a thousand years.'

'Let's go, baby,' he said. 'I suddenly feel like dancing too. I know a great place. Go there all the time.'

He paid the bill and they rushed outside looking for a taxi. They found one and he threw the door open for her, jumped in beside her, and told the driver to take them to the Black Cat Club.

'I can't get over how different you are now,' he said.

She slipped her arm around his neck and pressed her body close as she kissed him.

'Jesus,' he said, when she finally released him. 'I thought you wanted to dance.'

'I do.'

'Well, how the hell am I going to dance if you get me all worked up?'

She giggled. 'I forgot. I'm sorry.' She put her hands against his trousers and squeezed.

'Ouch!'

'Down, boy! Down!'

'Easy for you to say.' He put his arms around her again, but she wriggled away.

'Uh-uh! First we dance and have fun, then we go to a show, and later to your place and let the steam out of the boiler.'

She leaned forward and let her tongue dart out at the corner of her lips.

'You ought to rattle before you strike,' he complained.

At the Black Cat Club she rushed ahead while Eliot paid the driver. It was obviously a hangout for young singles.

'Hey, wait up,' he said.

'I can't wait,' she said. 'I've got to move fast, before the curtain comes down.'

He paid the admission and caught up to her breathlessly. 'Jesus, you're all of a sudden in such a hurry. Take your time, slow down. The evening is young.'

'Can't slow down!' she shouted over the amplified sound, moving her body to the rhythm. 'There's no time! There's only now, and I've got to spread myself around in the present, because there's no future.'

'I can't hear you!' he shouted, dancing with jerky motions like a wind-up toy.

'Never mind!' she shouted back.

The music filled her, but the more she danced the more she wanted. Every part of her body responded to the beat throbbing upward from legs to hips to the gentle pressure of her breasts massaging themselves against her bra. She wanted to tear her clothes off and dance naked.

'You're beautiful,' he said, when he finally got her back to the table.

'Tell me more.'

'You're the most exciting, most thrilling, wildest, maddest woman I've ever met.'

'Naturally,' she whispered.

'And also the most confusing, mysterious, changeable, seductive—'

'Who? Li'l old me? Y'all talking about li'l old Bella?'

'Just one thing that scares me, Bella.'

'What's that?'

'I'm afraid you'll change. I'm afraid you'll go into the ladies' room and come out different. Or if I turn my head or blink my eyes, you'll be someone else before I can hold you in my arms, before I can—'

'That's because I'm the world's greatest actress. But I don't want serious talk. I came to have fun.'

'But we have to talk about it.'

She stood up. 'If you're going to get serious, I have to leave. I'm not the serious type, Eliot. If you like me, you have to take me like I am. If you question who or what I am, I have to leave.'

'Jesus, Cinderella, hold it. I didn't mean anything. Please, don't go.'

She sat down. 'I'm *not* Cinderella. Don't *ever* call me that again. I play every other role, but not her.'

'Okay, okay. I'm sorry.'

'Tell me about yourself, Eliot. What do you do for a living?'

He looked at her hard, and right away she knew she'd made a mistake, and she started to get up. But he caught her wrist and said, 'I own the place where you work, Bella. I'm a partner in The Yellow Brick Road.'

'Of course, I know that,' she said, trying to cover her tracks. 'I was only teasing you.'

'Then you really must be one of the greatest actresses in the world.'

'That's what I've always dreamed of being. I always knew if they gave me the lead I could dance and sing my way to fame and fortune.'

'I believe it.'

'And not only dancing,' she said. 'I've had a couple of parts in plays, and readings off-off-Broadway and in coffee shops in the Village. People tell me I'm very good.'

'Hey,' he said, 'why don't you do some things for us at The Yellow Brick Road? We've had shows from time to time. You could sing or dance, or whatever, and entertain the customers.'

'I'd like that. I really would.' She pulled him over and kissed him on the lips.

'You want to go?' he asked.

'Where?'

'To my place? Your place?'

'I want to dance.'

'My God! You're not going to dance all night, are you?'

'Why not? The night is the best time for dancing. You don't go dancing in the morning, or in the afternoon.'

'My feet hurt,' he said. 'And I'm hungry. For food and for you.'

'Well, I'm hungry for dancing.'

She got up and danced alone, and then with other men. Her body, her arms moved with urgent rhythm. She had to hang on to the world by letting the music blot out every other reality but the here and now. She had the feeling that if she stopped the scene would change, the act would end, the curtain would fall before she was ready, and the thought scared her. Then she felt the pressure at the back of her head. She fought it. It wasn't fair, she hadn't been out that long. But it got harder to breathe. Everything blurred, and then she hit the floor.

When Sally opened her eyes, she was choking from the smell of ammonia.

She looked around, her mind blank at first, and then filled with fear. 'Where am I? What happened?'

'You collapsed on the dance floor,' the owner said, capping the ammonia bottle. 'You okay? Or should we call a doctor?'

'Dance floor? I – I thought I was in the bathroom.'

The owner looked at Eliot. 'The bathroom?'

'Yeah, she went to the bathroom. She wasn't feeling too good. I'll take her home in a cab. She'll be okay.'

'What time is it?' she asked.

'Eleven-thirty.'

'Oh, my God,' she said. 'Eliot take me home. Please take me home right now.'

The doorman got them a taxi. Inside the cab she saw Eliot studying her.

'You want to tell me what happened?' he asked finally.

'I passed out, that's all.'

'That's not all, Bella. Something else happened.'

She turned sharply. 'Why did you call me Bella? Did you drug my drink?'

'Jesus, what are you talking about?'

'We were in The Lion and Crown. You get me a Diet Pepsi, and the next thing I know I'm lying on the middle of a dance floor. Somebody must have put something in the drink.'

'Listen to me, Bella—'

'Don't call me that. You know my name is – is Sally.'

'Okay, Sally, listen to me. I don't know exactly how to handle this. But I've been watching you pretty close tonight. Todd was right. You're a regular Jekyll and Hyde, do you know that? One minute you're Sally, and you go in the john and you come out Bella, and then you collapse on the dance floor after dancing for three hours straight, and suddenly you're Sally again. Now you may be a great actress, but—'

'I don't know how to dance, Eliot. I never dance.'

He stared at her. 'Come on now, don't tell me that!'

'It's true. I'm so clumsy. I have no sense of timing, no feeling for rhythm.'

'And what about your promise to do a show for us? The readings and the performance?'

'Never. I'd die if I had to go in front of an audience.'

He leaned his head against the back of the seat. 'If I hadn't seen it with my own eyes . . . heard it with my own ears . . . the two ways you've been acting tonight are both different from the way you are at the restaurant.'

She was quiet, feeling the choking up inside her that made her fight back the tears.

'You seeing a doctor? You need someone to help you. You need a psychiatrist.'

She nodded. 'That's why I took the job. My alimony won't be enough to keep myself afloat while I see him . . .'

He was silent as they pulled up to her brownstone building on Sixty-sixth Street and Tenth Avenue. He paid the driver and followed her. As they walked toward the building he stopped in front of the darkened store window of the tailor shop next door.

'There's a cop in there,' he said.

'No,' she said. 'That's Mr. Greenberg's dummy, Murphy.'

'What?'

She led him closer to the glass door behind which Murphy, nightstick in his left hand, right hand raised, stood guard. 'He's Mr. Greenberg's security patrol. The shop was broken into four times in the last year and customers'

59

suits were stolen. So before Mr. Greenberg closes, he puts Murphy on night duty where people can see him.'

'But that wouldn't fool anyone who looked close.'

She shrugged. 'Mr. Greenberg says most people don't look very hard, and someone in a hurry to break into a store would just react to Murphy's uniform and pass it by. He says it has a psychological effect.'

He laughed. 'Jesus, it takes all kinds of people. Goodnight, Officer Murphy.'

She walked next door and sat on the top step. Eliot looked down at her.

'You going to be okay, Sally?'

She nodded and motioned for him to sit beside her. 'I don't want to go up just yet. Talk to me awhile. Tell me about yourself.'

He sat down on the step. 'My favorite subject. What do you want to know?'

'How did you and Todd become partners? How did you get into the restaurant business?'

He smiled and leaned his elbow against the next step. 'The restaurant was mine until the mid-seventies. My old man sent me to school to study to be a veterinarian. I got my degree. Then I became allergic to animal dander.' He slapped his knee. 'As far as I was concerned, that was just dandy. I was looking for a more exciting life.'

'How did you find it?'

'Just followed the yellow brick road down from the mountains of West Virginia.'

'What do you mean?'

'A yellow brick is actually what the swindlers used to make to fool the suckers, a gold brick. My father was a con man, but instead of worthless gold bricks, he traveled across the country selling stock in worthless coal mines. Coal with sulfur content so high it could only be burned in hell. Well, he ended up in New York. Just before he lost everything and went to prison he bought this place and put it in my name. This was my inheritance.'

'How did Todd get to be your silent partner?'

'I was having a bad time during the recession in the seventies. Remember the first Arab oil embargo? Almost lost the place. Todd had just made a big killing at poker. When he saw I was nearly going under, he decided to invest. Then he went on a losing streak that lasted until he gave it all up six months ago. This is the only thing he's got left. You wouldn't think two different generations could get along as partners, but we've got a great relationship.'

'I think that's wonderful.'

After a long pause he said, 'Now it's your turn. What really happened tonight?'

The smile left her face.

'You really don't remember anything between the time you went to the john in The Lion and Crown and the time you came to in that manager's office?'

She shook her head. 'It's a blank.'

'Does the name Bella mean anything to you?'

She looked down at her hands. 'I've been called that sometimes by people who claim they know me by that name. Usually strangers. There must be someone who looks like me—'

'You called yourself Bella after you came out of the john.'

'That's impossible.'

'And you behaved like a different person. You were wild and sexy and bubbling. You danced until you dropped.'

She stared at him, and then she began to cry.

'Hey, Jesus, I didn't mean to do that. I figured it was important for you to know what's going on so you can do

61

something about it. You ought to tell it to your doctor. He'll cure you, and then you'll get your head together, and you'll be okay. I want you to know you got a friend you can come to if things get rough. You call me up any time of the day or night, and I'll help out. And don't worry about the job. I'll back you up when the rush gets heavy.'

'Thanks, Eliot,' Sally said, wiping her eyes and smiling. 'You're one of the sweetest people I've ever met.'

He saw her to the front door and she held out her hand. He clasped it and said good-night.

She let herself into the apartment and looked around to make sure she was alone. She went directly to the mirror and looked at her face, to make sure it was familiar. She was afraid she might have forgotten.

'You're going crazy,' she told herself.

Then she lay on the bed and stared at the ceiling.

When she finally fell asleep, she dreamed she was dancing with Eliot on the beach – only it wasn't Eliot, it was Murphy, and it wasn't her because she had turned into a mannequin named Bella – and the two of them danced into the ocean until the waves closed over their heads and they both broke apart in the surf and drowned.

Four

SHE HAD THE SAME DREAM the next night, and when she told Dr. Ash about it on Friday, he asked her to lie down on the couch and free-associate to her dream images of the mannequins dancing. She followed a trail of mental images . . . dummies . . . clothes . . . smooth . . . hard . . . dancing . . . breaking up . . . naked . . . death . . . Cinderella . . .

And that was where she blocked. The association didn't go any farther.

'Let's back up a little. What does the idea of breaking up make you think of?'

'Nothing.'

'Something in your unconscious is trying to communicate with you, Sally. You've got to open yourself, to make yourself receptive to the forces in your own mind that are trying to help you.'

'I don't know what you mean, Dr. Ash.'

'I can help you, Sally, but the understanding and the cure will have to come from within you. What does Cinderella make you think of?'

'Death.'

'Why?'

'She was my kitten, and she died.'

'How?'

'I don't remember.' But as she said that the tears started rolling down her cheeks. 'There's so much I don't remember.'

'What does dancing bring to mind?'

She shifted uncomfortably, and after a long silence she said, 'Wait, I remember something about Cinderella. The name Derry came into my mind. I named one of my dolls Derry from the middle part of . . . Oh, did I tell you that before?'

'Do you remember telling me?'

'No. Just a feeling I might have. Did I?'

'Yes,' he said. 'While you were under hypnosis, but when you were brought out of it you didn't remember anything you said during the trance.'

'That's just the way it is during the blackouts. I have no memory of what I say or do, but just vague feelings.' She fell silent again.

'You were going to free-associate to *dancing*.'

She looked at him blankly. 'Was I?'

He smiled and nodded. 'And then you blocked it and went off on a tangent.'

She settled back in the couch and felt the weight of her body pressing into the leather, as if she wanted to sink into it.

'I can't dance,' she said. 'I never could. I'm clumsy. I have no sense of rhythm. I hate dancing.'

He waited, nodding. She squirmed. The dream images flowed into view – of a shadowy figure with long red hair dancing wildly, and the name Bella popped into her head.

'I was with one of my bosses last night. Eliot. He told me I was dancing and called myself by another name.'

'What was the name?'

'Bella.'

'Do you use that name?'

'No. Of course not. I had a doll once named Bella . . .'

'Why are you stopping?'

'I think I told you that too.'

64

He nodded. 'You told me your dolls' names.'

'Under hypnosis?'

'Yes.'

'Why don't I remember?'

'Because it's associated with pain. You didn't want to remember.'

'But I have to remember in order to get better, don't I?'

'In time,' he said. 'It will come to you. There's no need to rush.'

She looked at the floor. 'Did I tell you that those dolls later became my imaginary friends, that I would talk to them and pretend they would talk back to me.'

'You mentioned Bella talking.'

'They wouldn't talk to each other. Only to me. And I never told anyone about them. I formed a pretend club called "The Secret Five." There was Derry and Bella . . . and one called Nola . . . I – I don't remember the other one . . . the troublemaker. We'd have meetings and I'd serve imaginary tea in imaginary cups, and we'd have imaginary ladyfingers and talk about school and boys and important things.'

'What happened to those imaginary friends?'

'I don't know.'

'When was the last time you met them or spoke to them?'

'I think the club was disbanded when I started dating Larry.'

'When was that?'

'After I graduated from high school.'

'How did you disband The Secret Five?' he asked.

She turned to look at Dr. Ash, wondering why she trusted him to tell him this secret she had never shared with anyone else. He was watching her intently, his brow furrowed with concern for her.

'I told them I didn't want them anymore,' she said. 'But Derry said it wasn't that easy. She said once they'd been invented they weren't just going to disappear. And Nola said they had rights too.'

'What did you do?'

'I forced them out of my mind. I kept busy.'

He nodded for her to continue.

'And that's when the forgetful periods got much worse. I would lose track of long periods of time, and people would tell me I did things I had no memory of. Things I knew I never could have done . . . like . . .'

'Like what?'

'Like Eliot said the other night, about my calling myself Bella, and dancing all evening . . .'

'What do you think all this means, Sally?'

'I don't know. I thought I was crazy, but you say I'm not.'

He shook his head and said very firmly, 'You are not crazy, insane, or psychotic . . . all those words we use to speak of people who are so far out of contact with reality they can't function, or are such a danger to themselves and others they have to be institutionalized.'

'Then what am I?'

'What you have used to be called a neurosis. But now we in the profession realize it's much more serious than that. The category now referred to as "dissociative disorders" includes amnesia, fugue states, somnambulism, and a condition that has been much publicized recently called multiple personality.'

She nodded. 'I have amnesia, that's true. Can I be cured?'

He got up and went to his desk, 'I think so. But a first step in that direction is an acceptance of your condition. Intellectually, at first, but then emotionally as well. You have to believe and feel and know with all your being what you are. Only then can we change it.'

She knew he was trying to tell her something. 'Do you mean it's not just amnesia?'

He nodded.

'Not that other . . . not multiple . . .'

He put his hands reassuringly on her shoulders. 'I believe that's what we're dealing with, Sally. I think your imaginary playmates have taken on separate lives and become alter personalities. That's why you're accused of doing things you can't remember. You do them under the control of different people.'

She nodded. 'I see. That explains so much. It never dawned on me . . .' But she was thinking, That's not true. She didn't believe it, and nothing he'd say would convince her.

'It will take a lot of hard work,' he said. 'So little is known about multiplicity. The therapy is largely experimental. But as you develop insight into your condition, I think we can develop a strategy to cope with it – and possibly cure you.'

'Thank you, Dr. Ash. I'll do whatever you say.'

'See you next week.'

But as she walked out, she was thinking that she had no intention of coming back and squandering her money on a quack who was trying to convince her that she was a multiple personality. It was out of the question. There had to be another explanation.

Later that night in bed she tossed and turned, unable to sleep, and got up to look for something to read. There were so many books in the bookcase she didn't remember buying. Kant's *Critique of Pure Reason*, Joyce's *Finnegan's Wake*. She glanced through the pages and blinked her eyes. She couldn't understand a thing on those pages. She threw them to the floor. Why had she bought those books if she couldn't read them?

She turned to the front page of a pamphlet called *The New Woman: Equality NOW* and saw the name NOLA in a bold, printlike handwriting. *Nola*. She grabbed the other books she had thrown to the floor and looked, and those too had the name Nola written in them.

She had probably just done that and forgotten. Her mind was playing a joke on her.

Behind the books she found a box with a vibrator in it and an instruction sheet for firming and toning the skin. She didn't remember buying that either. Also behind the books she found two rolled-up copies of *Playgirl*. She opened the magazines, but when she saw the centerfold, she drew back and gasped. It disgusted her. Had she bought those magazines? Impossible. She would never even look at pictures of naked men.

Larry used to read *Playboy*. Pictures of naked women. And dirty pictures in those sex manuals. It was terrible to be married to someone with a filthy mind.

She tried to go to sleep, but every time she would doze off she would start to dream of the sea again. This time, instead of Murphy and Bella she dreamed of her twins, both floating on the water. Then she saw them washed up on the sand, draped in seaweed, their heads and legs twisted in unnatural positions.

She sat up gasping. She knew it was too early, but she had to call Larry to check on the children. When he answered, sleepily, he sounded annoyed.

'Don't be upset with me, Larry. I was dreaming about Penny and Pat. I had a nightmare – more of a vision – that they were hurt.'

'They're all right.'

'Can I talk to them?'

'They're asleep. God, it's nearly two A.M.'

'I have a right to talk to them.'

'You have no more rights, Sally.'

'Please, Larry, at least go check. I had a premonition.'

'You're always having premonitions. Just a minute. I'll look and let you know.'

She waited the few seconds while he was away from the phone, and listened for sounds. She heard a woman's voice in the background asking who it was.

Then Anna got on the phone. 'Why don't you leave him alone? All these calls, night and day. You're driving us nuts. We're going to call the police if it doesn't stop.'

'That's not true. I haven't called him in months.'

'You're a liar. Last night, and the night before. You're the one who makes those obscene phone calls. One day you want him back, the next day you threaten to kill him and your own son. I'll tell you this: The judge said if you keep it up, you'll never regain your goddamned visiting rights.'

'No!' Sally screamed. 'You can't do that. You wouldn't. They're my children – mine and Larry's. You have no right to—'

'You're the one who has no rights. You freaked-out, spaced-out nut. If you don't stop bothering and threatening—'

She heard Larry's voice whispering, 'Stop it, Anna. Leave her alone. She's crazy.'

'She's driving us both to an early grave.'

They argued for a moment, and then he was back on the phone. 'Listen, Sally, they're all right. Fast asleep. Now I know you're going through a bad time, but Anna's right. You've got to stop this constant calling at all hours.'

'But I haven't called, Larry. This is the first time in months. I don't know what she's talking about. I still love you, Larry.'

69

'You're starting that again? My God, I thought you were going to cut out this lying and manipulating. You woke me three times this month between two and four in the morning. You've called me at home, at the office, all hours of the day and night. What do you take me for, Sally? I mean, this irrational behavior broke up our marriage. It's been over a year now, so why do you keep it up? I thought you were going to straighten yourself out.'

'I'm trying, Larry. I'm getting better. I'm seeing a psychiatrist. And I've got a regular job as a waitress, so I don't have to ask you for more alimony. I didn't mean to bother you, but I think about you all the time. It hurts. And I was worried about the children.'

'Well, there's nothing to worry about. We're taking good care of them.'

'Anna's not their mother. I'm their mother and your wife.'

'Listen, that's over and done with, Sally. Anna's my wife now – and she loves them just as much as if they were her own children.'

'No,' Sally gasped. 'She can't. She can't. They're mine. I won't let anyone else have them. I'd rather see them . . .'

The vision of their broken bodies again. What was she saying? What was she thinking?

'Oh, Larry, no. I don't mean that. I'm sorry. I just wanted things to be the way they were . . .'

The sharp click at the other end told her he had hung up. She dropped the receiver into the cradle and put her head back on the pillow. At least the children were all right. She finally fell asleep.

I figured that was as good a time as any to get out by myself. I wasn't sleepy at all. My mind was going over what Roger had told Sally at that day's session. So I got dressed and went downstairs to talk to Murphy. Now I know it sounds crazy, talking to a window dummy, but there aren't too many people I can talk to about what's going on. Of course, now there's Roger. But I still find it very relaxing to talk to Murphy. He's *my* imaginary friend.

He was standing there behind the glass door, on duty, with his nightstick in his left hand, his right hand raised.

'I need someone to talk to, Murphy,' I said, sitting down on the steps in front of him.

'I know how you must feel, Murphy,' I said, 'standing there night after night, watching people go by on their way to having a good time while you're on guard, protecting this place. I'll bet you have the same dream I do, that God will make you a real person. Remember the story *Pinocchio*? I always loved that when Oscar read it to Sally. Pinocchio became real at the end. It could happen to you, too. There must be millions of imaginary friends like us who wish they could be the real people.'

He didn't say anything to me, and I didn't expect him to. It was enough just to have someone listen to me. 'The problem, Murphy, is that Sally doesn't believe what Roger told her. Is it good or bad for her to accept the fact that she's a multiple and to get to know the rest of us? Roger told me that curing her doesn't mean I'm going to die, and I believe him. But how does he know?'

Murphy just listened, with his sad smile.

'And what happens to the rest of us if Sally or Nola kills herself? I used to think that since the body is emptied after death, our souls – all of them – would be liberated. And then we'd each have our own way to salvation or damnation according to the lives we've lived, according to what we are. I don't think the Lord will let me suffer for what Jinx and Bella have done. Sally and I are pure. We deserve a place in heaven. What do you think, Murphy?

71

'I haven't figured out about Nola yet. She's basically a good person, and well educated, but she's an atheist. She takes the name of the Lord in vain and she says terrible things about the government. And I think she's for communal living and radical ideas. Take ERA, for example. When she thinks about it, I'm sure it's right and I'm all for freedom and equality. But then when Bella raves against it and says she's better off the way things are because women know how to make men do what we want them to do, I'm sure she's right and Nola's wrong. And Nola's pro-abortion, so I don't see how she can get to heaven. I don't say she's done bad things, except for shoplifting occasionally, but she has bad ideas. Do you go to hell for bad ideas if you don't do anything about them? What if you *try* to commit suicide, but you fail?'

I knew what Murphy would say if he could. That he didn't know, that no one could know for sure.

'Sometimes,' I said, 'I think with our kooky mental setup – what Roger calls *multiplicity* – it should be possible for one of us to die and go to the hereafter and the rest of us stay alive. Then I might know what comes after death without going through it myself. That would be something . . .'

I felt Murphy was agreeing with me.

'I should be the real person, Murphy, shouldn't I? Oh, God, I want to be the real person.'

I talked to Murphy until nearly four in the morning, and it got real deep and spiritual, as if I was almost praying to him to help me.

With his raised right hand Murphy blessed me, and I felt better. I learned a lot about myself talking to Murphy. And it gave me hope that even after Sally accepted the truth, there would be a place for me in the world.

*

The next morning Sally woke up feeling ashamed about calling Larry. She thought of calling back to apologize, but decided it would aggravate him. She went to pick out something to wear, but for some reason none of the outfits pleased her. She needed something new to raise her spirits.

She decided to shop at Horton's. All during the subway ride to Thirty-fourth Street she sat tight and frightened. She'd read so much about attacks on the subway that she watched every male face with apprehension – especially the young ones. Teenagers had become violent. No one was safe any more. They all stole to get money for drugs. New York had become a nightmare. She made the train changes, nervously clutching her large red purse under her arm. She watched to see if anyone was following her.

She breathed easily only after she entered the big, familiar doors of Horton's, but still she carried her large purse with her arm through the loops and her hand around it, the way the police anticrime bulletins on TV recommended.

Sally bought two dresses and a pair of slacks and a bathing suit. Not the kind of clothing she usually wore. She had the feeling her tastes were changing toward younger, more fashionable styles. The purchases left her just a little more than enough money to get home. One of these days, she decided, she would have to open an account at Horton's.

As she got on the down escalator she noticed a pockmarked man in jeans and a tan windbreaker watching her. She got off on the second floor and walked toward the elevator. He came in right behind her, his hands dug into his jeans pockets. She pressed against the back wall of the elevator, the headache starting at the nape of her neck. She would wait until he got off first, then she would go to another floor. She went to the top floor and he stayed on. The headache was subsiding, but her body felt trembly and cold . . .

73

Nola got off the elevator and wondered what she was doing in Horton's.

It was the first time she'd been out since the ocean. She remembered Nathan's, and the rain, and the damp sand between her toes, and three men dragging her under the boardwalk. She'd have to ask Derry what had happened since Coney Island.

She looked into the bag and noticed the brief bathing suit and decided it surely couldn't have been Sally doing the shopping. Either Bella or Derry. Well, as long as she was here she might as well pick up some art supplies. She looked through her purse and discovered a dollar and a half. Not even enough for a cab back to the apartment. And, damn it, she hadn't brought her checkbook.

She was furious at whoever had left her in this predicament. She went to the art supply section and when the clerk's head was turned, she slipped three large tubes of oils into the shopping bag. She needed some brushes, too. She shoplifted two of them very cleverly.

Certain no one had spotted her, she took the escalator and noticed a pockmarked man in jeans and a tan windbreaker right behind her. Well, if the jerk snatched her purse, he wouldn't get very much.

She had made it out the front door when he caught up to her.

'Lady,' he said. 'I'm a store detective. Will you please come back inside with me?'

She stared at him. 'What are you talking about?'

'Just come inside, please.'

'How do I know you're a detective?' she said. 'You might be a purse snatcher, for all I know.' She started moving on, hoping to tough it out.

'Lady,' he said, walking alongside. 'Just hold it. He pulled out his wallet and showed her an identification card that said

"Horton's Security Police." She noticed, when he reached for the wallet, that he wore a gun in a shoulder holster beneath his windbreaker.

'I didn't do anything,' she said.

'Just come with me, and we'll check it out,' he said.

She turned and started to walk back with him. 'You'll hear from my attorney,' she said. 'I'll sue you and the store for false arrest.'

He took her to an elevator marked 'Employees Only.' Inside, he turned to her. 'Now we can go up to the administration offices and call the police, or . . .'

His voice trailed off as he looked her up and down. She could tell by the look in his eyes that he was offering her a deal.

'Or what?'

'I can push the button to the basement. There's a small storage room in there where I grab forty winks from time to time. It's real private.'

'And then?'

'You're nice to me, I'm nice to you.'

'Can I keep the stuff in the bag?'

He shrugged. 'Why not? Don't cost me nothing.'

She reached over and pressed the button to the basement, thinking it would give her a little more time to talk her way out of it.

As the elevator went down, he reached over and put his hand on her butt, stroking and rubbing it.

'You're a beautiful woman,' he whispered hoarsely.

'I know,' she said. 'I'm just your type.'

The elevator stopped and the door opened at the basement level. He led her past corridors of cartons into a small room. There was no one else around. Nola's feelings of bravado disappeared. Suddenly she felt cornered. He put his hand on her breast. She felt the chill and began to shake. 'Hey, baby,' he said. 'You want it as bad as I do.' He unzipped his fly. Nola looked away and closed her eyes.

As the pockmarked man pulled her toward him with both hands on her buttocks, Jinx pushed him back. 'Get your fucking hands off my ass!' she snapped.

The sudden change of voice startled him, and he made the mistake of grabbing her by the arm. She caught his hand in a judo grip and flung him to the ground. In the same sweeping movement she was on him, jabbing her knee into his groin, pressing the heel of her hand into his throat.

'I oughta kill you, you fucking bastard.'

The young detective's eyes were popping as she choked him. She felt the gun and reached beneath his jacket and pulled it out of the holster.

'This'll come in handy.'

There was fear in his face as she brought the gun up and slammed it into his skull. He passed out.

'That'll teach you to fuck around with innocent women.'

She pulled his body over so that it looked as if he was asleep in the corner and put the gun into her purse. She closed the door to the room and wandered among the cartons until she found the employees' elevator. She got in and pressed the button for the main floor. Upstairs, when the doors closed behind her, she walked quickly into the crowd and out the Seventh Avenue exit.

Jinx took the subway back uptown to the apartment. She rummaged through the shopping bag to see what was in it, disgusted at the clothes and the oil paints. She checked the snub-nosed .38 service revolver, fully loaded. She would have to hide it where none of the others would stumble on it accidentally. She got a plastic bag out of the kitchen and put the gun in it. She waited until dark and then went down to the basement, grabbed a shovel, and went out through the back door into the small yard of the apartment building. Making sure no one was around, she selected a spot in the right far corner, near a telephone pole. She dug a hole about a foot deep, placed the wrapped gun in it, and then covered it and disguised the freshly dug hiding place with weeds.

Then she went back to the apartment and fell asleep on the couch.

When Sally woke up late next morning she looked around, trying to remember where she had been and what she had done. The last thing she remembered was being in the elevator at Horton's and afraid that the pockmarked man was going to snatch her purse. What had happened in between? For some strange reason, her hands were dirty. What had she been doing?

She looked around the room for the shopping bag and was relieved to find it in the closet. She took the dresses out and hung them up. Then she saw the two brushes and three tubes of oil paint: yellow, cobalt blue, and burnt sienna. Where had those come from? She dug through the papers and wrappings and found the receipts for the clothing, but none for the art supplies. How was that possible? If she had bought them and forgotten about it, she would have receipts. If there were no receipts, that could mean only . . .

She didn't let herself think the words.

She showered and dressed, putting on one of her old flowered prints. She went through breakfast in a mood of apprehension. She was trying. Really she was. But there was no improvement. The blackouts were worse than ever, and she was doing things, going places, with no memory of what went on. If Dr. Ash didn't come up with a solution very soon, she would be a candidate for the madhouse. She picked up a copy of the *Daily News* on her way to the bus stop and saw the page-two story about an attack on the detective at Horton's. She stared at the photograph of the store detective with the pockmarked face.

The story the store detective told, about being attacked by a woman shoplifter who had stolen art supplies and who carried a large red purse and a Horton's shopping bag, sent panic through her. He described her as being medium height and having dark hair and a frightened expression that had made him suspicious. When she got to the part about the gun and how she had turned into a vicious, violent tigress, she began to shake violently. She had to stop thinking about it. She had to go to work. She forced it out of her mind.

She was glad Todd was on duty today for the lunch hour instead of Eliot. She didn't want to answer any questions about the date or try to avoid Eliot's pressing up against her behind the counter. But she noticed Todd studying her very closely. Several times he approached as if to ask her something, but then he'd turn away, chewing fiercely on a toothpick. Had he seen the *News* article? Was he getting suspicious?

The lunch hour was slow, and I decided to let her handle it by herself. She didn't make too many mistakes, and no one made a pass at her, so I took the afternoon off.

When she left the restaurant, she didn't notice Todd following her. She was thinking about the pockmarked detective and the gun, and something in her mind whispered the word *church*. It wasn't me or any of the others. Just one of those thoughts that suddenly comes into a person's head. Though it did sound like a voice, even to me. I noticed Todd again when she stopped to cross at the light. He was across the street. She didn't see him. Saint Michael's Cathedral is just two blocks from The Yellow Brick Road, and remembering Dr. Ash's advice about her inner forces, she put on a kerchief and went inside.

In the close dankness of the church she shivered, peering to penetrate the darkness. The confessionals suddenly looked to her like a line of phone booths, and she imagined going inside one and making a long-distance call to God, to ask him why her mind got busy signals all the time, and why she was so often disconnected. But were there phones in heaven? She wondered what the area code would be. And could you dial God direct, or did you have to go through an operator? She was afraid God might have an unlisted number.

She should go and confess, but try as she might she couldn't remember any of her sins. It seemed unnatural that she would have none. There was the story of the shoplifting, but her heart and mind were clear. Still, if she hadn't sinned, why was she so oppressed? Why did she feel so helpless? Could she have done those things and not remembered?

She saw people looking at her standing there in the center aisle, so she genuflected, crossed herself, and slipped into one of the pews to kneel and pray. She felt someone move in beside her, and when she looked up she saw it was Todd. Maybe he knew. Maybe he had read the article and recognized the description of the woman as her. She opened her mouth to speak, but the pain in her head was too much. Her watch said 2:23. She put her hands to her face and bowed her head, and before she could finish the line, 'Hail Mary, full of grace . . .,' she was gone.

Five

NOLA WAS READY to run out of the little room and let the store detective call the police. But when she looked up and saw the altar and the flickering candles and the figure of Jesus on the cross, she whispered, 'Oh, no . . .'

'You all right, Sally?'

She turned. Instead of the pockmarked detective, a blond young man was studying her with anxious blue eyes. He was wearing jeans and a white shirt, sleeves rolled to the elbow.

She got up without answering him and walked out of the church. He followed close behind and when they were outside, he said, 'You've been acting strangely today, Sally. You need someone to talk to?'

She slowed down and turned to him. 'What makes you think I want to talk to someone?'

'You seemed different at work today. When you left the restaurant so upset, I followed you because I thought you needed help.'

'What was different?'

'There was a desperation in your expression, a kind of panic. It's gone now. You've changed again.'

'Be specific. How?'

'You're not like you were when you first came to me for the job. You seemed shy and ordinary, and then suddenly you were vivacious. At first I bought that story about being a photographer's model. But when Eliot told me about your date with him, how wild you were and how all you cared about was dancing, I began to feel something wasn't right.'

She had no idea who Eliot was, but she remembered Derry remarking once that Bella was a dancing fool. So Eliot must have been out with Bella.

'And now?'

'You're more serious. You speak differently – more articulate.'

'I'm a changeable person,' she said.

'I guess that's what's got me interested.'

'Interested in doing what?'

'In being more than your employer. I'd like to know you better.'

'All right,' she said. 'You can take me down to the Village and buy me a cappuccino.'

As they passed a store window, she saw the dowdy flowered print dress and cried out, 'My God! I can't wear this obscenity in the Village. I've got to get back to the apartment and change. Why don't we meet later?'

'Let me come with you.'

'Don't you believe I'll meet you?'

'Eliot warned me you're very unpredictable.'

'Look,' she said, 'if you want to come along and wait while I change, okay. I don't know how much time I'll have. But there's a lot I want to do tonight, and sex is not on the agenda. If that's what you're planning, you ought not to waste your time.'

'I just wanted to spend the evening with you,' he said. 'I can't figure you out.'

She decided she had to set him straight without spilling the whole thing. 'I have moods, Todd. There are times I act one way and like to do something, and then suddenly – without explanation – I do a one-hundred-and-eighty-degree turn.'

'You're different from other women. That turns me on.'

'Just so long as you don't turn *on* me.'

'Sally, I—'

'Call me by my nickname – Nola.'

'Another nickname?'

'Some people collect beer cans.'

They took a taxi and she insisted on paying for it. Outside the apartment, Todd peeked into Greenberg's store window and waved.

'Hi, Murphy.'

She turned to look at him. 'Why did you do that?'

'Eliot mentioned what you told him. You know, about Greenberg's security guard system.'

Nola stared. 'I think it's stupid to put a dummy on guard, and even stupider to dress it as a policeman and give it a name. Another hollow man.'

Todd nodded quickly. 'I agree with you – absolutely.'

'I wonder why he calls it Murphy?' she said.

'Well, you know Murphy's law,' he said. ' "Anything that can go wrong will." I guess old Greenberg is just a pessimist.'

Upstairs in the apartment, she had Todd sit in the living room while she went into the bedroom to change. She put on her favorite denim shirt and paint-spattered jeans and sandals.

Suddenly she noticed her books on the floor on the other side of the bed. God, why couldn't Sally leave her things alone? She went out of her way never to disturb Sally's things. She picked up the books, climbed on a chair, and hid them on the closet shelf. Damn it, books were important, one of the few ways of broadening her horizons, getting out of this mental trap. She felt caged with four invisible animals, and she had to be careful not to trespass on their territories. Well, she thought, clenching her fists, they shouldn't encroach on mine.

She stomped out of the bedroom, not even looking at Todd, and said, angrily, 'Let's go.'

'You sound upset.'

'Are you *coming?*'

They took a taxi. She hated the subways, the press of crowds, and she was pleased that Todd sensed her need for her own space, because he sat away from her. She insisted on paying for the cab, even though part of her wanted to let him pay. She didn't want to be obligated in any way.

'Where are we going?' he asked.

'To The Horseman Knew Her.'

'What?'

'It's a punch line, a double-entendre, and a coffee house in the Village.'

'Oh.'

'Remind me to tell you the joke sometime.'

'It must be funny,' he said. 'You're finally smiling.'

At The Horseman Knew Her, people came up to ask where she'd been because they hadn't seen her in ages and missed her literary readings. She loved to be there. It was the closest she'd ever get to the Left Bank, and it gave her the sense of living among writers and artists.

They were expanding the place, and there was the noise of hammering as workers pounded to break through to the empty store next door. You could smell the old plaster. The coffee shop itself was decorated to look like a French café. The table tops were old butcher blocks, and the walls were papered with yellowed copies of French, Italian, and German newspapers to give it that look of honest poverty, as if they couldn't afford to paper the walls with anything else. The chairs were a mixture, some wooden dining room chairs and others with wire-scrolled backs. One wall was lined with old park benches and small, round tables. The Tiffany lamps cast a reddish light on the bare wood floors. Behind the counter the giant espresso maker gleamed, with complicated levers and eagles on each of the urns.

She saw the disapproval in Todd's eyes, and that annoyed her. 'I know it's phoney,' she said, not bothering to lower her voice, 'but it's my kind of phoney.'

'I didn't say anything.'

'You didn't *have* to. Your face is very expressive.'

'So is the coffee machine,' he joked, smirking.

She groaned.

'Nola-darling!'

She recognized the voice before she saw who it was. Half-turning, she reached around and the short, fat man wearing his corduroy jacket over his shoulders as a cape, kissed her hand.

'Kirk-*darling*. How've you been?'

'I keep expecting you, Nola,' he said, staring at her through thick glasses. 'You keep promising you'll come to one of my Friday night soirées, but you never do.'

Nola introduced him to Todd. 'Kirk teaches economics at the Central Community College. But that's just to be able to afford his real profession, throwing parties at his apartment every Friday night. Everyone *raves* about them. Kirk wanders through the city and whenever he meets someone interesting, or at least different, he invites him or her or it to his Friday night get-togethers.'

'You both must come some Friday,' he said. 'Just bring a bottle of wine.'

He kissed her hand again and then he slipped off and cornered a very thin, round-shouldered young woman in a peasant blouse and very high leather boots, and Nola heard him say, '. . . Friday night . . . and bring a bottle of wine.'

The owner of the coffee house spotted Nola and came around the counter to hug her.

'Mason's been asking around for you,' he said. 'She needs the rent money.'

'I'm headed over there now to pay her,' Nola said. 'Just stopped by for a cappuccino and to see who was around. Abe this is Todd Kramer. Todd meet Abe Colombo.' Todd extended his hand, and Abe slapped his open palm against it, then gave Nola a peck on the cheek and headed back behind the cash register.

'Abe Colombo?' Todd whispered.

Nola smiled. 'Father is the black sheep of the local Colombo family in Little Italy. Married a beautiful Jewish girl. Then Abe did the same thing. Sarah's the one waiting on tables over there.'

It amused her that most people found it difficult to tell the waitresses apart, all of them with whiteface makeup matching the white aprons they wore over their black leotards and black tops. They all wore black ballet slippers and drifted silently, carrying menus on little chalkboards, with order pads dangling from their aprons by leather thongs.

Sarah spotted her and handed Todd the chalkboard menu. 'Nola, Norm Waldron's been in asking for you a few times. He's had some readings lined up and he thought you'd be interested.'

'Well, I don't have much time these days,' she said. 'I spend most of my free time painting, and I don't get out and around as much as I used to.'

Sarah took their orders for two cappuccinos and slipped back into the crowd.

'You've got a lot of friends here,' Todd said.

'Acquaintances, not friends. But as an artist I enjoy the company of creative people.'

'I didn't know you were an artist,' he said. 'I'd like to see your work.'

'You mean you'd like to come up to my studio?'

'Yes.'

'And, of course, then you'd like to have a little wine and fornicate on the floor by candlelight.'

'Look, don't confuse me with Eliot. He's the Don Juan. Ask anyone who knows me. I'm not a womanizer. But I will say you're the first woman who's really gotten me interested since my college days.'

She laughed. 'That's not so long ago. Okay, I'll take my chances. But I warn you, if you start anything it's at your own risk.'

When they left The Horseman Knew Her they headed up Houston Street to Soho, where she had rented a corner of a loft from an artist named Mason. Nola let herself and Todd in, and they found Mason sitting on the floor in front of an easel, smoking pot. Her pug nose and the brown hair framing her square face always made Nola think of a little Pekingese.

'Hi,' Mason said, staggering to get up. She ignored Todd and whispered to Nola, 'Come and look at my latest work. I'm trying new colors and shapes.'

Nola looked at the combination of squares and subway spray can-graffiti and nodded. 'Original. I like your technique. It's very now.'

'I agree,' Todd said.

Mason glared at him and turned back to Nola. 'I want to communicate to the young antiestablishment generation.'

When Nola took Todd over to her corner of the studio, Mason stalked out.

'What's the matter with her?' Todd asked.

'She doesn't care for men.'

'Do you?'

'About as much as I care for women.'

'What does that mean?'

'It doesn't *mean*. It just *is*.'

'God, I'm lost. I have trouble following your line of thought.'

'I'm sorry, Todd, I can't change it to suit you. If you can't follow, you'll just have to stay lost.'

He shook his head. 'You're the one who's lost. So why are you kidding me?'

'Just what do you mean by that?'

'Sally, Bella, Nola. Who are you?'

'I'm *me* – whatever name people call me.'

'Are you really?'

She looked away. 'I thought you wanted to see my paintings.'

'You're like quicksilver,' he said. 'Try to catch you and you slip between my fingers.'

'I did these paintings a while ago. But I haven't worked for some time. I don't get out much . . .'

She turned the canvases that had been stacked face to the wall and lined them up for him to look at.

He gasped.

She knew that to someone else, someone like Todd, these people, objects, and creatures of her dreams would seem like Dante's *Inferno*. She had no idea herself where the images came from. She painted in a frenzy of building up images on canvas. A woman with no face. A child with shattered planes of cheeks, forehead, and chin, staring at the viewer with dead eyes. A whole death series. Suicides never consummated. She'd finished them in oils. And then there was the multiple series: a face with many mouths – all screaming. A head split by a cleaver.

'Why?' he asked.

'A way to get a handle on my feelings. A way to control something inside me, by projecting it out of myself and fixing it long enough to look at it, to understand it. Control.'

He shook his head. 'Jesus! I know about being torn apart, of going through hell, but these are from the other side of Alice's looking glass.'

She nodded. 'You're different from the usual men that . . .'

'That what?'

'Never mind.'

'That Sally is involved with?' he said.

She stared at him. 'Who's been talking to you? Just how much do you know?'

He pointed to the painting of a girl with a face shattered into planes. 'Just what I've been able to figure out. I'll lay ten-to-one odds you're not who, or what, you appear to be at the moment.'

'I see. And what do I appear to be?'

'An intelligent, liberated woman interested in culture and the arts. Cold, sharp, intellectual.'

'And what am I *really?* Behind the appearance?'

'Humpty Dumpty,' he said.

'And all the king's horses and all the king's men—'

'But it's all a lot of Horsemen Knew Her.'

She was staring at the painting of a woman's face reflected from a broken mirror. '– couldn't put Humpty Dumpty together again.'

'You don't have to be together. I'm a hunch player. I'll take you as you are,' he said.

'What am I? What are you? Tell me who you are.'

'We're all different people at different times. In the sixties at Columbia, I was an anti-war activist. In the seventies

I was a gambler. Now I'm a businessman and part of the establishment. We're all many things.'

She shook her head. 'You're talking about different stages in a person's life. Most people are many-faceted, like the planes of a diamond prism that reflect light. I'm different. I'm a single teardrop on a five-pearl necklace.'

'That's what amazes me. Something about you has got me excited about life again. Without the stimulation of gambling, I went dead. You've awakened me. I don't pretend to know what it is. The way you keep changing turns me on. But don't get me wrong. I don't think of you as one of those neurotic women. I think of you as the most fascinating person I've ever met. Life with you could never be dull.'

She shook her head. 'You have no right to think of life with me.'

'I can't help it. You've been in my mind ever since that first day.'

His boyish blue eyes pleaded with her. She found him attractive.

She let him take her into his arms without resisting. He held her close, and though she didn't respond to his kiss, she didn't fight him off. But his hand on her breast startled her. She quivered, mentally backing off. She wanted him to keep his hand there, stroke her breast, kiss it, but she knew if he kept it up and she lost control, one of the others might slip through the revolving door.

Why? Why couldn't she stay out and give herself to someone she liked if she wanted to? It wasn't fair to be doomed to experience life only through books and magazines. She wanted the touch of his tender hands on her body.

He pulled her down on the cot. She wanted to stay out and let him make love to her. But the thought of being penetrated made her lose the sensation. The mounting feeling vanished and she grew cold, suddenly numb, and she knew she could experience neither passion nor pain. It made her angry as the door revolved and she was pushed through . . .

Jinx found herself pushed out. She looked up into a pair of strange male eyes, felt a hand moving between her thighs. She reached down and clamped his wrist, with nails digging into his flesh. She jumped up.

'WHAT THE HELL DO YOU THINK YOU'RE DOING?'

'I want you,' he said. 'I'm crazy about you.'

She pulled his hand away and slapped him hard across the face.

'YOU SON OF A BITCH! GET YOUR GODDAMNED HANDS OFF ME!'

Todd backed away quickly. 'Oh, Jesus!' he said. 'Another one.'

Jinx grabbed a chair and swung. She missed, and it crashed against a wall and bounced off, tearing a hole in one of Nola's paintings. Todd got hold of her wrists and pinned her down on the bed. She kicked and spat and screamed, twisting and rolling to get him off her. But Todd was strong.

'I'm going to kill you,' she screamed. 'I'll get my gun and blow your brains out.'

'Can't we discuss this?'

'You try to rape me and want to discuss it?'

'I wasn't raping you. Nola, what's wrong?'

Jinx felt the tension drain out of her body. She looked around quickly and realized what had happened. Usually she learned from Derry that it was Bella who got involved with a man. Now Nola was pulling the same goddamned crap. First with that department store cop and now this.

He tightened his grip and she felt paralyzed. She hated to be restrained. Not pain. She rarely felt that, and then only faintly, like a dull ache. But being immobilized made the panic sweep over her as if someone was choking her.

'All right!' she gasped. 'Get off me.'

He got off the cot, still holding her wrists. She felt herself breathing hard, as if she'd been running, but she knew it was her anger. God, she hated that feeling. Then slowly he let go.

She walked around the studio looking at Nola's paintings. They bothered her. The faces were people she vaguely remembered. When she got to the girl with the shattered face and empty eyes, she shuddered. It was like looking at herself in a corridor of mirrors. She picked up a knife and slashed them. Every time Todd came close to try to stop her she jabbed at him, but he managed to jump away each time. By the time she was done, she had destroyed every painting in the studio – Mason's included.

Todd gave up trying to stop her. He sat on the edge of the cot and watched. When she was done, she stood gasping in the center of the room, exhausted and limp.

'Does that make you feel better?' he asked.

'Drop dead!' she said.

'You've worked off a lot of aggression. You should be calm enough to talk about it.'

'To you?'

'Why not?'

'Because all you men are alike. You only think of one thing, using us and then dumping us, like old cars, in the junkyard.'

'Nola, that's no way to—'

'Shut up!' she screamed. 'I don't want to hear.' She lunged at him with the knife. He spun away, but she grazed his left forearm, leaving him with a bloody gash. 'There,' she said. 'That's a better color for you. Now, if you try to follow me, I'll finish the job.'

She threw the knife on the floor and ran out of the studio, passing a young dog-faced woman in paint-spattered jeans on the steps near the entrance. Jinx paid no attention when the woman shouted, 'Hey, Nola, where are you going? Where's the guy?'

Jinx ran and walked all the way to the south side of Washington Square Park, studying people's faces. When she neared the playground, she stopped and watched.

In the sandpile a little boy was tormenting a girl. Another vicious, disgusting male. He kept stomping on her sand-pies, and when the girl pushed his foot away, he pulled her hair. Jinx moved closer. The little boy headed toward the teeter-totter.

She remembered how Sally's stepfather, Fred, used to grab her by the hair when he wanted to punish her, how he would put her across his lap and pull her panties down to spank her. She recalled how hard he would become when he did that. She hadn't felt much pain even as a child, but he would keep at it until, when he finally let her up, his hardness would be gone and his eyes would be glazed. Like the little boy's eyes now. Jinx reached out and quickly grabbed him by the throat. She started to squeeze.

One of the other children shouted at her. She got distracted and I pushed out. I dropped the little boy and took off fast. I don't usually interfere, but kill a kid? God, I could just see the five of us spending the next hundred years in solitary confinement.

I got to a phone booth on MacDougal Street, called Roger's office, and told Maggie that Jinx had just tried to murder a little boy and Roger had better do something quick. He was at the hospital, Maggie said, and told me to meet her at the emergency entrance.

I was kind of shook up, trembling with the thought that these hands had slashed Nola's paintings and almost strangled a kid. Something had to be done, no doubt about it. But what? Maybe Nola had the right idea. Maybe we were better off dead. I shook that off. There had to be another way. Roger had to do something.

To be sure there was no confusion, in case Sally came out before I got to Roger's office, I tore a page out of Nola's little memo book and wrote: 'When you read this, go directly to the Midtown Hospital Emergency Ward, Maggie will meet you.'

I thought of taking a cab, but then I figured someone had to watch expenses, so I took the Fifth Avenue bus uptown. I kept the note folded in my hand so that if Sally came out she would know where she was going. It was all her fault. If she weren't so weak, she'd be able to hang onto herself and keep Jinx from taking over. I was always covering up for Jinx's meanness or violence, always coming out in time to soothe things over. Derry the trace, always happy-go-lucky, always there to pick up the pieces when Jinx did something nasty and got Sally into trouble. Like today. It wouldn't be that way if I could become the whole person. I closed my eyes and imagined myself soaring like a free, wild bird . . . higher and higher, swooping circles as I got closer and closer to the sun . . . and then I felt myself plummeting down . . . down . . . down . . . and there I was, caged again on the dark side of Sally's mind.

Sally turned to ask Todd why he had followed her into church, and was shocked to find herself on a bus wearing paint-spattered jeans. She looked around wondering if anyone noticed her embarrassment. Where had she been? What had she been doing? Where was she going? How long had the blackout lasted this time? She checked her watch. 5:31. The last thing she recalled was going into Saint Michael's at 2:23 and discovering that Todd had followed her. But was it the same day? Why was she wearing these paint-spattered jeans? Get hold of yourself, she thought.

When Sally sensed she wouldn't black out, she felt better. She relaxed and breathed easily, resting her head against the window. Maybe she should get off at the next corner and call Dr. Ash. Knowing how busy he was, she didn't want to bother him. But she had no idea what had happened since the church. She clenched her fists hard, and then realized she had something in her left hand. She opened it and saw the crumpled paper. Frightened, she smoothed it out and read the note.

Please, dear God, she thought, let nothing bad have happened. I'm a good person. I don't want to do bad things.

She looked up suddenly and saw the bus passing the Midtown Hospital stop. She jumped up and got off.

She walked from Fifth Avenue to Lexington, clutching the message. She glanced at it again. Not her handwriting at all. Bold, round – like printing – nothing like her tiny neat right-to-left-sloping letters, so small she used to be able to get notes from a whole lesson on one page in school when other kids used three or four. But this big handwriting was definitely someone else's. She pushed through the revolving door quickly, and Maggie was waiting to greet her in the lobby.

'How are you?' Maggie asked.

'A little shaky.'

'Who . . .?'

'I'm Sally.' She handed Maggie the crumpled note.

Maggie looked at it, shaking her head. 'You must be having a terrible time.'

'I'm sorry to be a bother. I know how busy Dr. Ash is.'

'You've got to feel free to call us any time of the day or night, Sally.' Maggie led her to a cold, white examination room. 'Now just rest awhile. Dr. Ash is with a patient. He'll be able to see you in about five minutes.'

'The amazing thing is I don't know why I'm here. I have no idea what happened. It might be nothing. I feel so ashamed.'

'You mustn't think like that, Sally. I know there was a good reason, and he'll help you work it out.'

'I hope so. I'm scared. Please leave the door open.'

Sally settled back and rested her head against the wall, feeling edgy. Hospitals made her nervous.

A few minutes later she was startled by the sound of voices. Two women passing the room glanced in. One, a nurse, had a white-lettered black name tag that said: P. Duffy, R.N. The other wore street clothes. When they saw her look up, they turned their backs. 'Is that the multiple?' she heard one of them say. Their voices sounded as if they'd gone into the room next door, and she could still hear them.

'Ash seems to think so.'

'The thought of it gives me the willies.'

'I don't believe in multiple personality.'

'But Dr. Ash—'

'Listen, you remember what Ash was like before he found this one? When a psychiatrist gets bored with run-of-the-mill schizophrenics and manic-depressives, he starts to look around for exotic new diseases.'

'You think she's a fake?'

'Not a fake. Everyone knows hysterical neurotics sense what their therapists want them to be and give it to them. It's common knowledge that Ash was on the emotional rocks before she came along. Listen, the burned-out syndrome happens to many fine psychiatrists.'

Then the door shut, and their voices were gone. Had she heard that, or only imagined it?

The door across the corridor opened, and a thin stringy-haired girl with pimples and a nervous look in her eyes came out with Maggie.

Sally looked down at her feet to avoid the girl's eyes. She didn't want to talk to anyone now. After what those women had said, she wanted to get up and run away.

A few minutes later Maggie came back and took her into Roger's office.

'Sally, what's the matter?' Roger asked. 'Are you all right?'

'I've got a terrible headache.'

Maggie looked at Roger. 'She was all right a minute ago.'

He got up and helped Sally into a chair. 'Did something happen?'

'I heard them talking,' Sally said. 'That nurse, Duffy, and that other woman were talking about multiple personalities. They said hysterical neurotics made up things for their psychiatrists. I didn't make anything up for you, Dr. Ash. I swear I didn't. I'm not acting or pretending. I don't know what's happening in my mind, but it's real. It's hell!'

'Duffy . . . God damn that stupid woman. If I had my way I'd—'

'My head, Dr. Ash! It hurts!'

She felt a knot pressing down at the top, and then as it twisted tighter, her hair pulled from all sides of her scalp into the center.

'It's happening. I can't hang on!'

He took her by the hand. 'Don't fight it, Sally. Just settle down. Forget about what those stupid women said. We'll be able to talk about it. Maggie, get some water.'

She saw Maggie moving, but she shivered and Roger blurred and their voices were distant, as if there were wheels within wheels in her head, each one turning at different speeds, and she could move from one to the other and be carried away from the center – herself – on which the others spun.

He was saying something to her, trying to reach her with words, but she couldn't stay in the center. She drifted out, caught the second spinning wheel, and then the third, whirling around and around. And then she lay back and the center became the blur. She grew dizzy, and then before she blacked out the thought occurred to her that someday she would have to ask what had burned him out.

Six

NOLA OPENED HER EYES and was about to return Todd's kiss, when she looked around and found herself in a hospital examination room being stared at by a doctor in a white coat and a woman she had never seen before. As usual, she sat silently, waiting for some clue as to why she was here and what was happening.

'Now, Sally,' the doctor said, 'I want you to tell me everything you recall since you left work this afternoon.'

So he thought she was Sally. If this was Sally's psychiatrist, the one Derry mentioned, she wanted nothing to do with him.

'Sally, are you all right?' he insisted. 'Why are you looking at us so strangely?'

'Because I feel strange. I've gone through a lot these past days, and I don't know why I'm here and it annoys me.'

'You're here because Derry made an emergency appointment for you. She called and said you nearly killed a child. Don't you think that's sufficient reason for you to be here?'

Nola put her hand to her mouth. 'Not me. I never did any such thing. Derry had no right to make any appointment for me.'

She saw them exchange troubled glances, and realized she had said too much. She settled back, crossed her legs, and looked from one to the other. Then she relaxed and shook her hair, running her fingers through it.

The doctor leaned forward and looked at her closely. 'Would you tell us your name?'

'First tell me who you are, where I am, and why I'm here.'

'Fair enough,' he said. 'I'm Dr. Roger Ash, your psychiatrist. This is Maggie Holston, my nurse, and more often than not my assistant. You're at the Midtown Mental Health Center because Derry called and said Sally was in trouble.'

She nodded. 'Well, I'm not Sally. I guess you've figured that out by now. I'm Nola. And you're not my psychiatrist.' She was amused by the surprise in his eyes. 'I can see you didn't expect *me.*'

'That's true,' he said. 'Derry made the call. Do you know Derry?'

'Yes.'

Roger said, 'May I ask you one question?'

She tilted her head and smiled. 'As long as I'm not paying you by the hour.'

'Thank you. Would you mind telling me why you've come out at the present time?'

She thought about it. 'I wanted to see what was going on.' She looked at her paint-spattered jeans. 'I guess it was just today. I was in my studio with, well – and then – here I am.'

'You mean you had no awareness of Miss Holston or me?'

'Well, I was aware of you indirectly, through Derry, like shadow figures on the wall.'

'Do you know the other people in Sally's mind?'

'Only Derry, directly. I know there are others. It's like bumping against people in the dark. I've been able to deduce from clues, from comments by people on the outside, and from what I can pick up through Derry. I've had to be a regular Sherlock Holmes, piecing together things from little bits of information. I'm the one who read about Eve and Sybil and told Derry about them. I've read articles about multiple personality. I guess you can say I put the idea we might be a multiple into her head, and she got the thought across to Sally to ask for help. Is that it, doctor? Is it multiple personality?'

He nodded.

'But Sally doesn't know yet, does she?'

'I've told her,' he said, 'but she won't really admit it to herself yet. She's going to have to face it. One of you should tell her the truth.'

'I can't reach Sally myself. The gulf between us is impassable. And things seem to be getting worse instead of better. I used to get out to read and paint a lot more often than I do now. Now, with the therapy and Derry's job, and the running around, and the dancing, and the men she and Bella are getting involved with, my God, I'm lucky if I get a chance to read the advertisements in the subways.'

'You say you've read about the treatment of multiple personality. Then perhaps you understand the therapeutic strategy in some of these cases.'

'Well, from what I gather, there are two approaches. In one, the therapist seems to cut off the other personalities from the host – sort of kills them. In the other, it's as if the doctor is putting them together – what they call fusion.'

He raised his eyebrows as if he was impressed. 'That's right.'

'Which are you planning?'

He glanced at Maggie, who was busy taking notes. 'A combination, possibly. I'll have to improvise as I go along. I'm sure you realize, Nola, that very little is known about multiplicity.'

She nodded. 'The books said how rare it was. Is that true? Are we so special?'

He smiled. 'Your – er, Sally's case has sent me back to the journals. The condition has been known since the early 1800s, but up to 1944 there were only about seventy-six cases available to most of us in the field. *Index Medicus* suggests that the medical journals of the world had about that many more. Let's say about a hundred and fifty cases in all of psychiatric and medical history up to 1944.'

'So it is rare.'

'But since then there have been thousands more. Strangely, almost every psychiatrist who diagnoses one case ends up with several others. The new third edition of *The Diagnostic and Statistical Manual of Mental Disorders*, put out by the American Psychiatric Association, now lists multiple personality under a new category called "Dissociative Disorders," along with such disorders as amnesia and fugue states. There's even been a "Multiple Personality Newsletter." It's now estimated that possibly three out of every hundred people have experienced some of the symptoms of the multiple personality syndrome. So instead of being such a rarity, we're discovering it's only the tip of the iceberg.'

She thought about that for a while. 'How do you explain this sharp increase in the numbers?'

He shrugged. 'Maybe we've been missing it all these years. Multiples have committed suicide, been executed, locked away as insane, or just hidden themselves in the big cities without ever having been discovered. Now that we know what to look for, we find more and more cases.'

She thought about it and shook her head. 'Or there might be another explanation. It might be the illness of our time. In a world exploded into fragments with the splitting of the atom, we might be seeing the results of our modern civilization – people splitting by mental fission. Or maybe it's a mutation caused by the mushroom-shaped fallout, a whole generation splitting in chain reaction.'

'That doesn't make sense,' he said.

She got up and walked to the window, looking at the people below. 'Why not? Maybe this is the way it's supposed to be. The human race has always adapted to its environment. You've got to admit that in this information-exploding world it's more logical to have the mind separated into autonomous compartments, a division of labor, like a mental assembly line.'

'But it's not efficient because you're working against each other, each personality constantly undoing what the other creates, and the result is chaos. It will destroy you all.'

'That's only because of the amnesia, the lack of inner controls,' she said, facing him with a haughty expression. 'Maybe these first attempts at developing a new mental species have been nature's early evolutionary failures. Perhaps someday a child with a predisposition to multiplicity will be born with a slight variation, able to create cross-over functions to deal with the amnesia, to control the alternating personalities. Then you'd really have a superior species of human being – *Homo sapiens multi-plus*. Splitting may be the wave of the future, instead of a defect.'

He struck the desk with his fist. 'It's my job to fight splitting because in almost every case the person who has the syndrome is at risk. Homicide and suicide. We've got to reverse the process.'

'You mean fusion?'

He nodded. 'That's right – the opposite of fission. How do you feel about that?'

'I'm not sure. From what I've learned about us from Derry, I know we're so different that I can't imagine how you could get us all together. But I'm willing to try because I'm enough of a realist to know that if someone doesn't do *something* we might as well be dead. God knows, I've wanted to end it, but something or someone keeps interfering. Maybe that's why I'm out now. But there's one thing you haven't mentioned in all this. How do you plan to work Jinx, with her violence and sadism, into the new Sally? Or do you have the illusion she's going to disappear if you ignore her?'

'You have good insights,' he said. 'You're right. I haven't yet figured out what to do about Jinx. I haven't met her yet.'

'Consider yourself lucky.'

'I'll have to meet her sooner or later. Do you think she'd talk to me?'

'Ask Derry. She's bragging about her new title – "the trace."'

'All right then, I'll work through Derry. And you can stay and listen in while I talk to her, if you like. I can arrange it through a posthypnotic suggestion.'

Nola thought about it. 'That would be fascinating, but it would be the start of co-consciousness, wouldn't it? Not yet. Maybe another time, when I'm sure you have control of the whole thing – including Jinx.'

'Whatever you say. I have no intention of forcing any of you to do anything except stay alive. You'll come together in your own good time, and I'll be here to help you deal with the problem.'

Then she felt his hand on her arm and closed her eyes.

'When I count to three, Derry will come out and talk to me. I have important things to discuss with her. One . . . two . . . three . . . Derry, *come into the light.'*

I opened my eyes and smiled at him. 'Hi.'

'Hi,' he said. 'Would you state your complete name for the record.'

'Derry Hall.'

'How have you been, Derry?'

'Not too bad. I enjoy the job. It's hard work, but it's fun.'

'Do you have any questions to ask me?'

'I wanted to ask you about what Sally overheard, before Nola came, about your being burned out.'

His face flushed, and he looked at Maggie and then back at me. 'What do you mean?'

'What that nurse Duffy and the other woman were talking about in the room next to Sally, that everybody knew you were *burned out*. What did she mean?'

'When I asked if you had any questions, I meant about yourself or the other personalities.'

I could see my question upset him and he was trying to avoid answering it. That got me all the more curious. 'Well, I'm always answering questions about me. But I'm so interested in other people. Of course, if you don't want to tell me . . .'

He looked at me sharply and then smiled. 'I guess you are entitled to an explanation. Physicians occasionally suffer from what's known as the 'burned-out syndrome.' The physician is always the last to know what's happening to him.'

'What's a syndrome?'

He didn't look at me. He was studying the veins on the back of his right hand. 'A pattern of symptoms that occur together. In this case it describes what happens to many psychiatrists who spend too much time with their patients, or as we call them now – "clients." Years of confronting people's fears, memories, dreams, and hallucinations take their toll. And the constant exposure to suffering dehumanizes the physician. He stops listening closely. His mind, to protect itself against constant exposure to suffering, forms a shell. Emotions harden. He goes through the paces, keeps up the false front and the bedside manner, but deep down he's stopped caring about the people he's supposed to be helping.'

My heart went out to him. I could understand what it was like to have to be constantly on the receiving end of everyone's problems, to live through everyone else's suffering. In a way that's what I had to do for Sally and the others. I wondered if I had become burned out too.

'I'm glad you told me, Roger.'

He looked directly into my eyes, and his voice became stern. 'You have to understand that I'm speaking in general terms about the syndrome, not about myself. Now enough theoretical talk. What happened after work today?'

'Happened?'

'You called Maggie and said something about nearly killing a little boy.'

'Oh, yes. Oh, my God, yes! Now I remember. You've got to do something about Jinx.' I told him what had happened, and he looked upset. 'You have to get rid of her,' I said, 'before she kills someone.'

He shook his head sadly. 'She's part of Sally, just as you are. You'll all have to learn to live with her.'

'No one can live with that evil woman.'

He thought for a moment and his brow furrowed. 'Do you think she'll talk to me?'

'I doubt it.'

'Could we try to get in touch with her?'

'I could try, but it won't do any good. She knows you're out to destroy her.'

'But I never said any such thing. Where would she get such an idea?'

'I guess she got it from me. I just assumed you wouldn't want a sadistic person like her in our new life when you brought us all together. She's vicious, Roger. Pure evil.'

'That's too easy to say, Derry. My job is to understand her, not to judge her.'

'But you couldn't intentionally accept the violent hatefulness and make us share it with her.'

'Nola seems to think we can't isolate her. She feels Jinx would always be there in the shadows, ready to break through. Aren't you better off making your peace with her, seeing if there's a way—?'

That made the hairs on my neck tingle. 'That's like making a deal with Satan!'

'Oh, come now.'

'You haven't met her.'

'Well, can you arrange it?'

'I don't think she'll go for it, but I'll try. You have to see and hear her for yourself.'

'All right,' he said. 'Jinx, *come into the light.*'

I closed my eyes and pressed my lips together for nearly a minute. But nothing happened. 'She won't come out. She doesn't trust you.'

'Tell her I just want to meet her face to face.'

I tried again. 'It's no use. She won't come out. God, she gives me the shakes. Look, I have goose bumps. She's going to kill somebody for sure.'

'Who does she want to kill?'

'She's wanted to kill Sally's ex-husband, Larry, for a long time.'

'Do you know why?'

'I guess so,' I said. 'I think it's because of the wife-swapping.'

'Would you explain that?'

'I just know about it secondhand, Roger. Larry used to get Sally to go out on dates with him and other executives from the garment industry – you know, buyers and sales managers and their wives. They'd have dinner, go to a nightclub or a show, and then the men would start talking about switching partners for the night. He told her if she did it, it would help him make big sales.'

'How did Sally feel about that?'

'She'd get a headache and ask Larry to take her home.'

'Did he?'

'Well, Roger, like I said, I only know about those things secondhand. Sally didn't go with those men, and I didn't, and I'm sure Nola didn't. If you really want to know what went on, you'd better ask Bella.'

'All right,' he said. 'Derry, *go back into the dark*. Bella, *come into the light*.'

'Hi, there,' she said, blinking as if a spotlight were blinding her. 'How've you been?'

'Bella, I sent for you because I was hoping you could give me some background information on Sally's ex-husband. Derry seems to think that Jinx wants to kill him because of some wife-swapping incidents. Would you know anything about it?'

'I ought to know something about it. She was too chicken to go along with the fun. I mean, she was Larry's wife, right? And he needed a woman who would help him get ahead. But when the time came for partying, she'd get her headache and I'd get to come out. Well, I'm not gonna bad-mouth it. It was a lot of fun, the dancing and the shows, and the parties afterwards.'

'How did Larry react to your switching?'

'He'd always be amazed. He'd say I was either the most changeable woman in the world or the greatest actress. I told him I was both.'

'Do you know why Jinx wants to kill Larry?'

'Derry told me Jinx got really pissed off at him the last time we ever swapped. That night we went to see the

Buddy Hackett show at the Copacabana. I just love Buddy Hackett. I mean, his dirty jokes are really outa sight. That was the night Sally got her headache early. What she calls 'off-color stories' really upset her. Shit, did you ever hear of such a prude? Well, anyway, I came out and caught the last half of the show, as usual. Later, when we swapped with an out-of-town buyer and his wife, I figured it was going to be a lot of fun. He had a beautiful white Cadillac, and he was staying at the Americana, and I just knew it was gonna be terrific.

'I wanted to go dancing, but he was drunk and in such a hurry to get upstairs to his room, that I figure it's gonna be a quickie and then we'd go dancing afterward. Well, the bastard catches me off guard and ties my hands together behind my back. When I start struggling, he gets my feet and ties me by the ankles. Hey! I tell him, You don't have to do this. I'll play. But he says this is the way he likes it, and he can't get his own wife to do it.

'Now I start begging him. Please, don't, I say. I can't stand being hurt. He says, you'll love it, honey. He says it makes him come on big, and he knows women really love to be punished. You're crazy, I tell him. I don't need no punishment. Keep begging me, he says. And then he takes his belt out of his pants and doubles it up like he's going to whip my ass. Don't do it, I warn him. You don't know what this can lead to. But he starts hitting me. Now I'm a coward when it comes to pain. I just can't take it. So I leave.'

'What happened?'

'I don't really know because, like I say, I left. But Derry told me later that Jinx came out and got her hands and feet loose. The guy wound up in the intensive care ward of the hospital, and Larry had to find a new job. Ever since that night, Jinx has been gunning for Larry.'

'All right, Bella. You've been a big help. I really appreciate it.'

'Any time for you, big fella . . .' She broke off the Mae West voice with a giggle.

'Now, Bella, I'd like you to *go back into the dark*, and when I count to five, Sally will come out and remember as much of these conversations as she wants to.'

He counted, and Sally came out, took one look around, and began to shake all over.

'It's this headache, Dr. Ash. I can't help it.'

'Do you remember anything that has happened in this office today?'

She looked around dazed. 'I just came in here and sat down, didn't I?'

'You blacked out, Sally. Don't you remember anything that happened during the blackout?'

'No,' she said. 'I never do.'

'We have to work on that,' he said. Then he told her what he'd told Nola and me about setting up lines of communication between us. 'That's the only way to break down the amnesia.'

Sally shook her head. 'I'm sorry, Dr. Ash. You keep telling me about these other people, and I try to accept the idea. But deep down inside I think I don't really believe it. I'm sorry.'

Her lips were trembling. She was about to cry.

'There's no need to apologize, Sally. Other psychiatrists working with multiples have discovered that the patient's first defense against treatment is almost always denial. So I'm not surprised by your disbelief. But you must prepare yourself to be confronted by the existence of the others one of these days.'

'I'll try, Dr. Ash, but it's hard.'

'Remember, Sally, it took a lifetime to develop these defenses. The walls won't come tumbling down just because we blow our horns at it.'

All the way home her lips kept moving. People turned to stare, but I was the only one who could hear what she was saying over and over in her head. 'There are no others. There is only me. I'm the only person. There are no others. There is only me. I'm the only person. There are no others . . .'

God, that depressed me.

Seven

THINGS WENT SMOOTHLY for the next few weeks.
I apologized to Todd for my unpredictable moods, and
he said no apology was necessary. Sally went to therapy.
Bella and Nola came and went for short periods without
any problems. Jinx kept away. I handled the job, and I was
getting to hope things could stay stable this way and maybe
we wouldn't really have to be fused. If I couldn't be the real
person, this was next best.

Then one evening after we closed The Yellow Brick Road,
Todd stopped me on the way out. He took a chewed up
toothpick out of his mouth and said, 'I know tomorrow's
your day off, Sally, but I need a favor.'

'Name it,' I said.

'You know that during the harness-racing season I set up
publicity campaigns for the special-events manager at the
New York Raceway.'

I nodded.

'Well, at the Memorial Day meet, before the last race we
always have a pretty gal dress up like a jockey. You know,
silks, helmet, goggles. We call her "Betty Wynns." The girl
that usually does it just called in sick, and Eliot suggested
you might fill in.'

'What would I have to do?'

'Betty Wynns just struts around on a moving float out
on the track before the last race, sings a couple of songs

– anything she feels like – and picks the prize-winning tickets out of a drum. There'll be fifty bucks in it for you.'

'Hey, you don't have to pay me for a favor.'

'Hell, that part's business. The raceway pays for it. We'd spend the evening at the track. I'd show you the setup. The whole gig shouldn't take more than fifteen minutes.'

'I'll do it,' I said.

He rubbed his mouth, watching me closely. 'You're sure it's okay? I mean, it's not something that would trigger one of those mood changes?'

I laughed. 'Just let me know when the spotlight goes on, and you'll get a performance. It sounds like fun.'

Todd picked me up at six the next evening in his black Lincoln Continental Mark IV, and he was studying me as if he was trying to psych out who I was. He was getting close to the truth.

'Hey,' I said, running my hand over the maroon leather interior, 'I could get accustomed to this.'

'That's the problem,' he said as he entered the Sixty-sixth Street entrance of Central Park. 'After you get accustomed to it, it's just transportation, no different from a beat-up old Chevy, but then you're still paying heavy installments.'

'Then why do you have it?'

'An executive has got to put up a front.'

He eased the car onto the FDR Drive and headed toward the Queensboro Bridge. I enjoyed the drive. We kidded around for a while and then he said, 'Sally, I—'

I knew he was going to get on the subject of my moods, so quickly I said, 'It's hard to believe you were a campus radical.'

'Why?'

'I used to look up to most older students during the war years. I've always admired idealists who cared more for causes than for material things. But protesters didn't want to be on the winning side. They wanted America to lose what they saw was an unjust war. Gamblers are different. They're out to win.'

He smiled. 'That shows how little you know about gamblers. Like the man once said, "It's not whether you win or lose, but how you play the game." For a gambler, it's not winning that matters. It's the excitement of the action.'

'How early did you start gambling?'

He stared straight ahead, and the car suddenly accelerated to eighty-five. 'As far back as I can remember,' he said. 'I was born on the West Side – Hell's Kitchen. I learned to play poker for pennies and nickels.'

'You gambled when you were a kid?'

'Gambling was my life until I went to Columbia. But even then I was hooked. I'd go around collecting money in those cans for different legal-defense funds or for Hanoi Relief, and I'd tell myself I could double or triple it at a crap game or at the track. Lady luck had to smile on me for a good cause, I thought.'

'Did she?'

'For a time. Once I had a run of luck that lasted nearly three weeks, and everybody thought I was the greatest fund raiser in the movement.'

'And when you lost?'

'I'd suffer the torments of the damned, but I had to keep gambling to give the wheel of fortune a chance to turn back in my direction.'

'But then you hit it big?'

'The best thing that ever happened to me was letting Eliot talk me into investing part of those winnings in The Yellow Brick Road. If not for that I'd have lost it all.'

'And where does Gamblers Anonymous come in?'

'After I invested in the restaurant, I went on a losing streak that took the rest of the stake I'd built up. Nearly ten thousand dollars. I panicked. I needed money, but Eliot didn't have the dough to buy me out. That's when he talked me into going to G.A. It's been six months since I've rolled the dice, or played cards for money, or bet my own money on a horse or a dog.'

I put my hand on his shoulder because my heart went out to him. I could imagine what he went through, and I could feel the same torment he must have gone through to overcome a mental sickness.

'What about this place?' I asked, as he pulled into a private reserved parking area. 'Isn't this temptation?'

'This is different,' he said. 'What I do here isn't gambling. It doesn't involve my own money.'

He saw my disbelief and laughed. 'You'll see in a few minutes.'

Instead of going through the regular grandstand or clubhouse admissions gate, we went through a special entrance. The guard nodded and touched his cap in a salute, 'Evening, Mr. Kramer.'

The elderly black man who ran the private elevator nodded as we got on. He was holding a marked-up copy of the *Racing Form Consensus*.

'Evenin', Mr. Kramer,' he said, glancing up. 'How does Prince of India look to you in the first?'

'He didn't even run in the money last time out, Jason.'

'Yeah,' said Jason, scratching his head with a stub of pencil he'd been using to mark the form. 'But that was a muddy track. Tonight's fast. I'm thinking of putting a deuce on him. I heard from the woman who cleans up the jockeys' dressing room that this jockey told her he's gonna win the first race.'

'You've been around here long enough to know better than that, Jason.'

'Yeah, I don't usually pay no never mind to tips, but this morning I was thinking of that horse anyway. I had a dream about that Indian prince who gets his weight in gold on his birthday. I figured that was more than a coincidence.'

'It's your two dollars, Jason. I guess losing it one way is as good as another.'

'You didn't always used to talk like that, Mr. Kramer.'

'You know I've been to the bottom, Jason. It's a long way back up, and I don't think I'll have many more chances.'

Jason smiled. 'Well, I don't have it bad like you used to, Mr. Kramer. I just bet a deuce now and then for the hell of it.'

'Keep it that way, Jason, and you won't need Gamblers Anonymous for the hell of it.'

We got off the elevator at the upper level and as Jason let us out, I realized that each of us had our own hell.

'What would a gambler's hell be like?' I asked Todd. 'Being roasted over a fire of losing tickets? Or being forced to crawl, forever looking for the winning ticket that fell out of a hole in your pocket?'

He looked out at the oval track as we approached the upper level. The bright lights reflected on the jockeys parading their silks. 'Why make it up when it's right here? For me, this is gamblers' hell, not being able to get a piece of the action for myself.'

As we walked along, people waved to Todd – window bet-takers, floor sweepers, concession stand operators. Everyone seemed to know him and like him. As he passed through the press room, several of the sportscasters greeted him. He waved back and looked at the clock.

'Fifteen minutes to the first race,' he said. 'Time to meet Stan.' He led the way through a small room below an outside gangwaylike staircase that led up to the booth of the race announcer.

We climbed the circular stairway to the glass and steel observation booth. A well-stacked brunette was sitting near the glass door, turning the pages of *Filmland Confessions*. When she saw Todd through the glass entrance, she gave no sign of recognition but reached over and unbolted the door to let us in, and then she went back to her magazine.

'That's Holly,' Todd said, 'Stan's girl. Two years ago she won the Miss Englewood competition.'

At the upper end of the booth, overlooking the track, Stan and his assistant were seated at a table behind a microphone. Stan was watching through binoculars as the horses paraded around the track.

'Fast track tonight,' Todd said.

Stan looked up. He had a boyish face with a deadpan expression like a sad-mouthed, whitefaced clown. He nodded, reached for a purse-sized leather case with a wrist strap, unzipped it, pulled out a roll of hundred-dollar bills with a rubber band around it. He handed it to Todd who counted twenty in all, replaced the rubber band, and put the roll in his trousers pocket.

'Anything in the first race?' Todd asked.

Stan picked up his binoculars and studied the trotters, now rounding the track and coming back to the paddock.

'No. There are four good horses – too close to bet. We'll wait for the second race. Call me.' When Stan spoke, his voice had a hard-edged, deadpan quality to it that matched his face. Miss Englewood looked up from her magazine long enough to let us out of the booth and lock it behind us.

'What was that all about?' I asked, following Todd down the circular staircase.

Todd said, 'At twenty-six, Stan is one of the youngest announcers in harness racing, and one of the best handicappers on the circuit. There aren't many people around here who know that the announcing job is only a sideline. He really makes his money following the pacers and trotters around the country.'

It was beginning to dawn on me. 'And you place his bets –'

Todd smiled and nodded. 'He's not supposed to bet at a track where he's announcing the races. For a five percent commission I handle his action. Either here or with my bookie by phone. Since I've got a reputation as a big gambler, no one suspects – no one who matters.'

When we got off the elevator, a waiter showed us to a table in the VIP lounge directly above the finish line, took our orders for dinner and drinks, and brought us the racing program and several handicap and tip sheets.

'I don't feel right, your spending all this money on me,' I said when the drinks arrived.

He smiled and shook his head. 'There's no charge for any of this. The raceway picks up the tab. It comes with tonight's favor.'

'Well then,' I said, hoisting my brandy alexander, 'here's to an exciting evening.'

He clinked my glass. 'With the most exciting and fascinating woman I've ever met.'

He was really so sweet, and I felt very close to him just then. Like a really good friend. Just then Stan's voice came over the loudspeaker. I couldn't believe it was the same guy. The post-time announcement sounded deep, rich, and nasal.

Several other people had come into the VIP lounge, and they seemed to know Todd.

'Has Stan picked one for the first race?' asked a florid man with an enormous cigar and diamond rings on three fingers.

Todd shook his head. 'He'll probably have something for the second race.'

'Shit!' the man said. 'I was hoping he'd pick us a winner in the first.'

Todd handed me a twenty-dollar bill.

'What's that for?'

'To bet.'

'I thought we weren't betting on the first race.'

'Stan and I aren't. You see, Stan isn't a gambler either. He's a handicapper, and like I said, there's a difference. A handicapper bets only to win. A gambler bets for the excitement – win or lose. So you gamble. Maybe some of your excitement will stimulate my adrenalin.'

'Who do I bet on?'

'Well, there's Jason's tip, Prince of India.'

I put the twenty on Prince of India to win, but even though I screamed my heart out, and Todd had a great time watching me jumping up and down and yelling, Prince of India broke stride and came in next to last.

Just before the second race, Todd picked up a red phone and called Stan. When he hung up, the man with the cigar and three rings, and three other wealthy-looking men in the lounge, crowded around him.

'Real McCoy in the second,' Todd said.

Each of the men slipped a twenty-dollar bill into Todd's hand. When they went to give Jason the money to place their bets, Todd handed me one of the twenties. 'See? Easy money. Go put it on Real McCoy.'

I went up to the betting window, and all that kept going through my mind was the song from *Guys and Dolls* . . . 'I got a horse right here, his name is Paul Revere . . .' Todd was at the fifty-dollar window, betting for Stan.

The post call sent chills through me and as they took off, I started screaming louder than I had before in my life. Real McCoy stayed in third place all the way to the final turn around the track, and then he made his move. It was a photo finish. We won. And the horse paid five to one. I cashed in my tickets, and when the man counted out the money, my hand was shaking. I shoved the bills quickly into my purse. This was the life. Todd cashed in four fifty-dollar tickets for Stan.

'It's really yours,' I told Todd, offering him the money I'd won.

He shook his head. 'That would mean I was gambling. What would my friends at Gamblers Anonymous say?'

The next horse Stan picked came in third, but he had three more good-odds winners, and I won $470.35 by the eighth race.

'Who should I bet on in the next race?' I asked.

He shook his head. 'Stan is letting the last two races pass. Too many good horses. And besides, you've got a job to do.'

Then I remembered why I was there. I'd have to fill Bella in on the deal so she wouldn't screw up. I looked around nervously. There were so many people around. 'Is there a place where I can have some privacy for a few minutes?'

'There's a dressing room next to the racing secretary's office. That's where the costume is. I'll give Stan his money and then I'll be back to get you.'

In the small dressing room, I got into the jockey's blue and red silks, brushed my hair in the mirror, tucked the money in my bra, and called Bella. I explained the deal to her.

She got sore. 'Me dance around in that thing? Wearing a helmet and goggles? I'm no clown.'

'Look, Bella. I promised Todd.'

'You promise, you deliver.'

There was a knock on the door. 'You okay?'

'Yeah, I'll be right out.'

'The driver is waiting for you.'

'Okay,' I said. I turned back to Bella. 'Tell you what. I'll share my winnings with you. I won four hundred and seventy dollars.'

'I want half, and you don't bump me for the rest of the evening.'

'Hey, that's highway robbery.'

'Nope, that's show biz. You don't like it, hire someone else.'

'Okay. Okay. The name of the character is Betty Wynns.' But before I switched I made a mental note out of Bella's hearing that I'd get even someday.

Bella looked at herself in the mirror, put on lipstick and a red silk scarf she found in the locker. 'Okay, Betty Wynns,' she said, wetting her lips. 'Your audience is waiting. Let's go knock 'em dead.'

The driver was outside the dressing room, and so was Todd. She slipped up and kissed Todd on the lips, catching him off guard. 'See you later, honey.'

'Jesus,' he whispered.

'I'll Betty Wynns too,' she said, giggling, and walked off behind the driver, wiggling her butt.

The driver, a good-looking Puerto Rican young man named Paco, led her to the flower-decked float hooked to a white pickup truck. The raised stage had a dummy horse and sulky and a wire-mesh drum filled with admission stubs. There were loudspeakers at each end of the float and a hand-held microphone attached to the cab.

'You know what to do?' Paco asked.

Doing her imitation of Mae West as she climbed into the sulky and took the reins in her hands, Bella said, 'Paco, honey, ah always know what to do.'

'Okay,' he said, laughing. 'I've got a mike in the cab too. I'll announce you and give the pitch. All you have to do after that is sing one or two songs – anything you want – and wave to the jerks while I drive real slow back and forth in front of the grandstand three times. Then I'll park in the center, and you do your stuff.'

As the truck entered the track, the crowd burst into applause, waving.

'Hey, Betty Wynns!'

'Hey, bet he loses!'

'Sing us a song, Betty!'

'Are those tits real?'

'Betty Loses it at the track!'

'Hey, Betty Eats it for breakfast!'

As they drove to the center of the grandstand, Bella took the mike and sang 'Camptown Races.' The audience roared appreciatively.

After the first number, Paco thanked the crowd for coming to the New York Raceway. Betty Wynns was going to pick the winning ticket stubs from the drum attached to the back of the cab. He parked the truck directly in front of the grandstand. TV news cameras were trained on her all the time.

'Pick mine, Betty!'

'Hey, Betty, you can ride me anytime!'

She waved, took off her goggles, turned the crank of the wire-mesh drum, and picked out the tickets.

'If the winners are good-looking guys,' she said, 'each one gets a kiss as a bonus.' And again the crowd roared with pleasure.

She mugged and joked for the audience. When she saw the TV camera she wet her lips and whispered in a sexy Marilyn Monroe voice through the mike, 'But I was hoping there'd be a casting couch to perform on.' She did a bump and grind, and the crowd cheered.

She picked the five winning tickets. The first three were men, and she kissed them. When the drawing was over, she sang 'My Heart Belongs to Daddy' and got a standing ovation. Then a bunch of young fellows jumped the fence and spilled onto the track. Paco drove the pickup away from the grandstand, and it took half a dozen security guards to round the men up and herd them back so the last race could be run.

'You were terrific,' Todd said, as Paco pulled back to the paddock entrance. She kissed Todd again, long and hard.

'C'mon,' he said.

'Where?'

'You can change, and then I'll take you home.'

'I want to bet on the last race,' she said.

'Stan hasn't picked anything for the last race.'

'Who's Stan?'

Todd looked at her for a long time and shook his head. 'Mood change again. You're the other one. I guessed it.'

'The other what?'

'The one who went dancing with Eliot, nickname Bella.'

'You got me fingered, honey,' she said, rubbing his chest. 'Now let me get outa these racing duds. I'm hot to trot.'

She changed, and I told her I wanted to get back out.

'We made a deal,' she said.

'I'll give you the whole four hundred and seventy dollars,' I said.

'Paying me off? Look, I'm the one who went out there to perform. I should have the money and the time out too.'

'You're going to regret this, Bella.'

'So what else is new? You made an agreement. I'm holding you to it.'

There was nothing I could do. Todd was waiting for her outside the dressing room. 'Don't bet too much on the last race. Stan thinks it's too close.'

'That's Stan's problem.'

She went to the fifty-dollar window and bet the whole four hundred and seventy on Sulky Sal to win. It was, she thought, a terrific hunch bet. Sulky Sal came in fourth.

'Well,' she said to Todd, stretching seductively, 'that was exciting.'

'You're a good loser,' he said.

'I always say about money, like I say about men, "easy come, easy go."'

He drove her home, and she invited him up for a nightcap.

He followed her upstairs, and I cursed myself for making that stupid deal with her not to bump her for the rest of the evening. I was afraid she'd come on strong with Todd and Jinx would break loose again. Jinx hadn't been part of any deal, but Bella wouldn't think of that.

That's when I got the idea that since none of the others had made a deal with her, one of them could do the bumping. Nola might cause complications. I decided the best one to take over would be Sally. She didn't know a damned thing.

Bella went into the bedroom to get into something more comfortable while Todd was fixing a couple of drinks. That's when I ran interference while Sally stumbled out, wondering what the hell was going on.

Bella started to say, 'That's not fair—'

But then she was gone, and Sally was tying her new pink bathrobe around her when she heard noise from the living room. It frightened her. She peeked through the crack in the door and saw Todd with a drink in his hand, turning on the TV set.

'Hey,' he yelled, 'you might be on the late news.'

She came out slowly, trying to make sense of what he was talking about. 'Why would I be on the news?'

'Well didn't you see those cameras down at the track?'

She looked dazed. 'What are you doing here? And why should cameras down at the track have anything to do with me?'

'Oh, no!' he said, putting down his drink and getting ready to run. He backed toward the door. 'God damn it, which one are you now?'

She glared at him. 'Look, I don't know what your game is, Todd. But I haven't been out of this apartment all day.'

'No?' he said, pointing to the TV screen. 'Well then, explain that.'

'—and tonight,' the announcer was saying, 'the folks at the New York Raceway had a great time winning prizes and being entertained by none other than Betty Wynns, who was in rare form tonight.'

The camera panned close and Sally's eyes widened as she saw herself.

'My God!'

'If you've been here all evening, who is that?'

'It's me . . .' she gasped. 'But I don't remember . . .'

She watched Bella dance, and listened to her sing and make wisecracks. Tears ran down her cheeks. 'It's not me. It can't be me. I don't remember.'

Todd tried to comfort her, but she drew away from him. 'Please leave me alone. I've got to think. I've got to sort this out.'

'Okay,' he said, 'if you're sure you'll be all right. No matter what happens, I just want you to know I love you.'

When he was gone she turned off the TV set and stared at the darkened screen.

She couldn't say it wasn't true any more. She'd seen it with her own eyes.

The silence was eerie, and she was in such torment I felt sorry for her. It was as if someone had ripped a mask off her face and she could suddenly see in the mirror what had been happening all these years of losing time and being blamed for things she knew she hadn't done, and being called a liar and being punished, and hearing the whispers behind her back, and people making circular motions near their foreheads with their forefingers.

'I don't want to live!' she screamed.

—You have to live, said the voice.

'Who are you? Whose voice is that? Which one are you?'

—I am here to watch over you.

'I'm a multiple personality. I'm a freak. I want to die!'

—Now that you know the truth, you're on the way to a cure. Don't give up.

'I can't stand this hell! Let me die!'

She broke a drinking glass and started to cut her wrist, but the voice stopped her.

—Now that you've seen Bella, you know the truth, and you'll accept the others emotionally as well as intellectually. Tell Dr. Ash. And then your treatment will go forward.

She fainted.

I didn't know where the voice came from. We'd probably all gone crazy.

At Friday's session in the hospital office when Sally told Roger what happened it upset him.

'I had planned to confront you with your other selves,' he said, 'but I expected to be present when you faced the truth. I never imagined you'd see it on television.'

'I wanted to die, Dr. Ash. I never felt so bad in my life.'

'This is a painful but necessary step on the way to getting better. We break through denial – your first line of defense – and now that you've been forced to accept the fact that there really are other people inside you, you can move toward co-consciousness. Once all of you learn to communicate with each other, you'll be able to function in relative safety. The greatest danger has always been that none of you knew what the others were doing.'

'I'm sorry I tried to kill myself, Dr. Ash.'

He looked at her thoughtfully for a few seconds. Then he leaned forward. 'That worries me.'

'I won't do it again.'

'We've reached a very delicate phase, Sally. You're in great danger right now. I think it might be best for you to admit yourself here as a voluntary patient. Just for a short while until we establish co-consciousness.'

She gasped. 'But why? I'm not crazy. You said I wasn't psychotic.'

'Of course you're not. But as I just said, the next step is crucial, and I want people around you twenty-four hours a day in case there are any more blackouts.'

She shook her head, frowning. 'But I've had blackouts all my life, and I didn't need hospitalization. What are you going to do?'

He leaned forward, took her hands in his, and looked into her eyes. 'Sally, up to now, every time I've put you under and left it up to you to remember, you've come awake with complete amnesia. You blocked the others so strongly we were getting nowhere.'

'What are you going to do?' There was alarm and fear in her voice.

'I'm going to give you hypnotic commands to remember what happens when I talk to the others. Not only will you hear them, as Sally, but you'll remember what you've heard. You'll start to accept them.'

'I don't want to accept them. Just get rid of them.'

'We can't do that. Now that you have knowledge of their existence, emotionally as well as intellectually, we have to bring you all together. You've all got to begin to communicate directly with one another.'

'I'm scared.'

'Of course. You created these people because you needed them, but then you defended yourself against the knowledge by amnesia. My approach is to break down the counter-productive defense mechanism, to have it out in the open so you can all work together. Remember, they were once your imaginary friends.'

She wiped away tears. 'Yes, but I never thought I'd have to meet them again.'

'It's the only way, Sally. I'm planning to begin group therapy with all your personalities, and I want you in the hospital where you can be under observation around the clock.'

'What about my job?'

'Tell Eliot and Todd you have to have a leave of absence – a week or two – for medical purposes. You don't have to go into details. I'll arrange things for you here.'

She nodded. 'Whatever you say.'

As she left the office, she sensed that her whole body was tense, every muscle knotted. She thought of packing a suitcase and running away. But she knew she wouldn't. She would face the nightmare people who were tearing her life apart, and meeting them all face to face would either make her well or it would kill her.

Part Two

Eight

THE FOLLOWING WEEK Sally signed herself into the Midtown Hospital Mental Health Center. She was in an open ward on the third floor that looked more like a modern hotel lobby than a hospital. But she felt terrified around the nurses and the other doctors and the patients, so she packed a mental suitcase and checked her mind out. I took over. Big-Mouth Duffy dropped into my room from time to time, sometimes waking me in the middle of the night, always asking me who I was. I knew she didn't believe in us, so I put on a big act and named some new names, pretending other personalities. She got real excited when I told her I was four-year-old Louise, looking for my mommy. And one afternoon I told her I was Martin Kosak, who had robbed a bank in Tucson. She wrote it all down.

I got to meet a lot of nice people in the bright, plant-lined dayroom, but when the word got around that I was a multiple personality, the other patients acted as if I was a freak.

'Which one are you today?' one white-haired old lady asked me.

'Jack the Raper,' I said. 'And I've raped a lot of old ladies in my time.'

She scurried away. I know it isn't very nice, but dumb questions like that get me riled up.

I became friendly with Maryanne, the stringy-haired, pimple-faced girl, who kept telling me how nice and friendly I was, and whenever I went into the dayroom to curl up on one of the rainbow-colored foam rubber couches, she'd come over and sit next to me. She liked to gossip a lot and I liked to listen because it gave her such pleasure to be the first one to tell news, and because we were both Roger's patients.

On my third day, I came back to the dayroom after a whole bunch of tests, including the one with the inkblots and one called the 'California Psychological Inventory.' I was tired and grumpy and I just wanted to play solitaire. But Maryanne came over and pulled her chair close.

'I don't want Dr. Ash for my doctor anymore,' she said.

I kept playing the cards without looking up at her. 'Why?'

'Everyone's talking about him. I overheard three doctors in the cafeteria, where I was cleaning off the tables, say they wanted him removed from the consulting staff, but they were afraid it would get them into trouble. Another one called him a dictator and said once Dr. Ash makes a decision, he doesn't listen to other opinions. He figures he knows it all.'

'Maybe he does.' I was stuck, so I cheated by sneaking an ace from the bottom of the deck.

'They said he's spending so much time on your case he isn't doing enough for his other patients and they have to cover for him. And they're right. He spends more time with you than with the rest of us.'

'Well,' I snorted, 'that's because there are five of me and only one of you.'

Her mouth fell open. 'You admit it?'

'Admit it? I'm proud of it. It makes me five times as smart, five times as beautiful, and five times as sexy as the rest of you.'

She glared at me. 'You bitch. Everyone says you're faking just to get his attention and taking up the time the rest of us should have.'

I laughed. 'Sure. I'm really an actress. They're gonna make a movie about multiple personality, and I'm practicing for the part. I'm gonna be a very famous person.'

'You're putting me on. You don't take me serious. You know what else I heard? The nurses were saying his wife hung herself from a tree in their yard because she couldn't stand living with him any more.'

'You're a goddamned liar and a pimple-faced two-bit whore.'

I guess I went too far. But what the hell, I was sick and tired of everyone dumping on Roger. She came at me suddenly, scattered the cards, and knocked me over backward in the chair. I hit the ground hard. And then she was on top of me, pulling my hair. I figured I could handle scrawny Maryanne on my own, because Jinx would as soon kill her as look at her. I didn't want any complications in the hospital.

We rolled over and over, and she tore my dress, but I got her in a bear hug and sat on her. She screamed at me. 'I'll get you! I'll make you sorry you ever started with me!'

'Me start with you? You were the one who—'

Before I could finish, I was yanked off Maryanne. Big-Mouth Duffy and another nurse pinned my arms and they were twisting. Maryanne jumped off the floor and kicked me in the stomach while they were holding me. Three to one wasn't fair, so I sent for reinforcements.

Jinx lashed out with her foot, caught Maryanne square on the chin, and knocked her unconscious. Then, sagging suddenly, Jinx took both nurses by surprise. When they relaxed she swung one hand free and caught one with a left jab, and then the other with a right cross. She heard the whistle and the alarm bell go off and saw the other patients cowering in the corner. But she kept after the two nurses. There was blood on the floor, and she knew it wasn't hers.

Duffy scrambled out of range and then tried to come back at her, but Jinx tackled her and kicked and bit her. The door to the dayroom flew open, and three male attendants came running in. One had a straitjacket. They surrounded her, and she let go of Duffy.

'Come on, you bastards! I'll take you all on!' The blood in her mouth nauseated her, but she didn't want to vomit now. She had to keep them from getting her.

The big attendant bear-hugged her. She kicked him in the nuts, but he got his leg in the way and squeezed her tighter.

'You're a hellcat,' he said, laughing.

'Hang onto her, Toby. I'll get this camisole around her.'

'Jesus, make it quick!'

She kept trying to claw him, but he ducked and bobbed. Finally they had her on the floor in the canvas jacket.

Why had they brought her to the crazy house? It was a goddamn lousy trick to lock her up in the booby hatch and then get her into a fight. She knew very well that meant trouble.

'I guess we ought to notify Doc Ash. It's his goddamn problem.'

The other attendant nodded. 'He's too easy on them, and then we got to deal with this shit. Look at that bite. I'll probably get rabies.'

Duffy got up from the floor and said, 'I'll take her now. And I'll do the notifying. Just help me get her back to her room and cuff her to her bed. Since her doctor left instructions that she's not to be given Thorazine under any circumstances, we'll let the bitch cool her ass in restraints a couple of days. We've got the situation under control. No need to disturb the good doctor over the weekend.'

'You're as good as dead,' Jinx snarled at her. 'Someday they're gonna have to let me out, and I'll come after you and cut your heart out.'

Duffy glared at her coldly, disguising her anger. 'It's a good act, Sally. But you overplayed it today. You may be able to deceive Dr. Ash, but you don't fool the rest of us.'

They half dragged, half carried Jinx into the room and pushed her inside. She fought as they fastened the leather bracelets and ankle cuffs to the bed. It infuriated her. 'The hell with it,' she snorted. 'It wasn't my goddamn fight anyway. Why should I stick around and put up with this crud? Take it back, Derry.'

'Not me,' I said. 'I can't stand being tied down.'

'Well, I'm taking off,' Jinx said, 'so give it back to Dumbo.'

I felt kind of guilty because none of it was Sally's fault. But better her than me. So I just watched while Jinx slipped away. Then I got this strange feeling someone else was there watching besides me, even though I knew that couldn't be, because I was the trace and I knew everybody. Well, anyway, when Sally came out and found her feet and hands tied to the bed she screamed and moaned and strained at the cuffs.

That's when the voice started talking to her again, a soft, friendly tone, saying, – Calm down, Sally. You'll do yourself damage if you struggle like that. You've got to have patience. Trust Dr. Ash. You must put your complete faith in him and meet the others. I agree with him that there is real danger for all of you if something isn't done quickly.

I figured the crazy house was getting to both of us. But Sally calmed down as she listened. And then she nodded and just lay there. She wouldn't resist. She wouldn't fight. And maybe whoever had done this to her would come back and take the cuffs off.

She tried blanking out, but that didn't work, so she began to think about her real father, Oscar the postman, who disappeared after her grandpa died.

She remembered the face she was looking for. She'd searched for it so often as she wandered the city streets, those sad, heavy-lidded eyes that made Oscar seem like a sleepwalker, shoulders stooped from carrying the mailbag all these years (but in her dreams he was the sandman, and instead of letters, the bag was filled with sand, like they'd always pretend after he told her a bedtime fairy tale). And she heard his mischievous laugh as if he were chuckling in his sleep. Or was it her sleep he was laughing in?

She was sure his disappearance was just an April Fools' joke, and some day he would come up behind her on the street and put his hands over her eyes and say, 'April Fool, Sally-girl.' Or he would point to something and say, 'Look at that duck over there!' and she would look, and he would sing gleefully, 'I made you look! I made you look! I made you buy a penny book!'

Always joking and playing with words when he took her along on his mail route. 'Look at that dog with two tails!' and then – 'April fool! Go to school! Tell your teacher you're a fool!'

Sad eyes, smiling when he woke her for school. 'Time to get up, Sleeping Beauty. Don't want to make your teacher angry.'

He always watched the time for her. Why did he rush onto the train that day and leave her behind at the station? Was he so deep in thought about delivering the mail he forgot she was with him? She cried when the policeman found her on the platform and took her to the station house to call her mother to get her.

And the other time when she and Mother went to the station house to fill out the missing persons report. But how could Oscar be missing? How could he lose himself? He had to be somewhere. She knew he had long been lost somewhere in his own mind when, after he wakened her every morning, she'd see him sitting alone at the breakfast table, staring into space as if his eyes were about to close. And just when she was sure he was going to nod off, he would chuckle out loud and rub his finger along his thin mustache and shake his head, saying, 'Oscar . . . Oscar!' as if scolding himself. And then his eyes would droop again sadly, as if he realized where and who he was.

In later years she wondered what he used to think in those days before he lost himself. Was he dreaming about the sea? Her mother once said Oscar had probably run off to sea, because when he was a boy he had loved ships and been a Sea Scout, and his father before him had been an able-bodied seaman, and he had always talked about going to sea. But they'd been married right after he graduated from high school, and her mother quit school, and Sally had been born six months later. She had always known her mother was ashamed and bitter about that.

But Sally didn't believe he had gone off to sea. She still imagined him as the sandman walking up the path with the leather mailpouch full of dreamdust, and someday she would see him and run up from behind and put her hands over his eyes and whisper, '. . . Guess who, Mr. Sandman. Guess who?'

She wished Oscar were here now. She wondered if he had gone somewhere to make a new life for himself. She'd heard of men doing that: find a new wife, have new children, take on a new name and completely different identity.

The more she thought about Oscar, the faster the thoughts tumbled through her head, mindgoingsofast I can't standit. I've got togetoff. The trainsgoingsofast. I have to slow it down. Why was it so hard for her to make simple decisions?

What to wear? What to eat? What floor to get off on from the elevator?

Oscar help me.

Dr. Ash help me.

God help me.

She had to tell Dr. Ash about Oscar. How, when she was six, she knew before anyone else that he wasn't coming back. How she knew something was wrong that night after the fairy tale when he thought the make-believe sand from his pouch had put her to sleep. He leaned over her bed and kissed her cheek and whispered, 'Pleasant dreams, Sleeping Beauty, until your Prince Charming wakes you with a kiss,' and nodding and smiling went out of the room. That was the last time she ever saw him.

Duffy kept Sally tied to the bed all of Saturday and until noon on Sunday. Then she came in and looked Sally in the eyes.

'Who are you?'

'Sally Porter.'

She moved real close and glared. 'And you've been lying about the others, haven't you?'

'What do you mean?'

'There are no other personalities. You made that all up, didn't you?'

The look of hate was frightening, and Sally didn't know what to do until the voice in her head said, – Agree with her. She's a vicious fool. Tell the bully what she wants to know.

'No,' Sally said aloud. 'I'm not a liar. Dr. Ash says there are others, and I believe him.'

'Ash gave orders for no tranquilizers,' Duffy said, 'and as far as I'm concerned you're still violent. So stay like that until tomorrow.'

But she sent someone in an hour later to take the cuffs off.

'I'm sorry,' said the big matronly nurse. 'Duffy is a vicious person. She shouldn't be a psychiatric nurse.'

Sally rubbed her wrists and ankles to restore the circulation. She peered quickly at the white-on-black plastic name tag. L. Fenton, R.N. That's what she should have, she thought, a name tag like that so people wouldn't always have to ask who she was.

'Thank you, Nurse Fenton. I'm sorry to be a bother.'

'Now don't you call yourself a bother. You need help, that's all, and you've got a fine doctor looking after you.'

Sally would have stayed in her room most of Sunday, but Eliot came with flowers and candy, and she was allowed to go to the visitors' lounge with him. He looked different. She tried to figure what it was, but she couldn't.

'It's sweet of you to come and see me,' she said.

'Todd would have come too, but he had to go down to the raceway to arrange the publicity for a group party. He told me what happened. I mean, about you seeing yourself on television.'

She nodded. 'Dr. Ash says that was good for me. All this time I've been refusing to accept the truth about those other people inside me.'

'I suspected from that first evening we went dancing. Remember, when you got sore because I called you Bella?'

She nodded.

'You're a beautiful woman, Sally. But more than that, you're a good person. Warm-hearted, alive, exciting. I don't have to tell you I'm crazy about you.'

'I'm a sick person.'

'But you're going to get well. One of these days you're going to get your head together. And I'll tell you something. I know I have a reputation as a swinger, but that's all over,

Sally. I'm willing to wait if you give me just a little bit of hope.'

'What do you mean?'

'After three failures, I never thought I'd want to get married again, but I've seen more goodness in you than in any one I've ever known. If you were married to a responsible man with a good business, the judge might reconsider about your kids. Think about it for the future.'

She blushed. 'That's very sweet of you, Eliot. The twins are the most important things in the world to me, but marriage. I – I don't—'

'Please don't say anything about it now, Sally. I just planted a seed, that's all. Maybe it'll grow. If it doesn't, and I can't be your husband, I'll settle for being a friend.'

She nodded. 'You're a wonderful man.'

When Eliot left, she thought about it. She tried to visualize herself married to a middle-aged swinger who flirted with every woman in sight. Maybe he could change. As she ate a chocolate-covered nougat she suddenly realized why Eliot looked different. His face had filled out. Eliot was obviously gaining back his weight. Was there a fat man inside him now screaming to get out?

On Monday morning at ten Maggie came to take her from the ward to Roger's office to begin the group therapy.

'We heard what Duffy did,' Maggie said. 'Dr. Ash is furious. He's sending a complaint to the hospital administration.'

Maggie walked with her out of the psychiatric wing, across the courtyard to the administrative and medical building where Roger had his hospital office.

When she entered the room, she noticed it was arranged with five chairs in a circle. Four of them had mirrors propped up in the seats. Roger rose as she came in and led her to the chair without a mirror.

'I'm sorry, Sally. Duffy's action was inexcusable.'

'I'm all right, Dr. Ash. Really I am. They told me you left orders for me not to be tranquilized. Duffy probably had no alternative—'

'That's absurd. She should have called me at home. I would have come right down. She could have locked you in your room. There was no reason for the restraints. We're not in the Middle Ages.'

'I was violent, Dr. Ash. And she knew I had a history of trying to take my life.'

He pulled a chair close to her. 'We've got to deal with that, Sally. We've got to dig out this background so that we can move more quickly. But, as I've said, you've got to know it as well as I do. You have to relive it, with all its pain and suffering. Now that you know the others exist, I've got to put you in touch with them.'

She looked around at the four chairs with the mirrors, terrified, as if looking for a place to hide. 'I'm not ready yet. It's too soon.'

'I just hope it's not too late.'

She sank into the chair, hunched forward as if to make herself as small as possible. 'I don't think I can take it.'

'I have faith in you, Sally, or I wouldn't go ahead. Let me tell you what I've planned for today.'

She nodded without looking at him.

'We'll try it first without hypnosis. I'd like you to bring the others out by an act of will, by calling to them and talking to them the way you did when you were a child.'

She shook her head. 'I don't think I can, Dr. Ash.'

'Just try, Sally. If it doesn't work, I can always induce hypnosis this first time to get things started.'

'What should I say?'

'I leave that up to you.'

She looked into each of the mirrors, seeing her own reflection, and feeling foolish talking to herself.

'Dr. Ash has asked me to speak to you . . .'

She fell silent for a few seconds. Then she tried again.

'We've all got to come together and cooperate, because Dr. Ash is trying to help us . . .'

She felt panicky. A headache started to grip the base of her neck and she felt the chill, but she knew that wasn't what Dr. Ash wanted. He didn't want her to black out. She had to stay conscious and confront those – whatever they were – inside her.

'Please come out,' she cried. 'Derry . . . Nola . . . Bella . . . wherever you are. Talk to me.'

Nothing.

'I'm sorry, Dr. Ash,' she said. 'I've let you down.'

'You mustn't say that, Sally. Or even think it. This is just a small delay. You're naturally upset and frightened over a big step like this – opening the lines of communication.'

'But they're not communicating.'

She waited another minute. I could feel Nola and Bella hanging around the edges, just as curious as I was to see what was going to happen. I had no idea where Jinx was.

I remembered Sally's fourteenth birthday, when her mother made a party and invited kids from the neighborhood but nobody came because all the kids thought she was strange. But Sally preferred being alone anyway. We all went up to her room and had our own party with the ice cream and cookies and cake. Bella blew out the candles and Nola made the wish. Later Jinx climbed down the drainpipe, swiped Fred's car, and took us joyriding. Sally got sick and threw up and got the beating, even though she didn't remember a thing about it. It's kind of a shame that she never got in on the fun but had to pay for it.

Now Sally was trying not to cry. She just waited, knees tight together, fingers clamped, and her voice trembled. 'You'd better send for them, Dr. Ash. They won't come for me.'

'All right, Sally,' he said, touching her arm. *'He knows what's in the darkness . . .'*

She closed her eyes and went under, waiting for his instructions.

'When I count to five, all your people will come into the room and attend the group therapy session. We have important matters to discuss, and it requires the attendance of everyone. By everyone, I mean Derry, Nola, Bella, Jinx, and of course – Sally. How high did I say I was going to count?'

'Five . . .' Sally whispered.

'All right, then. One-two-three . . . four . . . five . . . all *come into the light.'*

Sally heard him, and she was frightened as she waited to see what would happen. Then I felt something push me out.

'Hi, Roger,' I said. 'Long time no see. For the record, it's me, Derry.'

When she heard my voice she gasped and looked from one mirror to the other to see who it was. The only reflection different from her own was the one directly on her left. There, instead of her own brown eyes and brown hair she saw a blue-eyed blonde with a bright gaze and a way of glancing sideways.

'Hello, Derry,' Roger said. 'What's been happening lately?'

I told him about the evening at the races with Todd, and about Sally's reaction when she saw herself as Bella on the

TV evening news. She hadn't known about the early part of the evening, of course, so she was fascinated as I talked about Todd.

'The problem that's developing,' I said, 'is that Todd and Eliot are both making moves.'

'What do you mean?' Roger asked.

'Todd's in love with Nola, but he mistook me for her. Eliot's crazy about Bella, but he proposed to Sally.'

'Which one do you approve of, Derry?'

'Me? Neither,' I said, looking into his eyes. I hoped he could see he was the only one I cared for.

'Well,' he said, 'that's something we'll have to keep an eye on. But no decisions should be made until after fusion. The whole Sally should be the one to choose.'

'Well, she'd better choose right,' I said.

'Is there anything else I should know, Derry?'

I thought about it a minute, and then I remembered that nudge before I came out. 'Now that you mention it,' I said, 'there is something. I've been getting the peculiar feeling I'm being watched. Sometimes I hear a strange voice, but there's no one there. It stopped Sally from cutting her wrist after she saw herself as Bella. Normally I'd be scared, but I have the feeling it's something good, something or someone who cares.'

Roger nodded. 'I've been expecting something like this. It happens with most multiples. As long as the things it says are positive, it should be listened to. But I do want to be kept informed about it.'

I nodded. 'I'll put a tracer on it.' I giggled. 'Sorry, I couldn't resist that.'

He smiled, and I was glad he didn't get sore at my joke. 'There's one other thing you can do, Derry.'

'Name it.'

'I want your help in this group therapy effort. Can you ask the others to come out and join us?'

'I can try, Roger. Is there any one in particular you want next?'

'I leave that up to you.'

I thought about it and figured Bella would be the best bet. She was always aching to get out, and she'd never turn down an audience. I told her Roger wanted us out at the same time. She laughed and said she'd love to.

Suddenly Sally saw the face in the mirror change from her own to a redhead with false eyelashes, heavy stage makeup, and pouting lips outlined in bright red. Which, I wondered, was the truth? What she saw now, or the video tape on TV?

'Whew!' Bella said, stretching sensuously. 'I'm dizzy. It's like being whirled around and around under the bright lights.'

Sally looked so scared I thought she was going to black out. 'Let me introduce you,' I said. 'Sally, this is Bella.'

'How do you do?' Sally said.

'I do fine, when you don't upstage me,' Bella said.

Sally frowned, not understanding what she was talking about.

'Bella's in show business,' I explained. 'She's the one you saw on the TV news the other night – doing the Betty Wynns bit at the racetrack.'

Sally shook her head. 'That's not who I saw. I saw myself. How is that possible?'

Then it occurred to me that she was right. I'd seen it too. It was Bella's face when I saw it in person – like now – but on video tape it had been Sally's face.

'That's not too hard to figure out,' said the voice from the third mirror, on Bella's left, directly opposite the chair Sally was sitting in. Sally saw a new face fill the mirror.

High cheekbones, olive skin, and long straight black hair down to her waist made her look almost Indian.

'Leave it to Nola,' I said. 'The brain has an answer for everything.'

'It's really very simple if you know anything at all about psychology.'

She looked at Roger, but he smiled and said nothing.

'When Sally sees us,' Nola said, 'she is projecting images out of her unconscious. What she saw on the TV screen was a taped image that doesn't have her imagination.'

Bella got sore. 'Are you telling me that none of us really look the way we do? That we all look exactly like her?'

'That's right,' Nola said.

'I don't believe that,' Bella insisted. 'I know what my own face looks like.'

Nola looked to Roger for support. 'What do you say, Roger? Don't you think you ought to clarify things for them?'

'You're doing a good job,' Roger said. 'As the therapist in this group situation, I ought to keep out of it as much as possible.'

'That's something I've been wanting to ask you ever since I heard about this group therapy idea. It's not the kind of thing most Freudian psychoanalysts would do, is it? I mean, usually they use the couch, with the analyst in the background and the patient free-associating and dredging up all that unconscious material, right?'

'Right,' he said, smiling, 'but I'm not a psychoanalyst, and I'm not a Freudian. Although I believe in many of the things Freud taught and accept many of his ideas, such as repression, the unconscious, and some of his interpretation-of-dreams material, I also have incorporated ideas of others: nondirective therapy, psychodrama, and the concepts and techniques of hypnotherapy and group therapy.'

'In other words, you're eclectic,' Nola said.

'I guess you could say that.'

Nola felt strong. She felt on the edge of tossing her bombshell.

'Then I think you should move your chair and join the circle,' she said. 'If we are to let you in on our problems, we ought to know more about you.'

He shook his head. 'I don't think it's wise at this stage for me to—'

'I think Nola is right,' Bella said. 'If we're going to tell you everything, you shouldn't hold out on us.'

'This is your session,' he insisted. 'I have to keep out of it.' He looked to Sally for help, but she stared at the floor. 'Please, Sally, go on with the discussion,' he said.

'I – I think Dr. Ash is right,' she said. 'He's the doctor, and he knows what's best.'

'It's two against one,' Nola said. 'How does Derry feel?'

Roger got up and started pacing around the office. 'This is incredible!' he said. 'I've never heard of such a thing. It's not a thing you vote on. The therapist just doesn't introduce himself and his problems into the therapy situation.'

'Well then,' Nola said, 'there is a technique I believe you should add to your armory.'

He raised his eyebrows. 'And what is that?'

'The "self-disclosure" approach.'

'Where in the world –?'

'In a slender volume I picked up in the library. *The Transparent Self*, by Sidney Jourard. I assume you know his work. And Mowrer's. You surely know Mowrer's book on *The New Group Therapy*.'

'Of course,' he said. 'But I don't see what that has to do with us here.'

'Well, both Mowrer and Jourard believe that the therapist should provide a model for the patient, by self-disclosure, by opening up and revealing his own life and problems. Since you admit you pick and choose techniques and theories from different sources, we have a right to ask you to do what you're asking *us* to do.'

We all sat around and watched him squirm. Nola had set the trap, and he had walked into it.

'I vote with Sally,' I said, feeling like a traitor to Nola and Bella. 'If Roger doesn't want to disclose himself, he doesn't have to. I think we owe him plenty, and I don't think it's fair to put him on the spot. I admit I'm curious to know more about you, Roger. But if you don't think it's right or good for us, then I'm with you.' I looked Nola right in the eye and said, 'Two against two. It's a tie.'

The room suddenly got quiet. All of us were looking at the mirror in the fifth chair, wondering if Jinx was going to come out and get into it. There was nothing there. I was relieved, but I knew Jinx would pick her own time and place, that was for sure.

Nola finally said, 'You're the only one who can break the tie, Roger. That is, if you want to tell us why your wife hung herself from a tree in your own back yard.'

The color drained from his face as he stared at her.

'How . . . did you . . . find out about that?'

Nola tried not to smile. It wasn't every day you had your psychiatrist at the end of a string. They always made such an effort to keep themselves safe in the shadows, out of reach. She didn't want to hurt him. She was really curious about his wife.

'How did you find out?' he asked.

'I didn't find out,' Nola said. 'Sally heard about it at the hospital, and that's what Derry's fight with pimple-face was all about. She told Derry you weren't a very good psychiatrist, that it was common gossip among the nurses and doctors that your wife's suicide contributed to what they called a burn-out. Derry filled me in.'

'What else did they say?'

'That your heart went out of your work, and you had to carry on, putting up a false front, pretending you really cared about your patients and about what you were doing, when you had really blocked out all emotion so that you could go on. So you see, we have a right to know more about you before we put our lives into your hands.'

'All right,' he said, his voice thick and choked up. 'Maybe this *is* the time for self-disclosure. If it'll contribute to keeping you alive, it'll be worthwhile.'

He pulled his chair into the circle between me and Nola. Then he bowed his head and looked at the floor.

'Lynette was very young when we married. She was very beautiful, and we were very much in love. She worked and helped put me through medical school. Well, there's a problem among doctors not too many people know about. As I've told Derry, overwork and overexposure to patients lead to what's been called the "burned-out syndrome." You pretend you're deeply involved in your patients' lives when it's all really an act, because you've seen it all, and heard it all, and your own problems seem larger and more pressing than theirs. You harden yourself to the pain and suffering so that you can go on, but it spills over into your personal life . . . I mean into *my* personal life. I've always cautioned my patients against using the wrong pronoun, against saying 'your' when they mean 'my,' and here I am doing it myself. God, what a mess . . .

'Anyway, I believe that's why she killed herself. The exhaustion made me emotionally dead. Lynette blamed herself, and because she was such a delicate, sensitive thing with deep need for love and support, and because I couldn't give her those things, she . . . she . . .' He shook his head, forcing himself to go on.

'One morning, when I woke up and looked out the window, I saw her hanging, silhouetted against the sky. She chose the maple with our initials carved on it.'

He looked around at each of us.

'Our teenaged son blamed me for her death,' he said. 'After that he was in and out of reform schools for three years until he was sixteen. Then one day he took off and disappeared. I've never seen him or heard from him since. I've lived alone. I've never remarried. I've devoted my life to my work. Most of it just going through the motions – until now.'

He stopped talking and looked up at Nola, his hands hanging limply over the arms of the chair.

'So that's why you wouldn't take our case on at first,' Nola said. 'Because of my suicide attempt.'

And Bella said, 'And that's why now you're fighting so hard to keep Sally alive.'

He nodded, 'As long as you hang on, there's hope for change. Don't throw life away. No matter how bad it gets, no matter how black things seem, don't give up.'

Nola suddenly felt very close to Roger. 'I'm glad you shared that with us, Roger. Knowing what you've gone through, I feel more confident you'll find a way to pull us together. No more suicide attempts. I promise to cooperate.'

He sat back in the chair, stretching his long legs out in front of him.

'I believe it's important for Sally to recall what happened at the time each of you changed from imaginary friends to real personalities.'

'Sounds good,' I said, 'but I don't happen to remember.'

'Neither do I,' Bella said.

Nola shook her head.

'I can help any one of you to recall under hypnosis. It's a technique called age-regression.'

'It ought to be Nola,' I said.

'Why me?'

I thought about it. And then the idea popped into my head, almost like a soft, strange voice out of the fog answering her. 'Because you were the last one to be created,' I said.

'What's that got to do with anything?'

'Derry's right,' Roger said. 'It's logical for us to start closest to where you are and then work your way back.'

Bella nodded. 'That way we don't have to deal with Jinx until last, if and when she shows up.'

'Come on, Nola,' Roger said. 'I disclosed myself. It's your turn. You said you'd cooperate.'

'All right,' she said, crossing her arms. 'Go ahead and regress me.'

'Nola,' he said, *he knows what's in the darkness . . .*'

She nodded and closed her eyes. He reached out, uncrossed her arms, and took both of her hands in his.

'You're fast asleep, Nola, but you'll continue to hear my voice and follow my instructions. If you hear and understand, nod.'

She nodded, feeling her own breathing heavy and regular, feeling his warm hands holding her firmly.

'Sally, you must listen also. And the rest of you, too. Nola's going back to the time she was born. You'll recall it clearly, Nola, and you'll disclose it to us. Please tell us when that was.'

'Twelve years old . . . two weeks before the Thanksgiving holiday.'

'Where were you?'

'At Thomas Jefferson High School, in math class.'

'All right. You are now in the schoolroom at that time. Describe it in your own words.'

Nola talked with her eyes open, but she wasn't here with us anymore. She was in her head, long ago and far away . . .

'I feel odd. I'm sitting at my desk in the classroom and everyone is staring at me. But it's not me. It's Sally. The teacher has asked her a question and everyone is watching and waiting for her to answer, but she never learned the formula because she's terrible in math and afraid of geometry. The angles and arcs confuse her, and she's never understood the reason for studying such things. Usually she daydreams in math class or reads a comic book hidden in her notebook. The regular teacher knows, and she *never* calls on Sally. But today we've got a substitute, and he's called on her to solve an equation. Everyone is smiling because they know how bad she is in geometry and how difficult the proof is:

—Well, Sally. I'm waiting.

—I – I'm sorry, sir. I didn't do that problem.

—What do you mean, didn't do it? Your regular teacher assigned it for homework, didn't she?

—Yes, but—

—But, nothing. Did you do the others?

—No, I'm very sorry.

—*Sorry?* Sorry doesn't solve the problem. Please go to the blackboard and take a piece of chalk, and show us that you can work it out.

'Sally hated going to the blackboard with all the eyes on her, the kids giggling and snickering because she wasn't good in schoolwork. She wanted desperately to be their friend, to be liked by them. Now they would laugh at her, and it would be all over the school. *Dumb Sally made a fool of herself at the blackboard.*

'As she walked up to the blackboard and picked up the piece of chalk, hearing the snickering behind her and feeling her face redden, she suddenly felt a chill and a skull-crushing headache. That was the only time I knew what was in Sally's mind. Then I was out and she was gone. I was holding the chalk in my hand. I looked at the empty blackboard, and it was all very clear.

—Well, I didn't bother with it for homework, I said, because it's rather a simple problem.

'Quickly, I sketched the diagram and set out the formula. Then in bold strokes of chalk, I outlined the proof, and added the letters: Q.E.D. and said loudly, *"Quod erat demonstrandum!"*

'I turned and glared at the teacher and at the class, and saw they were all staring, some of them with mouths open. I held my head high, looked down at the poor fools, and walked in triumph back to my seat. Then the bell rang, breaking the spell, and everyone crowded around me and asked how I had done that.

'From that time on, I got stronger, got out more. I was the one who went to math class, got the A's. Then I started going to French and social studies and English, and I loved every moment of my existence. I didn't know about the other personalities in those days, but I noticed that I never got to go to gym, or theater, or home economics, or dance, or any of the social events. At first I thought it was that way with everyone, that life was just blocks of time where you suddenly found yourself in a situation and had the pleasure of figuring it out and dealing with it, putting the missing pieces together, using logic and deduction. But then I discovered, by things other people said, that it wasn't so, that I existed only during very special, limited periods where my knowledge was required.

'Once, when a student stopped me in the hallway and told me I'd baked a wonderful coconut cake from scratch in home economics class, I knew something was very wrong, because I'd never baked in my life. And another time, when a boy said I was a great cheerleader, I began to piece the truth together, using logical analysis.

'I came up with a plan. I saw posters announcing the dance after the Thanksgiving Day football game. So I decided to concentrate all my energies on staying out for the big game. Every time I found my mind wandering or daydreaming or blanking out, I would focus on something and start counting or concentrating on my breathing. I hung on through a whole day. That's when I met some of her other classmates. A lot of them looked at me strangely when I didn't recognize them or know what they were talking about. But I stayed out and went to the game.

'I had never been to a football game before, and this was the big event, the rivalry against Tilden, and when Sally's mother ironed her cheerleader's skirt and washed the white sweater with the big J, I knew there would be some problems. I hadn't the slightest idea what a cheerleader did. I rummaged through Sally's desk looking for a school handbook that might have the cheers, but there was nothing. So I got dressed and took the bus to the football field.

'That's when the headache began. It was like the one at the blackboard. But that had been Sally's pain. This time I felt it, as if the top of my skull was being pried off. But I fought it. I was going to have the experience or die trying. I got into the line-up of girls, and they looked at me oddly. I stood there and gasped, "I have this terrible headache."

'That's when I first heard Derry's voice.

—C'mon, Nola, she said. Don't mess things up for all of us.

—Where are you?

—In your head, Nola. Stop holding things up. Everyone's waiting.

—Who are you?

—Name is Derry. We don't have time to get acquainted right now. Just take my word for it that Bella is supposed to lead the big cheer and dance number, and you're about to make a mess of the whole thing.

—I want to stay out, I said, and watch.

—Well you can't. If you don't clear the road, I'll see to it you don't get out for another year. Now move it.

'I was stubborn. I held on, stumbling through the cheer by watching the other girls. But I felt the stabbing pain in my eyes, and Derry's voice said:

—I warn you. Pull over or I'll blind you so that you never read another one of those stuffy egghead books.

'So I got out of the way. And I didn't get to see the big game at all. I was told we lost, twenty-one to seven. That was when I became aware there were others, and that Derry was the only one who knew what was going on in all our minds. I came to learn about the others indirectly or through Derry.'

Nola became silent.

'I think,' Roger said, 'we've accomplished a great deal today. You have all learned a little bit about your history. I pronounce your first group therapy session a success.'

'Should we practice it on our own?' I asked.

'Definitely not!' he said in a quick, sharp tone. 'It would be dangerous. Sally's condition is still delicate. Don't rush things, and above all try to avoid stressful situations. I would like all of you to promise you'll cooperate, that you'll do your best to keep things on an even keel.'

We promised.

'When I count to five, Sally will be awake, and the rest of you will go back into the darkness. Sally will remember everything that has happened here, very clearly. You'll feel good – and relaxed.'

He counted, and when she came out of it she felt woozy and saw him studying her intently.

'Hi . . .' she said weakly.

'How do you feel?'

She rotated her finger.

'Do you remember what happened?'

She nodded. 'Like in a dream. Three of my imaginary friends came to the session, but they're not imaginary anymore. They've become real. And we've got to cooperate.'

'That's fine, Sally. You've done a lot of good work today.'

'Dr. Ash, you talked about keeping out of stressful situations. This place is very stressful to me. I'm afraid of Duffy, and I don't like it here. Can I be released and go back to my own apartment?'

He thought about it. 'You're here as a voluntary admission, Sally. If you feel you can work at it better outside, I guess there's no reason to keep you hospitalized any longer. You've met the others. You seem to handle it well. Wait another day to make sure you're under control, and then you can go back home.'

She smiled. 'You're understanding, Dr. Ash. You're the only one who really cares about me.'

'There are others, Sally. You're a wonderful and valuable person, and I feel certain you can have a full and meaningful life if we can solve your problem.'

When she was back on the ward, she remembered she had wanted to ask him about the fifth chair and mirror, and who it was who hadn't come to group therapy.

Nine

SALLY WOKE UP early Wednesday morning, packed her bag, and waited impatiently. Through the windows she saw it was raining. When Nurse Fenton told her it was all right to leave, Sally hugged her goodbye and rushed – almost ran – down the corridor.

All the way home on the crosstown bus, Sally kept wondering if the apartment would feel different now that she had met the others. She would have to be more thoughtful of their possessions, she told herself. They were individuals, and she should handle their things with respect.

She waved to white-haired, stoop-shouldered Mr. Greenberg as she got off the bus in front of the tailor shop. He waved back. He probably didn't even know she had been in the hospital for a week. Why should he? The poor man had his own troubles. All those robberies. This part of the West Side was a dangerous neighborhood. She saw Murphy off to the side with his back to her. Silly, of course, but on those rare occasions when she came home after dark, it was reassuring to see the police uniform through the glass door.

Suddenly she thought, what if her apartment had been burglarized while she was away? Her heart raced as she took the steps two at a time. Upstairs, she checked her door carefully for signs of forcing. Some dents and scrapes near the lock looked old, but she couldn't be sure. She opened the door, making loud noises – calling out, 'Hello! Anyone here?' hoping it would send any intruder out the window and down the fire escape.

Everything seemed in order, everything in its place. No one had broken in, thank God.

She made scrambled eggs for lunch. She was going to have french fries, but she remembered her promise to cooperate in keeping her weight under control.

Washing the dishes, she glanced into the darkened window of the oven. The reflection was her own. She paused with her hands in the soapy water. He had said not to get in touch with them unless he was around. Why? What could go wrong? Maybe he knew it wouldn't happen without him present. Maybe what Nurse Duffy had said about the psychiatrist creating the personalities was true. She probably couldn't reach the others even if she tried. Dr. Ash had made them come to group therapy under hypnosis. Maybe it was all a hypnotic fantasy that wouldn't work without him. But it might. After she vacuumed the rug, she turned the TV set on, spun the dial past her favorite game shows and soap operas, and settled on a discussion between three economists analyzing the recession and its causes. Not one of them had anything good to predict. The thought popped into her head – 'the dismal science.' Now what made her think that? She didn't understand what they were talking about, and it depressed her, but she forced herself to watch it for Nola's sake. When it was over, she sighed with relief and turned the set off.

How could it hurt just to have a short conversation with the others? They had all seemed so flippant when they talked at the hospital. None of them took it seriously. They had to be told it was a life-and-death matter.

She wandered into the bedroom to see if she could tell what belonged to each one. The brainy books were surely

Nola's. She picked up *Finnegan's Wake*, tried to read some of it, but slammed it shut in frustration. 'Nola, I know you're around somewhere. I have to talk to you. I have to see if all this is true, if I can see and hear you without Dr. Ash hypnotizing me.'

Later she rummaged behind the books until she found the vibrator. What was Bella really like? What did she do? As she turned the vibrator in her hand, the shape of it struck her, and she remembered something. The window of the sex shop on Times Square displayed vibrators like these. And other ones that looked like . . .

'Oh, my God, that's disgusting,' she said and threw it back into the box. 'What kind of perverts are they?'

Then she caught herself. 'I'm not supposed to judge them. Each one is an individual. I mustn't reject them. Try to understand them.'

She went back to the closet and took out the blue dress. 'Derry, I figured out that you bought this the day you got the job. I need to talk to you, Derry. I have to know the truth. Derry? Derry?'

Dr. Ash's telling her not to contact the group without him was like telling her not to scratch an itch. She couldn't bear the tension of it any longer. And hadn't he told her to avoid stress? She had to find out if she could really break through the barriers in her own mind. All it would take, she was sure, was some extra effort. Everyone always said she had no will power. Well, she'd show them.

First she took the phone off the hook and checked the double-bolted door. Then, methodically, she put the apartment in order, as if she were expecting company.

She took a warm, relaxing shower, brushed her hair, and put on the old flowered-print dress she hadn't worn in a long time. She arranged four chairs in a circle. Rummaging through the apartment, she found three mirrors and set them on the seats, propped against the backs of three empty chairs.

In front of one mirror she laid *Finnegan's Wake*. 'I've never read this, Nola, but I promise you one of these days I will. I resolve to read more and improve my mind. I'd like to talk to you, because you could guide me and show me what to do.'

Then she got my blue dress and folded it neatly on the second chair. 'Derry, I'll really try to have more fun and laugh more, the way you want me to. If you'll come and help me, I'll have more faith, and then we can show Dr. Ash we're cooperating. We can have fun together like good friends should.'

She put the vibrator on the third chair, holding it gingerly between her thumb and forefinger, trying not to show her disgust. 'I know I shouldn't be so afraid of sex, Bella. Come and talk to me. Tell me how to let myself go without the panic I always feel around men.'

She waited silently, not knowing how to go about bringing out the people she had seen and heard in her mind.

'I'm not crazy,' she said. 'I believe Dr. Ash. So you're all there. And you have to come out and reveal yourselves to me so the four of us can get better.'

The room was silent except for the rain on the windows. She got up and threw all the windows wide open, and then came back and sat down and waited. Still nothing.

'I know,' she said, suddenly jumping up. 'We'll have a tea party just as we used to when you were all my little dolls.'

She went into the kitchen and came back with the good teacups and the silver service, which was one of the wedding gifts she had been able to keep. She set four places on a TV folding table in the center of the room. And while the water was boiling, she opened a box of almond cookies and set them neatly in a platter. She never bought almond cookies, but from time to time she would find boxes of them in the cupboard. One of her personalities must have a yen for them.

The shriek from the kitchen startled her, and she caught her breath until she realized it was the kettle whistling. She jumped up again, made a pot of tea, and set it next to the cookies.

'Please come,' she begged, looking into one mirror after the other. 'I know I wasn't supposed to call you out by myself, but I can't stand it anymore. If one of you doesn't come to talk to me, I'll jump out of that window.'

I knew she was bluffing. She'd never break her promise to Roger. But I'd also given him my word I'd protect her. I could probably just have blacked her out and taken over, but I was so fed up with her childish behavior I figured I'd give her a talking to.

'This is stupid,' I said. 'You know what Roger told you. What do you think you're doing?'

She caught sight of me in the mirror on the left and recognized me right away. 'Oh, Derry, I'm so sorry. I couldn't bear it any more. My head was getting ready to explode, and I had to see if it was really true, if I could do it on my own.'

The panic in her voice was real.

'Settle down,' I said. 'What do you want?'

'Just to meet all of you, talk to you again. Know that we're going to be friends and work together.'

'Well, I don't know about that.'

'Please, Derry, don't reject me.' She looked around wildly. 'Would you like a cup of tea?'

'Yes. It's been a long time. Last time you invited us to a tea party, the cups and saucers were an aluminum play set. The tea was water and the cookies were pretend.'

161

'It's real tea,' Sally assured me, 'and those are butter cookies with almonds.'

'I know,' I said, 'my favorite kind.'

'So you're the one who bought them,' she said. 'See, I never knew. It's important for me to learn about those things.'

'Why?'

'So I'll feel closer to all of you and be better prepared for fusion.'

'If there is fusion,' I said.

She was watching me closely in the mirror, thinking she had to be careful because she knew now, from what Roger had told her, that I was the only one co-conscious with her and the others, and without me there would be no getting well. She had to win me over.

'You forget, I know what you're thinking, Sally.'

She was shocked. 'Of course, I forgot. I'm sorry. I didn't mean any—'

'You can't use me, or fool me, Sally. Maybe your therapy gives you an advantage, because now you've accepted us emotionally and you can communicate with the others. But I know what you're thinking, and only I know *all* the others and can reach them. So let's come to an understanding.'

Feeling my eyes on her, she deliberately kept her mind focused on drinking her tea. She didn't want to offend me. Not now.

'You're blanking intentionally to keep me out,' I told her. 'That's not going to work either. You've got to let me see and hear everything. If you want my help, you've got to make me a full partner.'

She looked right into my eyes. 'What do you mean full partner?'

I hadn't planned what I was saying. It just popped out and I decided – as Bella would say – to wing it.

'This is the deal,' I said. 'I help you get rid of the others. And we settle for a duet. Two for tea and tea for two. You for me and me for you.'

'Then we'd still end up a dual personality. Like Jekyll and Hyde.'

'Not exactly. More like Cinderella when her fairy godmother waves her wand and suddenly she's wearing a gown, ready to go swinging with the prince at the ball. We'll split our time, you up to midnight, me after, and we'll be free and happy as a bird with two wings to fly anywhere we want to. We could travel around the world – see London, Rome, Paris. We'd have a ball.'

'But Dr. Ash said—'

'He said we were special. Let's face it, if not for me, he wouldn't have paid a moment's attention to you. You'd be left to rot in a back ward somewhere. So I'm entitled to my share of happiness. I want to live and be a real person, too.'

Sally was thinking I was right, but it upset her to admit it. If I insisted on permanent partnership, she thought, there would never be a normal life, and she might as well kill herself now.

'Hold on!' I said. 'Whoa! Pull up. Now, I didn't say it had to be that way forever, did I?'

Sally looked up sharply, realizing I was responding to her thought of suicide. 'What do you mean?'

'I don't expect to live forever. I just want more time out to pack a few good years with romance, travel to faraway places, and a little excitement before midnight turns the coach back into a pumpkin.'

She realized she had a hold on me, after all, because the thought of suicide disturbed me.

'Yes,' I said. 'It does. I'm not sure how it'll work, but if you kill yourself, I might get the blame and maybe go to hell for it. I don't want to take chances. Well, you can't blame me for trying.'

She felt the headache coming on. From the base of her neck it flowed upward, turning her skull into a cap of pain.

'Relax. Don't fight it, Sally. Fighting it worsens the pain.'

'I don't understand.'

'You wanted the others to come out and join us for tea. But when you struggle against it, the neck tension gives you the headache.'

'Who's coming out now?'

'Hey, I'm not a fortune teller. I won't know until I hear her.' Sally sat waiting, trying not to fight. Today, unlike so often in the past, she felt she would remain instead of running away.

Then she saw the face in the center mirror, the false lashes, the stage makeup caked thickly, and sensuous lips.

'What the hell's going on here?'

'It's all right, Bella,' I said. 'She's decided to have a seance. Four charter members of The Secret Five are being called back from the great beyond.'

The name of the club puzzled Sally for a moment. The number five bounced around in her head.

'Oh, shit! A hen party. When I felt myself coming out, I thought there'd be some fun. I don't want another groupie session.'

'Please stay, Bella,' Sally said. 'I need to talk to all of you. We've reached a crucial point in the therapy. It involves all of us.'

Bella looked her straight in the eye with a disgusted expression. 'What the hell did you bring the vibrator out for? We going to masturbate?'

Sally was shocked, but she tried not to show it. 'No, I just thought if there were things each of you had touched it would help you come out.'

'It'll help me come, all right.'

'I didn't mean—'

'She's seen too many spook movies,' I said. 'Jesus, Sally, it's not like black magic or calling people back from the dead.'

'I didn't know.'

'You never do,' Bella said. 'That's why we're all in this mess.' Bella looked at the empty mirror. 'Who else is coming?'

'Just us and Nola,' I said.

'What about you-know-who?'

'Sally doesn't know about her yet. They haven't met.'

'Haven't met who?' Sally asked.

'Never mind,' I said. 'There's time enough.'

'She's going to be damned pissed off when she finds out she wasn't invited to the tea party,' Bella said.

'The hell with her.'

'If it concerns me,' Sally said, 'I have a right to know.'

'Who says so?' I asked. I didn't mean to be nasty, but I was getting fed up with her nagging.

'Please, Derry. You promised Dr. Ash you'd be cooperative.'

'And you promised him you wouldn't contact us on your own.'

Sally looked down sheepishly. 'I'm sorry. You're right. I won't ask.'

'Oh, hell!' I said, getting soft-hearted again. 'Bella is talking about Jinx.'

'Who's Jinx?'

'One of us.'

'Another one? I thought it was just the four of us.'

'Remember the name of the club? The Secret Five?'

Sally shook her head as if to clear it. 'Jinx? I've heard that name before, but I always thought people were just saying I was *a jinx.*'

'Not so far from the truth,' Bella said.

'Why don't you want Jinx to come?' Sally asked me.

'She's violent,' I said. 'No telling what she'd do if she was angry.'

'What could she be angry about?'

'She was born angry,' I said. 'She's a vicious, evil person, and the less we have to do with her, the better.'

'I agree with Derry,' said the mirror on the right. Sally turned and saw Nola's thoughtful gaze and her long black hair falling to her shoulders. 'Letting Jinx out now would be like opening Pandora's box. Trouble will fly out, and you'll have a time getting her back inside.'

'That frightens me,' Sally said, her voice choked up. 'If all of you feel that way, it must be true. And if Jinx is part of me, then I must be vicious and evil. Oh, my God . . . what am I?'

'You're a jerk,' said Bella. 'I'm leaving.'

'I don't think you should go,' Nola said.

'That's a crock of shit. I'll damned well leave when I please.'

'To do some street walking?'

Bella snickered. 'What would you know about it, smart ass? You've never been laid. That's why Larry finally walked out on us. Mostly your goddamned fault.'

'That's not true,' Nola said.

'It is so. You'd never go drinking with him. You'd make a stink about his friends.'

'And you'd get stinking and end up in *anyone's* bed like a two-bit whore.'

'Look out who you're calling names, you shit!'

'Hey,' I said. 'We didn't come here to fight. Sally, you started this. You're the hostess. You handle it.'

'Yes,' Sally said, obviously flustered by the name-calling. 'I called you together. I mean, I arranged this party. We have to discuss the future. We have to cooperate with Dr. Ash . . . I mean . . .' She choked up, unsure of what to say next, and she saw her fingers lacing around each other. The chill was quickly followed by tension in her neck, building into pain, and she looked at me in desperation. She knew what the aura and the headache meant. We all knew. Sally tried to hang on, but the pain was too intense, splitting her skull, cutting her in two. In the mirror on the wall she saw the face, wild, with hair like snakes.

'Derry . . .' she whispered. 'Help . . . I think it's . . .'

'All right,' I said. 'Relax and let me in. Jinx can't force me out.'

Sally looked quickly at the clock. 8:43 . . .

Well, I was wrong.

Jinx came out screaming, 'What the fuck is going on here?' She saw the faces in the mirrors, and one by one she smashed them. She tore down the drapes and wrecked the furniture. God, I was glad I didn't have to spend the night there. She scrawled the letters J-I-N-X on the wall mirror with Bella's lipstick, and then she smashed it too. All of which, I figure, including the three small ones, adds up to twenty-eight years of bad luck. Jesus! I really tried to take over, but she'd become far too strong for me.

'That,' screamed Jinx, 'is for openers! You goddamn assholes!' and ran out of the apartment.

Jinx went through the basement kicking aside cartons, pictures, and toys, and ran into the back yard. She was furious at all of us, especially me. She knew I didn't like her dressing up in men's clothes, so she was going to do it to spite me. Climbing the fence to the adjoining yard, she realized she hadn't broken into Greenberg's Tailor Shop in a long time. She worked on the back door and then saw the lock had been changed. Well, it would take her just a few seconds longer to jimmy the door frame and spring it. She returned to the basement and hunted until she found a metal bar, and then went back to work on the doorjamb until she'd pried it away from the lock. The door came free, and she slipped into the back room.

She rummaged among the men's suits – freshly steamed, still smelling of cleaning fluid – discarding one after another because they were too big. But when she pushed aside the curtain to enter the front of the store, she backed up in shock.

A goddamned policeman! Standing right inside the door with his back to her. He must have heard her prying open the back door. She dropped behind the counter and watched his reflection in the side mirror. The nightstick in his left hand, as if he was ready to use it. No movement. No shifting from one foot to the other.

'Son of a bitch!' she whispered. 'A goddamned dummy!' Then, for some reason, the name Murphy flashed through her mind.

She pulled the dummy to the back of the store, stripped off its jacket, and tried it on. A little tight around the chest. She found a strip of satin lining in a drawer and tied her breasts flat. Then she tried the jacket again, over her dress. Perfect fit. She pulled the trousers off the dummy, and snorted, 'You don't have a goddamned thing either, so what're you smirking about?' She put on the trousers and the cap, slipped the thong of the nightstick around her wrist, and checked herself out in the mirror. Great. They'd think a cop killed Larry. And that would send them off on a wild goose chase.

She let herself out the back door and climbed the fence. She clawed at the dirt around the telephone pole until she felt the plastic bag she'd wrapped the gun in. She wiped the mud off and pulled out the snub-nosed .38 service revolver she'd taken from that pockmarked bastard at Horton's Department Store.

First she would kill Larry, and then the goddamned shrink who was planning to do away with her. That one would come under the heading of self-defense.

She shoved the pistol into her belt, and retracing her steps through the basement, walked out onto the street twirling the nightstick. Though it was only nine-thirty, Tenth Avenue was deserted. But she moved with confidence. No one would try to mug or rape a cop. She had a nightstick and a gun to protect herself with.

She walked north, trying car doors with no success. Then, on Riverside Drive, she saw a bald, middle-aged man with horn-rimmed glasses getting into a new Mercedes. Walking alongside, she tapped on the passenger-side window with her nightstick.

He pressed the button, lowering the window. 'Yes, officer?'

She showed him the gun. 'I won't hurt you if you don't panic.' She opened the door and slid in alongside. 'Move it the hell out of here,' she said.

His eyes opened wide, and he tried to protest. 'Don't shoot. Don't hurt me. Here, take the car. Just let me—'

'Drive, you bastard!' she said, jabbing the gun into his ribs.

He turned the ignition and hit the accelerator. The car screeched from the curb. He ran a red light and swerved as a pickup truck nearly hit him. A few blocks away she told him to drive down a deserted street.

'Now stop right here.'

'What are you going to do?'

'Get out!'

'Don't shoot me!' he said, scrambling out of the seat.

She slashed the barrel across his bald head, knocking his glasses to the ground, and he stumbled backward. 'I wouldn't waste a bullet on you,' she said, slipping behind the wheel. 'Goddamned men drivers.'

She sped off, cruising north on Riverside Drive to the Henry Hudson Parkway. She took the George Washington Bridge and on the Jersey side began weaving in and out of highway traffic, leaving open-mouthed drivers in her wake. Some cursed as she cut in ahead of them. Others shook their fists as she grazed their bumpers. Driving fast cars gave her more pleasure than anything else. God, she'd love to put this thing through a demolition derby and then see old baldy's face when they brought it back. The bastard probably had plenty of insurance on it anyway.

Suddenly she realized how foolish it was to attract attention and take a chance on getting picked up. All she needed now was to be caught impersonating an officer and carrying a loaded gun. She got off the highway and slowly took the streets toward Englewood, New Jersey, searching for the right address.

She parked across the street from Larry's ugly red and yellow split-level ranch house, with its four Roman pillars and on the lawn a replica of a nineteenth-century gaslight. As she got out of the car and crossed over to his driveway, she saw a woman pass back and forth in front of the living room picture window. She guessed it had to be Anna. She wondered if he lied to his new wife, too. The bastard would pay for the pain and suffering he caused women. Oh, yes, he'd pay. He'd pay for pretending at first that Jinx was the one he really loved, that he tolerated Sally just to be with her. That night when she came out and found he'd been screwing Bella she tried to kill him, but he was too strong, and he'd been able to wrestle the knife out of her hand. And then the wife-swapping. That degraded her. Well, he'd pay for all her suffering now.

She saw a man's form pass in front of the window. Damn! If she'd gotten there a minute sooner she could have blown him away. There was a full moon, so she hid behind the yew tree bordering the lawn, where she couldn't be seen from the street. She watched through the picture window and saw Anna again, and then other people. Larry came into view again, but someone else was blocking him. Jinx braced the gun, steadying it with her left hand. If he came into view just once more . . .

But the lights went out.

She cursed under her breath. Seconds later she saw the upstairs lights go on. Slipping the gun back into her belt, she thought it through.

She would wait until all the lights were out, give it another half-hour, and then slip in through one of the downstairs windows. She'd move upstairs carefully and slide something in front of Penny's door to keep her from coming out and interfering. She didn't want to hurt Penny. Then she would slip into the master bedroom and kill Larry, and, of course, she'd have to shoot Anna. By that time the noise would bring Pat running, and she'd blow him away, too. Then downstairs and away before Penny could get out and see who it was. If Penny caught sight of her through the window, all she could report was that a policeman had taken off in a black car. Then Penny would have to go and live with Sally, and the suffering and the nightmares would stop.

The lights went out. The whole house darkened, except for the imitation gas lamp on the lawn. She waited another hour and then tried the front door. Locked. She walked carefully around the house and tried the side door and the back. All locked. She tried three windows, unable to budge any of the screens from the aluminum storm windows. Finally, on the fourth side of the house she noticed a basement window. She kicked at it hard with her heel and the catch gave way. Swinging the window up with one hand, she slipped into the basement. She heard a noise from upstairs. And then another. Footsteps. Had someone heard her? She walked up the basement stairs, determined that she would kill whoever she met in that hallway. As she opened the door from the basement into the foyer she heard the side door of the garage. Someone coming in? She hadn't heard a car. Then she realized Larry must be going out.

She peered through the window, and in the moonlight she saw a man's shadow across the lawn. He got into the car parked in the driveway. Where the hell was the sonofabitch going at this hour? Probably tomcatting. She could catch him in the act. She ran out the back door and around the house in time to see him pull away from the curb. She jumped into the Mercedes and followed him for a couple of blocks without her lights. When he turned a corner in the direction of the Washington Bridge, she put her lights on and followed him.

Forty-five minutes later he pulled into an underground parking garage on the East Side close to Third Avenue, with her right behind him. He would be suspicious by now, but this was the time and place to do it – while he was on the way to meet someone. Probably another wife-swapping. God, it would be good to see his face before she did it.

She found a parking slot and waited. She saw him lock his car and head toward the elevator. When he passed close by, she threw the door open and pulled the gun out of her belt.

He stopped, and seeing the gun, he put his hands up. 'I live here, officer. I have identification. I—'

It wasn't Larry. He was a pinch-faced man with gray, close-cropped hair and a gray mustache. Son of a bitch, if she hadn't followed the wrong man. 'Who are you? What were you doing in Larry's house?'

'A woman? You a woman cop? Why are you following me?'

She put the barrel of the gun to the side of his head. 'You goddamn cocksucker. You'd better talk fast or I'll spray your brains all over the wall.'

'You're not a cop! Hey, lady, I – okay, don't shoot. I – I was visiting. I'm Larry's director of sales. He knows I was there. This is some kind of a terrible mistake. You can check with the—'

'You goddamn sons of bitches are still at it.'

She thought of shooting him, but Larry was the one she wanted, and shots might bring the attendant or the guard around and she'd be put away and not get the chance to do what she had to do.

'Look, if you want money, I have about a hundred in my wallet. You can have it. Just don't do any—'

She brought the pistol barrel across in a wide arc, slashing his face, and then back on the other side.

'Oh, my God!' he screamed, clutching his bloody face as he passed out.

She got back into the Mercedes and raced out of the garage. She drove toward the highway, muttering, 'Shit! Shit! Shit!' over and over again.

By the time she hit the FDR Drive and headed south, she was so frustrated and disgusted with herself that she was doing ninety. Then she heard a siren behind her and saw the flashing lights. God damn. That's all she needed now. She pulled off at the Forty-second Street exit with the patrol car still behind her and went careening up one street and down the next, clipping fenders, turning corners too sharply, going the wrong way up a one-way street toward Central Park, and cutting back across town, losing the patrol car before she doubled back to the apartment. Across the street she pulled to the curb and jumped out of the car.

She made it to the apartment building, and as the front door clicked behind her, she heard the siren and saw the flashing light through the window and saw the police pull alongside the battered Mercedes. Laughing, she ran down to the basement and out to the back yard and buried the gun in the same spot. Then she slipped back into Greenberg's shop. She stripped off the uniform, dressed Murphy, and shoved him back behind the glass door. That's when she realized she had lost his nightstick. For a minute she didn't know what to do with his empty hands. So she turned the right one palm up, and the way his middle finger stuck out it looked as if he was giving the world the finger.

When she got back up to the apartment and saw the mess she'd made before taking off on the wild goose chase, she said, 'Shit, you can have it back, Derry.'

'Not me,' I said. 'I don't clean up after you.' I didn't tell her I was scared and completely drained. Adventures I like, but this was too much. I was glad she'd gotten rid of the gun, though I had half a mind to dig it up and throw it away. But I knew I wouldn't. Weapons scare me. Anyway, I figured it was Sally's place to handle the mess. It was all her fault. If she hadn't been so stupid in the first place, Jinx wouldn't have crashed the tea party.

Ten

ON FRIDAY I let Nola go to therapy to tell Roger about the tea party and about Jinx coming out. She didn't tell him the part about the gun and Jinx trying to kill Larry because she didn't know about it. That's why I kept away. I was afraid I'd have to tell him, and then he'd send us back to the hospital.

When she told him about Jinx's tearing up the apartment, he got up and paced around his office, slamming his fist into his palm. She'd never seen him so worked up. 'This is terrible. I told you. I warned you not to do it alone.'

'It wasn't my doing!' Nola said. 'I'm not Sally. Jesus, you don't have to shout at me.'

'Forgive me, Nola,' he said, throwing himself back into his chair, 'but a miscalculation like that could have cost your life. All your lives. I'd never have forgiven myself if something had happened to you.'

She had a strong feeling of guilt, yet she was pleased that he cared so much. He didn't look burned out to her now. He was different. If he was only pretending to care then he was doing an Academy Award job.

Nola said, 'Just before Jinx took over, Derry said to Sally, "Jinx can't force me out." Well, she was wrong. Either Derry is getting weaker or Jinx is growing stronger.'

Roger nodded, the tips of his fingers touching his chin. 'We've reached a flashpoint. I think it's time to take the next step.'

She knew what he meant, and that sent chills through her. 'I shouldn't have told you about the tea party.'

'Nola,' he said, leaning forward across the desk, 'this isn't an intellectual game. There's real danger here. We mustn't delay any longer. It's got to begin with you.'

'You're talking about fusion, aren't you?'

'Yes.'

'Now wait *just* a minute,' Nola said. 'I never gave my approval.'

'That's what I'm asking for now.'

'But it doesn't always work, does it?'

He toyed with the gold pen on his desk and shook his head.

'And when it does work, there's no guarantee it'll stick,' she said.

'That's right. Most other multiple personalities have only appeared to be successfully fused, but then under extreme stress the patients have split apart again. In some situations, new personalities have appeared. Nola, we have no guarantees. We can only try.'

'I'm no guinea pig,' she said.

'The method has been successful in some cases, Nola. It's all we've got. Let's face it, my one overriding purpose is to keep you alive. We've reached a crisis that puts all your lives in danger. It's my professional opinion that this is the best way.'

'But why me?'

'The best strategy is to move backward in time. As the last to be formed, you should be the first to merge. Besides, your education, self-control, and pride, added to Sally's good nature and humility, will strengthen Sally's ability to handle the other fusions to follow.'

'Would I – if I agreed – be aware of what's going on after fusion?'

'I can't be sure, but my theory is that as part of the new Sally you'll have a permeating awareness.'

'What about Jinx?'

'I'm hoping that, at first, the combination of the two of you will erect an intellectual barrier against her excesses. Later, when Bella's sensual and Derry's emotional qualities are added, there will be enough of a release valve that the four of you should be able to repress Jinx's anger and aggression.'

'So that's what you meant when you said the other time that you might be using *both* techniques – fusion *and* cutting off. You fuse four, and cut one out.'

'Not necessarily cutting out. Repression is a normal part of all human mental states.' He leaned back in his swivel chair and looked directly into her eyes. 'I need your permission, Nola.'

'I just don't think you have the right to destroy an individual. I'm a mental reality. *Cogito ergo sum.*'

He slapped the arms of his chair, got up, and began to pace back and forth.

'I don't deny your existence, Nola, but each of you could argue the same right to go on living a separate life. Now if it were a physical multiplicity, like Siamese twins, we might be able to cut you apart and give you each a separate existence. But there's no way to cut your minds and give them separate bodies. Attempts to do away with alter personalities don't seem to have worked. You're like disembodied spirits. So we've got to try the other way – fusion. What we're going to do won't destroy you, it'll—'

'Change me.'

'That's inevitable.'

'But I don't want to change. I'm satisfied with myself the way I am.'

'I can see that. But just because you're educated and proud doesn't mean you're complete.'

'I resent that.'

He held his hands out, palms up, imploring her to understand. 'A complete human being also has emotions and sexuality and empathy for others, and some degree of humility. I'm not going to destroy you, Nola. I'm going to help you reach the human level beyond books and films and classical music and painting. To be perfectly frank, you need to merge with the others as much as they need to merge with you.'

'I have to think about it.'

'Of course,' he said. 'Consider it over the weekend. You may want to consult with the others, or you may handle it alone. If you agree, we'll try our first fusion on Monday.'

He let her leave without changing her back to Sally.

We all sort of agreed, without really saying it, to give Nola the weekend out. She needed to make the decision, and I pointed out to the others that it might be her last couple of days. Fair is fair.

Well, she went on her own kind of binge. God! All Friday night she played her records. Beethoven and Bach. I thought I'd go out of my mind, but I realized she needed her kind of music to help her think things through, so I put up with it.

Saturday she went to the Museum of Modern Art and the Metropolitan, and then in the evening to a dull-dull play on off-off-Broadway, ending up with late supper alone at a small French restaurant. When she ordered escargots, I was curious, but when I saw what it was I nearly got sick to my stomach. I mean, it took me a long time to get used to her eating oysters and clams, but I drew the line at snails. Ugh! But to tell you the truth, I have to admit they weren't half bad.

Sunday was the topper. Bagels and lox for breakfast and the whole day reading the *New York Times* – all ten pounds of it – from the first page to the last. Like it was the last time she was ever going to read it. For me it was a weekend in hell.

But even then she still hadn't made up her mind to agree. Sunday night she really got depressed, sitting around moping, and she began to think about killing herself again.

It really worried me. I'd never seen her so down. She was visualizing herself going up on the roof and jumping, and then she thought of slashing her wrists. Then a poem by someone named Dorothy Perker or Parker went through her head, and she started to laugh. She was really torn between giving up her life by merging or giving it up by throwing it away. She went to the medicine cabinet looking for her Librium, but luckily I'd thrown them out last week. She sat down at the table, pulled out a sheet of her own beige letter paper. Then she started to write.

I cannot consciously accept this fusion. I've asked myself Hamlet's question over and over again, but his dilemma was simple compared to mine. It's not just a matter of being or not being. It's a matter of being someone other than myself or not being, and frankly I prefer the second alternative. I know it's selfish. The problem is compounded by the new knowledge that in taking my own life, I take the lives of others as well. And in that sleep of death what dreams may come . . . in that undiscovered country from which no traveler returns? Thus conscience does make cowards of us all . . .

As she wrote, she had a double feeling – one of depression, and at the same time one of watching herself and realizing she was being very sentimental and maudlin. The double feeling got stronger, so that for a moment she drifted out of herself and saw herself sitting there, as if part of her were something hovering over her from a distance, watching her write. She turned and saw a figure. The face was blurred and she couldn't tell if it was a man or a woman – shoulder-length hair, an Indian headband, and a flowing white garment like a sheet wrapped around him or her.

—Who are you? she asked.

—Your Helper.

—I don't remember you.

—I've been in existence for only a short while.

—Why are you here now?

—To keep you from harming yourself.

—I have a right to take my own life.

—But it's not your own life. You know that. You've been thinking of your responsibility toward the others.

—What should I do?

—Listen to Dr. Ash. He's a good and wise person.

—He wants to debase me by fusing me with those mindless creatures he calls my personalities.

—Trust him when he says it won't be your debasement. Your life of the mind reaches noble heights at times, but it's still empty, a partial life. The only hope is if you surrender your individuality to the greater need.

—Help me to surrender.

—It lies within yourself. I can only guide you.

—Show me the way then. I'm frightened.

The figure moved toward her. She saw it glow and then slide into herself like a double image being brought into focus. Then she no longer saw the outlines of the Helper as someone separate, but as part of herself.

—That didn't hurt at all, did it, my child?

—No. And I still feel as if I'm me. Is that the way it will be?

—That's the way.

She sat there and thought about what was happening to her, and then she remembered reading an article by a psychiatrist in California who had described how something like this existed in most multiple personalities.

—Are you the *Inner Self Helper?* What they call the ISH?

—I'm here to help whenever I'm needed.

—Are you one of our personalities?

—No. I'm not a separate being, as the rest of you are. I'm here only as helper and protector. I reside within you, but also out in the universe. I manifest myself only when I am needed.

—I need you. Tell me what to do.

—Dr. Ash says the decision must be yours and it must be voluntary. I can only help you be strong enough to make the choice for good.

—You're my fairy godmother!

—I've been called that. Also guru, guide, ISH, teacher, Helper. It's all the same.

—I'm glad we have an ISH. It makes it easier.

—It's time to decide, my child.

Nola sat there for a long time feeling the warmth steal over her body, and then she picked up the pen and added, at the bottom of the note she had written,

I ACCEPT FUSION . . .

Then suddenly she felt a lightness, and the ISH was gone, and she was alone in the room, feeling good.

I couldn't help myself. I was so happy and excited I sneaked out and got on the phone right away before she could change her mind, and told Roger.

Monday morning, in Roger's office, she started to backtrack.

'I'm afraid of losing what I've got – the things I love. I've always felt that a part-time existence of a quality life – an examined life – was better than seven days a week of mediocrity.'

Roger suddenly looked very tired. 'Yet you keep trying to kill yourself.'

'I get depressed.'

'Nola, there's no reason to believe you're going to sink to a common denominator. Your mind isn't going to be strained into a purée. Think of it more as a kind of mental bouillabaisse, where each of you adds ingredients to the whole but at the same time maintains an identifiable quality.'

She shook her head. 'You're good with words, Roger. But you forget that the *abaisse* derives from the Latin *abassare*, meaning to lower or humiliate.'

'It was a poor example.'

'I think it was appropriate. Humiliation is part of the background of most multiples, isn't it? Knowing you were unwanted and humiliated and abused in your childhood and adolescence?'

'True, but you have no reason to feel humiliated by being fused. You're not being cut out, but being taken in.'

She glared at him. 'You say that, but I still have the feeling of not being wanted. Of shame. Of degradation.'

'We all care for you, Nola. You're needed. And in helping cure Sally, you make a contribution larger than just healing one individual. What we learn from this procedure might help relieve the suffering of thousands of other recently discovered multiples who live secretly in a chaos of time because they're afraid or ashamed to come out of hiding.'

'I'm supposed to sacrifice myself for closet multiples?'

'Not sacrifice. Think of it as moving from part of a self to a whole self. You wanted to end your life many times. Instead of throwing it away, make your existence count. For God's sake, Nola. Give yourself to the whole. You're needed.'

She was quiet for a while, never taking her eyes off him. Finally she said, 'Can we use the name Nola Bryant instead of Sally Porter?'

'That's not practical,' he said. 'The birth certificate is in Sally's name. So are the Social Security number, the insurance policy, the pension credits from jobs she's held. And there are utilities, medical records, tax records, credit cards, and bank accounts. You'd have no way of establishing credit without her legal name.'

She felt something tugging inside her and then, almost against her will, she told him about the Helper.

He listened thoughtfully, and then he clasped his hands and nodded. 'To tell you the truth I've been wondering when something like the Inner Self Helper was going to manifest itself. At first I thought it was Derry, but as one psychiatrist who has worked with many multiple personality patients has pointed out, the ISH is different from the usual personality, not fully developed, but more of a personification of the conscience. What Freudians would call the superego.'

'I think there's more of a religious dimension to it,' Nola said. 'Though I've been an atheist most of my life, I had the definite feeling of the Hindu concept of Atman – that part of the individual spirit or soul residing within us – and merging with Brahman, the universal soul or mind. It came to light in a moment of desperate quietness, and now I'm wondering if my fusion will be like what wise men of India call nirvana – the blowing out of the flame of life that allows us to extinguish our individual existences and merge with the supreme spirit.'

'There's only one way to find out, Nola . . .'

She felt herself weakening and clenched her fists.

'Oh, come on,' he said softly. 'What's in a name? A rose by any other name would smell as sweet.'

She looked up and laughed. 'He who steals my name steals everything . . .' But after a long silence she spread her fingers, looked at them, and nodded. 'Do it quickly.'

'All right then,' he said, holding up his gold pen. 'Sally, *come into the light*. Nola, stay too. Both of you have learned that to solve this problem you've got to join forces and become one person. That can happen only if your two minds merge, permeate each other, and fuse into a single mind with the characteristics and qualities of both, as things were before Nola split off. Think of yourselves as two ponds. You, Nola, are one, filled with education, culture, and pride. You, Sally, are another, deprived of those things that have been diverted into the pond called Nola, but filled in your own right with maternal longing, a sense of right and wrong, and humility.

'Now I'm going to dig a trench between the two ponds. You can see it in your minds' eyes. I'm starting from Sally's pond. It's hard work, but I'm digging closer and closer to Nola's pond. In a moment I'm going to reach Nola, and you know what will happen when both ponds are connected by the trench. Tell me what will happen, Sally.'

'The . . . waters . . . will mix . . .'

'And you tell me, Nola, what will happen when the waters mix?'

'The qualities will intermingle.'

'And you agree to this mixture, Sally?'

She nodded.

'And you agree to this mixture, Nola?'

She hesitated.

'Nola, you must commit yourself now, without reservation. Once the waters are mixed there is no separating them. You and Sally will be one mind as well as one body. Do you agree, Nola?'

'Yes.'

'All right. Now I'm digging with your Helper's guidance. There. We've broken through. The waters are rushing from both ponds to the center of the trench. Sally's awareness is rushing toward Nola. And Nola's awareness is rushing toward Sally. You can see the swirling current as the waters mix and disperse their qualities throughout the one overall body of water. From now on there is no more Nola, no more Sally. There is only a second Sally – one person, educated, proud, and confident that she can handle her job and life and those who may try to interfere with her, but also humble and sympathetic toward others. When I count to four, she will open her eyes. Sally, you'll remember as much or as little of this session as you need to. You may remember parts of your separate lives, but only as history. In the present, and for the future, you have fused into one mind, in one body, one person, different from either of the two minds. You are a new woman, the second Sally. And you've made us all and your Helper very happy. One . . . two . . . three . . . four . . .'

Her eyes flickered. She blinked a few times, and then opened them wide.

'How do you feel?' he said.

'Woozy. As if I've been in a whirlpool, spun around and around before going over a waterfall.'

'Relax, and then tell me what you remember.'

She took a deep breath to steady herself. 'Not much.'

'What is your name?'

'Sally Porter.' She said it with a long sigh.

'What's the last thing you recall?'

'Inviting the others to tea. And then *everything* went blank.'

'How do you feel about what happened?'

'It was a terrible mistake. I should have known better than to get involved.'

'Do you want to clarify that?'

'I've always been a loner. Please forgive me, Roger, I don't mean to appear snobbish, but the things I've always liked and succeeded at have been things I've done by myself. I know I still have problems, but I have a strong sense that if I can be left *alone* to think things through, I'll be able to work them out.'

'I see.'

'Of course, I'm not referring to you. Don't misunderstand. I mean, we'd be better off if you and I could handle the important decisions instead of bringing the others into group therapy.'

'Thanks for clarifying it. I thought you meant you wanted me to leave you alone for a while.'

She looked at Roger directly. 'Not at all. I think you're the most intelligent man I've ever known. I find your company stimulating.'

'Thank you.'

'I – I don't know what made me say that. I feel odd.'

'In what way?'

'Unsure of myself, of what I'm saying, and why I'm talking this way. I have the peculiar sensation I'm sounding differently from the way I've ever sounded – saying things I've never said before.'

'That's to be expected after fusion. I'd like you to do something for me.' He handed her a pad and a pencil. 'Please write your name.'

Without hesitation she wrote *Sally N. Porter*.

'I didn't know you had a middle initial,' Roger said. 'What does the N stand for?'

'I don't know why I did that. I've never used a middle initial.'

'What does it stand for?'

'I guess it's Nola.'

'That's a lovely gesture. Did you make a conscious decision to take that for a middle name?'

She shook her head. 'It just came out, but somehow it *feels* right. Do you think it's okay for me to use it?'

'I don't see why not, for the time being. Do you think Nola would mind?'

She thought about it for a long time. 'I have the strangest sensation. Just a feeling – I don't know why – that Nola is gone, vanished out of my life. It makes me a little sad, like losing an old friend you've just rediscovered. Does that mean the fusion was successful, that I'm getting better?'

'Let's hope so,' he said. 'I think it's a good sign, but we'll have to wait and see.'

'I hope you don't mind my saying this,' she said, 'but there aren't many men who have your insight into women.'

He laughed. 'I've learned a lot from you.'

She stood quickly.

'What's the matter?'

'A strange phrase keeps popping into my head. I keep thinking: *The second Sally*. Isn't that peculiar? What could it mean?'

'It might mean you've reached a second stage in your development – or in your reintegration.'

'I have the crazy impulse to go to a French restaurant and try some new gourmet dishes,' she said. 'Would you care to have dinner with me?'

He smiled. 'I guess I should keep a close watch on you for a while.'

'That wasn't what I meant,' she said.

'I know. But allow me the luxury of a professional excuse for doing something I want to do.'

She laughed and shook her head. She knew he was speaking to her differently – no longer talking down to her, and she liked being respected for her intelligence.

'A man who's just played God shouldn't have to rationalize his desire to take his creation to dinner.'

As soon as she said it, she wished she hadn't. She hadn't meant the barb to hurt him, but she'd felt the need to puncture him. His frown showed she'd succeeded. 'I'm sorry. I shouldn't have said that.'

He looked at her thoughtfully. 'It was to be expected. Mad scientist plays God . . . Maybe I should just see you home and take a rain check on dinner.'

'You've got the rain check. But I can get home alone.'

He nodded. 'I respect your wishes.'

As she walked out, her stride was firmer, her head more erect. Sally's cringing slouch was gone.

I can tell you the whole thing gave me the creeps. I tried to reach the old Nola. But Sally was right, Nola was gone. As if she'd been kidnapped or murdered or something. I remembered one of the books she loved so much, and the thought kept running through my head that she'd drowned herself after all and her body was somewhere at the bottom of Walden Pond. Scary. And another thing bothered me. I could tell by the look in Roger's eyes that he found Sally number two a very attractive woman.

When Sally left the office, everything looked out of kilter – as if she was seeing it all through new lenses. In the past, facing the panel of buttons in the elevator had made her panic. Never sure which one to push, never sure what floor to get off. Now, she confidently jabbed LOBBY and enjoyed the plunge down.

Outside, she watched the crowds moving in both directions. Passers-by glanced at her as if confused by someone in the city standing still and taking it all in rather than rushing off somewhere. Then slowly, catching her breath like a swimmer slipping into cold water, she moved from the doorway and plunged into the downtown current.

She found her senses heightened by the anonymous closeness of the crowd. Not having to communicate with anyone gave her a feeling of isolation – something part of her had always enjoyed – being and not being there. *With* but not *of*. She kept thinking of pools of water and herself floating along. It made her giddy and she laughed. She was glad Roger wasn't taking her to dinner. It would be more exciting to spend the evening alone. A walker in the city! She loved the double vision of being in the crowd and observing herself in it. She would move to the sound of her own drummer.

Drifting toward Times Square. She had always avoided the ugliness of the sexploitation movies and porno shops. She had always scorned the hustlers and the hookers. But now, for the first time, she saw them as people, each distinct and unusual. She was no longer above them, no longer quick to judge them. She had, she suddenly realized, been a snob.

She turned east on Forty-second Street toward the main library. A couple of drunks in front of Bryant Park tried to touch her, but she avoided them. In the past men like this had made her so fearful that she would panic and black out. Now she felt in control, and getting stronger. She knew she could talk her way out of trouble if they tried to bother her.

Instead of going in the Forty-second Street entrance she went around to Fifth Avenue to look at the lions. Suddenly it was important to see the guardians flanking the steps as she walked between them. They would protect her. She remembered her first school excursion through this library, when she had believed that if she read hard and long enough she would finish all the books in the world and know everything. Now she smiled at her foolishness. She went to the circulation room and browsed. She found one of her favorite books, turned the pages, and soon found herself lost in the lush prose and rolling cadence of Thomas Wolfe's *You Can't Go Home Again*. She caught herself sinking into the pounding rhythms and rich images of the city and she closed the book, put it down, and walked out. There was, she agreed, no going back.

But she'd better go back to the apartment and shower and dress to go down to The Yellow Brick Road. As she got out of the taxi, she couldn't understand why she felt sad. And then suddenly it hit her that what she was feeling now was only temporary. Soon there would be another merger and another . . . a third and then a fourth Sally. And she would see the world in a new and strange way after each fusion. Each time it would be someone else walking the city, dreaming and wondering about the future.

She saw the store dummy in the policeman's uniform and stared at it as she passed. It looked as if he was giving the world the finger. What was it Todd had said? 'Murphy's Law. Anything that can go wrong will.' That was foolish nonsense and superstition. Nothing would go wrong. She was stronger than ever. She was in control.

In the apartment, she took the stuffed rabbit and panda from the bed, wrapped them in one of Greenberg's plastic garment bags, and shoved them into the back of the closet. She chose a striking white and yellow dress to wear that evening. Then she went to the bathroom and stared at herself for a long time in the mirror.

'You know who you are,' she said. 'You're stronger now. No more blackouts. No more switching. You'll maintain *control* and show Roger there's no need to fuse the others.'

The idea delighted her. The more she thought of it, the more she felt that was the answer. She could stabilize her life on her own and *prevent* blackouts or conversions, and there would be no need for other mergers. That was it! Wonderful!

She stepped into the shower and the water hit her back, warm and delicious, and she let it swirl around her, and while she was luxuriating in it, I realized that Bella and Jinx and I were going to have a fight on our hands, because it wasn't going to be only this new Sally. Now she had the ISH on her side.

Part Three

Eleven

THINGS WENT OKAY for a few weeks. Sally two was different from before. A lot smarter – well, I don't know about that – maybe I should say a lot more educated. She also kept thinking she was going to stay out and control her own life and never black out again.

What bugged me was all the time she spent seeing foreign films (God, I hate to have to read the titles at the bottom and miss the expressions on the faces!) and going to art museums, and reading . . . reading . . . reading . . . The TV set went on the fritz, and she didn't bother to have it fixed, so I couldn't even get to watch late shows. It wasn't the deal I'd agreed to, I can tell you that.

Then one day she decided to make a big try to handle the rush hour at The Yellow Brick Road herself. I started to come out as usual, but clonk! I hit a stone wall.

Okay, I figured, you can probably handle the orders now that you got yourself some brains, but what are you going to do about Bella's performance? But the new Sally was thinking about that, telling herself she'd keep control until the lights went down, let Bella out on a short leash, and then take over again as soon as the show was over. She didn't know that Bella had decided that once she got out, we were going to stay out and have us a ball.

Todd came over to her table, where she was relaxing after she changed into her uniform. He studied her seriously.

'You seem different tonight. More cool and above it all. Are you Nola?'

She shook her head. 'I'm Sally.'

He raised his eyebrows. 'The stay in the hospital must have done you good.'

'It really did.' She saw Eliot watching them anxiously from the far end of the bar.

'Sally, ever since that night you saw yourself on the TV news, I haven't been able to get you out of my mind.'

'Todd, I really don't want to—'

'Hear me out. You're a wonderful person – kind and thoughtful. I find you fascinating, and I'm in love with you.'

'You're looking for trouble, Todd.'

'Let me be the judge of that.'

'You don't really know me. I have weaknesses.'

'Listen, now that I've overcome my own gambling sickness, I'm strong enough for both of us. I'll learn all about you and your problem, and I'll help. You don't have to struggle with it alone. You need someone to talk to, someone to help you pick up the pieces when you fall apart.'

Sally looked down at the table. 'Please, Todd, give me time to sort myself out.'

He looked at her thoughtfully and nodded. 'All the time you need.'

When he left the table, she struggled with the notion. She didn't love him, but then maybe that could come later. Or maybe love wasn't even necessary. Two people could make a relationship work on other levels. As Todd left, she saw Eliot heading for the dance floor to announce the nine o'clock show. His clothes looked tight. He was putting on more weight. Sally got up and headed for the center of the dance floor, thinking she should be able to handle it on her own. But then as she felt the swirl in her stomach and the chills and headache, she had the flashback memory of trying to stay out during Bella's cheerleading days, and at the last second she let go.

Bella bounced onto the dance floor. The lights went down, and as the spotlight embraced her, she raised her arms over her head and laughed. 'Folks, you're going to have a show tonight like you've never seen before.' She grabbed the electric guitar and started singing and swaying, feeling she was going to make up for all the times Sally hadn't let her out. The crowd got worked up, tapping their feet, clapping their hands. She built it up to a wild beat, until she felt confined and restricted. Suddenly, she pulled off the emerald-sequinned halter top, threw away her bra, and danced topless.

She could see Todd, shocked, start toward the dance floor, but Eliot held him back. They both stood by the cash register and watched. She knew her body was beautiful, and she knew how to use it, bumping and grinding to make the short skirt come down to the floor. She was finally dancing in her panties. She felt wild and free again. She had a right to excitement, to the limelight, to applause.

What was wrong with showing her body? It was a performer's equipment. The happiest moments in her life, as far back as she could remember, were in front of the crowds, feeling herself reflected in their eyes, sensing the approval, hearing the applause. *Mirror mirror on the wall, who's the fairest of them all?*

Lost in the beat. Stepping high. Arms, legs, head, breasts throbbing. Oh, God, she was happy! This was the way to reach out and share herself with strangers who appreciated her.

I hadn't expected Bella to do a striptease, and I thought of moving out and stopping it, but Jinx beat me to it. She forced Bella out of the spotlight, and then stopped suddenly. She stood quite still, glaring, the perspiration streaming between her breasts. The crowd was shocked into silence.

'You want to see a naked body?' Jinx shouted. 'You want to see a woman parading her flesh so you can jerk off under your tables? Then let's have a real performance of female degradation!'

She stepped to one of the tables and snatched a cigarette out of a customer's mouth.

'Look at this body,' she sneered, 'and see how we can brand it like cattle.'

She pressed the lit end of the cigarette about an inch above the nipple, and the crowd gasped. They couldn't know she didn't feel the pain. It was Sally's pain, but Sally wouldn't feel the burn until she came back.

'And another one here!' She pressed it above the other nipple, and there was the smell of singed flesh.

'Ohmygod! She's burned herself!' shouted a woman at a ringside table. She jumped up to leave.

'It's all part of the act!' shouted a man nearby, clapping his hands.

Then others around him applauded, and finally the whole audience was cheering.

'You ain't seen nothing yet!' Jinx shouted. 'The fucking show has just begun.'

Todd and Eliot started toward her, finally, but she threw the cigarette butt down and grabbed a wine glass from one of the tables. She spattered the contents into the customer's face and then broke the glass against the side of the table. She held the broken stem against her throat and shouted, 'Keep back both of you, or I'll end it quick.'

They stopped, and she moved to the center of the floor and said, 'Now you'll see the first live performance of a suicide on stage. I dedicate this to Nola, who is no longer with us.' She strutted up and back, raised her left arm above her head, and sliced the broken glass across her wrist. The blood flowed down her upraised arm onto her body.

'For God's sake, stop her!' someone screamed.

'It's fake blood!' someone else shouted. 'I seen shows like this before.'

Then she cut her other wrist, threw the broken glass into the crowd, and paraded up and back, hands above her head, trying to bump and grind like Bella. But she knew she had no rhythm, and she couldn't use her hips the way Bella could, and it made her furious.

Someone shouted, 'More! More!'

'Watch me, you bastards!' she roared. 'Every one of you is bleeding to death. You're all a figment of my imagination, and when I die, the whole world will be destroyed in one big rush. That's what I'm doing, don't you see? I'm not killing me. I'm destroying you. When my blood runs out and my mind is drained, not one of you will have any existence.'

The crowd laughed and applauded.

But as she danced near the ringside tables, a woman leaned over and touched the drops of red with her napkin and looked at it closer.

'It's real!' she screamed. 'It's blood! She's really killing herself.'

More applause. But then as Jinx strutted around, the applause died, and the whole crowd watched in fascinated silence. It dawned on them they weren't just watching another sadistic punk-rock performance. Waitresses stopped. Busboys froze. All watching a bloody dance of death.

Stupid bitch! She was really trying to kill us all. I pressed and struggled to get through without success until she slipped on her blood, and that distracted her. Then something pushed me from behind, whispering, *You're on*.

For a moment I froze in the spotlight. Audiences scare me. Then I laughed and shouted, 'The magic show is over for the evening, ladies and gentlemen. There is no blood. There is no wine. There isn't even any body. I don't exist. I'm a trace of an illusion. It's all sleight of mind.'

I bowed, turned, and wiggled my fanny at them, and they applauded with a standing ovation. Off stage I handed a couple of napkins to Todd. 'You'd better bandage my arms before I get this place any messier. I guess they all believe it was an act.'

But Todd and Eliot knew the burns and the cuts and the blood were real. They had the first-aid kit out, and Todd put on antiseptic and bandages.

'You crazy broad,' Eliot said. 'What'd you want to do a thing like that for?'

'I wish I knew,' I said.

'I'll get you to a hospital,' Todd said when he finished bandaging my arms.

'Won't be necessary,' I assured him. 'Things are under control now. Just take me home.'

After some argument he got me a cab, but he insisted on coming along. At the apartment he didn't want to leave me alone. 'Maybe I should call a nurse to stay with you,' he said.

'I'll be okay, Todd, really I will.'

'Sally . . . Nola . . . Derry . . . whichever you are. If anything happened to you I don't know what I'd do.'

'Nothing will happen.'

'It almost did. I can't stand the thought of your being in danger. Marry me and let me take care of you.'

'That's not possible, Todd. I'm no good for you.'

'Good? You're the best thing that ever came into my life. I've never known a woman like you. Good, intelligent, vital—'

'What about my violent moods? You saw what happened tonight.'

He shook his head and paced back and forth. 'When you get well, you'll be able to deal with that. All it takes is self-control. You changed tonight and stopped whatever it was that possessed you. That shows your goodness is stronger than your destructiveness.'

'I'm not so sure anymore,' I said.

He took my hand. 'Marry me.'

'Don't press me, Todd. I'm not myself tonight.'

'All right,' he said, 'but whoever you are, you've made me alive again, and that's all I care about.'

When he left I tried to go to sleep, but I kept tossing and turning, half-scared that once I dozed off I had no idea who might come out.

I went down and talked to Murphy about it. 'I'll tell you, Murphy, I'm surprised this hasn't made me a nervous wreck by now.'

But it was hard to confide in Murphy ever since Jinx had turned his hand around and made it look like he was giving the world the finger. Somebody ought to tell Mr. Greenberg to change it. It wasn't nice.

Twelve

BELLA LOOKED AROUND, ready to take her bow, expecting to see an appreciative audience. When she found herself in bed – alone – daylight streaming in the windows, she shouted, 'Aw shit! Not again!'

Then she noticed her bandaged wrists, looked into the mirror and saw the burn marks on her breasts, and she thought . . . Jesus, someone really got messed up by a sadist.

She jumped up and looked around, furiously, hands on her hips. It was too goddamned much. She knew she should be used to it by now, but it really bothered her not to be able to finish a performance. She was sick and tired of being upstaged all the time – in one situation after another – in the spotlight or in bed. So what was all this shit about cooperation? Whoever had taken over ought to respect the things that were important to her. Well, God damn it, she'd get even if it was the last thing.

She caught sight of the desk calendar and the appointment notation: *10:00 A.M. Therapy. Roger's office.*

It was nine o'clock now. Only an hour left to stay out? It wasn't fair. Then, thinking of Roger, she had an idea. She would stay out, go to his office and – pretending to be the new Sally – she would throw him completely off guard. The new Sally hadn't been around that long, but I had told Bella about her, and Bella was a quick study. She knew she could do it. And if she blew a few lines, Roger wouldn't be any the wiser – he didn't know the new Sally that well yet.

Giggling as she went to put on one of Sally's dresses, she visualized the big seduction scene. She would play the new Sally to the hilt and get Roger worked up. She saw herself lying on his black leather couch, in tears, playing on his sympathy, and when he bent close to comfort her, she would show him her burned breasts, take him in her arms, and make love to him. It would be a great performance. As she waited for a cab, she imagined herself holding a bouquet of flowers and bowing to an enthusiastic audience.

Just before Bella walked into Roger's office, I tried to take over, but she was so single-minded right now that I couldn't push out. The trace was definitely getting weaker. It bothered me that Bella was going to make a play for Roger. I'd told her how I felt about him, and she'd promised to keep hands off. But who can trust Bella with a man?

She walked into his office on the stroke of ten as if making an entrance into a scene, head high, Nola's haughty carriage softened by Sally's weak gaze. I've got to admit Bella can act. It was a great imitation of the new Sally.

The best I could do was make her stumble against Maggie's desk.

'Sorry, Maggie,' she said, 'I was so deep in thought about a new book I've been reading on the women's liberation movement, that I didn't notice the desk had been moved.'

'It hasn't been moved,' Maggie said.

'Well then,' Bella ad-libbed, raising her eyebrows the way Nola used to, 'it should be.'

I could see right away that Maggie noticed the bandages on her wrists and tried not to react. But when Roger spoke to her he treated her differently from the way he used to. It's like when you listen to someone you know very well talking to someone else on the phone, you can tell by the way they talk and the tone of voice who they're talking to.

Well, Roger used to talk to the old Sally slowly and carefully, watching her face closely to see if she understood. Now it sounded just the way he used to talk to Nola.

'Do you want to tell me about it?' he asked.

'About what?'

'Those,' he said pointing to her wrists.

'Complete blackout,' she said. 'I don't remember a thing. I must have cut myself. I guess someone tried to kill me.'

Then, remembering who she was supposed to be, she shrugged the way the second Sally would have. 'There are times when I still think life isn't worth living.'

'You promised you wouldn't speak like that. Suicide is not an acceptable solution. You know how I feel about that kind of talk.'

'Yeah, because of your wife, huh . . .'

He looked up at her, his brow furrowed as if he sensed something off-center in her replies.

'I wasn't trying to commit suicide,' she said. 'I know I've changed. I feel different, more aware of what's going on around me, but I guess I don't have as much control as I thought.'

'You've got to take it slowly,' Roger said, 'you're getting stronger, but the others are fighting for survival.'

'I don't blame them,' she said. 'But I have my rights too. I want my twins. A mother goes through hell, thinking about her kids. I've got to get well and show the judge I can make it.'

'I've got confidence in you, Sally. And I know Derry's going to help you pull through. Not only Derry, but Bella's cooperating, too. I know it's hard to think of her that way because she gets you into trouble so often. But just as Nola used to dwell on death, Bella thinks of life.'

'I never thought of her that way. Of course, I can see

now it's probably true.' She crossed her legs and smoothed her dress. 'But I think Derry's afraid of what you're going to do. You know, the cure. Fissioning us together. That's the right word, isn't it? Fission. Or is it fusion?'

He studied her closely. Then he suddenly picked up a yellow legal pad and a pencil and handed them to her. 'Would you please jot something down. I want you to have a message on paper in the event of another blackout. Put down, *In case of emergency, call Dr. Roger Ash. Midtown Hospital*. Now, let me see it, please.'

She handed it to him, and when he saw the handwriting he said, 'I don't like this behavior.'

'What do you mean?'

'All right, Bella, where's Sally?'

She was amazed that he'd caught on. She looked down. 'Away somewhere.'

'Can I talk to her?'

'Not now.'

'I have to speak to Sally,' he said. *'He knows what's in the darkness . . .'*

Her eyes closed, her head nodded gently, her hands fell relaxed into her lap.

'I have to speak to Sally. It's very important. Sally, *come into the light.*'

She opened her eyes and wet her lips. 'It's still me.'

'Why won't Sally come out?'

'She's very upset, and she doesn't want to talk right now.'

'When will she talk?'

Bella stretched seductively. 'Oh, when she's ready. She's all confused and ashamed of the things she's been doing. She wants to work things out in her own mind. She says you can talk to me instead, like you used to do with Derry. Only Derry isn't so strong anymore.'

Roger thought for a moment. 'All right, Bella, I've been planning for a long time to get into deep therapy with you. As long as you're here, we might as well start now.'

'That's just what I had in mind. Deep therapy. I need it.'

'How do you feel about these blackouts, Bella?'

'It's like when I was a teenager. Even though I was broke, I used to go to see Broadway shows all the time. I'd hang around out front, and when they'd come out to smoke during first act intermission, I'd slip inside with the crowd. I'd almost always find a seat. We called it "second-acting." Well, I knew the middle and end of every play and musical on Broadway, but never how they began. I'd have to fill in by guessing. That's the way it is with my life. I come in on the second act all the time – usually on the dance floor or in bed with a stranger. But the crummy thing is that most of the time I don't get to stay for the climax or the final curtain either.'

'You don't like that very much?'

'Would you like it never to know how things turned out? Let's face it, Roger. I could use a few curtain calls, too.'

'What if I could help you find a new role, Bella? A great part. Maybe you wouldn't be the star, but you'd be in a show that would run for the rest of a long, happy life.'

She laughed. 'Hell, Roger, I always figured this was your casting couch.'

'I'm serious, Bella. As a performer you know it's often necessary to submerge yourself in the character – to become someone else for the benefit of the whole show.'

She rubbed the bandage on her wrists thoughtfully. 'Sure – like they say, playing around is the thing.'

'I think it's time you got to share the lead.'

'The lead? You mean I get top billing?'

'Not quite. You get to play the lead, but you give up the billing. Just as you did when you came in pretending to be

206

Sally. You'll be fused with the character, submerged into a part that we'll call, for the time being, "the third Sally."'

She wasn't sure what he was getting at, but somehow she trusted him. 'Is there dancing in it?'

'There can be.'

'And good-looking men?'

'I don't see why not.'

'Are you gonna be in it?'

'I'll direct, but I'm not a performer.'

'You'd be a great leading man, Roger. I bet you could perform great. I'd love to play opposite you.'

He smiled and shook his head. 'Thank you, Bella, but I assure you I'm a lousy actor.'

'How do we get this thing into production?'

'We use the Stanislavsky method. First we'll go back into your memory to when you first began to act on your own, apart from Sally. I think it's important for you to relive that period. Once you've done that, I'll help you get into the role of the third Sally. With hypnosis, you'll put yourself into her place, see things from her point of view, and finally – as with any good actress – you'll submerge your own identity into the character you're playing.'

'Hey,' she giggled, 'sounds like a great part. I'll play as long as it has music and dancing and sex, and some good Italian food from time to time.'

'Let's make that a clause in your Equity agreement.'

'Okay, maestro. The show must go on.'

He used his gold pen to induce hypnosis and told her to go back to when she first had split off. She'd forgotten it, but when she saw the school auditorium on that winter night in her mind, she remembered how it happened.

Roger said, 'Tell me where you are, and what's taking place.'

Bella felt herself drifting back in a fast current, but then, like an actress picking up her cue, she jumped to Sally at eleven years old in sixth grade. Sally was getting ready to go on stage for the Christmas play, a musical version of *Snow White and the Seven Dwarfs*. Her part was Bella, the new queen-witch wife of King Absent-Minded. Sally was trembling. She knew she would forget her lines. She knew her voice would get stuck on the high notes. She knew she would black out and forget what had happened and be punished for doing something bad. Jinx had already been around for about four years, causing trouble, though not nearly as bad as she was now.

Her mom and Fred were out front. Sally hadn't wanted to do the play, but her mother had insisted that Sally would become an actress some day.

The headache began at the bottom of her neck and slowly built up to her head. She leaned against the wall. She couldn't go on. There was no way she could do it. But the boy who played Sneezy pushed her, and she was on the stage, facing the glare of the spotlight, her teacher in the wings, the blur of the audience in front of her. She froze and blacked out.

Before Sally could fall, Bella caught herself.

Bella sang and danced and got the biggest laughs, and when the curtain came down everyone stood and applauded, and she took four curtain calls. Everyone said Sally was a natural actress, because the minute she got out on that stage in the role of Queen Bella, she was transformed from a shy little girl into a star performer. The teacher said she was the best actress they'd ever had. The audience went out buzzing. Even Fred came by afterward and said that out there on stage she looked real pretty. He put his hand around her waist and said it looked like there was going to be a real actress in the family.

The touch of his hand and the look in his eye did something to her and she smiled back at him. He gave her a wink and a squeeze, but her mother suddenly came up and yanked her away.

'Go ahead and get out of your costume,' her mother said. 'We got to go home.'

And that was all Bella remembered about that night . . .

Roger brought her back to the present, still under hypnosis, and asked her what her feelings were about that memory.

'It was my first time out,' Bella said. 'I never forgot what it was like to be the center of attention. I was in plays from then on, all the way through high school. And only on stage was I really alive – really me – in front of the audience admiring me, listening to every word I said, gasping, laughing, applauding. I wanted that forever. I never wanted the curtain to fall. I never wanted to walk off stage. Without singing and dancing and acting, I'm nothing. Later I became a cheerleader – but even that wasn't the same.'

She thought about what she had just said. 'I'm nothing. And if I fuse with her, I'll be something?'

'That's one way of looking at it,' he said, 'but you have to make the choice. Think about it. Let me know on Monday if you agree to go through with it.'

'Will it hurt?'

He shook his head. 'I'm sure you'll never know what happened.'

'Will it be permanent? Derry told me that you explained to Nola it might not be permanent, that someday we might all get unstuck again.'

'That's a possibility. But we've learned a lot from other cases. I believe my combination of intensive hypnotherapy and behavior modification goes beyond what the others in this field have done.'

'I want to live, Roger.'

'I know. And I think this is the single best chance to keep you alive.'

She went over it in her mind during the weekend, asking me again and again what did I think. I told her to make up her own mind. I respected Roger, I said. I was sure he was trying to do what was best, but I wasn't about to take the responsibility for a decision like that on my shoulders. I don't go in for heavyweight thinking about serious problems.

She wanted me to ask Nola's advice, to get an idea what it felt like, but I told her that ever since Nola became Sally two, I couldn't communicate with her at all.

'Is it like she's dead?' she wanted to know.

'How do I know what it's like to be dead?'

I told her Nola just disappeared, vanished, poof! One minute she was here, and the next minute she was gone. I told her about the two ponds and the merging water, and that got Bella nervous because she can't swim a stroke.

It was just imaginary, in her mind, I said. That calmed her down. But I told her the important thing was that Sally seemed to have shifted part-way over to Nola's style of thinking. 'If you merge,' I said, 'you'll probably make a big change in their attitude toward sex and dancing.'

'And the theater,' she said.

'That, too.'

'I'm torn,' she said. 'I never had to make a decision like this before.'

She spent Friday night listening to her old rock 'n roll records. Saturday afternoon she took in a matinee called *Dancing Feet*, and that night she went to a disco. She went by herself and just danced with a lot of strange young men, but something was different. Her heart wasn't in it. She kept trying to throw off the frightened feeling by moving to the beat of the music, but the swirling lights made her dizzy.

She drank too much, and when a good-looking young guy with a pony tail danced very close and kissed her neck and whispered that he'd like to make it with her, she figured, why not? This might be her last performance as herself.

'Take me home,' she whispered into his ear.

The boy – he couldn't have been more than nineteen or twenty – had an old beat-up Dodge, and he drove with one hand on the wheel and the other between her thighs. She snuggled up close, unzipped his fly, and played with him.

Up in the apartment, he kissed her, and she pulled him close.

'Oh, baby, yes . . .' she groaned. She put both hands behind his neck, held his pony tail, and pressed his face deep into her breasts. 'Give it to me hard!'

She wanted to feel him inside her . . . the friction . . . the rising to a climax . . . But just as he was starting to enter, she felt his body shuddering.

'No!' she shouted. 'Not yet! Wait!'

But he was done, and he shriveled and rolled off her and looked away. 'I'm sorry,' he said. 'Oh, God, I'm sorry.'

Bella lay back, disgusted. Curtain time, with no climax, and a lousy ending as usual. 'That's all right, kid,' she said. 'I came fast, too, at the same time.'

'Really?' He rolled toward her and looked at her desperately.

'Yeah. Hey, listen, I wanted you as much as you wanted me. You were great. First time?'

He nodded, blushing, and put his shorts and pants on.

'Hey, where you going? I thought we'd spend the night.'

'I can't,' he said, looking at his watch. 'It's late already. My folks'll kill me.'

He kissed her and said, 'You're beautiful. Thanks for everything.'

She let him out and locked the door behind him. 'Thanks for nothing . . .' she said when he was out of earshot.

Then she threw herself on the bed and lay there limply, watching her breasts heaving. She put her hands to the nipples, circling them, feeling them firm under her touch. She wanted it. Somebody, anybody. She rubbed herself, trying to recapture the feeling, but that wasn't any good now. She got up and rummaged through the drawer for the vibrator she had bought a couple of months ago. Dumb Sally used to think it was for firming the neck and cheeks. Where did she hide it?

Bella tossed things out of the drawers, desperately looking for it. She could never find a goddamned thing. Always changing things around, always neatening up. If only they'd keep their goddamned hands off things that didn't belong to them.

She used her finger, stroking herself first slowly and then desperately. Just as she reached a peak of excitement, the headache began again.

'Shit!' she said. 'Leave me alone. I'm not finished. I've got to get off . . .'

Let me help.

'Who the hell is that?' Bella said, sitting up.

I told her it was Jinx.

'Hey, that's an idea,' she said.

I told her I was keeping out of it. If Bella wanted to play with herself, that was her business, but I didn't approve of mutual fooling around. Bella was thinking that she had never been with a woman before and the idea interested her. I told her I didn't even want to hear about it.

'But you're the connecting link,' Bella said. 'I only know about Jinx through you.'

'Well, I'm just not going to have anything to do with it. Jinx gets her kicks out of sadism.'

'Dog in the manger. Just because you're frigid, you don't want anyone else to have any fun.'

'I'm not frigid. I'm normal.'

'A virgin . . . normal?'

'I just don't believe in premarital sex.'

'You waiting for Prince Charming to come and kiss your ass?'

'Leave me out of this. I don't believe in orgies.'

'Orgies? What orgies?'

'Well, if three people are involved in sex, what else would you call it?'

'Oh, for God's sake. That's just a technicality.'

'Never mind,' I said. 'It's sick, and I don't want any part of it.'

'*We don't need her,*' Jinx said, and I realized it was the second time she had communicated directly with Bella.

'Now that we can deal directly with Sally,' Jinx said, 'we don't have to go through Derry.'

Bella seemed impressed with the idea. 'But Sally wouldn't—'

'It's two against one,' Jinx said. 'We won't always have this advantage. Why should we always do what she wants?'

'You're right,' Bella said. 'There's a lot I haven't tried yet, and now it's starting to look like maybe there won't be much more time.'

'You can't,' I said. 'Roger told Sally the fusion is still delicate. Something like this might set her off.'

Jinx's laugh gave me chills. 'The hell with her and the goddamned fusion. We'll be better off without it. We were better off before Roger started this crap.'

Then I understood her real reason for egging Bella on. She knew the fusion was delicate, and she wanted to throw a monkey wrench into the works.

'How do we do it?' Bella asked.

'Get your vibrator,' Jinx said. 'Sally hid it in the bottom drawer of the dresser, under the electric blanket.'

Bella got it and tested it. 'Works fine,' she said. 'Now what?'

'Now we bring Sally into the light.'

'Can you do that?'

'She brought the rest of you out for the party. So why not?'

She sat down in front of the three-mirrored vanity table. Bella's naked body appeared in the left mirror.

Slowly, Jinx's hard face, lined and tight-lipped, came into focus in the right-hand mirror. Her black hair still made me think of snakes. Then, in the center mirror I saw Sally looking around dazed and confused, like someone startled awake from a deep sleep. She looked from the left mirror to the right, surprised to see herself nude except for the bandages on her wrists.

'What's the matter? What's going on?'

'This time I'm throwing the party,' Jinx said, 'and you're invited.'

Sally recognized Bella, but Jinx's face and voice were strange. 'What do you want?'

Bella said, 'We just want to have some fun.'

'You're stronger now,' Jinx said. 'You don't have to be afraid any more.'

'I want to go to bed,' Sally said.

'So do we,' Bella said. 'We'll three spend the night together. Like old-timey pajama parties.'

'Look, I don't know what you two want,' Sally said, 'and I don't care. So just go back to wherever you came from and leave me alone.'

'She wants us to leave her alone,' Jinx said.

'That high and mighty tone sounds more like Nola than—'

'I'm Sally,' she said sharply, 'and I don't want anything to do with either of you. So leave.'

'It's not that easy,' Jinx said.

'That's right,' Bella said. 'It's not that easy.'

Jinx picked up the vibrator and pressed the button.

Sally heard the soft hum and looked at her sharply. 'What are you doing?'

'We belong together,' Jinx said. 'We're part of each other. Together and yet separate. We don't need anyone else to satisfy our needs and desires.'

She stroked Sally's leg and ran her hand up between her thighs.

'Don't do that!' Sally said sharply. She wanted to slap the hand away, but Bella was holding her left arm down, and she felt Jinx's fingers stroking her, with gentle circling motions.

'No,' Sally said. 'I don't want you to do that. I don't use that thing.'

'I do,' said Bella, 'as often as I can. But it's more fun with the three of us than alone.'

Bella stroked Sally's breasts, rubbing the nipples gently with saliva-tipped fingers. Sally struggled for a while longer, but her breathing became heavier and heavier. Her eyelids fluttered, then glazed. I got scared and tried to break through, but there was no way. They were concentrating too intently.

Then Jinx picked up the vibrator and rammed it in. The vibrations sent quivers through Sally's body so that she began to twist, and that made it tighter, and her whole body tingled with the very gentle electric shock. Sally's *no's* became softer and more liquid as her lips twitched. Bella slipped her tongue out and wet them. Jinx picked up speed. She thrust the vibrator harder and harder, pounding away, whispering obscenities into Sally's ear. 'Come, you goddamned bitch. That's what you've been needing. To be raped. All these years you've put it off on Bella, or left it to me to fight my way out. Now you can join us in one good big fuck.'

Sally came with such throbbing violence, that her back arched, and then she passed out.

Jinx laughed and slipped away. Bella lay there, thinking she should feel better – loose and easy. Instead, she felt guilty. She got a bottle of Johnny Walker out of the closet and started some heavy drinking.

'Damn it, no matter what I do it doesn't come out right.'

—That's because this isn't the way.

—Who's that?

—You're feeling bad because you know you did the wrong thing.

—It wasn't me. It was Jinx's idea.

—The time has come to stop blaming others.

It bothered Bella that she couldn't tell if the voice was that of a man or a woman. She was seeing a face, but it was blurred.

—Well the others deserve the blame.

—You shouldn't be drinking so much. You need a clear head to make your decision.

—Who are you?

—You know.

—Are you the one Derry calls the ISH?

—Yes, your Inner Self Helper. And you must let Dr. Ash help you fuse so that what happened tonight will never happen again.

—Maybe now Sally won't want to fuse. Maybe it broke her up.

—No, she'll be all right. I helped her blank it from her mind. It's buried deep in her unconscious.

Bella talked with the Helper half through the night and went to sleep without making a decision. Sunday morning, with the worst hangover in her life, she decided she never wanted to see the world through those bloodshot eyes again. She spent most of the day in bed with an icepack on her head, not caring if she lived or died.

'Okay, ISH,' she said out loud, though the Helper wasn't around just then. 'I'll merge. But if I lose my mind, it's your fault.'

On Monday Sally went to therapy all upset and jumpy without really knowing why. Then Roger explained about Bella's joining them.

'I don't *know*,' Sally said. 'I thought I was doing a good job of handling things.'

'What about that performance on stage, and the self-inflicted injuries?' he said.

'All the more reason not to let Bella have more influence than she already does.'

'That's not the way it works, Sally. When you incorporate Bella into yourself, you should be able to control her and yourself and possibly also resist Jinx. Let me just point out that what you are doing now is a defense mechanism predictable in cases like this. First denial. Then resistance. But we've got to go forward.'

'Why so soon? It's been less than a month since I've felt this new sense of intellectual exuberance. Why can't we wait?'

'I'd planned to give you another month before going ahead. I'd hoped that after curbing the suicidal tendency we could risk developing more slowly as we uncovered the past. But the part of you that's filled with anger has moved into the foreground. You'll need more power on your side to control it, and I think it's best to speed things up.'

She was silent.

'Do you agree to this merger with Bella?' he asked.

She nodded.

'Say it out loud. It has to be wholehearted and without reservation. Not for me, but for yourself.'

'I *agree* to the merger.'

Then he called Bella out and asked her if she had thought about it and if she was still willing to go through with it. She said she had talked it over with me and the ISH and had decided to take the part.

He used the gold pen. 'All right, Bella. The houselights are going down. The curtain is rising. When the footlights go on, you'll be blinded for a moment, but you'll know the audience is out there. You're going to be one of the great performers of the world, but your stage name will be Sally Porter, and you'll never again recognize a separate exist-ence. Your mind will be locked back on the track it was on before that night you performed in the Christmas play, and everything that has been a separate Bella will now be fused as history into the wonderful character of Sally.'

She nodded, feeling the excitement of the opening, the tension and stomach fluttering as the audience became hushed, her Helper smiling from the wings . . . waiting . . . waiting . . .

'When I count to three, you'll open your eyes. You won't remember any of this, but you'll know you're Sally Porter. How high did I say I was going to count?'

'Three . . .'

'All right, now. One . . . Two . . . Three . . .'

She opened her eyes, blinking, and looked around. For some reason she half expected to find herself on stage under the bright lights she loved. But she was here alone with Roger and he was looking at her anxiously.

'How are you?' he asked.

'Fine. Excited.' She realized that excited was too weak a word. She felt exhilarated, as if she could soar above it all.

'What kind of excitement?'

She laughed and ran her tongue over her lips. 'I feel like dancing. That's peculiar, because I *never* dance. I don't even know how. I'm so clumsy.'

'You'll discover that you dance well, Sally. Don't be surprised and don't fight it.'

'I've never even thought about dancing before. Yet . . .' She got up, and hearing a melody in her head, she began to move and sway around the room. 'Would you like to take me dancing, Roger?'

'I don't think it would be a good idea, Sally. With so many changes taking place in your life, we ought to keep our relationship limited to this office.'

'You don't like me,' she pouted. She wanted him, and she knew she could get him if she worked at it.

'That's not true.'

'Well,' she said, 'I've heard some therapists spend time outside the sessions with their patients. I'm not making a pass at you, and I don't plan to seduce you, if that's what you're worried about. I just think that with these new feelings you ought to chaperone me the first few times I go out on the town.'

'Chaperone?'

'To make sure I don't get into trouble. We can have dinner, take in a show, go dancing afterward, and you can leave me at my front door. I swear I won't entice you inside.'

'I don't think it's a good idea.'

She put her hand to her head.

'What's the matter?'

'I'm getting one of those headaches.'

She was lying. She didn't have a headache at all, but now she knew how to get Roger to sympathize with her. I felt like coming out and warning him, but I decided not to. After all, Sally three was his doing, and his responsibility. It would be fun seeing how she wrapped him around her little finger. I assure you, I wasn't jealous. If I had thought she was really after him, I might have interfered. But she just wanted to play games. And that was okay with me. Now that I realized the ISH was helping Sally, I was glad for her, and glad to be relieved of some of the responsibility. Sally was glowing as if she was ready to go anywhere and do anything. She loved life.

I felt a little relieved too, because with Bella gone there was less likelihood of Sally getting into trouble with men. The third Sally would be able to control those urges. But it was sad to know there would be no more separate Bella. With all her faults, she'd been fun to have around. Those wild things she got us into were exciting, and something was going to be missing. I told myself her spirit lived on in Sally. And that was like an afterlife, wasn't it? Still, just to make sure, I searched and searched. But it was true. No more Bella. And with Nola and Bella gone, Sally was brighter and sexier than she had ever been. When she got home she couldn't figure out why the vibrator was lying on the bed. Blushing and laughing, she dumped it into the garbage can. She wouldn't need that anymore.

I called for the ISH to see if it would talk, but I didn't get an answer. I figured he or she wasn't ready to start helping me.

Part Four

Thirteen

TWO WEEKS LATER, early in September, Sally phoned Roger and begged, 'I know my session isn't until tomorrow, but please take me out tonight. I need to be with someone I can trust. I've been good, I've controlled my impulses, but I need a night out.'

He thought about it for a long time, and then pressed the button on his intercom. 'Maggie, I have no patients scheduled this evening, do I? Good. Cancel any other appointments. I'll be going out.'

'I'll be ready at six,' Sally said.

I know it sounds nosy, but I wasn't about to leave Sally alone with Roger. No way. I figured I'd just trace along. Before the show, Sally couldn't decide between a Jewish delicatessen and a French restaurant. Roger suggested a little Italian place he knew, with red checkered tablecloths. In memory of Bella, I guess. It was so romantic, with dripping candles in Chianti bottles.

Sally didn't think it was romantic. She said it was sentimental.

Jesus, that made me want to punch her one. Always putting things down. I had a good mind to give her a headache. If she kept it up, I'd get Jinx to help me knock her on her butt.

'How are you feeling?' Roger asked.

'Terrific,' she said. 'But kind of restless. As if I should be going somewhere, doing something.'

'We are doing something.'

She smiled at him. 'That's not what I mean. I'm talking about doing something exciting with my life.'

All the time she kept talking to him, she kept looking around to see if there were other good-looking men in the place, almost as if Roger weren't there. God, she got me sore. She was more phoney now.

The show was great – a musical with a sad ending – and if I had been out, it would have brought tears to my eyes. But not Sally. She kept analyzing the story and criticizing the singing and the dancing. I liked it, but I guess I don't have very good taste.

When he took her home she whispered into his ear, 'You don't really have to leave me at the front door, Roger. You could spend the night.'

'We've got an agreement, Sally.'

I was glad he said that. If he'd fallen for her phoney come-on, I would really have sicced Jinx on them. It made me respect Roger more to know he wouldn't fall for a woman just because she was beautiful, intelligent, and sexy. I mean, he knew she didn't have deep, honest feelings. She couldn't love and she couldn't hate, so with all her brains and beauty she was still only part of a person – and not necessarily the best part.

But she was shrewd. When he took her back to the apartment, she kept insisting if he didn't come in for a nightcap and keep her company, she might be tempted to go out again and find other male companionship.

'Well, just for a few minutes,' he said.

When she took off her wrap and put on a slow dance record, she expected him to take her into his arms. Instead, he pulled out what looked like a cigar case.

'I had a feeling you might have difficulty sleeping tonight,' he said, 'so I brought along something to relax you.'

That surprised her. She was sure she had him. 'I don't want to relax, Roger. Not that way.'

'It's the only way tonight, Sally.'

'I have a right to go out and find other male companionship if I want to.'

'Yes, but as your doctor, I prescribe bed rest tonight – alone.'

She felt the anger rising. 'You don't want me, but you don't want anyone else to have me either.'

'That's not true. I'm just trying to keep you from harming yourself while you're in this delicate transition stage.'

'Transition to what? I'm satisfied the way I am.'

'But you won't stay the way you are. You're still unstable. There's more to do, and we've got to be careful not to let you tear yourself apart with impulsive behavior.'

'Let no man put asunder what Roger Ash hath joined together? Is that it? You think you're God, Roger?'

He took the hypodermic out of the case and tipped it upward into a vial of clear fluid.

'I don't want it!' she screamed, knocking it out of his hand. They both stared at it on the floor. 'You don't have the right to make moral judgments for me now.'

He pulled out his gold pen and said sternly, *'He knows what's—'*

'No!' she screamed, clamping her hands over her ears. 'You mustn't do that just to control me. I'm not a child, and you said yourself I'm not crazy. You know it's not ethical.'

He stared at her.

'You're doing that just to dominate me,' she said, 'so how are you different from Svengali? Am I just a puppet in the hands of a hypnotist? Is that how you dominated your wife – until she killed herself?'

His face reddened and he slowly put the gold pen back into his breast pocket. 'I'm sorry. I guess it really isn't my place to govern your behavior, as long as it's not self-destructive.'

'I didn't mean to hurt you,' she said. 'But if I'm not free to make my own decisions, to come and go as I please, then I'm your prisoner. And that's not what this is all about, is it?'

He said softly, 'I stand corrected.'

She put her hand on his arm. 'I'd still prefer you to stay with me.'

He picked up his jacket, started for the door, and then glanced back. 'Just promise me you won't harm yourself.'

'I promise. What I want now is the opposite of death. I want to live life all the way, as a free person, to make my own choices.'

'Well, then, Sally, good-night. I'll see you for a session tomorrow morning at nine.'

After he left she stood there, uncertain what to do with her newfound freedom. Something inside her suggested she make popcorn and watch the late show on TV or else finish *Moby Dick*. But she shrugged both thoughts off, mumbling, 'That's not what I had in mind.'

She knew it would be best to stay home, but she paced restlessly around the apartment. She wanted to go and she wanted to stay. She knew there was nothing out there for her. Wandering the streets would make her lonelier and more depressed. But still, she might meet someone interesting. Decisions. Decisions. It used to be so simple. She picked up the phone and started to dial Eliot's home number, but stopped halfway. Then she dialed Todd's number instead. When he answered, she stared at the phone and hung up quickly.

'Shit!' she said, finally, grabbed her purse and coat, and ran down the steps and out onto the street. It had started to rain. She ducked under Mr. Greenberg's awning, fished around in her purse for her plastic rain hood, and put it on, using the store window as a mirror. Murphy was still there, but oddly enough his nightstick was gone. His empty right hand had been turned as if making an obscene gesture. Stupid idea, she thought. As if a burglar would be put off by a window dummy in a policeman's uniform.

She waited on the corner for a cab, but the crosstown bus came first and she took it. No sense in throwing money away. She got off at Third Avenue and walked along, feeling the excitement of being out on the street with the night people. She was amazed at herself, feeling this was risky but wanting to do it anyway. Before the evening was over she might have a great adventure, might meet someone who could turn her life around. An accident, a chance encounter, and everything would take a different direction from then on. It was wrong. It was stupid. But who the hell gave a damn? She was going to have a good time. She was a night person, too.

She heard music from the Shandygaff and wondered if 'shandy' really came from 'shanty.' She would have to look up the derivation sometime. Inside it was crowded, and she saw hungry eyes turning to look at her. At first she was pleased and slipped over to the bar to order a scotch, but when someone rubbed against her behind, she felt her skin crawl and pulled her arms close as if to protect herself.

'Hey, you here alone? Can I buy you a drink?'

He was good-looking. Blow-dried hair and a turtleneck sweater.

She started to say yes, but caught herself shaking her head, unable to get the word out. He drifted away. What was wrong with her? She didn't know what she wanted. She rummaged in her purse for a cigarette and discovered

227

she had none. She wanted one, but at the same time the smoke in the air oppressed her. It had never bothered her before, but now it smelled sickening. Did that mean she wanted to give up smoking? She downed the scotch quickly, paid for it, and pushed through the press of bar patrons. Outside, she paused and leaned against the building to gulp the rain-freshened air.

Well, did she smoke or didn't she? It was too confusing, and she shook her head, trying to sort it out as she walked. Through the brightly lit window of Bargain Books she peered at the people rummaging among the tables of remaindered books. She drifted inside and looked at the dollar table. *Home Canning Made Easy*. She picked it up, thumbed through it, and then put it back. The thought of cooking and baking no longer appealed to her. *Budget Gourmet Restaurants in New York* sounded more interesting. She reached for it, but a bright red dust jacket caught her eye. *Sexual Awareness for the Liberated Woman*. She reached and froze. She wanted to pick it up, but it was as if her arm had become paralyzed. A stack of *The History of Avant-Garde Film* lay next to it, and she managed to slide a copy over on top of *Sexual Awareness* and pick them both up, hands trembling. As she thumbed through the photographs of the sex manual, she felt herself blushing. Seeing naked bodies entwined, she remembered Larry showing her pornographic photos, suggesting positions he wanted her to take, things he had wanted her to do. She remembered screaming and crying and throwing up all over the bed afterward. Perverted and disgusting. But now, seeing it, she felt her breasts tingle and ran her tongue over dry lips. She was both repelled and fascinated. It would have to be with a stranger, she decided. She could do all the forbidden things she wanted to do, and then walk away from it and not feel he would look at her afterward

228

in disgust. But would she have to reveal it in confession? She felt eyes behind her and turned to see an elderly man grinning.

'Looks interesting,' he said. He reached over and picked up a copy of the same book and thumbed through the pictures, glancing sidewise at her from time to time as if trying to picture her doing those things. 'I'd pay a lot for a liberated woman with sexual awareness.'

He made no attempt to hide the bulge in his trousers, but faced her and ran his hand down his stomach. 'A woman who could take it into her head to please an old man could name her price. I've got money.'

She laughed. 'Grandpa, your heart couldn't stand it.'

'A beautiful way to die,' he said, nodding.

'For you,' she said, 'not for me.' She threw both books back on the table and walked out of the bookstore laughing, but also blushing and angry all at once. She let the cool drizzle bathe her face and waited, as if expecting something to happen. No sign of a headache. Sexual embarrassment used to give her a headache, but not now. That must be a good sign, she decided. She was getting better. She would have to remember to tell Roger about that at tomorrow's session.

She wanted something to happen, but she knew she should grab a cab and go back to the apartment before something did happen. Suddenly she felt depressed again. What was the use of going through this charade if every action was going to paralyze her with indecision? She might as well be dead as living this torment. She could just dash out into the middle of the street and let an oncoming truck make her final decisions for her. So definite. So easy. So final. Whoa, there! She pulled herself up. She'd signed a no-suicide contract, hadn't she? No. That had been someone else, in another country, and besides the whore was dead.

Oh, shit on this self-pity and self-analysis. She was out to have a good time. Get laid. And then kill herself if she goddamn well pleased. It was her body, her mind, her life, and she'd do what she wanted with all or any part of it.

Standing outside a liquor store, she caught sight of the bottles of wine, and that reminded her of something. She looked at her watch – 11:55. She asked an old woman what day it was. 'Friday,' the woman said, looking at her strangely.

And Friday was Professor Kirk Silverman's party night. That was what she needed. One of Kirk's kooky kinky parties, where she'd heard there was booze and pot and stimulating conversation. Maybe it would help her pull herself together. She remembered the price of admission and went into the liquor store for a bottle of Chablis. Then, seeing a taxi with its light on, she dashed out into the street and hailed it.

'Hey, lady!' the cabbie shouted. 'You nearly got yourself killed.'

'That's what life is all about,' she laughed. 'Second Avenue and Bleeker Street.'

She settled back, pleased that she had found something better to do with the evening than kill herself.

It was a dimly lit fifth-floor walk up, and she was out of breath by the time she reached the apartment. The door was scarred and dented where it had been pried repeatedly near the lock. A steel plate had been bolted in place, and a gleaming lock cylinder looked brand-new. She rang the buzzer. Seconds later she heard the click of the peephole and then the slide of a chain being drawn back. The door opened and Professor Kirk Silverman peered up at her through thick lenses.

'Nola-darling,' he said. 'How wonderful. You finally decided to come to one of my parties.'

He was wearing tight-fitting flare jeans and a cable-knit white turtleneck.

'I was lonely, and when I remembered it was Friday night, I thought it was a good time to keep my promise.'

'And I have promises to keep, and miles to go before I sleep . . .' He put his arm around her waist and hugged her close as they walked down the long, narrow hallway. The sound of talk was overshadowed by the beat of bongos.

'We have a varied crowd tonight, Nola-darling. You'll find some of them interesting. I'll introduce you to a couple of people and let you make your way on from there.'

'I know it may sound odd, Kirk, but I don't use the name Nola-darling anymore.'

He peered up at her quizzically. 'Oh? What do you call yourself?'

'Nola was a nickname. I'd rather be known as Sally-darling from now on. I'm making a break with the past.'

'Sally? I've never thought of you as a Sally. Nola is so much more exciting. But it's your name, darling. Sally-darling it is. A break with the past? Fascinating. Fascinating. Maybe there'll be room for a short, near-sighted professor of economics in your unbroken future.'

'Why not?' she said, laughing. 'You're a fascinating man.'

He peered up at her, eyes blurring behind thick glasses. 'You're different somehow. Your voice. The way you carry yourself. Your laugh is vibrant. You have a kind of magnetism.'

'I'll bet you tell that to all the lonely strays you invite to your Friday nights.'

'Not all. Only those in whom I see a spiritual kinship. There is something about you, Nola – Sally – that sends out

231

confusing vibrations. There is torment beneath that armor. I know a massage technique to penetrate that shield and you can experience a release you have never known before.'

She was about to say she'd love a massage, but he must have sensed her sudden repulsion because he backed away and pushed aside the beaded curtain that separated the kitchen from the crowded living room.

'No time to talk of those matters now,' he said. 'Have a good time. Let me introduce you to Eileen, here, who writes beautiful erotic poetry.'

Eileen sized her up, and Sally sensed an immediate hostility. She chatted briefly and excused herself to get a glass of wine. Couples were sitting on couches around the room, kissing and caressing, while others stood nearby in close conversation. In the far corner a young black man, stripped to the waist, was softly beating the bongos while a group of admiring middle-aged women sat around him rocking their bodies to his rhythm.

She drank one glass of wine, and then another and another, and the smell of pot and the insistent pounding of the bongos began to excite her. She had the impulse to pull off her clothes and dance with the black man. She saw herself with him in the jungle, dancing, biting, copulating, and then she caught herself. *Racist*, she thought.

In the dim light, she saw someone familiar across the room. It was Sarah Colombo, on one of the couches, a man's hand between her thighs. She couldn't understand why it made her angry, but *wife-swapping* burst into her consciousness, and she remembered Larry telling her that there was nothing wrong with a wife going to bed with the head of the sales department if it would help her husband get ahead. She'd been horrified at the suggestion, disgusted. She remembered refusing. They were at a party at the sales manager's house. Larry and the man's wife had disappeared. Sally had had too much to drink, and the sales manager had gotten her down on the couch, and very quickly he slipped his hand between her thighs, and before she could push him away she got a headache and blacked out.

Only now the blackness lifted, and she remembered the rest of the evening. It was as if the amnesia veil had parted like that beaded curtain, and there she was, passionate, responding, tongue meeting his, pelvis responding. She didn't want to think of it, but the memory was becoming clearer, like a recalled dream. She was ashamed of it, and yet she identified with Sarah Colombo there on the couch, with that man's hand between her own legs, his fingers exploring.

God, what had happened to her? Was she becoming so debased and perverted? She had never done those things. So how could she suddenly remember them all so clearly now? History, she kept thinking. It's someone else's history.

She had another drink and thought of staying behind after the party with Kirk Silverman. She started to get another glass of wine, but stumbled.

I caught her.

This was as good a time as any, I figured, while she was drunk, to get out and stretch myself for a while. I felt Jinx trying to get out too, but I said, Hey, it's my turn. You were out on stage and nearly got us all killed, and you had your orgy. I'll stay out and have some fun myself, if you don't mind. I hung on with all my strength and she backed off.

I went back to the kitchen and helped myself to some eats (the hell with the calories – I love beer and cheese). There was a good-looking guy with a shaved head and a ring in his ear giving me the eye, and for once I felt grateful Bella wasn't around anymore to cause trouble. She'd have made a play for him. I just ignored him, and finally he went away with a woman whose hair reached down to her butt.

I'm not an alcoholic or anything like that, but I enjoy a buzz now and then. It lifts my spirits and lets me do the wacky things I like to do. I went around from group to group talking and listening, and I saw Kirk Silverman watching me.

'You all right, Sally?'

I started to tell him I was Derry, but I figured why confuse the poor guy. 'I'm all right, as all right as I'll ever be. And you have a lovely place here, and a beautiful party with all these beautiful, kooky people, and I'm very honored to be here among all you intellect – intellect –' But I kept hiccuping and never got out the whole word.

'Let's go into my study, Sally, away from the crowd awhile so we can talk.'

Now, I knew he wanted to do more than talk. I mean, I'm no fool. But he was so short, and with those thick glasses his eyes looked so sad, I felt sorry for him, so I went along. He had a couch in the book-lined study, but I expected that. What I didn't expect was the thing standing right in the middle of the floor that looked like a telephone booth covered with sheets of lead.

'Where's the phone?'

'It's not a telephone booth. Haven't you ever seen one of these before?'

'What is it? One of those modern sculptures?'

'It's an orgone box.'

'You play music on that? Where are the keys? You play. I'll sing along.'

'Surely you've heard of the work of Wilhelm Reich, who discovered the orgone.'

'Huh? Oh, yeah. Sure. Here today, or-gone tomorrow.'

He looked puzzled. 'You change from one moment to the next, Sally-darling. Even your voice sounds different.'

'It's the booze,' I said. 'Affects different people in different ways.'

'No, Sally-darling, it's more than that. There's an aura of warmth about you now. A glow, an essence of goodness.'

'Oh, my goodness, it shows, huh?'

'I'm very glad you came tonight. I've thought of you often.'

'Tell me about this Oregon box. Is that where it's from? How does it work?'

'The great Reich showed us that the energy of the libido is concentrated in electrical matter known as orgones. If you stand inside the orgone box, the shielding helps concentrate your sexual power.'

'You're pulling my leg.'

'Step inside with me, Sally.'

He said it again, like Charles Boyer, in that deep French accent, 'Come wiz me into ze orgone box . . .'

'For a professor of economics, you sure do come up with the wildest stories and gimmicks.'

He looked at me sadly. 'When you're short and nearsighted you need gimmicks to attract beautiful women. But I assure you, I have abilities and talents that will never bore you – I'm attracted to you, Sally-darling. Passionately, deeply. I want to hold you and—'

'You were going to tell me how it works.'

'It focuses the orgones and builds the energy in the body until it reaches a kind of critical mass. Fusion, like in a hydrogen bomb. And then there is a sexual explosion that is far beyond anything you've ever known, setting off a chain reaction of orgasms.'

'Sorry I asked.'

'Let me share it with you, Sally.'

He grabbed me and pulled me into the orgone box. With his pot belly, it was a tight squeeze. He got his legs wrapped around one of mine, and started rubbing against me.

'Stop it, Kirk.'

'The orgones are building up.'

He was hanging onto me, pumping my leg like a fat puppy, and I couldn't shake him loose. I didn't know what to do. I could have just let him keep going, building up the orgones, but I was getting worried about that nuclear sexual explosion. I figured I'd better head for a fallout shelter.

But that was all the excuse Jinx needed. She elbowed me aside, and the next thing I knew, she knocked Kirk out of the orgone box and toppled the whole damned thing over on its side.

There were tears in his eyes. 'You didn't have to do that, Sally.'

'You goddamned sonofabitchin' little pervert, you're lucky I don't rip your balls off.'

His mouth opened and closed several times, chewing the air, and I could guess what he was thinking. Jinx stormed out of the place, pushing people left and right and leaving a trail of astonished expressions and open mouths. I don't think Sally-darling's going to be welcome at one of Kirk's Friday nights for a long time.

Jinx went down the five flights two steps at a time, almost falling several times, but catching herself against the wall. She ran out onto the street, trying to get her bearings. When she discovered she was on Bleeker Street and Second Avenue, she thought of a cab, but decided against it and went down the side streets looking for an unlocked car. She found one near Astor Place, and it took only a few seconds to hotwire it. She pulled away from the curb with tires screeching.

I knew what she was going to do. We had talked over this fusion business more than once, and she said she'd never let it happen to her. 'I'll kill that shrink first,' she said. 'I swear it. And then things will be the way they were before he came along.'

When she swears things, I take it seriously. Jinx always keeps her word. She was going to dig up the buried gun. She was thinking about staying in control all night, up to the time for tomorrow's nine o'clock appointment. Then she'd walk into Roger's office with the gun in her purse and keep her word. I tried to get out again, but even though I knew what she was planning, I couldn't find a crack to squeeze through.

The gun, she remembered, was buried in the back yard, near a telephone pole. She was thinking about it all the way uptown, and jammed the brakes as she nearly ran a red light. Mustn't get stopped now, or picked up in a stolen car. She had work to do. Getting out was becoming harder, and she had to take advantage of every break. She drove slowly, resisting the impulse to floor the accelerator.

I kept trying to get out, but she blocked every opening. And there was no way to give her a headache. The only way to get past her and take control would be to wait till she was exhausted from pouring out all her anger and viciousness. Then she'd just let go. But she was determined that wasn't going to happen until after she killed Roger. I tried to communicate on the drive to the apartment, nagging on the edge of her mind, thinking words that might let us talk. Maybe because she was overflowing with anger, or maybe because she was enjoying the chill, drizzly weather, she decided to let me through to her.

'Let's call it a night,' I said.

'Not until the shrink is dead.'

'But why?'

'Because he's like all the other bastards. He's trying to wipe you and me out, the way he did Nola and Bella. And then, you know what? . . . He's going to wrap us all up in one neat, female package and use her.'

'I wouldn't mind that,' I said.

'Well, I don't want any man's hands on me.'

'He's not just any man. He's a warm-hearted guy. Bella made passes at him, and the third Sally threw herself at him, but he resisted. Doesn't that prove he's different?'

'It only proves he's biding his time until you're fused into Sally, too. You're the one he's after. But I have no intention of letting it happen. I'm not giving up my freedom to serve Sally.'

'Then there's going to be hell to pay.'

'There always is.'

'Look, I care for Roger,' I said.

'That's your problem.'

'It's yours, too. Without my help, you're cut loose. You have no idea what Sally thinks or does. Even though you can communicate with her a little now, you can only remember the bits and pieces of when you're out. You know what they'll do to you if you kill him?'

'I'm not afraid to die.'

'But that's just it. You won't die. They'll pour you into a straitjacket and lock you away so that there's no freedom for anyone. And all you'll be able to do with your hate and spite is bang your unfeeling head against rubber walls.'

That got to her. She was visualizing what I said, but it got her angry and she blotted me out and floored the accelerator. I felt sure she was going to smash us up. But she didn't. She's a damned good driver.

'Why do you hate men so much?' I asked her.

'They've broken promises.'

'Who are you talking about?'

I knew who she was referring to, but I figured if I could keep her talking, I might get her off guard and slip through.

'Larry.'

'He was Sally's husband, not yours.'

'Maybe.'

'What do you mean by that?'

'He used to beg her to whip him, but she couldn't do it.'

'Oh, that . . . I didn't pay much attention. I don't care for kinky lovemaking.'

'Well, he and I got along just fine. That was the closest I ever came to loving a man, and he said he'd never care for anyone else. I'm the one he gave that silver flying-fish pin to.'

'Well?'

'I found out he was fooling around with other women.' She drove right through a red light.

'Well, Jesus. He cheated on Sally, not you. He couldn't have known about you. He just couldn't understand the changes in mood.'

'I thought he and I were friends, pals. And then I discovered that Bella had been coming out and sleeping with him, and she was the one he really cared for, not me. And that hurt. It really hurt.'

'You don't hurt.'

'That's a stupid thing to say, Derry. I may not hurt physically, but I have more pain in my heart than ten people. I hurt so bad that all I want to do is hurt others back. When he started the wife-swapping that hurt me more than anyone could imagine.'

Of course she was right. I knew how tormented she was all the time. I don't remember her ever being really happy in all the years I've known her. It just doesn't seem fair that I should have so much happiness and fun out of life and she should be so miserable. She stopped at the next light, one foot on the brake and the other on the accelerator. When the light turned green, the car screeched and lurched forward.

'I feel bad about that, Jinx. I wish I could trade places with you some of the time and give you some of my happiness.'

'Oh, shut up. You're so big-hearted, you make me sick.'

'Okay, but you're not as bad as people say. You do those things because you're suffering. But hurting Roger isn't going to stop that suffering.'

'Maybe it will. If he's dead, Sally will split up again, and Nola and Bella will get out, and things will be as they used to.'

'There's no more Nola and Bella. I've searched and searched for them, and believe me, they're gone.'

'Where could they go?'

'I like to think they've gone over the rainbow,' I said.

'Huh?'

'Didn't you ever see Judy Garland in *The Wizard of Oz?* That's where I've always wanted to go, somewhere over the rainbow, where somebody can help all of us and give us the things each of us is missing. In my dreams I see myself like her, but instead of a dog I've got my cat, and my ruby slippers, and the five of us going somewhere over the rainbow.'

'Jesus,' she said. 'You're really a cornball.'

'I just like to feel that someday I'll be a real person, with someone to love and care for. I still wonder – whatever happened to Cinderella?'

'She's dead, and you know it,' Jinx snapped.

'A cat has nine lives.'

'She's dead and rotted.'

'She has eight other lives. I'll find her someday.'

We drove in silence for a while. She was thinking of the gun, and I kept trying to figure a way to keep her from killing Roger.

'I hope you're not going to dig up the gun in Sally's beautiful new dress,' I said. 'I insist that you be careful and not get mud on it.'

'Go to hell!' She left the car a block from the apartment and went directly to dig up the gun. It was five in the morning.

The gun was still there. No one had found it. I cursed myself for not digging it up and throwing it away. I had to think of something.

'I don't want you to get Sally's dress dirty,' I pleaded.

'Leave me alone now!' she shouted, and she smeared her muddy hands on it. 'There. Her goddamned dress is filthy now. If you say one more word about it, I'll tear it to shreds.'

I was relieved. Now she would have to go upstairs and change. When we got up to the apartment, I suggested a drink, but she refused. She just sat there looking out the window, waiting for daybreak. It was a beautiful sunrise. At seven-thirty she got up to dress. I was sure she'd put on her favorite black suit. She did. And the silver flying-fish pin. At least, now Maggie and Roger would know it wasn't me or Sally.

Jinx was going to take the stolen car at first, but then she realized the police might be looking for it, so she took a cab instead. I kept quiet now, hoping she'd forget about me and maybe I could catch her off guard. Again and again I tried sneaking out, but she had the place filled with hatred, and there was no way to get through.

I could warn Roger if only I could get to a phone. But she wasn't about to let me tip him off.

If she killed Roger, then Sally would unfuse and Nola would kill herself. I thought of telling Jinx that, but it wouldn't stop her. She didn't care if we lived or died. Well, if Roger was dead, I wouldn't care either. That would be the end of the five of us. It was all my fault. If I hadn't come out at the party, Jinx would never have gotten out.

She took the elevator up to his office and told Maggie she was here for her nine o'clock appointment. I could tell by the look of alarm on Maggie's face that she knew it was Jinx. She and Roger knew that only Jinx wore black, and they knew about the flying-fish pin, and I hoped they'd realize there was danger. But Maggie nodded and pressed the intercom and told Roger that Sally Porter was here. I tried to scream, *It's not Sally. It's Jinx and she's going to kill him.* But no words came out. I couldn't control my arms or legs or voice. I could only watch helplessly as she opened the door and walked in.

Roger reacted to the black suit and the flying-fish pin. He looked into her eyes with a glance of disapproval. So he knew. But he couldn't know what she had in her purse. I tried to budge her arm so the purse would fall to the floor, but there was no way. I was a helpless witness.

'Come in and sit down,' he said.

She ignored the chair he pointed to, took the one across from his desk, and placed her purse in her lap. She wouldn't do it right away, she thought. She'd play with him first. She wanted to see surprise on his face, and then fear.

'How have you been?' he asked.

She toyed with the clasp of her purse.

'I'm glad you decided to drop in and have a talk, Jinx. I've thought about you a lot.'

She was annoyed that he'd found her out. She stopped pretending. 'I don't believe you. You don't care about me. I know goddamned well what you're planning.'

'Would you mind telling me?'

'Oh, shit! You wouldn't admit the truth if I did.'

'Give me a chance,' he said. 'Tell me what you think, and I'll tell you if you're right.'

'Okay. You're going to fuse Derry and create a fourth Sally. And then I'll be locked in forever, like one of those lost souls in – what do they call it, where the lost souls of unbaptized children wander?'

'Limbo?'

'Yes. With all the others fused and Sally strong, I'll be lost in limbo forever. I have no intention of letting that happen.'

'What if I told you that I haven't made any definite plans regarding you, that I've decided to keep all options open, including the possibility of merging you last?'

'I wouldn't believe you. You don't like any part of me. I'm the black sheep everyone would like to ignore. I'm the skeleton in the closet, and you want to lock me in and throw away the key. I've been hurt so much in my life that all I've got left in me is hate, and you don't want that in your wonderful new Sally.'

'That's not true.'

'You're lying. Sure, Derry is part of the plan. You'll add her happiness and good-naturedness to the cold-blooded, intellectual sex machine you've created, and then you'll stop. You're not about to let me spoil your perfect woman.'

'I won't deny I've thought of it that way from time to time.' She was surprised he'd admitted it.

'But,' he went on, 'as a psychiatrist I had to reject the idea.'

'Bullshit.' She stood up and backed away from him.

'Hear me out. Every psychologist knows all human beings have anger and hatred in them. We ignore the evil in us at our own peril. We've learned we can't really get rid of aggressive feelings by hiding them and locking them in the closet, as you say – what we call "repression in the unconscious." They always return to haunt us. Our job is to bring those feelings, born in pain and frustration, out into the open. Then they don't fester and destroy everything.

'I don't think of you as evil,' he said. 'I think of you as someone who's suffered more than a person can bear. All your conscious life you've been the receptacle for the emotional pain and bitterness the others couldn't face. Now it's time to spread that over the whole Sally. What you can't tolerate alone might be handled if shared by the five of you.'

'God, you're a smooth talker, but I don't believe you.'

She had the purse open and slipped her hand inside. She felt the metal of the handle in her palm, her index finger touching the trigger, pulling the gun out, releasing the safety.

He looked at the gun.

I screamed with all my power. I called on the Helper to help me force Jinx's hand down. I screamed until I thought my mind would burst. Jinx sensed something. She hesitated and put her free hand to her head in astonishment.

'I've got a headache.'

'You feel it?' he asked.

I kept screaming at her. Screaming . . . screaming . . . screaming . . . I felt her weaken just a little. She was trying to pull the trigger, but the pain of the headache amazed her and paralyzed her hand. Slowly I forced the gun to turn away from Roger's direction until it pointed at me. She stared at it, not believing her hand was moving against her will. 'Don't stop me, Derry!' she grunted.

'Let me . . .! Let me . . .!'

'Jinx!' he shouted. *He knows what's in the darkness . . .*'

But it was too late. Her finger twitched and we both heard the explosion, and I felt the sharp pain, and in the flash of light everything grew quiet, and I went over the rainbow . . .

Fourteen

WHEN SALLY OPENED her eyes, she found herself lying on the couch, feeling lousy. She turned her head and saw Roger and Maggie looking at her anxiously.

She struggled to raise herself. 'Roger what happened? I was at a party, and—'

'Don't try to get up,' he said. 'You were wounded. Not seriously, but you lost some blood.'

Then she saw the black suit. 'Oh, my God . . . It was Jinx!'

'Everything's all right now.'

'What did she do?'

She saw his face was pale.

'Jinx wasn't able to do it. She pointed the gun at me, but I think, somehow, Derry interfered and turned the gun on herself. The important thing is that Jinx felt pain for the first time.'

Sally dropped back to the pillow. Her left shoulder was numb. 'What am I going to do? If Jinx can come out and do things like this, I'll never be able to live a normal life. She might as well have killed me.'

'It was my fault, Sally, not yours. If I had put you to sleep last night, not let you talk me out of it, Jinx might never have come out. I almost lost you. We have to move more quickly. She didn't get out through you, I'm sure. She emerged through Derry. If we close the last escape hatch by fusing you with Derry, I'm sure you'll be strong enough to repress Jinx.'

'But what if that doesn't work?'

'There'll be time to try other things. I don't think Jinx will come out for a while after this emotional release.'

'By "other things," you mean merging Jinx, too, don't you?'

'As a last step – if it's necessary. Bringing her violent impulses out into the open with all your other feelings, thoughts, and emotions might make her anger and aggression controllable, but that would be only a final, desperate gamble. And *she'd* have to agree.'

'Do you want her viciousness to be part of me?'

'What I want doesn't matter,' he said.

'It matters to me.'

'Let's decide after we've given Derry's emotions a chance to become part of your new personality. I want you to go home and think about it. Talk to Derry. Sleep on it. If your answer is yes – and both of you agree – we'll do it tomorrow. I'll have Maggie set up a special appointment.'

Then Roger said he wanted to talk to me, and he called me out into the light. I was surprised and glad because I was anxious to tell him what had happened.

'Hello, Roger,' I said. 'Glad she didn't get my favorite doctor.'

'You had something to do with stopping her, didn't you?'

'I didn't think I'd be able to. Jinx has gotten much stronger.'

'I didn't know,' he said. 'That makes a difference.'

I told him what happened after he left Sally, how she went to the party, how I slipped out to have a good time, and what happened when Jinx took over.

'Do you know why I've brought you out at this time, Derry?'

'Because you finally decided you just can't live without me?'

He laughed and took my hand. I gripped his to keep him from taking it back.

'You know what I told Sally.'

'I'm not ready to go yet, Roger. I'm still young. I want a few years more as me.'

'There isn't time, Derry. Jinx is unstable, and you said yourself she's getting stronger. We've got to tighten things up so there's no chance of her doing again what she did this morning.'

'I'm afraid, Roger.'

'There's nothing to be afraid of.'

'But you need me. You said so yourself.'

'The time has come to give that up. We have to strengthen Sally and break the connection to Jinx.'

'Does that mean I won't be the trace anymore, and I won't know what's going on in their minds?'

'It won't be *their* minds. It'll be *your* mind. You'll *be* Sally instead of just a separate part of her. You'll be whole and complete, the way you always wanted to be.'

'I just can't think of myself as a brain. Whenever people try to talk to me about serious things, what's going on in the world, or art or culture, I put on a wacky act so they won't know how dumb I am.'

'You're not dumb, and you won't have to do that any more, Derry. You'll know all the things Nola and Bella and Sally have learned. It'll become your knowledge.'

'I've always been scared of sex. My kidding around is a cover-up.'

'Sex will become a normal part of your life.'

'I've never cried, Roger. I've never felt real sadness, like other people. I've watched Sally so unhappy, and crying all her life, and I said, that must be like death. I never wanted that, Roger.'

247

'But that's what being a whole person means. It's more than just laughter and good times. It means mixed emotions, and responsibility, and deep feelings, and highs and lows. We all lose things or people in our lives, and that makes us sad. I've got to help you become strong enough to hang onto life and not be ashamed of tears. Human beings are born crying.'

'Is that how I was born?'

'Let's find out how you were born.'

'I'm frightened.'

'So am I, but you won't be alone. Are you ready?'

'Yes. But hold on to my hand, Roger. Don't let go.'

I saw his eyes go watery. He squeezed my hand and his voice was choked up. *'He knows what's in the darkness . . .'*

I swam out of myself. I heard him off in the dark distance saying, 'We're going back to the time Derry came into existence. There was once a time when it was only Sally and Jinx, and then something happened to split you off into a separate personality. When I count to three, you'll relive that day, bringing the same emotions out into the open. And you and Sally and I will know how you came to be.'

I moved out of the darkness, through the clouds and gloom into the rain, wandering the streets looking for Cinderella. And I remembered it was Easter Sunday and Sally was ten years old. I hadn't been born yet. That happened three days later, but through Jinx's memory I knew how it had happened, and I told Roger.

Sally had found a crippled kitten a few months before, and she named it Cinderella because one paw was missing. She said it had lost one of its slippers at the ball and was waiting for her prince to find her and bring her slipper back. She was always acting out the fairy tales Oscar used to tell her at night, and 'Cinderella' was one of her favorites. But this was the first time she had ever had a real pet of her own to help her pretend, and she talked her mother into letting her keep it, even though Fred was against it.

She brought it milk and scraps and made believe that Fred was the wicked stepfather who kept Cinderella hidden down in the dirty cellar and wouldn't let her go out and have fun.

She liked to hold Cinderella close and feel the purring against her cheek and the soft fur tickling her nose. And Cinderella would run up to her and rub her back against Sally's leg.

And she and Cinderella would play together whenever her mother and stepfather locked her up alone in the house. She would tell Cinderella all her problems, and Cinderella would listen carefully and purr to show she understood how mean people were to Sally.

Now in those days Sally believed she was a very forgetful little girl. She would deny she had done bad things, and she would be punished by her mother and her wicked stepfather, who called her a terrible liar and locked her up in her room or in a closet. Then she would pretend she was really a princess and her real father was a king who wandered his kingdom disguised as a postman, and he had left her temporarily with a servant named Vivian. Someday, if she was a very good girl, King Oscar would come back and reclaim her. But as long as she did these bad things she couldn't remember doing, she was trapped here in the closet. It was very clear, she told Cinderella, that a bad witch had put a magic spell on her and made her forget and lose time. All she had to do was wait until King Oscar came back and carried her off in his magic mail pouch, and then she would be free to turn back into the princess. But she had to stop doing bad things. Of course, she didn't know then – nobody knew – that a mean little girl named Jinx had done all these terrible things.

I didn't know where Jinx came from. She never told me that. But she did tell me later that whenever Sally had to be whipped, she would black out and Jinx would get the beating. She didn't know why it was, but Sally could change in a second, and the whipping wouldn't hurt Sally at all, and she wouldn't even remember being hit. Later Sally would see the red welts of the strap on her arms and legs, and they would sting. And she would wonder where they had come from. She wondered if everyone had those magical things happen to them.

According to the way I can piece it together from Jinx's and Sally's memories, Sally went to church alone with Fred that bright Easter Sunday when her mother was off visiting her grandmother in the hospital.

Sally was so fascinated by the story of the Resurrection that she sat there with her mouth open and Fred had to nudge her to close it. When the sermon was over and they walked out, Fred plopped his tweed cap on quick. He always wore it tilted way over to the right to cover the dent in his bald skull.

'Is it true,' she asked, 'about the Resurrection?'

'Of course it's true. You don't think Father Anderson would preach a lie, do you? It's the Gospel.'

All the way home in the car she wondered about how a person could die and be brought back to life. It was just like in the fairy tales. 'And is it true,' she asked, 'that on the Judgment Day all the dead are going to be resurrected back to life?'

'Sure,' he said. 'We believe in that, and unless you're a heathen, you do, too.'

She nodded. So there *was* magic in the world.

Later that afternoon, she was talking to Cinderella about it when Fred came out of the house. He had changed into his working clothes, but was still wearing the tweed cap tilted over his right eye, and he was going to turn over the soil in the garden and put in some fertilizer. She noticed that the minute he started with the shovel, his face got flushed, so that when he grinned, his missing teeth made her think of a jack-o'-lantern on a pole.

'Talking to your kitty about that sermon are you?'

'It sure does sound amazing.'

'Well, that's the miracle of the Resurrection. You're a good Catholic like your mother, aren't you?'

She nodded.

'And you believe in miracles, don't you?'

'I guess so.'

'What do you mean, you guess? You either do or you don't, and if you don't, you'll go straight to hell when you die and not get resurrected.'

That scared Sally, and she said, 'I do believe. I do.' It wasn't that she believed Fred, but after all if the Bible said so and the priest said so, then it must be true.

'Well, then,' he said, 'do you want to see a resurrection happen before your very eyes?'

She looked up at him, surprised.

'Well, you know it does happen quite often with cats.'

'How come?'

'Haven't you ever heard that cats have nine lives?'

She nodded.

He opened his palms. 'Well, that's what it means. It's the Lord's way of showing us the miracle right here on earth. You want to see it don't you?'

She nodded.

'Well, then. Bring Cinderella over here, and we'll make the miracle of the Resurrection happen right before our eyes, and when she's reborn, her missing paw will be good as new. You'll get to see it.'

She wasn't sure what Fred was going to do, but she hugged Cinderella close and rubbed her face in her fur.

'We're going to see it, Cinderella. Miracles and magic are real, and we're going to see a resurrection.'

'But don't tell your mom. Let her be surprised when she sees Cinderella with a new paw.'

Fred dug a hole in the back of the garden near the fence, and then he put his shovel down and picked up a rock.

'Now, Cinderella is going to be just like Jesus on this Easter Sunday.'

'How's that?'

'Well, she's going to sacrifice one of her nine lives for all of us, the way the Lord did. She'll die, and we'll bury her, and then she'll be resurrected good as new.'

Sally was frightened at the word *die*, but she was curious too. She had never seen death. And she tried to imagine what it would be like to be brought back. 'Are you sure she'll have a new paw?'

'Well, of course. You don't think the Lord would resurrect someone with missing parts, do you? The Bible tells us that on Judgment Day we'll be made whole, and the infirm shall be made well, and stuff like that. She'll be good as new, running around and playing like a normal kitten. You wouldn't deny her her natural born right to be a whole and healthy kitten, now would you?'

Sally agreed that would be very selfish of her.

He handed her the rock. 'Here. The Lord said to build his church with a rock.'

'What do I do?'

'Just bash her in the head a few times, good and hard. And she'll go to sleep. Then we'll bury her in this hole, and then she'll be resurrected. You'll get to see the whole thing, and you'll understand what that sermon was all about. It won't hurt her a bit.'

She held back.

'It'll be like Sleeping Beauty in one of those fairy tales you're always telling her before you go to sleep. Remember? She pricks her finger and there's blood, but it doesn't hurt her, and then she awakes back to life? Now go ahead and bash her,' he said, 'or I'll do it.'

So she lifted up the rock, and said, 'Goodbye, Cinderella. When you're resurrected, you'll have all your paws.' She brought it down with all her might on Cinderella's head. She heard the screaming howl at the same instant she saw the bashed skull and the blood on the white fur.

'There's blood!' she gasped.

'Of course,' Fred said. 'I told you there'd be. Ain't you seen pictures of Our Lord on the cross, with the nails in his palms and the blood dripping down? There's got to be blood for the resurrection, so she can be washed in the blood of the lamb. Blood causes the magic.'

'When does she get resurrected?'

'First we bury her.'

He dumped Cinderella into the hole and covered her with dirt, packing it down hard. Then he found a large stone and put it over the grave.

'How will she get out of there?'

'Same way the Lord did.'

'How long will it take?'

He put the shovel away in the shed and walked back to the house, calling back over his shoulder, 'Took Jesus three days. Guess that's about how long it usually takes. Either that, or until she gets kissed. You just keep your eye on that there grave, and don't forget to call me when you see that stone start to move. I want to be here when you see her all resurrected and better than new. And when your mom comes, don't tell her what we did. We want to surprise her with Cinderella's new paw and all. Just tell her she died and we buried her. That's all.'

Sally kept vigil by the hole until it was very dark and her mother made her come in.

'I don't understand how it happened,' her mother said.

Fred called out from behind his paper. 'Well, Viv, it surprised me. Sally just up and killed that little kitten with a rock. Just bashed her head in.'

Sally's mouth opened to protest that he had told her to do it, but Fred called out, 'You know that kid does mean things, and lies and pretends she don't remember. I seen it with my own eyes, and I buried it there in the back yard.'

Sally was sent to bed, but she couldn't sleep as she tried to puzzle out why Fred told it that way. Maybe so it would be all the more surprising when Cinderella was transformed into her second life, all whole and better. Wouldn't her mother be amazed?

The next day in school she couldn't concentrate, and the teacher scolded her for daydreaming. After school, she went out to the back yard to sit and watch by the grave, until her mother came out and snapped at her for being such a vicious child and doing such a terrible thing.

'You wait until tomorrow,' Sally told her mother 'You'll be surprised.'

Vivian shook her head and said that she was acting crazier every day.

The next day it rained hard. Sally's teacher let them draw pictures. Sally drew a picture of Cinderella with all four paws, but one of her classmates said the picture wasn't right because Cinderella's left front paw was really missing.

Sally explained that the picture was to show what Cinderella would look like when she was resurrected, because she had just used up one of her nine lives and she was going to be reborn with all her paws . . .

One of the other children said cats didn't really have nine lives. They argued, and the teacher finally interrupted and said, 'Sally, I have to agree with Nancy. That's pretending – like Santa Claus and the Tooth Fairy – and you're old enough to know the facts of life—'

Sally stared at her. 'What about the Bible? What about Christ being resurrected on Easter Sunday? Is that pretend too?'

'Are you asking what I believe?'

Sally nodded, tears forming in her eyes.

'Personally, I don't believe in the Resurrection, Sally. Those who have faith believe. Those who don't, say it's a beautiful fairy tale to help us accept death.'

Sally's lips quivered. She stared wildly around her. 'You're lying. You're all lying. Cinderella's going to be reborn. Today's her resurrection. I'm going home to see if she's trying to come out of her grave.'

'Sally, wait!'

But she left her books and sweater on the desk, and before the teacher could stop her, she ran out of the classroom and down the street. Though it was nearly a mile, she ran breathlessly in the rain all the way home. She thought her chest was going to break, but she couldn't stop. She had to get there. She had to see for herself.

When she got to the yard her wet hair hung down into her eyes and her whole body was shivering. She stared at the stone. But it wasn't moving. It had been three days. This was the time. Cinderella had to come out.

Maybe the stone was too heavy, she thought. She pushed it away and watched for signs of movement in the wet earth. Soon Cinderella would claw her way out of the hole and come bouncing into her lap with all her paws, and Sally's dress would get muddy, but she wouldn't care.

She waited. She hoped it would happen before her mother and Fred came out. She wanted to be the first to see it.

Thinking Fred might have packed the earth too tight with the back of the shovel, she loosened the mud to make it easier for Cinderella to get out. She scraped at the dirt with her fingers. It came away easily, and as she dug, she paused from time to time for a sign of movement from below. And she dug . . . and she dug . . . and finally she felt the wet fur and smelled the rotting body. She brushed the mud from the stiff paws and from the head . . . and saw the hole where she had smashed the skull.

Maybe if she kissed it, it would get all better and the miracle would happen and wake her up. She put her lips to the wet fur. She felt something move – something tickled – it was alive! Then she pulled back and saw the maggots crawling out of the bloody gash. She couldn't cry. She couldn't breathe. She screamed . . .

Her scream turned into my laughter.

Sally's mother and stepfather came running out of the house because of the screaming, and when they saw me standing over the uncovered grave, laughing, they didn't understand what had happened.

'Sally, what are you doing? Are you crazy?'

How could I explain that I wasn't Sally? That I was Cinderella. Not only had I been resurrected, but I had been changed from a kitten into a little girl by a magic kiss, and that was the greatest miracle of all.

'She's out of her head,' Fred said. 'I always told you. Look at that. No feelings. No heart. Kills that poor little kitten and then digs it up and laughs. That kid belongs in the nuthouse.'

Her mother snatched the shovel and covered the kitten with mud. Then she grabbed my smeared hand and said,

'Go to your room and stay there the whole day. Sally, you're an evil child.'

I didn't know why she kept calling me Sally. I knew I wasn't Sally, but someone else. Then I had a thought. I was really Derry, after the middle part of Cin-*der*-ella, the heart of her name. Derry – that's me. So when her mother called me Sally, I just laughed and said, 'You don't know anything – either of you.' And I went skipping off to explore Sally's room and see all the things she had. And I lived happily ever after.

Fifteen

ROGER BROUGHT ME OUT of hypnosis, looked at me thoughtfully, and shook his head. 'The amazing thing is how you survived that childhood at all.'

I laughed and said, 'Do you mean me or Sally? I had a lot of fun in those days. But I didn't remember my name was from Cinderella's second syllable. The funny thing is I went and dug in that spot a few days later, but the kitten was gone. Vivian or Fred must have dug her up and gotten rid of her. All my life, I've been looking for Cinderella, and now I find out Sally brought her back to life through me, with a kiss.'

'You know what happens at midnight,' Roger said.

'I don't want my story to end, Roger. I want to live happily ever after.'

'You will, Derry, but in the real world, fused with Sally. Your happiness won't die. It'll merge into the heart and mind of the child who lost her faith that day in the rain and created you. Now it's time to give up another one of your lives to make Sally whole again.'

'I'm afraid, Roger—'

'It's all right to be afraid. But now you know it'll take more than magic and fairy tales to make you real.'

'I've always wanted to be the real person.'

'But do you want it badly enough to overcome fear? It won't happen unless you agree to fuse with Sally.'

'And then I'll be dead.'

'—or resurrected into the fourth Sally.'

'Whose mind will it be? Whose feelings?'

'If my theory is right, you'll still have awareness.'

'And if it's wrong?'

'I just don't know.'

'But you really want me to do this?'

'*You* have to want it, Derry.'

'Part of me does, part of me doesn't. Jesus, here I am with parts of my own already. Who's the party of the first part?'

He laughed, and I ached for him to touch me, to hold me in his arms, gently. Not sexual, or anything like that. Somehow, I knew if he kissed me I would become the real person with all the feelings and thoughts and emotions.

'I'm sure you heard what I told Sally and Nola and Bella. Think about it. Let me know your decision by tomorrow.'

'Do we decide separately, or should we talk about it together?'

'That's up to you. It might be good to be in contact with each other tonight. And perhaps your ISH will help.'

'Like a farewell meeting, huh?'

'You might think of it as a hello meeting.'

'You sure do like to play with words.'

'I'll change that shoulder dressing tomorrow.'

He explained that he was going to give Sally a prescription for something in case the pain got too bad, but nothing too strong or narcotic. He didn't want to chance a blackout before the session. Then he brought Sally out and told her the same thing.

Sally moped around the apartment that evening. She played all six Brandenburg Concertos, and it nearly drove me out of my mind. I mean it was bad enough when Nola used to do it, but if that was what she had planned for our future, I didn't think I could take it, even for Roger.

The fight came over what we should have for our last dinner as separate personalities. She wanted to go out to La Petite Maison, and I wanted to go to Hoy's Place. She said she was getting sick of Chinese food, and I said ditto for French. So it came down to, should we compromise and have something neither of us wanted? I suggested a kooky idea, that we have two last suppers. I mean, what's the sense of counting calories in your final meal? She insisted on French first because she didn't trust me to keep my promise. I pretended to get huffy about that, but she's right. I do break promises. Let's face it, all my life I've had to get what I wanted by sneaking out for a few minutes of reality. I knew she'd never break her word. God, it was going to be dull, keeping promises and telling the truth all the time. I had the sneaking suspicion that if I did merge with her, I'd be limited to only a few little white lies now and then. But I didn't tell her that. I said, 'We ought to have Chinese first, because – you know – an hour later you get hungry again. The other way around it won't work.' She couldn't argue against that, so we went to Hoy's Place, and I stuffed myself with fried wontons, spare ribs, and butterfly shrimp. Then we went for a long walk to work some of it off and talk things out.

People turned to look, but I told her not to pay any attention. What did they know? They probably just thought she was crazy.

She was feeling kind of low and I tried to rile her up. 'Sometimes I think you like feeling depressed,' I said.

'What's that supposed to mean?'

'Well you feel glum more than anyone I've ever known. So it must give you pleasure.'

'That's stupid.'

'Now don't start calling me stupid. You start that with me and I'll refuse to fuse.'

'What makes you think I want to fuse with you?'

'Because you've got more to lose than I do.' She didn't answer, so I had the feeling I was on the right track. 'I'm not real,' I said, 'so death or madness won't bother me. You, on the other hand—'

'You're lying as usual, Derry. You've always wanted to be real, and this is your chance. I'm the one who tried to kill herself at least five times that I remember, and you and Bella stopped me. So don't pretend to be so blasé.'

'What's blasé mean?'

'It's French for—'

'I should have known.'

'It means weary and bored of the pleasures of life.'

'Okay, you're right. I'll never get bored with life.'

'I do.'

'I guess that's another reason Roger thinks fusion will be good for us. I mean, I'll give you the love for living and being happy-go-lucky, and you'll settle me down.'

Some guy was handing out massage parlor handbills. I held my hand out for one – just to be funny – but she yanked me away. Kill joy! We walked silently for a while, and then she said, 'So what do you want to do tonight?'

'Let's pick up some guys and double-date.'

'Come on, Derry. Don't kid around.'

'It would be fun.'

'Some fun. Then we run into trouble, and you-know-who will do you-know-what.'

She was right, as usual, but I hated to give in. 'Wait a minute. I know who we can double-date with, and they'd understand and it wouldn't cause trouble.'

She stopped because the idea hit her at the same moment it hit me. 'That would be something,' she said. 'They'd flip.'

'Go ahead. You call Todd, and I'll call Eliot, and we'll meet them.'

'It won't work,' she said.

'Hey, come on,' I said. 'One last fling. We'll have a ball.'

'It's crazy – but okay. Better if I call Todd, tell him I'm lonely and depressed and want to go out, and say I've got a blind date for Eliot.'

'Wow,' I said. 'Terrific. But let's not plan what we're going to do. Let's play it by ear, or – what's that word? – imp – imp –'

'Improvisation. I'm good at that.'

'We'll improvisation the evening away. But how will you explain the shoulder?'

She'd forgotten about it. 'Tell them the truth, of course.'

'Never mind,' I said. 'Leave the explaining to me. I'll improvisation an explanation that'll curl your teeth. You just get Todd and Eliot to meet us at La Petite Maison.'

She called The Yellow Brick Road and told Todd she was alone this evening, and asked if he and Eliot would like to double-date after the restaurant closed. He checked.

'Eliot wants to know what she's like.'

'A lot like me,' I chimed in.

'I mean she *looks* a lot like me,' Sally added. God, she's such a stickler for the truth.

Todd said it was okay with Eliot and they'd meet us at La Petite Maison at one in the morning.

It was only ten now, so Sally suggested a movie to kill some time. She wanted to see a classic about the great famine in India by the director of *Pather Panchali*. I wanted to see a rerun of the Marx Brothers' *A Night at the Opera*. We tossed a coin, and she won. I felt lousy watching starving people in India, with the flies and the sores and the begging, at a time when I was full of Chinese food. So I went to sleep and let her see it.

When it was over, I also felt guilty about killing time when I had so little of my own left. I mean, I might be sleeping forever pretty soon.

We went to La Petite Maison to wait for Eliot and Todd. Sally ordered a Harvey Wallbanger and I ordered bourbon. The waiter looked at us as if we were crazy, and I had to hold in my giggling or he would have thought we were too drunk to be served.

When the guys showed up, they saw the two drinks on the table and then looked around for the other person.

'She went to the ladies' room,' I said.

'But she's here,' Sally added.

Todd slid in next to Sally, and Eliot sat down across from me. Eliot's gold silk sport shirt, unbuttoned to show his hairy chest, matched his gold slacks. He was putting on even more weight, and everything puckered. Todd still wore jeans, but tonight he had a denim sport coat as well.

'Well, what's she like?' Eliot asked.

'I told you, like me,' she said.

'There's only one you,' Todd said.

When she gave him a dirty look, he got flustered. 'I didn't mean to be funny. That wasn't the right way to put it.'

'Yer damned tootin!' I said.

They looked confused at the change of voice. Not that they could put a finger on it, but something was off kilter, and they couldn't figure out what it was.

'I'm practicing a new act,' I said, laughing.

Todd smiled. 'You seem in a real good mood. I hope your friend is, too. What's her name?'

'Derry,' she said. I guess she forgot they knew me.

They looked at each other and then back at Sally. 'Derry?' Eliot asked.

I started to make a wisecrack, and she kicked me under the table.

'Excuse me a minute,' Sally said. 'I'll check out the ladies' room. Be right back.'

She slid out of the booth and moved out of range before they could ask any more questions. Once we got inside the ladies' room, she couldn't help but start laughing. Me too. I was relieved to see how much of Bella there was in Sally now.

'Did you see that look on Todd's face?' she giggled.

'When you said, "Derry,"' I added.

'I didn't know they knew your name,' she said.

'Well, for God's sake, I'm the one who works for them, remember?'

'What do we do now?'

'We dance and have our second dinner. Isn't that what you want?'

'That's not all I had in mind.'

'Hey,' I said. 'Don't start anything. I'm saving myself.'

'For Roger?'

'Yes.'

'You won't get Roger,' she said. 'To him, you and I are a fascinating case. That's all.'

'I'm more than a case to him,' I said.

'Look, it's a terrible mistake to confuse transference for love, it's not the—'

'I don't want to hear about it,' I said, putting my hands over my ears. But that was dumb, because she wasn't talking out loud. The words kept coming through her head.

'—and even if he did care for you, he's too ethical to fool around with a patient. You're heading for a fall.'

'It's my fall.'

'Mine too,' she insisted.

'I suppose Todd's the one you're interested in.'

She smiled. 'He cares for me. He's young, well-off, and good-looking. You got a better prospect?'

'Eliot's more fun than Todd. Gamblers take life too seriously, always figuring the odds.'

'Eliot's a middle-aged reconstruction job,' she said. 'A recycled Don Juan, and look at the weight he's put on. He's backsliding.'

'So what? He's still more fun. He knows about us, and about the problem, and he accepts it.'

'Todd knows, too.'

'That's just it,' I said. 'I think Todd's gonna be disappointed to find that there are only two of us left. For him the five of us were an exciting poker hand – a full house.'

'Well, we're still three queens.'

'You're counting the wild joker,' I said.

There was a knock on the bathroom door. 'Sally? You okay?' It was Todd's voice.

'Yeah, I'll be right out,' she said.

She brushed her hair quickly, and when she pushed out the door, Todd was waiting.

'You sure everything's all right?'

She took him by the hand and pulled him back to the table.

'I'm sorry, guys. My girlfriend skipped,' I said. 'I saw her giving this good-looking fella the eye. Then after she ordered her drink, she pretended she had to go to the ladies' room. Someone said they saw her leave with him. I'm really sorry.'

I don't know where I got the story, it just popped into my head, and Sally was squirming. Eliot looked downcast. I guess he'd been planning on a big evening, and now he must have felt like a third wheel.

'Look,' Sally said. 'Why don't the three of us spend the evening together. I mean we're all friends. We can have as much fun with three as most people can have with four. We can still dance and after we eat, we can go up to my place, and have some fun.'

Now that shocked me. She was thinking, *Manage a twah*. I didn't understand, but it sounded French, and from her feeling, I knew it was dirty. I told her privately I wasn't going along with it.

Sally and I took turns dancing, and I know we had them thoroughly confused. As long as we kept them apart it was okay, but when we were at the table together, the conversation got hairy. They must have thought she was the most scatterbrained person on earth, saying something one minute and contradicting herself the next. I'd lie, and she'd cover it up. Then I'd uncover it, and she'd turn it right back into the truth. It was a lot of fun, and I began to think it wouldn't be so bad to be fused with her. I mean, she was a long way from the old Sally.

We left the club at three in the morning, but by this time I was beginning to get worried about how the evening was going to end. I knew Sally was going to invite them up for a nightcap, and I had the feeling they each expected the other one to leave. But from Sally I kept getting vibrations that said *orgy*. I had no intention of letting it come to that, but I was afraid if I blacked out, Jinx would break through.

I tried to convince Sally, but she was turning me off. I could only imagine she felt that being a combination of Sally, Nola, and Bella all rolled into one, she had more votes and the right to make the decisions now, where before I used to do that because I was the trace. Well, I can be stubborn, too.

When we got out of the taxi, I said quickly, 'Well good-night, fellas. It's been a wonderful evening, but I've got an important appointment early tomorrow.'

'Hey, I thought we were coming up for a nightcap,' Eliot said.

'That's right, you are,' Sally said. 'Sally Porter always keeps her word.'

'For a minute, you had me confused,' Todd said.

'That's better than being Kung-Fused,' I snorted.

'Or re-fused,' Eliot said.

'Oh, Jesus!' Sally said.

'Hey,' said Eliot, pointing to Greenberg's window. 'Look, Murphy is giving us the finger.'

'Where? Let's see,' Todd said. 'Oh, yeah. Look. That Greenberg has a sense of humor. Where's Murphy's nightstick?'

'It got lost,' I said.

Sally frowned, because she didn't know anything about Jinx's escapade dressed as a cop.

'Hey,' I said. 'Why don't we invite Murphy up for a nightcap too?' I figured Greenberg might be right about a police uniform having a controlling influence.

They thought that was a terrific idea. I showed them how to get in through the basement and spring the back door. We sneaked Murphy out and Todd and Eliot carried him upstairs. They sat him in one of the easy chairs with his legs crossed and his arms hanging over the sides. Then Sally broke out a new bottle of Irish whiskey and we all had a drink.

'It must be awful to be a window dummy,' Eliot said.

'I dunno,' Todd said, 'it's a quiet life. Like being a night watchman.'

'He wants to be a real person,' I said.

'What?' Eliot was refilling his glass.

'Like Pinocchio, the wooden boy who wanted to be a real boy,' I explained.

'Oh, yeah,' Todd said. 'When he lied, his nose got long.'

'That's not all that got long after he became a real boy,' Eliot said, laughing.

'Poor Murphy has lost his stick,' Sally said.

Eliot giggled. 'Is it wicked to stick it?'

'Hey, this party's getting dirty,' I said. 'I'm putting on my pantyhose and going home.'

'You are home,' Todd said.

'Then you guys better put on your pants and go home,' I said.

'Aw, it's the shank of the evening,' Eliot said.

'Then get on shank's mare and hoof it,' I said.

Todd laughed and kissed me.

At that point I stopped laughing. He kissed me hard and deep, and I felt his body against me. I was torn between pushing him away and pulling him toward me, and then I realized it was I who wanted to push and Sally who wanted to pull, and it was getting all mixed up. Is that the way it would be when we were fused? *If* we were fused. Here I was, almost accepting it.

Then Eliot tapped Todd on the shoulder and said, 'May I cut in?'

Todd backed away with a sweeping bow, and Eliot kissed Sally, and I felt his hand on her breast and his hard-on against her thighs.

'Hey, Eliot,' I said. 'Let's not get carried away. The party's over.'

He nuzzled my ear. 'I thought it was just beginning.'

'Well you thought wrong.'

'Which one are you now? Bella?'

'Or Nola?' Todd asked.

I pushed Eliot away and stared at both of them. 'What do you mean?'

Todd said, 'There was no other friend, right? You wanted to date the two of us. You're all confused, and the Sally we know would never pull a stunt like this.'

'I think you guys had better go now,' I said.

They both protested, but I insisted. 'Look, fellas, I'm sorry if you got the impression you were going to score tonight. You both know about Sally's problem. It's been a lot of fun, but I have to tell you that Nola and Bella are gone. They've been fused into Sally. And tomorrow morning I'm going to be fused with her, too. And we'll be a normal person after that.'

That sobered them up. Eliot scratched his head and nodded. 'Gee, that's great, Sally. I'm real glad for you.' But his expression told me that for him the fascination and the excitement would be over because Sally would be an ordinary woman – just one possible conquest.

Todd seemed genuinely pleased. 'Hey, the odds are coming down, and I'm betting on your goodness to take you down the home stretch,' he said. 'I think I understand what's been going on tonight.'

'What's that?' Eliot asked.

'Never mind,' Todd said. 'But I got the feeling Sally'd rather be alone the rest of the evening. She's probably got a lot of thinking to do. Sally, take the rest of the week off. We'll have Evvie cover for you.'

Sally started to protest, but I squeezed Todd's hand and kissed Eliot on the cheek. 'Thanks, guys. It's great to have friends. I don't know how I'd have survived the last six months without the two of you.'

When they were gone, Sally sat down in the chair opposite Murphy and stared at him for a long time. 'What are you thinking about, Murphy?'

'He's trying to decide whether or not we should agree to fuse,' I said.

'How do you know what he's thinking?'

'I'm the trace, remember?'

'Murphy's not one of our personalities.'

'He could be.'

'What's that supposed to mean?' she demanded.

'Let's face it,' I said. 'You started each of us by pretending we were real. Then we each took on a life of our own. Roger says other multiples have personalities with different ages, different races, even different sexes. You could imagine Murphy was real, and then just for tonight you could have a man even Jinx couldn't do anything about.'

Sally thought about it. The idea fascinated her. All I had to do was plant the seed. I know I'm a troublemaker, but I always wanted Murphy to be a real person, too, even if it was only for one night. Tomorrow I would lose my identity. Tonight was Murphy's last chance to find his.

She pretended Murphy was real. She talked to him, offered him a drink. Stroked his head. 'Let's dance, Murphy.'

She put on a record and took him into her arms and danced a slow and dreamy dance around the room, like in the old movies, the way Donald O'Connor dances with a mop, and Costello does it with a girl window dummy. But Sally was pretending Murphy was a real man who loved her.

Then I heard a voice in her head. It was spooky, because even though I instigated the whole thing, I didn't really know it would work. He had a soft, low voice, real sexy, with an Irish brogue.

'I've been watchin' you through the window,' he said, 'and wantin' you for ever so long.'

His face had softened. Blue eyes searched hers with tenderness. She wanted his arms around her, and she was thinking it would be like being caressed by a demon-lover.

'Do you have a first name?'

'Just Murphy. That's all Mr. Greenberg calls me.'

'Don't you get tired, standing there in the doorway all the time, with your hand up in the air?'

'It's my job. No use complainin'.'

'But it must be boring. No one to talk to, no one to be with.'

He shrugged. 'Derry keeps me company sometimes when you're asleep. We have good long talks about life and politics and the problems you face with all these people in your head.'

'You're in my head now, Murphy.'

'Just for tonight,' he said. 'I'm not like the others. I wasn't with you since your childhood.'

She knew he was watching her undress with love in his eyes, and she felt he was the most loving, kindest, most understanding man she had ever known – the kind of man she had been searching for all her life. She undressed him and took him to bed with her. He touched her tenderly, tracing her skin, kissing her eyes, her throat, her breasts, touching her all over with fingers as light as cobwebs.

'I can't . . .' he said. 'You know I can't –'

She kissed him back. 'It doesn't matter, Murphy. I've done it all my life in fantasies and dreams. It doesn't matter how love comes, as long as you hold me in your arms.'

When it was over, he thanked her for making him come alive, even if it was only for one night.

'It doesn't have to be just for one night,' she said. 'I can keep you hidden, and you can visit me when I'm lonely or sad.'

—*No, Sally. You mustn't think that way anymore.*

271

She sat up in bed and looked around. It was a familiar voice.

—You're going to undo all the good you've done with Dr. Ash. You're falling into your old habits again of trying to solve your problems by creating people in your head.

—Are you the Helper?

—Yes, but I haven't come to scold you. I've come to help you prepare to fuse with Derry.

—Derry talks to Murphy, too.

—But Murphy isn't one of your people. And it's going to set things back if you make him real. You'll start splitting all over again, into more parts, and then more and more. There's no end to the number of people who can crowd up inside you if you don't change your way of facing reality.

—What is reality?

—We won't get into that discussion, Sally. As Nola, you always were clever with words. But she let words dominate her life. Now we've got to use them to untangle the web, not to create more twisted strands.

—What shall I do?

—Let Murphy go. Let him be what he is – a window dummy.

Sally nodded, and she felt a sadness, knowing she was never again to use her power to create people. She got up and dressed him in his police uniform and sat him in the chair.

'I'm sorry. I mustn't make you a real person,' she said.

After she went to sleep, I came out and turned on the TV set. At first all I saw was the test pattern, but then after a while the Helper came on, and we talked.

—Are you a man or a woman?

—A little bit of both.

—How come?

—Everybody is a little bit of both.

—I never knew that.

—What have you decided, Derry?

I squirmed around in my chair, looking at Murphy, with his half-smile and his cap tilted over one eye. I straightened it because it made him look like Fred, and that got me nervous.

—Well?

—I don't know. I'm afraid. I don't want to die.

—You know it isn't death. You know Dr. Ash said it means you'll be part of Sally.

—But it's a kind of death because I can't tell what it'll be like. I don't know if I'll be awake, or asleep and dreaming. If I'll be the one having the thoughts, or if I'll just disappear and not know anything. I can't get in touch with Nola or Bella anymore to ask them what it's like, so even though I see traces of them in Sally, that's just like seeing parents' ways and features in their children, although the parents are dead.

—I'll be there to hold your hand, Derry, and show you the way. Instead of thinking of it as death, it'll be a kind of resurrection.

—I've heard that one before.

—But not from me. I'm on your side.

—Mine or Sally's?

—Well, Sally's and—

—Aha!

—You both are really one.

—That's not true. You know that's not true. Other people keep saying that because they can't accept that different persons can exist inside the same mind. But you know better. You're here and you see into us, and we're not really one. I'm me.

—It's a matter of defining reality.

273

—Now hold on. You put Sally in her place when she started using that word, talking about reality. Not fair using it on me.

—You're right, Derry, but unless you proceed along the lines Dr. Ash has laid down, you'll come apart.

—Does that mean Nola and Bella would be back?

—Not them. They're fused. But others might be created. New personalities.

—Strangers?

—Yes. It becomes an easy way of avoiding frustration and anger. The power to create people runs rampant.

—Oh, Jesus!

—If left unchecked, the mind will divide again and again, creating more and more people, until existence becomes impossible.

—Sounds like cancer.

—In a way it's very similar.

—I see.

—The choice is yours, Derry. It must be an exercise of your own free will.

—Right now, huh?

—Right now.

I sat there in the dark, staring into the TV picture tube, wishing I could see if the Helper was a man or a woman. The voice sounded so damned familiar. And even as I was squirming about giving an answer, I knew I was going to have to do it because Roger wanted me to. I had hoped to stall until the last minute. Maybe do some horse trading with him. But now the ISH had me up against the wall, pressing hard.

—All right.

—You've made the correct decision, Derry. You won't be sorry.

—If I am, I'll come back to haunt you.

Then I turned off the TV set and went to bed.

I got up very early and took Murphy back down to Greenberg's shop before he opened. I kissed Murphy on his cold, hard cheek and said, 'If not for the ISH, you could have become a real person. Well, I'm glad you had at least one night alive, even though it was just in Sally's mind.'

He didn't say anything, but there was a twinkle in his eye as I set him back behind the glass door. Then I adjusted his hat and raised his right hand, turning it outward to direct traffic. I went upstairs, hoping I'd remember all this after Sally and I became fused. I wondered just how much memory there would be – if I would remember Nola and Bella and Jinx and myself, or if it would be like in *Heaven Can Wait* or the original version, *Here Comes Mr. Jordan*, where the hero – killed before his time – gets blanked out at the end so he doesn't remember his past when he gets a new body and a new life. God, that would be awful. I wanted my past. You had to have a past to be a real person. I should have asked the Helper.

Back upstairs I talked to Sally while she showered. 'So we've both decided, huh?'

She nodded. 'I think last night proves we can get along. We're different, but not incompatible. We'd better get down to Roger's office.'

'You go ahead,' I said. 'I've got a few last minute details to take care of. I'll join you later.'

It was a beautiful October afternoon. The air was crisp and the sky was deep blue. Sally decided to splurge on a taxi. She was glad Roger had given her a day to think it over. She was sure now that fusion would work.

Up in his private office, he studied her quietly as he changed the bandage on her shoulder.

'How are you feeling this morning?'

'Wonderful,' she said.

He gave her a pad to sign her name and nodded when he saw it. 'So tell me about what happened yesterday, and what you've decided.'

She told him about the double-dating with Eliot and Todd, and he thought it was funny. She told him how they swiped the window dummy from Greenberg's store and had it sitting there all during the party.

'So you and Derry got along.'

'I'd say so.'

'And what's your decision about fusing?'

She nodded.

'I'm pleased,' he said. 'I'm going to put you under hypnosis now and bring Derry out. You can share the experience with her.'

'Will I remember it?'

'Partly. Her memories will merge with your own, but you probably won't recall the actual fusion experience any more than a child recalls being born.'

'Some people say they can recall the trauma of birth.'

'But most of us don't.' He held out his gold pen and said, 'And now I want to talk to Derry. Derry, *come into the light.*'

'Hello, Roger,' I said. 'Glad you called me out.'

'You must have heard what we were talking about. Do you agree to fusion?'

I nodded. 'But there's one thing I want you to do for me, Roger. I know it's not very professional, but at the last moment, I want you to kiss me. A real kiss. And then it'll be like in the fairy tales where the kiss erases the witch's spell.'

He smiled and nodded. 'All right, Derry. I'll be your Prince Charming. My kiss will break the enchantment, and your dream of being a real person will come true. *He knows what's in the darkness.'*

I slipped away, and behind the darkness I heard Roger saying, 'We'll go back, Derry, to the time when Sally was tricked into killing Cinderella. But now we can make the fantasy of nine lives real. As you stand there looking at your kitten lying in the mud, you can see she's come back as good as new, and with all four paws. It's getting close to midnight. And now that we know Derry is really the heart of Cinderella, you'll change back to what you were before the transformation took place. Horses into white mice. Coach into pumpkin. And you – Derry – back into Sally. In another moment the clock will strike twelve, and on the final note you'll be merged forever into the Sally you once were.'

He began to count, and I saw Sally at the ball, beautiful, intelligent Sally in a lovely white gown, dancing with Roger. As the clock began to strike, I heard his voice, deep but choked up. I knew he was sorry I'd be leaving forever.

'One . . . two . . . three . . .'

She fled from the palace and ran down the steps, brightly colored like the curve of a rainbow.

'Four . . . five . . . six . . .'

Running so fast she lost her glass slipper. She had to get home before she was transformed.

'Seven . . . eight . . . nine . . .'

Into the coach, hearing the coachman urging the white stallions down the road to get back before the stroke of midnight, before she turned back into an ordinary person.

'Ten . . . eleven . . . twelve!'

The Helper waved a wand. Roger leaned forward and kissed me tenderly on the lips, and that was the last thing I ever knew as Derry. I flowed into her, gave up my life, and became the fourth Sally.

Part Five

Part Five

Sixteen

WHEN I OPENED my eyes, I saw Roger leaning over me looking anxiously into my face.

I said, 'So you found me, Prince Charming.'

'Just for the record,' he said, 'tell me your name.'

'Sally Porter,' I said.

'And how do you feel?'

'As if I've been running in the darkness for a long time. As if I've lost something, and found myself at the same time. I know I'm Sally, but I'm Derry, too.'

The words didn't really express my feeling. It was a sense of fullness, excitement. The world was beautiful, and I loved everyone in it. Not that I was a Pollyanna or a fool. I knew there was suffering and loss and evil, but they were far away from me. I felt safe and happy.

Then I noticed the shoulder bandage. 'There's something I've forgotten, isn't there? Something I've repressed.'

He helped me sit up. 'You've been through a painful experience. There'll be emotional as well as physical scars.'

'I thought I was cured. For a moment I felt so happy, so complete.'

'And you should. You've accomplished a lot, and you'll go on feeling that way. Memories buried deep may surface from time to time. Long-forgotten experiences will be painful to recall. Loves. Losses. Hatreds. But you will know them only as history.'

'I don't know what you're talking about,' I laughed. 'I've never hated anyone in my life.'

He nodded. 'That's because you're a kind and wonderful person.'

I could see something was troubling him, but he wasn't ready to tell me about it yet.

'I want to give you some tools to help you control yourself from blacking out. There's a lot of talk in our society today about "letting go," allowing the inner person to dominate and push aside the cognitive or intellectual processes. For you, that romantic attitude could be dangerous.'

'I doubt that I'd get swept up in something like that,' I said.

'Still, there'll be times when you'll feel on the edge of losing yourself. You're pretty much on your own now – no one to come to your rescue, no one but yourself to keep track of your thoughts and actions—'

'ISH and trace.'

'What?'

'Those words popped into my mind. Isn't that what you once called it? The ISH and the trace?'

'That's right,' he said. 'And in their place you'll have to be your own conductor and switchman to keep the main track open when you're going full speed ahead.'

'I'm crazy about your figures of speech. As long as I don't have a loose caboose as an excuse.'

'There are some exercises I want you to learn.'

'Can I be the Orient Express?'

He studied me for a moment, looking deep into my eyes, as if trying to see behind my irises.

I hunched forward on my knees and put my face close to his. 'I see two of me,' I said. 'One in each of your lenses.'

He put his hands over mine, turned them upward. 'You've got to understand that there are still two of you,' he said.

282

I tried to pull my hands free. 'Don't say that,' I said. 'Even as a joke.'

'It's not a joke. You've got to face certain things before you leave here.'

'I don't want to hear.'

'Only knowledge can protect you. You've undergone a kind of mental surgery today. Someone's going to try to fragment you again. Someone inside you who magnifies your suppressed anger. You need weapons to fight her.'

'I liked it better when you said tools. Weapons frighten me.'

'All right. Tools,' he said. 'But I don't want to dwell on names for these things. There has been enough naming. Names have a way of creating realities to fulfill themselves. But there will be feelings, intuitions, subtle perceptions. You are a very sensitive person, Sally. You'll still sense what you've often described as a chill or aura before the headache and blackout. You've told me the warning lasts only a few seconds.'

'I don't remember saying that.'

'Until your memories return, you'll have to trust my tapes and notes. During those few seconds of warning, you'll have a chance to retain control. I'm going to give you a posthypnotic suggestion that when you clasp your hands tightly together and squeeze three times, you'll be able to prevent yourself from blacking out. Whenever you feel the aura, you will do this, and it will make the feeling of tension and headache subside. You'll stay in control.'

I told him I understood.

'All right then, Sally. *He knows what's in the darkness . . .*'

Then he looked into my eyes as I came out of it. 'How do you feel?'

'In control,' I said. 'With a sense of presence. Of hereness. As if I have a definite weight, solidly resting in the

283

here and now. I don't know why, but it's a new feeling. As if before I was light and airy.'

'Is it a good sensation?'

I thought about it and nodded. 'It makes me feel more real, somehow.'

He squeezed my hand, and I squeezed back. 'That's what I mean,' I said. 'Solid, real, good.'

'That feeling should continue, and flourish. Oh, there may be moments when you feel unreal. Everyone experiences that sense of lightness . . . fantasy . . . illusion. But if it comes with the blackout warning, you'll know what to do. Do you remember what that is?'

I clasped my hands and squeezed three times.

When the session was over, I couldn't resist leaning over and kissing Roger on the cheek. 'I feel wonderful,' I said, 'and I owe it all to you. You're the most wonderful doctor in the world.'

He beamed. 'And I owe you a great deal, Sally. Have a good day, and we'll meet again same time the day after tomorrow.'

Outside I thought, This must be the way children see the world. With fresh eyes. Looking into every face. Taking in every shop window, gazing up to see the rooftop architecture we've passed a thousand times and never seen. On Fifty-seventh street I stared into art galleries. The airline offices on Fifth Avenue made me think of all the places Roger and I could visit, all the things we could see. Of course, he had probably been to Europe before. But showing it to someone, he would see it through new eyes, too. Through my eyes. And I would see it through his.

I knew Roger loved me. And part of me had loved him from that first day in his office. So what, if he named it transference? I would show him it was more than that. He had changed during these past few months. Warmer, more considerate.

Seeing a mother pulling along two youngsters, I suddenly realized I had changed, too. I hadn't thought of my own children since my last call to Larry. That bothered me. Time. Like a knotted elastic string. Some days stretched into ages. Other days, even weeks, were just missing and everything twisted and tangled. But how could I have forgotten Pat and Penny? I thought I should really go see them. A surprise visit. But that wouldn't work. I had the vague notion I had been bothering Larry with phone calls I never even recalled making. I still loved and wanted Larry. No, wait. I didn't love him, and certainly didn't want him. What was it? I stopped at Rockefeller Center and sat down on one of the benches. Part of me loved him because he had married me and taken me away from that terrible place I called home. But it wasn't love. It was dependence. Was it that way with Roger, too?

I found a phone booth and rummaged through my purse for some change. I dialed and after three rings, Anna answered.

'Don't hang up,' I said. 'This is Sally.'

'Oh, my God!' she said. 'Not again.'

'Listen, Anna. I've changed. I'm calling to apologize to you and Larry for all the trouble I've caused you. I realize how patient you've been, but I promise you won't have any more trouble with me. I've been in therapy with a wonderful doctor, and I think I'm cured. It wasn't insanity or anything like that. It's something I'm sure you've read about, or seen on television, called multiple personality. I had it. And my problems were because of my other people. Most of the time I never remembered what I did.'

'*Sally?*'

It was Larry's voice. He must have picked up an extension.

'Yes, the whole and complete Sally this time, in full control of her faculties. I have most of my memories back, and—'

'You sound different,' he said.

'It's another one of her tricks,' Anna said.

'I don't blame you for being suspicious,' I said, 'but you have to understand that those other times, I was really several different people. Someday maybe I can visit, and I'll explain it all to you. But most of all, I'd like Pat and Penny to know about it, to understand why things were the way they were. If they could realize that I really loved them and never wanted to hurt them, that would satisfy me.'

'A likely story,' Anna said.

'Just a minute,' Larry said. 'Sally, would that really satisfy you?'

'I swear it.'

'But you will want them back, right?'

'I'd be lying if I said I didn't. But now I understand it wouldn't be best for them. They need a stable home, and I know you and Anna are raising them with love.'

'Well,' Larry said, 'I thought you called to wish them a happy birthday. If you want—'

'I forgot!' I cried. 'Oh, my God, Larry, I completely forgot. Is it today? No, wait. Tomorrow.'

'They're having a little party tomorrow afternoon at one. If you wanted to come by, I think it would be all right.'

'Oh, thank you Larry. I'll have time to shop for their presents. And you don't have to worry. There won't be any trouble. I've got myself under complete control now.'

I hung up and walked quickly toward Sixth Avenue, wishing I knew what they already had, what they needed, what they wanted. I knew so little about them. Hard to admit that my own children were strangers to me. I had been so wrapped up in my own problems I had never really seen them growing up.

I wandered in and out of stores, trying to find things they would keep for a long time and would mean something special. At first I thought of an ivory and ebony chess set with an inlaid chessboard for Pat, but then I realized I didn't even remember if I had ever taught him to play. Oh, my God, I wasn't even sure how old they were. Wait. I could figure it out. The year after I graduated from high school I must have been nineteen. Or had I been eighteen? No, nineteen. So the twins were eleven. No, tomorrow would be their tenth birthday. Well, if I was twenty-nine . . . Or was I twenty-eight? I fished in my purse, desperately looking for my driver's license. And then leaned weakly against the counter. I was twenty-nine, and the twins were ten. But it scared me to realize how great the gaps were in my memory.

I finally decided on a set of oil paints for Penny and a camera for Pat, and two contemporary novels. I had them gift-wrapped and then went back to the apartment to have an early dinner and prepare myself for meeting my children and my ex-husband.

On the bus to Englewood, I had the disturbing sense of déjà vu. Though I reassured myself that I'd never made this trip to Larry's new house before, nor ever met his wife, Anna, I imagined it as an ugly, red and yellow modern split-level ranch, with four Roman pillars and on the lawn an imitation gas lamp.

When I arrived I was startled to see it as I had visualized it in my mind's eye. It couldn't be déjà vu. I must have been there before. Buried somewhere in my memory, it had now been uncovered, as when the ocean washes away layers of sand from the beach, exposing the bleached skeleton of a sea creature.

I was sure I'd never been there before, but the vision of a policeman in a battered Mercedes flashed into my head. The house, a car chase, a policeman.

I quickly covered the mental skeleton over, yet the outline remained, like sand sculpture.

As I walked up the driveway, Anna came out on the lawn to greet me. I was amazed at how small she was and how round her eyes looked. She moved in quick starts, with small sharp gestures, like a squirrel ready to scamper at the first loud noise.

'Larry went to get the cake,' she said. 'He'll be right back.'

'Lovely house,' I said.

'Glad you like it. I think the gas lamp gives it the latest nostalgia look.'

'I'm early, I know,' I said. 'But I have to admit I was eager to get here.'

'Come on in. You can see Pat and Penny before the other children arrive.'

I followed her into the living room, cluttered with figurines, knickknacks, and artificial flowers in imitation Ming vases. The walls were covered with awful romantic landscapes of Roman ruins set amidst Victorian gardens.

'What a lovely place,' I said. 'So many beautiful things.'

'I've always felt the children should be exposed to art.'

Pat and Penny appeared in the living room doorway, curious but hanging back, as if uncertain how to greet me. I was startled at how they'd grown in a year. They both still had much of their summer tan. Pat's auburn hair had been cut short. He wore tan slacks and a navy blue blazer. Penny's hair had been set into sausage curls, and she wore a green organdy dress. They both looked as if they'd stepped out of a back-to-school catalogue. I hated Anna for doing that to them.

I held out my arms, and they came to me reluctantly. I hugged and kissed them, but I was hurt by their unyielding stiffness.

'Show your mother your rooms while I go ahead and finish setting the party table,' Anna said. 'I'm sure she'd like to see all your nice things.'

I was pleased to see by the open books in their rooms that they were both still readers. We talked about books and sports, and Pat was impressed with my knowledge of football. I said I was sure the Dallas Cowboys would be in the playoffs and get to the Superbowl again this year. Pat was a Giants fan, but he agreed that it was exciting to see Roger Staubach load up the shotgun to pass on third down, or watch him scramble out of trouble during a pass rush.

'I've always loved football,' I said. 'I was a cheerleader in high school.'

'You never told me that,' Pat said. 'How come?'

'Oh –' I laughed – 'I must have mentioned it. You probably just don't remember.'

'I'd remember!' he said defiantly. 'I've got a good memory!'

What was I saying? I'd never liked football. I didn't know a thing about it, who Staubach was, or what the shotgun was. Yet it made sense to Pat, so what I'd said couldn't be complete nonsense. Where had I gotten it from? When had I ever been a cheerleader?

'I hate football,' Penny said. 'It's too violent.'

'That's what Anna says,' Pat complained. 'She doesn't let me watch.'

'Dad should be back soon,' Penny said. 'Are you gonna act strange when he's here?'

289

'What do you mean?' I asked.

Pat nudged her with his elbow, and she became silent.

I decided not to pursue it, but after a few thoughtful moments while Pat was showing me his new stamp collection, Penny blurted out, 'I don't remember you telling us about being a cheerleader, either. If we both forgot it, does that mean we're becoming like you?'

'What do you mean?'

'Anna says Dad told her that after you do funny things, you forget. If one of us forgets something or lies, she yells at us and says, "You're taking after your mother."'

Pat gave her another warning jab with his elbow, but she glared at him. 'Well, it's true. That's what she says.'

I stood there, stunned, my face feeling hot, not knowing where to turn, where to hide.

'You okay, Mom?' Pat said.

'Yes, just a little dizzy spell. I guess I did have a kind of sickness that made me forget a lot. But I wasn't a liar. It's just that when I forgot things I did, people accused me of being one.'

'Are we going to become like you?' Penny asked.

'Of course not, darling. Just because a parent has an illness doesn't mean the children get it. I'm sure you have a very good memory.'

Penny rubbed her fist against her cheek. 'I forgot my homework assignment last week.' She started to sob. 'And I lost my allowance, and Pat forgot to answer the last question on the back of his math test.'

'That doesn't mean any—'

'We're becoming like you!' Her voice was shrill. 'I don't want to be like you! Please, don't let me be like you!'

Pat hit her, and she howled and kicked him. He caught her by the hair and shouted, 'Shut up! Dad said not to get her upset or she'd do bad things to us.'

I felt the chill, the tension in the air, the ache starting at the base of my skull. There was something I was supposed to do. What was it? I couldn't remember. The aura was strong, as if cold static electricity was passing through my body.

Looking at Pat and Penny going at each other, I felt a sudden revulsion for my son. I wanted to get my hands on him, around his throat, and I wanted to choke him.

Then I remembered. Hands clasped and squeeze three times. I squeezed, and squeezed, and squeezed. And then the aura faded, and my body, which had become numb and icy, began to warm.

'Look at her!' Penny shouted.

They were both staring at me.

'You gonna faint?' Pat asked.

'Don't hurt us!' Penny screamed.

Pat dashed out of the room. 'I better get Anna!' he shouted.

'No!' I gasped. 'I have no intention of hurting anyone. I'm all right. Just a spell of dizziness. Please don't disturb her. I've got to go anyway.'

I ran down the steps of the split level, back to the cluttered living room that gave me claustrophobia. Anna came out of the family room.

'Larry should be back by now. I can't imagine what's keeping him.'

'I can't stay,' I said. 'I've got an important appointment.'

A questioning look, and then relief in her eyes. 'Are you sure? Penny and Pat were so looking forward to sharing their birthday cake with you.'

I wanted to scream *liar!* but I forced a smile. 'That's all right. I'm counting calories anyway. Better not put myself in the way of temptation.'

'Well, I can understand,' she said. 'I'll tell Larry you were here.'

'Give him my regards.'

'He'll be sorry he missed you.'

I had to get out of there before Larry got back. Something told me that if I saw him, not all the self-control exercises in the world, not all the hand clasping and squeezing would keep me from blacking out.

As I walked to the bus stop I saw a car with a driver that looked like Larry. He turned his head and called, but I looked straight ahead, pretending not to see or hear. I walked faster, almost ran. The car backed up.

'Sally? The house is the other way. Get in.'

I didn't trust myself to answer or look at him.

'Are you all right, Sally?'

I kept walking. Eyes ahead. Then I saw the disgusted look on his face, and he put the car back into forward gear and sped off.

When I got on the bus, everyone turned to look at the lady who was squeezing her clasped hands and crying.

Seventeen

ROGER SAID it was a good sign that I had been able to keep from blacking out and switching.

'Switching to what?'

'I don't think we should go into that,' he said. 'For now some things are better kept in the dark.'

More skeletons covered with sand.

'I thought the whole basis of depth therapy was to bring out the repressed material so that it wouldn't cause disabling symptoms.'

'I agree,' he said, 'in most cases. But you need time to get used to the new Sally. You're still fragile. Your feelings with the twins suggest that the hostility is close to the surface.'

'Then I was right to run?'

He nodded. 'It was the first test of the self-control exercise. Like a new dam, you don't subject it to overwhelming pressure all at once. Build your resistance progressively to prevent collapse.'

'I can tell you that seeing what was happening to my kids hurt so much I thought for sure I was going to break up.'

'Well, you held together, and I think you should be rewarded.'

'Still using behavior modification?'

'In a way. Reward what we want to reinforce, punish behavior we want to alter. A lot of people are against it on moral grounds, but I've been in touch with other therapists working with multiples. They say it's a useful tool.'

'Okay,' I said, 'reward me.'

'What would you like?'

'Go out with me. Let's just go walking in the city, right now.' His eyes clouded, and I backed off quickly. 'Of course, if you think it's wrong . . .'

'Oh, no. I'd love to go out with you. It's just that I have other patients this afternoon. And you know how painful it is to have an appointment canceled.'

'Of course. I'm sorry. How insensitive of me. I've got some time off, so I just didn't think.'

'But I have the evening free,' he added quickly. 'What would you like? Dinner? The theater? Or dancing?'

'How about all three? Or is that too greedy?'

'You've got a date.'

I wanted to kiss him, but I held back. I had to budget my display of happiness, spend it a little at a time. As F. Scott Fitzgerald had once observed, the emotional bank account was getting low. I didn't want to overdraw my good feelings. 'Okay,' I said. 'I'll wander the city by myself, keep my mind occupied until this evening. I suspect the city is going to look different to me now, because I'm different. Do you know what I mean?'

'I can speculate,' he said. 'But I can't really know. I'm guessing it'll be like coming back to a place after being away for many years. A person changes and then notices everything from the perspective of new knowledge and new experiences. The same and yet altered.'

We arranged to meet at The Horseman Knew Her for dinner and go from there to an Off-Broadway show. Roger saw me to the door, but before he could turn I kissed him. He flinched. I felt the tension in his arms, but then he relaxed. Though he didn't return my kiss, I was grateful he didn't pull away.

Since we were going to meet in the Village anyway, I decided to spend the afternoon there as well. I took the subway to Washington Square, delighted to find a late autumn outdoor art exhibition.

Looking at the paintings gave me another chill of recognition. I shook it off, watched the chess players, and then the children in the playground sandpile.

At five I went to the coffee house to meet Roger.

The Horseman Knew Her was celebrating its expansion, and as I stepped through the crowd down into the new addition, I noticed these walls, too, were papered with European newspapers, but unlike the yellowed ones in the main dining room, these were new and gave the place a phoney atmosphere of mock impoverishment. The old and the new didn't mix. Maybe when the new papers yellowed they would blend into the old.

Abe Colombo saw me and came out from behind the counter. He looked upset. 'You're not welcome here, Nola.'

I wasn't sure I heard him right. 'What?'

'Anybody who would cut up another person's paintings is a shit.'

'What are you talking about?'

'You want to destroy your own work, it's okay. An artist has that right. But to ruin someone else's is the lowest kind of—'

'I don't know what you're talking about.'

'If Mason catches you here, she'll kill you. I don't want any trouble.'

'I swear to you, I never did anything to her paintings.'

'Mason says you did. So just get out.'

'I'm meeting someone here,' I said.

'I told you, if Mason sees you, she'll go for you. She comes here every night. I'm asking you to leave before she gets here.'

Anger was building. I felt myself breathing hard. 'This is a public place, and I've done nothing to be treated this way. Go ahead and throw me out if you want to, but you'll have to put your hands on me to do it. And then I'll see you in court.'

My fists were clenching and I made a conscious effort to keep them open, though I felt the clammy moisture in my palms.

Abe stared at me. 'I used to like you, you know? I warn you, if you get into a fight with Mason here, I'll be the one to press charges.'

He walked away, and I sat down at a small, round table near the window. My body was trembling, and I had a headache. I wanted to throw the ashtray and the salt and pepper shakers, but I didn't. I had to keep control. I sat at the table, hands clasped tightly as if at a school desk, and stared out the window. I prayed that Roger would get there soon.

Abe's wife, Sarah, in her black leotards and white apron, started toward me with her chalkboard menu, but then changed her mind and went by. I was sure everyone was watching me, whispering. So there was something still lost, memories still buried. I recalled having seen Mason for the last time when I showed Todd my paintings. I remembered his kissing me, pushing me down on the couch. And that was all. But something else must have happened to make me feel as I felt now – like tearing the place apart. But I wouldn't. I would sit there and simmer, and when Roger came we would go somewhere else for dinner.

Kirk Silverman came in. I started to wave to him, but he pretended not to see me. I remembered going to his party, but not leaving it. Still second-acting . . . God, when would I fill in the gaps and learn my own history?

Then, through the side window, I saw Mason's stocky figure plowing toward the coffee shop at about the same time she saw me.

I didn't know too much about Mason, except that she was a member of the Gay Coalition, and now I remembered liking her right away when I rented part of her loft for a studio. She was a masculine-looking woman, and though I used to think of her as a tough-but-friendly little Pekingese, now she looked ready to bite. My first impulse was to go out the back door, but she was already inside the annex now, pushing through the crowd, straight for my table. Sarah Colombo saw her, too, and intercepted her. They were too far away for me to hear what Mason was saying, but her face was red as she pushed by Sarah and came toward me.

'I've been looking for you, you goddamned bitch!'

I sat there controlling myself, but my heart was beating fast, my palms sweating. 'Abe told me what you said. I swear I have no memory of destroying your paintings.'

'Lousy liar! Come on outside, and I'll help you remember.'

'I have no intention of getting into a fight with you,' I said. 'If you say I did some damage, I'll pay for it. I've always liked you, Mason. Please try to understand, I've been sick. I wasn't in my own head, I—'

She slapped my face.

'That's for openers!' she shouted. 'Now I'm gonna tear you apart!'

I felt the chills, the beginning of an aura, but I fought it. I had to keep control. There was too much at stake to black out. I clasped my hands.

She grabbed my arm and yanked me out of the chair, pulling my hands apart, dragging me into the crowd that parted and made a ring around us. Abe came toward us, but when he saw Mason had me, he stopped and crossed his arms.

'Mason, don't!' I begged, trying to clasp my hands. 'I swear. So help me—'

She swung with her free fist and hit me in the stomach, knocking the wind out of me. I went down, and she landed on me and pinned both arms out on the floor. I didn't want to fight, God knows, I didn't want to fight. But there on the floor, I had the sudden feeling that if I didn't defend myself, someone else would. I struggled to get my arms free, and then, with the headache starting, I jabbed a knee into her side and pulled free.

I rolled over, got an arm around her throat, and pressed down in a headlock. I had no idea how I'd learned that wrestling grip. I heard her groan and gurgle. Someone said, *Snap it! Break her neck!* and I knew I could pull my arm sharply and do it.

I clasped my hands, palms facing each other, fingers interlocked, with my arm still encircling her neck. I squeezed once.

Kill her! Kill the bitch!

First I thought someone in the crowd was urging me on. Then I realized it was inside my head. I was slow and deliberate, but around me everything moved quickly and jerkily, like an old movie.

Mason flailed, trying to reach my head, but I avoided her. I was calm now, and in full control. I pulled my left arm with my right hand, just enough to cut off her breathing momentarily, but made no attempt to hurt her, as I squeezed a second time and then a third.

'I want to talk to you,' I said slowly. 'I'm going to loosen my grip enough so you can breathe, but I want you to listen to me carefully. Nod if you agree not to struggle anymore.'

She gurgled and nodded. I relaxed my grip enough to let her breathe, but kept control.

'I didn't start this fight, but I'm a lot stronger than I look. If I want to, I can jerk quickly and snap your neck. Do you understand?'

She nodded.

'I've been ill. I can't explain right now. You'll have to take my word that I blacked out and never knowingly did anything to your paintings. It's like when you're stoned and don't remember afterward. The difference is that you choose to get stoned, but I never chose to black out. I want to apologize for what she – I – did, but I want you to promise, in front of all these people, that if I let you up, you won't attack me anymore. If it happens again, I might lose control and really hurt you. Not that I'd want to, but sometimes I do things without knowing I do them. Right now, I'm hanging over the edge.'

I heard the desperate hardness of my own voice. Mason's head turned slightly and as she looked at me, the hate in her eyes changed to fear. She nodded and gasped, 'Okay . . . let . . . go. I . . . won't . . . do anything . . .'

I let go, and she rolled over and rubbed her throat with both hands. I stood up, and she did, too.

'I'm leaving now,' I said. 'And I won't come back here anymore. If we run into each other by accident some time, let's just pass without talking. I'll say it again – I'm sorry.'

She backed away, and I went to the table and got my purse. Then I took one last look around and walked out.

Roger caught up to me crossing MacDougal Street. He looked at my face. 'What happened?'

Suddenly the strength, the coolness, the confidence drained out of me. I felt I'd collapse. He caught my arm and held me up.

'What is it, Sally? What's wrong?'

I started to cry. 'Take me home, Roger. I'm cold. Oh, please get me home.'

In the taxi I sobbed out what happened. 'I wanted to kill her, and then run and find a dark cellar to hide in to cut my own throat.'

'But you did none of those things,' he said. 'A few weeks ago, maybe even a few days ago, you'd have blacked out. But you stood your ground, defended yourself, by yourself, on your own. I'm proud of you.'

'But I wanted to kill her.'

'Wanting to kill is human. Controlling your impulse is mature and civilized.'

When we got to the apartment, he paid the driver and started to say goodnight to me on the stoop.

'You've got to come up, Roger. I can't be alone now.'

He hesitated, and then nodded. I slipped my arm through his as we went upstairs.

'Why can't I remember what happened with Mason's paintings? Why am I blank?'

'We're all blank about many things in our lives, Sally. We repress painful experiences. We blot out traumas and dreams, leaving gaps in our memories. Over the years, some of them close, like scabs on scrapes, sealed away forever. Others seep out, like draining wounds. Both are painful, but you're learning to handle them.'

'I'm not cured, Roger. Am I?'

'You're on the way, Sally.'

'But not yet. There's something I don't know.'

'You can't rush knowledge.'

I sat down on the couch beside him and put my head on his chest. I heard his heart beating very fast.

'But I have to rush it, Roger. I have this terrible premonition that something is going to happen to me. I have to live every minute of every day because someone or something is going to steal time from me. I always used to lock my door so people couldn't steal my money or my possessions, but I never realized that all the while someone was stealing the hours and days of my life. I can't buy any more. I can't save it, or collect interest on it, or invest it. I can only spend it, one second at a time. And these other people were sneaking into my mind all hours of the day and night, stealing it from me. So much has been taken away that I feel I have to rush to make up for it.'

'You're trembling, Sally.'

'Hold me close, Roger. I'm falling apart.'

He held me tight. 'It's the shock of what happened with Mason. Shhhh. It'll pass. Try to relax. I'll do what I can to calm you. *He knows what's—*'

I stopped him with a kiss. I clung to him and forced my lips against his. His mouth responded long and deep.

Then he pulled back and looked into my eyes. 'Why did you stop me from putting you under?'

'Because I want to be in control, Roger.'

'I shouldn't have kissed you.'

I put my finger to his mouth. 'I kissed you,' I said, and kissed him again, this time lightly, just brushing his lips.

'I love you, Roger.'

He shook his head and pushed me aside as he stood up to face me. 'This is wrong, Sally.'

'You want me too. I know it.'

'I've got to go.'

'You can't leave me like this. If you don't want to take me, at least give me love.'

'I can't!' he shouted. 'Don't you understand I can't. For God's sake! That's why my wife killed herself.'

It came like a slap in the face. I stared at him. 'What are you talking about?'

'When a man is exhausted, it affects his whole life, not just his relationships with patients. When you become tired and jaded, you stop caring for others. You go through the motions. But you're really dead inside.'

He paced up and down, shaking his head and pouring it out. 'For years, I was able to hide it from my colleagues, even from my patients. But I couldn't hide it from my wife. I tried to make her understand it wasn't her fault. It wasn't because I loved her less. I was burned out physically as well as emotionally because the mind and the body are *one thing*. You can't drive part of yourself, day and night working with the mentally ill, driving your mind beyond its limits, and not expect your body to be affected. It consumes you slowly. In the beginning you care for people and give yourself to them. Then the sameness, the constant assault, day after day after day, year after year, creates emotional dulling, and you become callous. You've given all your compassion away, and there's none left for yourself or your family. But you hide it. Because you know compassion is expected, you pretend compassion. And you begin to despise yourself for being a hypocrite. You rationalize and say you're doing this because people need you. But that's a lie, too. People sense your coldness. People sense your withdrawal. Especially the schizophrenics. They are so sensitive. Oh, my God, they know when you're only pretending to care. And the guilt for living a lie shrivels your soul.'

Tears brimmed in his eyes, and though I wanted to put my arms around him, I didn't dare break the spell of his outpouring.

'My wife knew. Lynette was a delicate, vulnerable woman, and when I was no longer able to make love to her, she blamed herself. My words of love couldn't contradict my body's lack of response to her needs.'

He stared at me. 'Don't you understand? She didn't commit suicide. I killed her just as if I'd tied that rope around her neck and looped it around that branch, and then kicked the chair out from under her. I did it. Because I'm a fraud. A gutted, hollow man, parading around pretending to be alive.'

I took his hands, and he let me pull him down beside me. 'I'm glad you told me, Roger. But just as you say the mentally ill know when you're pretending to care, we also know when you're pretending *not* to care.'

His eyes probed mine, and he started to protest, but I covered his mouth with my hand. 'Let me,' I said. 'Maybe you *were* burned out, but I've sensed the change in you. I know you care about me. And if you can care for one person besides yourself, then you can care for others. Can you look into my eyes and tell me that you don't care for me?'

He shook his head. 'You know I do.'

I stroked his face. 'Then if what you say is true, and the mind and body influence each other, you should be able to care with your body as well.'

'Sally, no . . .'

I kissed him gently. I opened his shirt and touched his throat. I felt him quiver under my lips and I knew he was torn between fear of failing and guilt at the possibility of succeeding. I undressed him slowly, and he started to respond hungrily. When I pushed him aside, he stared at me with amazement.

'Slowly,' I said. 'Very slowly, and very gently. No rushing . . . Let's just touch for a while . . .'

I touched him all over, and it was as if warm fluid passed through my fingers to his body and between his fingers and mine. He kissed my breasts, explored my skin, and soon he became alive, taut and ready.

'Sally,' he whispered, 'it's been a long time. But we must not . . .'

'I'm a real person now, Roger. A whole person. And I want you to be, too.'

I guided him to me, but then, as I felt my body accepting him, I sensed the aura. I clasped my hands behind his head and squeezed. But my skull began to throb. Each thrust of his body pounded and smashed as if it reached all the way to my head, hitting me with a rock, over and over again.

I wanted to scream, but I knew it would stop him, shrivel him. So I screamed in my mind, squeezing my hands, fighting the headache that threatened to break me. *No! Leave me alone! I have to be the whole person!*

Roger made love to me, and I loved him back in pain. But when it was over and he kissed me tenderly, I unclasped my hands and my headache split me. I heard a familiar shriek echo in my mind. Then I remembered who I'd forgotten, and I had to let go.

Jinx screamed.

Her hair had become snakes, and I feared that looking at her face would turn me to stone. She fought me like the angel of darkness and wrestled reality out of my grasp. The world became an optical illusion. One moment I was an urn – a receptacle for his love – and then I split into two facing profiles and she took over. She was here. In full control. And I was looking up from the dark abyss, watching, hearing, feeling what was going on inside her.

Jinx looked at the middle-aged doctor holding her in his arms and spat at him.

He put his hands up to protect his face. She clawed the back of his hand with her nails and caught his hair, pulling, kicking, screaming . . .

'You bastard! Dirty old lecher! Get off me! You son of a bitch! I'll tear your eyes out! I'll kill you!'

Naked, she ran for the kitchen and found the carving knife. He wouldn't get away from her again. And once he was dead it would be her body, her mind, her life controlling her own existence. She would go on a killing spree. She was invulnerable. She would kill strangers with impunity, and then she would disappear and the others would pay. But instead of five, now there would be two. The fourth Sally would be punished, and Jinx would be free to do it again.

First there had to be ashes and blood. The blood of Ash.

She saw him staring at her from the doorway. He had pulled on his trousers. Seeing the knife in her hand, he grabbed a cushion from the leather chair. So they were going to battle! She would flay his corpse and then nail his skin to the wall. She wanted to hear him scream. She wanted to refuse his pleas for mercy, wanted to sever his body from his soul and cast it into the pit.

'Suffer!' she screamed, 'and then die!'

She swung the knife and cut into the leather.

'Jinx, please,' he said. 'Calm down. Let's talk.'

'You kill with words,' she croaked. 'You shove words down people's throats and choke them the way you choked your wife, with a rope of words from the tree of knowledge. You masturbate words. They spurt out of you slimy and venereal, and they kill with hidden meanings, and lies . . . lies . . . lies!'

'It's all right to hate me, Jinx, but a knife isn't the answer.'

'Then it's the question. The cutting edge of truth.'

She slashed and jabbed, cut his chest, caught his fingers, and he dropped the cushion. Then surprisingly he stopped retreating and threw himself at her. She gashed his shoulder twice before he knocked her down and got his knee on the wrist of the knife hand. Then she felt his hands on her throat.

'You bitch!' he roared. 'I'll kill you first. You don't exist! You're a nightmare out of hell!'

There was no pain, but she felt his thumbs digging into her throat, and the choking sensation made her feel light-headed. The lights dimmed. His face blurred. And she knew she had to leave the body to keep from dying. Let Sally die. Let him choke the life out of her, and when Sally was dead, Jinx would be free, and he would be so tormented by what he had done he would kill himself.

Suddenly she felt him let go and heard him say, 'Oh, my God, what am I doing? *Go back into the darkness!*'

It would do them no good, she thought as she slipped away. Now she was strong enough to take over again anytime, for as long as she pleased.

Because only she could face what was in the darkness . . .

Eighteen

I WOKE in a hospital room, my arms and legs spread-eagled and bound with leather cuffs fastened to the head and foot of the bed. The odor of urine gagged me. Overhead the light bulb was encased in wire mesh, and the windows had chain link covering. Outside it was snowing.

I screamed for help but my throat was hoarse and sore, and it came out rasping. A key turned in the lock, and a nurse padding on crepe soles carried in a dinner tray. Keys jangled in a leather key guard at her belt. It was Mrs. Fenton.

'Okay . . . okay . . .,' she said. 'Lunchtime, Jinx, but if you spit food in my face again, I'll shove a tube down your throat and pour it into you.'

Be calm, I told myself, and find out what's happened. It was obviously a case of mistaken identity. Mrs. Fenton just didn't recognize me.

'Understand me, Jinx?' She glared, and her voice threatened. I nodded.

'I'll be good, Mrs. Fenton.'

Her eyebrows went up. 'Oh? That's a change.'

'I'm sorry if I've been causing problems.'

That confused her, and she peered at me more closely. 'What's your name?'

'Sally Porter.'

The harshness went out of her eyes. 'Well it's about time, Sally. Thank goodness. We've been waiting a long time for

307

you. Just a minute. Dr. Ash asked to be notified as soon as you came out.'

'Do I have to stay tied down like this?'

'Just till I get back. Hang in there and we'll get you more comfortable.'

Mrs. Fenton left and came back with Big-Mouth Duffy, whose face was bandaged.

'I don't trust the bitch,' Duffy snorted.

'It's all right,' Mrs. Fenton said. 'This is the other one.'

'I still don't buy that Jekyll-and-Hyde crap. It's a put-on. If she goes for my face again I'll let her have it. I say taking the cuffs off is a mistake.' Duffy glared at me as she unfastened my left leg, pausing as if expecting me to kick. When I did nothing, she snorted, 'Playing possum.'

'Dr. Ash's orders are to remove the restraints as soon as she calls herself Sally. Now get her out of them.'

'I'm sorry if I hurt you,' I said. 'I don't remember.'

By the time Duffy had finished unlacing the cuffs, Roger came in. When I saw him, I started to cry.

'That's all right, Sally. Go ahead and let it out. You've lived through a nightmare. But you're back out now, and that's what counts.'

'What happened, Roger? We were together and then . . .'

He nodded for Duffy to leave and indicated that Mrs. Fenton should stay.

'Mrs. Fenton will help you shower and dress, and then she'll bring you to my office. We'll go over the whole thing.'

'What happened to me, Roger?'

He looked into my eyes. 'We made a mistake. It's as if you've been asleep for a long time, Sally. I'll explain it in my office. We have a videotape. I think it's time you finally saw it with your own eyes.'

After my shower, Mrs. Fenton helped me brush my hair and got me a dress from among my own clothes, which had been brought to the hospital. I asked for the blue one I knew Roger liked best. Though I was in a hurry to talk to Roger, she insisted I eat some lunch first.

I told her I felt dazed and strangely sluggish.

'That'll be the drugs they gave you – or her. Demerol didn't have any effect on – on the other one – and Dr. Ash said they can't use Thorazine on multiples, so they used something new, but you may be reacting to it differently. It'd slow you down all right.'

Out in the corridor, a pair of shoes stood in front of each door. It gave me the feeling ghosts were on guard. We had to go through the dayroom to get to the exit. Some of the patients screamed obscenities when they saw me, and others faced the wall as if terrified. What kind of monster had I turned into that I could affect them so?

Mrs. Fenton made me wait outside the nurses' glass-walled station while she phoned ahead that she was bringing me down. The attendants having coffee inside looked at me with curiosity. One of them got up and came out and stuck her face close to mine.

'What's your name?' she demanded.

'Sally Porter,' I said.

'You're a liar,' she said. 'You may fool the others with your act, but I'll keep my eyes on you.'

Mrs. Fenton pushed by and told her to leave me alone. Then she unlocked the door to the corridor, and we went out of the dayroom.

It was a long walk, then an elevator to the lowest level. From there we passed through an underground tunnel complex blocked by wire mesh gates at every intersection.

'Where are we?'

'This is the tunnel route from the maximum security ward. All the buildings are connected underground so we don't have to take a patient outside to go from one to the other.'

'From outside all the buildings look separate, you'd never know they were connected. I never knew about these tunnels when I first came here.'

'You were a voluntary patient then, Sally. You never had to be in maximum security.'

'Was I very bad this time, Mrs. Fenton?'

She nodded without looking at me. 'The worst I've ever seen.'

The tunnel sloped upward, and we came to a heavy double door that Mrs. Fenton unlocked with one of the keys from her belt. On the other side I found the cool, familiar fluorescent-lit halls of the admissions wing.

Maggie was waiting and she hugged me. 'Sally, it's good to see you. How do you feel?'

'A little sluggish,' I said.

'I'd better get back to the ward,' Mrs. Fenton said. 'You'll call an attendant to return her?'

'I'll take care of it,' Maggie said. 'Thank you.'

Mrs. Fenton patted my shoulder. 'Good luck, Sally.'

Maggie took me into Roger's hospital office. He got up when we came in. 'Sit down, Sally. We've got a lot of work to do.' He nodded to Maggie. 'Get the video tape cassette we made last week.'

'Last week?' I whispered. 'Has it been that—?'

He nodded. 'Nearly a month.'

'My God. What are you going to show me, Roger? I'm frightened.'

'That's natural, Sally. But the time has come for you to see what happens when you black out. It must seem as if you've been asleep. But your body wasn't. As we've fused your other personalities – we won't mention their names anymore – you've developed amnesia for them and the whole experience. And I think that's good.'

'Then why are you going to show me the tape?'

'Because the other mergers have taken place only after you've been in touch with each one.'

'You're not going to change me again, are you?'

'I thought we could avoid it, Sally. I'd hoped that when you became a more fully rounded individual, deeper and more complex, you could repress the other one. But just as you've become stronger, she has, too. As if she's matched you step for step on the other side. She can't be locked away and forgotten. We've got to deal with her, bring her into the open, ventilate her growing hatred and violent urges.'

'I thought you cared about *me*, Roger.'

'I do, Sally. Believe me I do.'

'I'm not sure, Roger. Maybe the scientist, the researcher in you has taken over, fascinated by the notion of seeing what will happen. I think completing your work has become more important than your feelings for me.'

'There's no other way, Sally.'

'There is. Love should be able to do it. Love should be able to overcome hate.'

'That's Derry talking. Sorry, I shouldn't have used her name. What I mean to say is, if you use your intellect, you'll realize that's sentimental. I know you don't really believe "Love conquers all," any more than I do.'

It hurt when he said that, but he was right.

'I'm afraid, Roger.'

'We're all afraid of our violent impulses. But we control them and rechannel them into positive actions. In isolating your suppressed anger, separating it from the total self, your child's mind developed a pocket – a mental boil – gave it a name, and thus created your first alter personality of violence and evil.'

'I didn't think psychiatrists used that word.'

'You're right. That's a moral judgment, but what other way is there to describe the person thrashing around in the dark side of your mind?'

'What if afterward I hate you?'

'That's a chance I have to take. If I have to give you up to save you, that's my moral obligation.'

'Now who's being sentimental?'

'Let's put it another way. It's my professional opinion that if we don't go all the way, she'll destroy you.'

'And you don't want that on your conscience.'

The look in his face showed I'd hurt him. 'I'm sorry, Roger. That wasn't fair.'

'You're partly right.'

'You mean it's a gamble either way.'

'Yes.'

Maggie came in with a video cassette, and Roger slipped it into the TV monitor. I couldn't bring myself to look at first. Then I heard the voice: harsh, low, unfamiliar, spitting out obscenities. I put my hands over my ears and closed my eyes. But the sound came through, and slowly I took my hands away and looked at the screen.

The face I had dreamed of but never seen in control of the body before was twisted in anger, the eyes glared. She was saying, '. . . When I get out of these leather bracelets, I'll tear your eyes out, you goddamned sonofabitch! All you ever wanted was to use her, to fuck her. You thought you could isolate me and nullify me. Well, I'll fool you yet. When you least expect it, I'll kill you. And then I'll kill Sally.'

'And what becomes of you, Jinx?'

'Then I'll be free as the wind.'

'You'll be dead, too.'

She laughed. 'I believe in an after-death, Ash. I'm a child of the devil, and my soul will enter someone else. You see, I'm all mind, all imagination, and I'm not bound by a body. When hers ceases to be, I'll find another . . . and then another . . . I may have been born here, but I've always had the desire to travel. Witches live forever. I was burned in Salem and reborn in her body.'

I was repelled and fascinated. It was incredible to see my likeness glowing with hatred, my mouth pouring out filth. And I realized I had to accept the blame. To avoid pain, I had created that monster out of my imagination, and then rejected her. She'd taken the punishment, born the brunt of other people's lies, hypocrisy, and sadism. As she spoke of her aloneness and suffering, I felt the tears in my eyes. I know it sounds foolish, but I wanted to hold her in my arms and say, 'You don't have to hate or be lonely anymore.' I had to make it up to her.

'I have no right to deny her,' I said. 'I'm responsible. But do it quickly before I change my mind.'

He turned off the monitor and said, 'I thought you'd feel that way.'

He hypnotized me and sent for Jinx. But she wouldn't come out.

He said, 'If she won't cooperate, maybe we can find out why, through you.' He regressed me to the time Jinx was born, and I remembered . . .

I was seven. It was a morning in December just before my grandfather died. I saw myself in Grandma Nettie's apartment above the grocery store on Sutter Avenue in Brooklyn, where Mom took me to stay sometimes when she had to work at the dress factory. Alone in the kitchen, I heard

Grandma get up and come out of the bedroom and put on her galoshes and the sheepskin vest she always wore when she delivered milk on winter mornings. She said I had to stay in Grandpa's room in case he needed anything. I told her I didn't want to stay alone with Grandpa. I was afraid of the bad things he tried to do to me.

She slapped my face and told me not to tell terrible lies about a respected old man who taught Sunday School. Then she told me to sit near the bed so I could tell if he needed his bedpan or his medicine, and she locked me in his room.

I shouted through the door that I was afraid, but her footsteps moved away, and the outside door opened and closed, and I cried and cringed against the locked door. I needed help, but there was no one to hear or help me. I turned back and saw Grandpa propped up against three big pillows, looking at me, his face yellow, his cheeks sunken, his mouth all wrinkled and puckered without teeth. He told me to get him a glass of water. I screamed that I wouldn't come near him or let him touch me. He said I only imagined he did bad things to me. He was my grandpa, he said, and he loved his pretty little granddaughter, and he would teach me some games. He struggled to lift the blanket, and the bottoms of his pajamas were down below his knees, and his thing was standing straight up. I closed my eyes and begged God to make him die so I wouldn't have to look at him and I wouldn't have to touch it and do the terrible things he wanted to teach me . . .

The next memory was the smell of roses. When I opened my eyes, he was in his coffin, his face no longer yellow but white and filled out, like a mannequin in a store window, and people were standing around with tears in their eyes.

I sat very still because I didn't know how the magic had happened. I had wanted him to die, but I hadn't known you could make someone die by wishing it.

I heard people say he was a good man. And how the Sunday School would miss his teaching. And how well Sally took it after being in the same room with a dying man who looked as if he'd had convulsions. I remembered nothing, but I knew better than to tell anyone.

It was my first forgetting.

Roger brought me back to the present, and I said, 'So that's when Jinx came out – when my grandfather tried to abuse me.'

He tried again to bring Jinx out, but it didn't work. Then he tried a third time, saying that Jinx would be there the day Grandpa died – and she'd remember being alone in the room with him.

Jinx opened her eyes, and this time it was as if I was there, watching her. She didn't know how long she had been in that room. She tried to open the door and threw herself against it with all her might. Grandpa motioned for her to come to the bed. He'd uncovered himself, and she hated him for doing that.

'Come to Grandpa, Sally. Be a good girl and be nice to your old grandpa. It won't hurt.'

She glared at him and looked around the room for something to protect herself with. She came closer to the bed, pretending she was going to do what he wanted. But as he reached for her, she pulled back. Finally, he caught her by the hair and pulled her close to him and pulled down her panties.

'You have to be good to your grandpa. I'm an old man and I don't have much longer to—'

She struggled and screamed, but there was no one to hear, no one to help. And then her hands went under his arms and she tickled him. He pulled back, laughing. She did it again, under his arms, on his sides, and he let go of her hair.

'I'll teach *you* a lesson!' she screamed.

'Don't, Sally!' He was laughing, gasping for breath, and he rolled from side to side on the bed trying to protect himself from her flying fingers as she tickled him all over. He choked and coughed, and she realized that as long as she kept it up he couldn't do anything to her. The choking became a rattling, and a gasping, and then he threw up. She backed away because the smell was so awful. He lay there across the bed, his eyes bulging, his mouth in a frozen laugh with vomit trickling down his chin.

She put on her panties, sat on the floor near the locked door, and waited.

Later, her grandma came and took her out of the room, and said, 'Oh, my poor child, what a terrible thing for you to see.'

Jinx said, 'He tried to do bad things to me. I'm glad he's dead.'

Grandma slapped her again and screamed, 'Don't you ever say a thing like that, you wicked child. Never tell anyone things like that or you'll go straight to hell and burn forever. You're bad, you're evil . . . you're a spawn of the devil.'

But Jinx pulled away and ran out of the house into the cold, running to get away from the smell and Grandma's slaps and Grandpa's dead bulging eyes . . .

I heard Roger's voice calling Jinx back to the present, but she didn't want to come. She wanted to keep running forever and never see us again. She didn't want to go back into the dark and let me out. She was thinking that I didn't deserve to be out all the time while she was trapped inside.

But Roger had the power to bring her back, and now I felt her being pulled, and she heard the words . . . *You can remember as much of this as you want to. All of it, some of it, or none of it . . .*'

I opened my eyes and felt the tears rolling down my cheeks. 'I never wanted to do those things, Roger. I tried to tell my grandma and my mother, but no one would listen to me. No one would help me. No one cared that he made me do those things. I tried to tell them, but they called me a wicked, lying child. I'm so ashamed. So ashamed . . .'

'You mustn't blame yourself for his death.'

'I created Jinx out of fear and anger. I've got to accept her back into myself,' I said. 'Do it quickly, Roger. It wasn't fair for me to run away and hide and leave her to bear all my pain and sorrow and hatred alone, and have none of the happiness.'

Roger told me to clasp my hands. 'You were born in torment and anger, Jinx,' he said. 'But now Sally wants you to rejoin her.'

I heard her voice shout, 'I won't! I'll stay myself until hell and heaven merge first.'

I felt the pain of my nails digging deep into the back of my hand. I looked down and saw it bleeding.

Roger stared, as if uncertain how to proceed. 'The others merged willingly,' he said. 'I might have known Jinx would refuse. There's no way to force her to yield her identity. She has to want to give up her separateness.'

'So it was all for nothing,' I said. 'All the others, the struggle, the fusing. I'd be better off dead than try to live an existence that changes me like an optical illusion every time I blink my eyes.'

'Don't ever give up!' he shouted. 'There has to be a way past her barrier. Maybe if we go far back in time, past her defenses.'

The laugh that came out of my throat, without my control, was hers. 'You'll have to go back to the dawn of human consciousness.'

Then I heard the words of the ISH inside my head, saying: – That's the answer and the key. Go back to the beginning.

I told Roger what my Helper had said.

'All right,' Roger said. 'If that's what the ISH feels it takes, we'll do it.'

That scared me, but I sat quietly and listened.

He held up his gold pen. 'Your mind is a time machine, and you'll go all the way into the past. When I count from seven to zero, we'll have turned the dial back to the dawn of human consciousness. When you arrive there you'll describe it.'

He counted, and my mind fell back into itself.

Back into the mind of Jinx, hating, thinking, remembering . . .

Once upon a timeless time, she thought, back far enough. Before defenses. Before the splitting off into human self-consciousness, when all minds were one and there was no separateness of personalities, but one universal Mind, all knew and communicated without speech. All minds interpenetrated. Each shared thoughts open to all. No fear. No pain. No anger. Commands unspoken. Mind moving like the great wind, and all souls drifting like wind-blown leaves. Nothing hidden. No suspicion or jealousy or hate . . . Each mind open to the totality. No troubled unconscious. No nightmares. The universal spirit moved upon the land.

Then something unforeseen happened. Winters grew longer and colder than ever before. In the tens of thousands of years of human memory, we never recalled such cold. Countless more bellies ached, tugging at the Mind, urging it to get more food. But there was not enough.

So the great Mind decided that some of the mouths would be fed and the rest pruned back like branches. Mind would limit itself to a few tens of thousands of bodies and let the others go.

And then a single resistance. Among all the females, one had isolated a corner, a pocket of self-conscious privacy, pinched out of its portion of the total Mind. The community didn't know where, or who, but only intuited a raw edge of closure somewhere in the universal consciousness. That woman was me.

I was born different. When they took me from the breast, I wanted more. Later, I felt a troubling, a sense of passing time. I was incapable of knowing that I alone felt anger when my stomach ached from hunger. Mind sensed it, and for a time the community pushed more food my way. When I copulated the first time, I felt a strange body-quaver, and the Mind was startled. Never had one of its parts been so preoccupied with its own body.

When I nursed my own child, I felt the warmth and the throbbing as it suckled, and I resisted when another female reached to nurse the child, too. I refused to accept another's child. At each stage of my life, Mind punished me for my feelings of self-ness. There is no separate *you*, the Mind whispered. There is only the whole.

But one day I found a thin spot at the corner of my awareness and poked a hole in the frayed fabric of consciousness. The dark unknown beyond it terrified me at first, and I retreated quickly before the Mind could find the break. But it was difficult to keep away from it, and I would probe from time to time, like a tongue seeking a lost tooth. I discovered I could put self-thoughts through the gap, outside the tent of the communal mind, and keep them secret in my own pocket of awareness.

I collected private ideas and feelings and hid them, stored like the collected berries wrapped in leaves outside the cave, and put the knowledge out of the group-mind and into my private-mind. When my female infant cried in hunger, I fed her secretly, without letting myself think it, so the Mind wouldn't know. I did the same for the male who had first copulated with me. We became special to each other.

My baby grew up preferring me to all the others in the tribe. Mind was troubled at such perversion, but though it swept through the consciousness of the race like a whirlwind, it couldn't find the private mind-place I had created for myself. I and my male and my child had food for our bodies while others went hungry. I taught my child how to make her own secret mind-place for her thoughts, to keep knowledge from the others, so that memories and learning could be hoarded. My mate was strong and found meat and hid it in the forest, and hid the knowledge. And the two of us taught our child how to do the same.

But Mind suspected. It listened and searched and probed, and one day it found us. The entire community lashed out. We were in agony, but I would not bear the torment of the conscious Mind. We had done nothing wrong. We would bear it no longer. We would escape from the Mind and live each in our private, secret places.

So we stepped through the hole into our own consciousness, blocking out all the pain and suffering the great Mind was visiting upon us. Then the great Mind drove us farther away, and the waters rushed in a great flood and sealed the hole and locked us out forever – excommunicated from the great swirling spirit of thought. A reversal of knowing. Our secret places became our conscious minds, and the great shared Mind became our unconscious.

I became the mother of a new race of humans, each an individual with a consciousness of its own, eternally split off from the great shared being of the human race, slipping back secretly, visiting sometimes in dreams or insanity or mystical revelation to draw sustenance, but never to be co-conscious with the human over-spirit.

My split-off descendants multiplied and, because of body consciousness, became physically strong. They developed secret ambitions, greed, and lust. Generations begat generations and developed fire, and the wheel, and the knife, and the gun, and overwhelmed the earth because they proliferated, while the great Mind – unconcerned with these outcasts – still pruned. And the New People learned hatred and war. Each of my isolated heirs called his or her memory of the great Mind 'the Soul,' or 'the Spirit,' and was driven by a longing to find his or her way back. But no longer was the whole earth of one language and one speech and one thought. It became The Great Babel.

Thus the human race created its own multiples of personalities and lived unhappily ever after . . .

Jinx poured her fantasy out, and I shuddered. Surely she was insane. As I had come to know more about Jinx, I'd begun to believe she had cut herself off from the human race by free choice, and that to isolate myself from that evil I had shut her out. I had refused to accept the angry, tormented side of my soul. I was responsible. But now, according to her, it had happened to the human race that way from the beginning . . .

Since I was the larger entity, I knew I had to open the passage to the dark place and let her rejoin the rest of me, accepting her *as she was*, with her anger and frustration and hatred – born of her lonely suffering. I trembled, knowing that until I asked her forgiveness and gave her my love, I could not become a truly complete human being.

Roger touched my arm and said, 'You'll have to be the one to ask Jinx to agree. I don't think she'll respond to me.'

I opened my mind and said, 'Jinx, forgive me.'

She didn't answer.

'Jinx, I know now what you've suffered, why you were cut off from me. You're the anger I could never express. I want you back. I want to be a whole person, a real person, and only through you do we have the power to do it. This way we're dead, destroyed, torn apart because we can't live in time anymore.'

'I'm satisfied the way things are,' she said.

'But things can't stay that way,' I told her. 'I'm too strong now, and you're too strong, and we'll tear ourselves apart. We can't live torn in two, Jinx, and we can't live in the world of make-believe anymore. And we can't live the rest of our lives waiting for a sleepy-eyed postman to carry us off in his mail pouch to the magic castle. We've got to join forces and live in the here and now. The Helper wants it that way.'

Jinx sighed, and it was the deepest, saddest sigh I ever heard.

'I ask your forgiveness, Jinx. For all the suffering I've caused you. I heaped it all on your head, and then when you lashed out in pain, I called you evil. I beg your forgiveness for that, too. Come back to me. I want you, Jinx. I need you. I love you for the things you've suffered, and I swear to you I'll never drive you away again.'

She sighed again, and I heard her voice. 'All right,' she said, 'I've been cold and frightened. I don't want to be alone anymore.'

'Do you agree?' Roger asked.

'I agree,' she answered.

'Then, *come out of the darkness.*'

She came out of the dark cave and stood beside me. I took her trembling hand.

'When I count to six,' Roger said, 'Jinx will no longer resist fusion. You will both take a new journey, but in the present. How high did I say I was going to count, Jinx?'

'Six . . .' she whispered.

'You are no longer a landlocked body,' he said. 'Your consciousness is like a stream that flows downward from your mountain of frustration and despair, flowing down through other springs and brooks . . .'

She saw that she was a stream. At first in the frosty air of the mountain peak, and then following the contours of the land, flowing, falling, feeling her way down, over dead trees, around boulders, into holes and gaps in the earth.

'. . . Now the flow of frustration mingles and merges into one angry river moving like the great Mississippi, down across the continent of Sally's mind . . .'

She saw the anger, rushing, turbulent, carrying the debris of waterlogged memories and threatening constantly to overflow its banks and flood the plains of my mind with hatred and violence. Roaring southward, rushing to join the waters of the great gulf.

'You are now merged once and for all,' he said. 'Jinx's anger and hatred and sorrow are bathed forever in Sally's love. There is no separate Jinx. Sally opens herself to you. There is only the fifth Sally, who will express her own emotions – if need be – of hostility and aggression. When I count to *five*, Sally will awaken and never again need a separate consciousness. You will be fused into one person for as long as you both shall live. And you will remember . . .'

I waited with fear for the counting.

'One . . .'

I heard the sound of crying.

'Two . . .'

It was the ISH.

'Three . . .'

I saw its face in agony, mouth open, eyes on fire.

'Four . . .'

It was absorbing all of Jinx's anger to save me. It was Oscar's face.

'Five . . .'

I tried to stop the fusion, but it was too late.

And then Oscar and Jinx were both gone and I knew my first Helper had given up his life to make the fusion. My father was really dead.

I cursed and shrieked at Roger, pausing only to catch my breath. I poured it over him, clenching and unclenching my hands, gripping the table top to keep from clawing at him.

'It's all right, Sally,' he said softly. 'I expected you to hate me.'

'Hate is too mild a word! You sicken me. You disgust me. You killed Oscar.'

I no longer held myself in check. I trembled. I felt the tears rolling down my cheeks, and then I cried until I was exhausted.

'I love you and I hate you, but I don't understand why.'

'You have all your emotions back, Sally.'

'But I don't want to hate you.'

'In time you'll learn to express it, Sally, and then channel it. You won't be an easygoing, eternally sweet-tempered person anymore. You'll get angry when you have to and direct it at those things that deserve it.'

'There's more to it than that. I'm capable of doing terrible things. I could lie, cheat, steal. I could kill.'

'All humans are capable of those things. But it's only a fifth part of Sally. The rest of you shares the conscience of the human race, and it'll hold you in check.'

'What will happen to me?'

'A fresh start. You get to know yourself in all your complexity. You rejoin the human race. You'll stop looking for Oscar. You'll build a new life.'

'Oh, God,' I said. 'It doesn't feel the way I thought it would. I thought it would be beautiful. I thought I would spend the rest of my life having fun, enjoying love, exploring the world. But now most of the things I cared about don't seem worthwhile anymore.'

'That's to be expected. You're seeing everything from a new perspective.'

'I used to be so sure of right and wrong, good and evil. But the world is still a rotten place. People are still betraying, robbing, killing each other – individually and as nations. Once I thought I knew all the answers. One world. The melting pot. The dream of oneness, my oneness and the unity of the human race. But now I'm not sure anymore. There are all these shadows and differences and exceptions. It's as if I've been reborn into a fragmenting world that changes the questions as soon as I think I've got the answers.'

'You're not alone, Sally. Others are searching for solutions. Good people.'

'And some compounded of good and evil,' I said.

He nodded. 'You're strong enough now to face yourself. I think Todd will be waiting to see what happens.'

I shook my head. 'Not Todd. He wanted only the good parts of me and the excitement of an unpredictable woman. Oh, maybe he was titillated by the odds that something in me might explode at any time. But he was betting only on the goodness. And that's too easy. Anyone can love goodness. Sentimental, pious, hand-wringing, sanctimonious goodness.'

'Eliot?'

'A sweet guy, but I think he was attracted by the thought of loving five women for the emotional price of one. No, I'm breaking off with both of them. I'm going to look for a new job.'

'Well, of course, but there's nothing wrong with—'

'You accepted all of me, Roger. The good and the bad. You made me whole. You're the only one.'

He shook his head. 'We've talked about transference.'

'The hell with abstract theories. Transference is a form of love. I'll take it any way I can get it.'

'I'll tell you what. Let's not see each other for a while. Let's see how well the fusion holds and how you feel in a year. After the transference has worked itself out, if you haven't switched or created new personalities, and if you still want to come back, we'll give it a try.'

I was shocked. I didn't expect him to stop seeing me now. 'I'm not ready to go out on my own. I have to tell you about my feelings, other memories that are flooding my mind. My plans for the future—'

He handed me the gold pen he'd used for hypnosis. 'Write it, just for yourself. Put your life into perspective. While you were in maximum security, they brought me a new multiple personality case, a six year old, a little girl with seven other personalities, two of them suicidal, one violent, one a child prodigy who plays the piano and composes music. Now, because of my work in this field, she's been sent here.'

'Another one? My God, it's frightening.'

'Right now this child needs my help, and thanks to the knowledge I've gained through treating you, I should be able to help her. I have a session with her in a little while.

I'm discharging you. I won't say goodbye. I'll come to see you off in the morning.'

'No, don't,' I said. 'I'd rather leave here by myself.'

He kissed me on the cheek and then left me in his office. I sat there awhile, until Maggie came to take me back.

The next morning it was snowing. Nurse Fenton helped me pack, but I left alone. In the elevator I punched the LOBBY button. I waited, half expecting to shatter again, but I stayed myself. Downstairs I looked at the clock behind the receptionist's desk. 10:32. In a sense it was all a matter of time: remembering the past, experiencing the present, anticipating the future. All the fragments and splinters of the hours had to be there so you could – if you wanted – put each in its own place and examine the history of your existence, the chronology of yourself. I looked at my watch again as the bus pulled up. 10:37. Could I make it all the way crosstown, and into the apartment, without losing time?

I watched the snow fall, saw people shoveling it into white mounds. I walked gingerly. As I got on the bus, a boy threw a snowball at me. I got angry and shook my fist at him. I waited to feel pain at the base of my neck, but the headache never came. The bus let me off at the corner, and the clock said 10:59. Twenty-two minutes across town, and I owned every second.

Up in the apartment I had the overwhelming feeling that from now on I would keep every moment of every day as one person. That was something a real person, a whole person, could call happiness.

I decided to go jogging in the snow. On the way out of the building I saw Murphy in Greenberg's shop. 'I made it, Murphy,' I said, as I started to run. 'I'm a whole, real person.'

His nightstick was still missing, but now, instead of giving the world the finger, his right hand had been turned palm forward to direct traffic. It looked to me as if he was waving at the world.

I waved back.